THE GUARDIAN

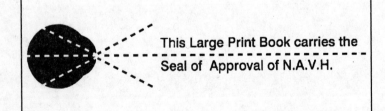

This Large Print Book carries the
Seal of Approval of N.A.V.H.

THE GUARDIAN

BEVERLY LEWIS

THORNDIKE PRESS
A part of Gale, Cengage Learning

GALE
CENGAGE Learning·

Detroit • New York • San Francisco • New Haven, Conn • Waterville, Maine • London

LIBRARY OF CONGRESS CATALOGING-IN-PUBLICATION DATA

Lewis, Beverly, 1949-
    The guardian / by Beverly Lewis.
        pages ; cm. — (Home to Hickory Hollow series ; #3) (Thorndike Press large print Christian fiction)
        ISBN 978-1-4104-5537-6 (hardcover) — ISBN 1-4104-5537-8 (hardcover) 1. Foundlings—Fiction. 2. Amish—Fiction. 3. Lancaster County (Pa.)—Fiction. 4. Large type books. I. Title.
PS3562.E9383G83 2013b
813'.54—dc23   2013003392

Published in 2013 by arrangement with Bethany House Publishers, Baker Publishing Group.

Printed in the United States of America
1 2 3 4 5 6 7 17 16 15 14 13

To Edwin and Marion Rohrer,
cousins ever dear.

PROLOGUE

Something about heading for home at nightfall tugged at my better judgment that Thursday evening. And my squirmy youngsters weren't helping my concentration one bit as I picked up the reins and signaled for the mare to move forward.

"*Psch!* Be still back there," I called over my shoulder. All four of them had managed to squeeze into the back of the carriage.

"*Ach,* but Sarah's hangin' over the edge with her doll," tattled nine-year-old Benny.

Leda, his twin, complained, too. "*Jah,* she's awful *rutschich* tonight."

"*Kumme* sit with me, Sarah, won't ya?"

"My dolly wants to look at the sky," little Sarah said in *Deitsch. "Sei so gut, Mamma?"*

Please? Sarah had a way of adding sugar to her pleadings. Such mischief she was! How many times in her four years had Sarah gotten her way simply by making her perty blue eyes do the talking? *"Please,*

7

Mamma," she'd say in Deitsch and warm my heart yet again.

Soon I could hear Sarah and Leda chattering and laughing softly, playing their hand-clapping game. Their brothers, Benny and seven-year-old Tobias, grew quiet, most likely watching the fireflies twinkling on the roadside. *Must be wishing they were catching them in a big canning jar.*

It was beyond me why they'd bunched up together back there, all sticky and sweaty from the long, hot day at the benefit auction in Paradise. We'd raised money to assist two Mennonite families with children who suffered with fragile X syndrome, a genetic disease. We did this twice each year.

Mine were the only Amish *Kinner* present, but that didn't seem to bother a soul. And the children played cheerfully, jabbering in Deitsch. At the end of the day, once all the money was counted, many families were reluctant to leave, enjoying the good fellowship. My great-aunt Heddy Hoover, Mennonite matriarch, suggested we make strawberry ice cream. So the young folk took turns cranking the old ice cream makers brought out from the summer kitchen, and we sat and talked. There was some gossip, too, including news about Rosaleen Yoder, the preacher's twenty-year-old daughter and

8

the teacher at our Hickory Hollow school. Due to her recent engagement, Rosaleen would not be permitted to teach this fall.

In the end, we'd lingered much longer than planned. And I'd thought for sure my children would be fussing over who'd get to sit up front with me during the trip home to Hickory Hollow. *Little Sarah always wins out. . . .*

Looking back at them again, I saw my precious girl kneeling to peer out the back of the buggy, holding up her cloth doll, Kaylee, and talking to it. I couldn't help wondering what thoughts buzzed round in her head.

My last baby with Benuel . . .

The sweet scent of honeysuckle mingled with the oppressing humidity as I made the turn onto Harvest Road. A few more *clip-clop*s of Dandy's hooves on the pavement, and just that quick, the family carriage fell still. The children were sound asleep.

I breathed a grateful prayer, thinking how far my young ones had come since their father's farming accident three years ago. *"Children are ever so resilient, Maryanna,"* Great-Aunt Heddy had whispered today as we stood under the immense green canopy of a tree, watching Sarah and her sister and brothers as they played happily with all the

9

other Plain youngsters present. *Jah, resil-ient . . . more so than their own Mamma, just maybe?*

Tender thoughts of Benuel filled my heart anew. Although many expected me to re-marry in due time, someone to share the responsibilities for this family, I could scarcely consider it. At thirty-three, I be-lieved no one could ever replace my dear husband, so why should I receive another man into my life? Although I missed Benuel terribly, we were all doing fine, with the Lord's help. In all truth, I was rather content as a single mother.

Honestly, it had never crossed my mind that our lives would take such an unforeseen turn the year after Sarah was born. I'd been taught to lay down my own wishes and desires to accept God's sovereignty. The events and circumstances of our lives were enveloped by this heavenly covering.

A shelter, of sorts . . .

So I'd set out to be a young woman who lived cheerfully and worked hard under the shadow of the Almighty, as the psalm de-clared. And for the most part, I had not questioned what happened to Benuel. At least not to God.

The sound of Dandy's hooves on the road calmed me. *Ah, twilight . . . such a pensive time of day.* On a similarly tranquil evening, baby Sarah was born as healthy as can be, free of the fatal genetic disorder that plagued many of our Old Order communities due to generations of intermarrying. Right from the start, little Sarah's life seemed like a divine miracle, God's gracious gift. How thankful Benuel and I were, and ever so relieved. With three healthy children at home, we'd feared that eventually a babe would be born with the disorder . . . that little Sarah might be the one.

"Sarah?" I called softly to her now. *"Boppli?"*

No answer.

I didn't call again, lest I awaken her . . . and the others. My girls sometimes curled up next to each other and slept on the ride back from a family or church gathering. But this night, I wanted my youngest one's company — *needed* her near. Oh, to have Sarah's head resting against me, her tiny hands folded prayerfully in her lap as she slept.

Sarah . . . God's little princess.

"Once we're home, I'll tuck her into bed," I whispered. Now that my children had no earthly father to care for them, it was up to me to be the best Mamma they could have. *A sacred and blessed calling.*

11

CHAPTER 1

Maryanna Esh directed the mare onto the familiar road, the carriage lights showing the way. Hickory Lane was indeed a welcome sight. She gave in to a deep sigh as a nearby owl *hoo-hoot*ed at the glistening white half-moon.

In just minutes, Bishop John Beiler's farmhouse appeared on the left — its tall, ancient trees adding to the air of dignity about the place . . . a quality the People affixed to the man of God and everything surrounding him.

Farther down Hickory Lane, beyond Nate Kurtz's vast cornfield, the spread of land that had belonged to widowed Ella Mae Zook came into view. Known as Hickory Hollow's Old Wise Woman, Ella Mae was one of Maryanna's dearest friends and confidantes — Ella Mae liked to say she always had time for peppermint tea and a prayer. The land had been parceled out to

Ella Mae's adult children, including her daughter, the Amish midwife, Mattie Beiler, and her husband, who'd lived in the main farmhouse for more than two decades now.

The stretch of road eventually led to the stark white clapboard house built many years ago by Benuel's grandfather, Simeon Esh, once a well-respected carriage maker in the hollow. The rustic outbuilding where some of the first carriages were made and repaired still stood on the north side of the property, flanked by thick underbrush and wild flowers and nearly obscured from view.

Maryanna relaxed as she rode into the tree-lined driveway, relieved to be home. The solar-powered yard light shone brightly, and for that she was grateful. Someone, possibly her father, who resided with her mother in the *Dawdi Haus* next door, had gone over and lit the gas lamp in the kitchen.

She stepped down from the buggy and tied Dandy to the hitching post, then called to the sleeping children. "We're home now. Leda, you and Benny unhitch the horse an' stable her, won't ya?"

After a moment, the twins climbed out and stumbled toward the mare. Tobias came next, rubbing his eyes as he followed his older siblings. "I can help, too, Mamma,"

14

he said in a husky voice.

"Jah, right quick," Benny said, seemingly more awake than the others.

Maryanna made her way back inside the carriage for Sarah, glad for the slight breeze this warm night. "Kumme, little one . . . Mamma's gonna take ya off to bed." She couldn't remember a time when she hadn't carried Sarah into the house while the older children unhitched after an evening trip. Not since Benuel's accident, anyway. "Sarah, honey . . . time to open your peepers, ya hear?"

"*'Tis best not to show partiality,*" Ella Mae had once chided her privately after Maryanna repeatedly sought out Sarah at a picnic gathering following Preaching service. "*Ain't good for her, nor you,*" Ella Mae had said, her milky blue eyes mighty serious.

Maryanna hadn't realized she was even doing it, but she supposed if Ella Mae thought so, then it surely must be.

"Sarah . . . where'd ya go?" whispered Maryanna, looking about. Then she realized her youngest must have crawled out when no one was watching.

She exited the carriage again, making her way around it to the children. "Did ya see Sarah wander by?" she asked Leda, who'd already unhooked the back hold strap on her side of the mare.

"*Nee* — no," said Leda.

Benny merely shrugged.

"*Des Haus,* maybe?" Tobias piped up.

Maryanna glanced at the house. "Jah, prob'bly."

She made her way across the driveway and through the large backyard. The grass felt comforting on her bare feet, and she made a mental note to mow tomorrow. *Right after breakfast, while it's still a bit cool.* Goodness, but it seemed like yesterday little Sarah had taken her first few tentative steps here — just weeks before her first birthday. Benuel had knelt right down in the grass, egging her on and wearing the biggest grin on his mischievous bearded face. He'd clapped his callused hands as Sarah tottered into his open arms, and Maryanna couldn't help but notice his twinkling blue eyes.

Like Sarah's own . . .

Maryanna entered the house by way of the west-facing side door, where the well pump was attractively enclosed in white gingerbread laths. Clipped shrubs flourished along the edges, as well as hollyhocks and petunias. That particular back door led directly into the kitchen, and just inside, she noticed again that the linoleum was beginning to show some wear. Maryanna pushed a throw rug over the worst of it. *No extra money for new flooring.*

There was a second back door, as well, which opened into the long utility room, where work shoes and boots were neatly lined in a row. Maryanna was fairly sure Sarah would've wandered in this way, sleepy and eager for her bed.

The house was downright stifling after being shut up all day, and she hurried to the kitchen windows, opening them as wide as they'd go.

Pressing the back of her hand to her face, she longed to slip away to the shower. What a treat on such an oppressive night! But she didn't dare indulge herself till the children were settled inside once Dandy was stabled for the night.

Stopping to light a lantern, she then carried it up the stairs. Heading past Leda's room on the right, Maryanna moved to Sarah's room on the left, at the far end of the hallway. Sarah liked her bedroom close to the street because she loved the sound of the *clippity-clopp*ing, she'd whispered in Deitsch one night when Maryanna tucked her in with the Lord's Prayer and a hymn.

Slowing her step, Maryanna wondered how the children always managed to find their way up the long, dark staircase without

17

a flashlight or lantern. *Young eyes.*

In Sarah's room, she raised the lantern high. The bed was still made, the room uninhabited, as best she could tell. She set the lantern on the oak dresser, built by Benuel himself, and looked under the bed skirt. "Are ya hidin', little one?" This wasn't the time for a game of hidey-seek.

But Sarah was not there, either.

She snatched up the lantern. Calling louder, she made her way back down the stairs. "Sarah, are ya here?"

Maryanna searched the entire main level of the farmhouse, every possible hiding spot Sarah and her siblings had ever used for rainy-day fun.

Wurum is sie? — Where is she?

Maryanna headed back outside. She set the lantern on the porch steps and ran across the yard, retracing her path to peer into the carriage. But she found it as empty as before.

It would do no good to alarm the other children, yet she rushed back to them and helped insert the tugs into the harness around the back of the horse. "Have ya seen Sarah anywhere?" Her voice was a wavering thread.

"She ain't inside?" Benny asked.

"Can't seem to find her." Then, thinking

18

she ought to have done it sooner, Maryanna grabbed the lantern from the steps and made a beeline to the stable. Not finding Sarah there, Maryanna moved on to the greenhouse, where she and the children spent many hours planting vegetables — and garden flowers, too — ofttimes dividing and potting plants to sell at their roadside stand.

"Dear one?" The lantern flooded the familiar corners with light — the nooks and crannies her youngest knew so well. Where Sarah pretended there were little fairy creatures living amidst the cobwebs she refused to sweep away.

Picking up her pace, Maryanna made her way to the Dawdi Haus to check with her parents. On many occasions, Sarah liked to pad over there in her long white nightgown and say *Gut Nacht* to *Mammi* Emmie and Dawdi Zeke, who sometimes slipped candies to all four children. *"Our secret,"* Sarah had told Maryanna with a playful smile. And sure enough, the next morning, Maryanna found the wrappers under bed pillows.

Tapping lightly on the screen door, Maryanna looked into the small house where her parents lived, snug and contented. *"Mamm?"* she called through the dark utility room that led to the small kitchen. "Are ya still up?"

She heard rustling, and then the downstairs bedroom sprang to light. Maryanna realized she'd likely awakened her parents and felt bad, wondering what she might say, not wanting to worry them needlessly.

Her mother appeared in the hallway, hair hanging loose to her waist. "Maryanna . . . what is it?"

"Chust lookin' for Sarah — thought she might've come over here."

"Ain't she with you?" Mamm replied, a wrinkle forming on her brow as she motioned Maryanna inside.

"Checkin', is all." Maryanna waved goodnight and turned to leave.

But her mother called after her. "Maryanna?"

"Not to worry." She kept going, moving faster now as a nameless fear settled on her.

When Leda saw her coming from the driveway, she must have known her little sister was still missing. "Mamma . . . did ya find her?"

"Sarah's got to be round here somewhere."

"I'll have a look-see in the house," Leda said, her skirt tail flying as she dashed back before Maryanna could stop her.

"Mamma?" It was Tobias's small voice now. "I looked in the woodshed."

20

"How 'bout the springhouse?"

"Ain't there, neither," he said.

Maryanna struggled to catch her breath, her hand on her heart. Her pulse pounded in her temples as she looked out to the dark road and beyond, to hundreds of shadowy acres of cornstalks, and she couldn't help but tremble.

O, Lord Jesus, where's my darling Sarah?

CHAPTER 2

Jodi Winfield pulled her shoulder-length hair into a loose twist and reclined as she situated her laptop for her upcoming Skype session with her fiancé, Trent Norton. Lounging indoors against peony-red pillows on this sultry July evening was the best way to avoid the miserable heat. It was her first time house- and cat-sitting at her cousin's modest country home in Lancaster County, Pennsylvania. Certainly, the place was a step up from Jodi's tidy apartment in Arlington, Vermont, where she shared two walls with other renters.

Plenty of time to regroup before school starts!

She recalled the text message a teacher friend had sent yesterday, just as Jodi arrived. *Are you up for teaching a third-fourth grade combo next fall?* Jodi had winced at the thought. It was not her ideal setup, but she was willing to do whatever it took to get tenure.

Reaching for a tall glass of lemonade, she relished the pleasant surroundings. Scattered about were silver-framed wedding pictures of her first cousin — policeman Scott Winfield — and Paige, his winsome blond bride of two years. There were candlesticks in graduated sizes placed on the barnwood coffee table. A large framed pastoral print graced the entryway. Cozy was the best word to describe Scott and Paige's bright, homey place . . . Jodi's home away from home for the next two weeks.

The room overlooked a fruitful landscape to the south, where lush fields and a picturesque barn with two silos stood in the distance. The unique setting and comfortable furnishings made it impossible to refuse the couple's request to spend some time here.

Eyeing the clock, Jodi awaited the specified time to contact Trent. She curled her toes, attempting to relax, but it was impossible to dismiss the trauma of the past six months. At one time, she and Trent had been knit together by their faith. Now it was all Jodi could do to whisper an occasional prayer — not that it mattered. As it turned out, God didn't hear them, anyway.

23

And now there were Trent's recent remarks to contemplate. Just two days ago,
Trent had stopped by her apartment to say
good-bye while she was packing. He'd
mentioned their mutual friends' new baby
boy. *"Such a handsome little guy."* Trent had
sounded almost wistful. *"Sometimes I find it
hard to believe we'll never have one of our
own, hon."*

She hadn't known what to say. Sure, she
loved kids — *other* people's children, particularly in a classroom setting. But after a
long day in the trenches, it was great to
return to a peaceful home.

Thankfully, Trent had moved on to another topic, but Jodi had remained rattled.
She hoped she'd concealed her concern,
especially since it was to be their last visit
before Trent left for Japan in less than two
weeks.

As for herself, Jodi wasn't up for revisiting
the idea of having children someday. Not
with her only sister's passing still so fresh.
Jodi's life had flown into a tailspin from
which she had yet to recover. Some days, if
it hadn't been for Trent's encouragement
and support, she felt she might not have
survived losing Karen.

Jodi recalled her fiancé's look of exuberance when he'd talked of the infant. Trent's

soft green eyes — nearly blue — twinkled at her, though not in jest.

So was he having second thoughts?

Presently, she signed into her Skype account. *Don't complicate things further,* she decided. As it was, Trent had to have noticed her frustration with God these past months, although she couldn't tell by his demeanor — he was the same patient Trent as always. Eventually, she would have to come clean about that matter, as well. Right now, she never wanted to set foot in church again.

When Trent's handsome face came into view, Jodi thrilled to see him. She couldn't help smiling.

"Hey, pretty lady. You look cute with your hair up."

"Thanks. Trying to keep cool."

"So how are you?" His light brown hair was combed neatly, and his five-o'clock shadow was beginning to appear. Trent's grin and confident voice nearly dispelled her earlier concern.

"Livin' the good life," she admitted. "Attempting, anyway."

"Well, I miss you, too." He chuckled.

She nodded slowly. "Yeah, sorry."

"You sound tired."

"Just a little."

He tilted his head. "You sure?"

She was tempted to say nothing, but that wasn't fair. "Just deep in thought, I guess."

"Missing Karen?"

"Some, yeah." She mentioned having talked recently with Karen's husband, Devin, and hearing the pain in his voice. "He's really struggling . . . as we all are."

"Well, once school starts you'll be very busy again," Trent suggested kindly, "which might be helpful."

Nothing helps, Jodi thought, recalling how difficult it had been going to school and teaching all day, weighed down by wrenching sorrow.

Trent continued talking, referring fondly to his own teacher friends in Bennington, Vermont, where he'd already acquired tenure as a fifth-grade teacher, though he'd taken a one-year leave for the upcoming job overseas. The decision had thrown her for a loop, although technically, they'd made it together.

Trent was fired up to teach English as a second language in the Japan Exchange and Teaching Programme, also known as JET. The plan was to make some extra money to set aside for their honeymoon next summer. And, too, Trent had always wanted to do something "to spread some cultural love around," as he liked to say. More recently, it was also tied to spreading "the Good News."

Deep down, Jodi was secretly crushed. But she'd pulled herself together, refusing to stand in the way of his dreams, even if it meant they had to wait another year to marry.

Presently the conversation lulled, and Jodi mentioned her cousin's delightful home and their beautiful white cat with gray-blue eyes. "Oh, and you should see the stocked fridge — enough for the whole block. Scott and Paige have spoiled me."

"You deserve it." He grinned. "Be sure to invite them to the wedding."

"Don't worry." She paused, wondering how to proceed. "And Trent . . . uh, I've been thinking about what you said the other day . . . before I left."

He smiled knowingly. "About kids, right?"

She nodded.

"I didn't mean to upset you," he said.

"You didn't," she lied. "I mean, I guess I should ask you . . . are *you* having second thoughts?"

"Jodi, I want you to be happy."

"I know, but —"

"Honestly, this is the kind of thing we should have taken more time to discuss."

She fell silent. So there *was* something

more to talk about.

"In the meantime," Trent continued, "we'll trust God for the future."

She cringed, saying nothing, but felt dishonest in her silence.

"You okay, Jodi?"

She couldn't bear to tell him the truth. Trent's faith was rock solid. She held her breath and forged ahead. "It's just that I've been struggling . . . a lot."

"Go easy on yourself, Jodi. You're plowing through deep waters."

She took a breath.

"Remember, I'm praying for you," he said, but it sounded patronizing, and Jodi wanted to reply that prayer certainly hadn't helped Karen, her older and wiser sister. And dearest friend.

Jodi twisted the thin twenty-four-carat gold bracelet Karen had given her before she died. It was a keepsake present her sister had purchased with her first paycheck, fresh out of grad school.

Jodi willed away her tears. "Oh, before I forget, I received an email from George Stringer, my principal. He plans to call me later this week. I guess the district's in a financial crunch."

"Like most school districts in the States."

"Still, teaching two grade levels might

present a challenge."

"You're an amazing teacher, hon. You might love it. I've seen you in action, remember?"

Jodi smiled, feeling more optimistic. "Speaking of action, I've been logging a bunch of miles here." She honed in on her training for the half marathon in Boston in October. "Sometimes I wish I could run with a group or an instructor."

"Well, you ran with me for a while." He winked, winning her heart all over again. "Just remember to warm up and don't push it — it's easy to overtrain, you know."

"Tell me about it."

He reminded her to take the supplements her doctor had recommended and to eat plenty of fruits and vegetables. "But keeping hydrated is key."

"That's not hard here."

"Exactly." He chuckled. "You're *breathing* water, right?"

They said their usual I-love-yous and good-byes. And Jodi was relieved they'd avoided more talk of babies — and prayer.

A lot can change in a year, she reassured herself.

CHAPTER 3

Jodi chopped a few tomatoes and sliced a cucumber into a bowl of baby greens and spinach leaves, then tossed the salad, looking forward to a late supper. Gigi, the fluffy white cat, meowed up at her, begging. Smiling as she remembered what Paige had warned about the fastidious animal, she checked the food dish and saw that it was still full.

"So you want fresh food, is that it?"

Gigi meowed again.

"Um, you're not spoiled at all, are you?" She chuckled, thinking she'd like to have a cat of her own to keep her company while Trent was gone.

Gigi rubbed up against her ankles, going in circles between her feet.

That's when Jodi noticed the loaf of homemade bread on the far end of the kitchen counter, with a note: *Delish! From a local Amish stand. Enjoy!* ~*Scott and Paige.*

Unable to resist, Jodi decided to have a piece with her light supper. But only one. She wondered about the person running the roadside stand, having never actually met anyone Amish. A copy of the June issue of *The Mirror,* the newsletter published by the Lancaster Mennonite Historical Society, was lying on the counter nearby. Circled in red was a blurb about a discussion and tour featuring Amish businesses without electricity. Jodi was curious how that was even possible and read further about four summer field trips offered by the local historical society, guessing Scott and Paige were members.

Breathing in the homey smell of the bread, Jodi recalled that the couple had referred to the "Plain" people quite frequently since moving here from the outskirts of Chicago. Jodi had also noticed a number of Amish novels in the corner of the downstairs family room, which additionally included a collection of old Dickens books that Paige had acquired at a rummage sale. And as a trusted policeman, Scott had mentioned interacting with nearby Amish during the course of his job, including at the annual Gordonville Fire Company Fall Mud Sale and Auction, where he often helped with parking and checking in vanloads of Amish from other states. From their many chats, there was no doubt in Jodi's mind that Scott and Paige were Amish aficionados.

Jodi hadn't the faintest idea what their attraction was to the horse-and-buggy crowd. *What's the big deal, anyway?* She turned and spotted Gigi standing by the food dish, just staring down at it. Jodi laughed and shook her head. "You're missing Mommy and Daddy, eh?"

She crouched to stroke Gigi, who purred into Jodi's open hand. *I miss someone, too,* she thought. Her big sister's memory was planted firmly in the middle of Jodi's heart. Even though she was six years older, Karen had always understood what made Jodi tick. *Like no other . . . not even Trent.* Her constant confidante and close friend, Karen had promised to always be there, though in the end, through no fault of her own, she couldn't keep the promise.

Gigi stepped away and looked back at her. She tilted her fluffy little head.

"Give me a chance, okay? You'll like me soon enough." With that, Jodi washed her hands and set the table for one.

She wondered what Trent really thought of her struggles. *What if I can't recover spiritually? Will he still want me?*

The answer seemed obvious. *Why would a*

wonderful guy like Trent want to marry a faith-less basket case like me? Jodi thought as she picked at her food. *Poor guy needs a good wife . . . someone normal who trusts God, wants kids, and doesn't cry on cue.*

Jodi blew out a breath, dabbed at her eyes, and began to eat. *Enough of this,* she thought.

When she finished eating, she cleaned up the few dishes and relaxed for an hour or so. She was eager to get out and jog first thing tomorrow, to explore the unfamiliar Pennsylvania back roads. She enjoyed losing herself in the effort of putting one foot in front of the other, her ever-attendant companions — despair and regret — slipping away with each stride. At this stage of her life, running beat prayer any day. It was Jodi's only dedication now, her sacrificial altar.

Maryanna strained to remember when she'd last seen little Sarah in the back of the carriage. Wasn't it right before turning onto Harvest Road? Sarah had been looking out the back with her dolly. And Benny and Leda had both warned Maryanna, hadn't they? *"Sarah's hangin' over the edge,"* Benny had said. But then everyone had quieted down, and Maryanna had assumed that all of her children had fallen asleep.

Everyone but Sarah.

Startled, Maryanna did not want to admit the appalling possibility that she had not noticed the goings-on in the buggy while concentrating on the drive in the ever-dimming twilight. It struck a blow to her very heart to consider her young daughter might have fallen out of the carriage and onto the road while her older siblings slept. Could it be? Yet what other explanation was there?

"Go quick an' fetch Jake Lantz and his father," she told Benny. "Run!"

Her eldest grabbed a flashlight and took off out of the house barefoot. "I'll be back in a jiffy, Mamma."

Ever-willing Benny, she thought, thankful not for the first time that he was named for Benuel.

"Will Freckles Jake tell all the men?" Leda asked softly.

Maryanna nodded. "Jah, for certain."

"I can run over to the other neighbor's, if ya want," Tobias offered, his pale blue eyes blinking up at her as they all stood in the kitchen, Leda's arm wrapped tightly around her. "Joshua will be glad to help."

Maryanna shook her head. She didn't want to involve him if she didn't have to. In due time, Josh would hear the news of miss-

34

ing Sarah, just as all the other farmers would.

Tobias frowned. "Mamma, Joshua's mighty *schmaert* — we should tell him. He's just next door!"

Maryanna sighed. Tobias was right. Regardless of her aggravation with the young widower, they needed everyone's help tonight, including her father's. "Fine, then, Tobias. Go an' tell him."

Eagerly, the boy nodded and headed for the door.

"I'll wait here with you, Mamma, in case little Sarah comes home." Leda breathed in spurts, like she might cry.

"*When* she comes home," Maryanna said, leading her to the long bench near the table. She simply didn't trust her emotions tonight. Yet she needed to be strong for her children all the same.

Think, she told herself. *What would Benuel do?*

Oh, if only her husband were still living! *"You've got a good head on your shoulders, Maryanna . . . and don't forget it,"* he'd said the morning before the accident that took his life. Out there in the field just across from theirs — helping with the corn harvest in Josh's brother Ned's absence. Maryanna hadn't ever let herself think Benuel

35

shouldn't have offered to help that day. No, it wasn't for her to question God's sovereign will. Even though there were times when the loss hurt as surely as if her arm had been the one crushed and severed.

"Mamma?" Leda asked, her light blue eyes solemn. "Remember Sarah's guardian angel is with her."

Maryanna nodded and pressed her lips together. " 'He shall give his angels charge over thee,' " she quoted.

"Will the angels lead Joshua and the farmers to our sister?"

Maryanna reassured her that men from all four corners of Hickory Hollow would come and help search. And all night if necessary. They'd done the selfsame thing when Mary Beiler's elderly grandfather, Abram Stoltzfus, wandered off one night last summer.

"Let's pray Sarah won't be too frightened." Maryanna leaned her head on her older daughter and felt Leda's wet cheek against her face. The vision of her little one walking around crying, nowhere near home, wondering what to do — it was all Maryanna could do to suppress her distress. To think they hadn't even noticed Sarah had fallen out of the carriage. *If that's what happened,* Maryanna thought, still aghast at the idea.

"The Lord *Gott* sees just where she is," she added, partly to comfort herself.

"Right now?" Leda whispered, looking up at her.

Maryanna smiled faintly. "Jah, this very minute."

With that, they bowed their heads, ending by reciting the Lord's Prayer together. And the all-important words *"Thy will be done"* lingered in Maryanna's mind long into the night.

CHAPTER 4

Keeping the night watch, Maryanna thought as she silently talked to God into the wee hours of Friday morning. She stood with clenched hands, her eyes fixed on the land beyond Hickory Lane. Dozens of men organized by Joshua Peachey, including Maryanna's own father, had headed south through the field and on the narrow road hours before. With every wink of their flashlights and lanterns, Maryanna had beseeched God for help as they linked arms and combed the area.

Now the house was ever so still — too quiet. Leda, dear girl, had been the most reluctant to go to bed, sitting in her room and brushing her long blond hair for a good half hour before kneeling at her chair to pray. Benny and Tobias, on the other hand, were too quick to head for their bed, the mattress squeaking as they leaped in. She'd heard Tobias saying his prayers under the sheet, and the remembrance of his small, trembling voice brought tears to her eyes even now.

Unable to sleep, Maryanna moved through the kitchen and out to the back porch, standing beneath the partial moon. She felt as dazed as the night of Benuel's Homegoing, numb and unable to think clearly. *"Fuzzy-headed"* is what her sister Mollie had gently called it back then. Maryanna's parents and all eight of her siblings had sought to soothe her in one compassionate way or another.

Moving away from the house, she wandered aimlessly to the little springhouse, then out to the edge of her lane, where she stood near the road and scanned the darkness, unable to see the men any longer. She shivered at the thought of her little one so far from home.

"I must do something," she murmured, raising her hand to her cheek and leaning into it.

As a small child, Maryanna had learned hymns and read verses from the Psalms that brought the peace that passes understanding. Later, when Benuel's untimely death came and the toil and the responsibility for their medium-sized farm — and the greenhouse he'd built — became wholly hers, the

Scriptures she'd heard repeatedly as a girl buoyed her heart.

Maryanna had, in turn, determined to pass on the faith in the same way to her own children. Sadly, she felt she'd failed to do much with Sarah, the spiritual guidance falling through the cracks when Benuel died. It was all Maryanna could do to get out of bed and go through the chores of her day back then, when Sarah was just a one-year-old. Maryanna had sung to her and tucked her in with a prayer, but she hadn't had the energy to continually instruct her in the ways of the Lord, as with her older three — she still didn't. *Yet teaching my children to obey and respect almighty God is my utmost duty,* she thought, knowing she alone was now accountable before the Lord for watching over the souls of their youngsters for as long as they were under her roof and care. *We will give an account of our household to God one day.*

Maryanna leaned against the old mailbox to steady herself, feeling uncommonly weak. But how could she rest, not knowing where her sweet baby girl was? "Dear Lord, hear our prayers for Sarah," she whispered to the night sky.

Oh, if only she could be out there looking right along with the men, doing something

40

besides standing here. It was all she could do to stay put at home, waiting for word. *And in case little Sarah shows up here.*

She trudged back to the house and up the long stairs to Sarah's dark bedroom. Moving to the row of wooden wall pegs, lantern in hand, she touched the newest Sunday for-*gut* dress she'd sewn for Sarah — a soft rosy color. *Like her little cheeks.* She recalled Sarah running across the lawn and straight into her arms.

"Oh," she gasped softly. Her mother-heart quivered at the thought of Sarah alone in the night.

Where?

Poor little thing, she hadn't gotten into a car with an *Englischer,* had she? No, Maryanna couldn't let herself dwell on that. Benuel's distrust of fancy folk still overshadowed her. And the memory of Benuel's failed business agreement with an Englischer years before made her flinch.

"He who looks up to God cannot look down on people," Bishop John Beiler had cautioned Benuel.

The whole thing had upset her husband no end, and because of it, Maryanna remained leery of getting too familiar with outsiders.

Now, staring out at the darkness, she

thought of all the men and teenage boys searching up and down Harvest Road, and Old Leacock Road beyond. Josh Peachey had brought a map of the county and laid it out on her kitchen table as more than a dozen farmers looked on, quickly determining a plan of action. Buster, his big watchdog, had waited silently on Maryanna's porch.

Surely, Sarah would be found soon . . . before morning's light. The Lord's all-seeing eye would guide the men, leading them as a loving shepherd cares for the smallest lambs.

And Sarah's angel. She recalled Leda's sweet reminder.

Jah, it's just a matter of minutes. . . . Maryanna was ever so sure.

Maryanna Esh's anxious expression had strangely energized Joshua Peachey, and he took lengthy strides as the horizontal line of men picked their way over the quiet field. The conscientious assembly included the blacksmith and his new young partner from Indiana, as well as Hickory Hollow carpenters and dairy farmers. Even Michael Hostetler, raised Amish but recently moved to the outskirts of Hickory Hollow with his English bride, joined in the search. More than forty strong, and the number of men grew as news of Sarah Esh's plight spread from house to house like a grass fire.

The sooner we find her, the better. In one hand, Joshua gripped the leash for Buster, his energetic German shepherd. He wielded his large flashlight with the other, trusting the Lord God for help and guidance. He was thankful for an exceptionally clear night.

No one conversed as they picked their way over one acre after another, though Joshua heard an occasional whispered prayer, especially from Ezekiel Mast, Sarah's maternal grandfather, and their ministerial brethren, including Bishop John Beiler. In his midforties, John was a younger bishop than most, yet as stern as any of the brethren in the area. But when it came to young children, his heart was soft. Joshua had observed him playing with his two youngest and was struck by the bishop's affectionate side.

Joshua, too, had a tender spot for children. He particularly enjoyed Tobias Esh's eagerness to assist him around the farm — the boy seemed drawn to him. He did wonder, though, if the main interest wasn't Shadow, the black rabbit that had belonged to Joshua's deceased wife, Suzanne. He sometimes let Tobias take the rabbit out of the cage in the kitchen and let it roam free. There was no doubt Maryanna's young son was over the moon about the gentle animal.

On the other hand, Toby's pretty mother was not at all interested in the dwarf rabbit. Come to think of it, she was not enamored with any of Joshua's pets . . . nor with Joshua himself. Sure, they'd been neighborly, especially while Suzanne was living. But since her passing, Maryanna had changed from being the cheerful hostess — inviting them for supper and ice cream get-togethers — to being withdrawn. Keeping to herself, for sure.

Just then someone in the middle of the search line halted, and the whole bunch of them stopped, shining their flashlights toward Smithy Riehl, their longtime black-smith, as he stooped over and picked up something that looked like a work boot. Nothing of consequence.

"How'd that ol' boot get out here?" he asked the man next to him, Nate Kurtz, who merely nodded. "And only *one,* yet."

This struck Joshua as rather humorous, although there was no chuckle left in him.

Buster pulled hard on the leash, nosing his way toward the boot. Joshua directed him back, and they continued plodding forward, a few more of the men talking occasionally now. It was as if they viewed the search as a sacred mission — or so Joshua felt. Sarah Esh was the dearest little girl ever . . . and not just because she favored her fair-haired mother. Sarah was exceptionally bright and quite the charmer, too — he'd observed her more than a few times at market, smiling up at the English tourists. In fact, her older sister, Leda, had told Joshua's own mother that she figured one day little Sarah would grow up to be a teacher at the one-room Amish school, or something that required an outgoing personality and a mighty *gut* wit, too. Spunky as Sarah was, some even wondered, himself included, if Maryanna's youngest might eventually push the boundaries of the community.

Doubtless little Sarah would require a steady hand in the years to come. *She needs a father figure, for certain!*

CHAPTER 5

The very last thing Maryanna thought she was capable of was drifting away to slumber. Yet when the knock came at the back door before dawn Friday morning, she started and nearly toppled off the chair where she'd sat in the front room near the window. She'd been having a fretful dream, and it took several seconds till she realized where she was, or just why she was sitting up to sleep, of all things.

Then swiftly, it all rushed back. "Ach, has my Boppli returned?"

Maryanna staggered a moment as she stood to make her way through the front room and into the kitchen, to the main back door.

There on the walkway stood Joshua Peachey and his father, Stephen. Her eyes darted away from Josh's thin, bearded face to his white shirt, grimy from the search. Stephen was every bit as disheveled. Mind-ing her manners, she motioned them inside, glad she'd left the gas lamp burning in the kitchen.

In the light, she gasped at the sight of the small blue dress in Josh's callused hand. *Sarah's!*

"Maryanna . . . I'm awful sorry." Josh looked down at the garment. "We found it next to Old Leacock Road a little bit ago." His soft hazel eyes were serious as he handed it to her.

She reached for it and pressed the dress to her pounding heart.

"Found these, too." Josh's father held out his hand.

"Hairpins," Maryanna muttered absently, receiving them and closing her fingers around the hard pins, squeezing them for dear life.

"The men are still out lookin'," Josh said, a deep frown on his tanned face. "Till morning."

"And for longer, if need be," Stephen added, his expression grim.

She didn't have to ask if there was anything else of Sarah's. The men's somber faces told it all. *"Denki"* was all she knew to say.

Josh's gaze lingered, his care and concern evident. She looked away, and it struck her just then that the two of them must be thirsty.

"I'll get you something to drink," she managed to say.

"No, no, we'd best be gettin' back to the others," Stephen said, dark circles beneath his eyes.

"Why not get some rest?" she urged the older man.

Josh agreed, suggesting his father return home. "You won't be any *gut* tomorrow."

"Ach, tomorrow's already come," Stephen firmly replied.

Maryanna felt weary — she had not wanted the day to arrive before Sarah's return. "I appreciate everything you're doing. I truly do." She stared at the little dress. Its fabric suddenly felt flimsy, and she was overcome with emotion, struggling not to cry. "Ach, forgive me," she whispered, her lower lip trembling.

"Will you be all right here?" Josh was quick to ask.

He means alone.

There was no good answer — Maryanna was alone without Benuel each day and every agonizing night. Losing her daughter simply emphasized her sadness and loss all over again. Oh, she wanted to sob now, wail as she had when these same men had

48

brought Benuel to her, carrying his broken, bleeding body across the field and placing him gently on the back porch. As tears filled her eyes, she stared blindly at this little dress she'd made with her own stitches. *For my precious girl.*

She gathered herself as best she could. For absolute certain, she was all right in her own house, where her other children still slept soundly upstairs. Where good-hearted Benuel had worked diligently to turn this old farmhouse into a home and the greenhouse into a family business. Where little Sarah had come into the world, all dimpled and pink cheeked, with the assistance of Mattie Beiler, the local midwife.

Maryanna felt dizzy and reached out to steady herself. Josh's face turned white — could he see the anguish in her eyes?

What does it mean? she asked herself, terrified of the answer. *Little Sarah's dress, here in my hands?*

But, no, she couldn't let herself succumb to fear or doubt. She must not give up hope. *I will not.*

Such were Maryanna's last thoughts before her legs turned rubbery and she lost her balance, falling toward Josh as if in slow motion.

The doorbell rang at six o'clock that morning, during Jodi's early breakfast of fresh fruit and carrot juice. *Who's this?* She hurried to the front door, hair still damp, and Gigi the cat scampered in the opposite direction. At the door, Jodi discovered a young brunette woman holding what looked to be a bag of clothing.

"I saw your light," said the woman, who wore a lavender skirt and soft pink blouse. "I'm Alesa Weaver, a church friend of Paige's . . . hope I'm not too early."

"No . . . you're fine." Jodi glanced at the bag.

"I'm afraid I'm lagging behind," Alesa explained, shifting her weight and the bag of clothes. "Paige is so great about organizing benefits and clothing drives and such. I'm just now getting my act together." Alesa held out the big bag.

"I'll see that she gets it."

"Oh, would you?" Alesa smiled broadly.

"Sure." Jodi reached for the clothes.

"Thanks so much." Alesa wiggled her fingers and turned to leave, then looked back. "Where'd they go on vacation?"

Jodi replied, "The Oregon coast."

"Must be nice."

"It's certainly cooler there." Jodi smiled.

Glancing again at the bag of clothes, Jodi turned and carried it into the house. She knew how picky Paige was about clutter, so she hauled it into the laundry room and closed the door. She'd text Paige later about Alesa's donation — find out what to do with it.

Jodi proceeded to the hallway near the back door to do her stretches, recalling Trent's friendly reminder. He loved her; she knew he did. But what might happen if she said no to his sudden openness to having children someday? And if she agreed despite her fears and they married, would she begin to resent her husband?

Jodi sighed and wished things might return to normal again, the way they were prior to Trent's mentioning children. But, no, she wanted to go back even further than that, back to the way they'd been a year ago, before her sister's diagnosis.

In spite of Jodi's efforts to stay focused, memories of Karen could jar her when she least expected. Sitting on the floor, Jodi brushed away tears at the thought of her sister's horrific battle with leukemia.

Six months ago, she and Devin and her parents had scattered Karen's ashes on a treed hillside overlooking the Connecticut River, an area Karen had loved since childhood. Yet the open wound in Jodi's heart was still oozing. How could she ever effectively move forward with life without her sister and best friend?

Jodi raised the fragile bracelet to her lips. "I'll never forget you, Karen."

She returned to her stretches. When she was adequately limbered up, she filled her hydration pack with ample amounts of ice and clipped her cell phone onto her shorts, thankful for these first few hours of cooler temperatures.

Gigi reappeared, padding down the stairs. "I'm heading out for my run," she told the cat while she put up her hair. "You'll have the place to yourself, so mind your p's and q's, okay?"

Then Jodi was off, out the back patio door and down the gently sloping lawn to the narrow road. Her goal was fixed clearly in her mind: nine miles without stopping. *No matter what!*

CHAPTER 6

Maryanna felt outright humiliated later, when she realized she'd fainted into her neighbor's arms. Goodness, she hoped Josh didn't think anything of it. *Wasn't like I planned it,* she thought, busying herself now with serving the oatmeal she'd made for breakfast. Mamm had always said cooking and baking were good for the soul, as well as the stomach. And in doing so, Maryanna attempted to keep her mind off her worst fear — that somehow Sarah had disappeared for good.

Why on earth had Josh felt it necessary to bring her Sarah's dress? Maryanna brushed a tear off her cheek, and despite her heavy heart, the thought of the man's pet rabbit came to her. While she'd never actually seen it, she'd heard plenty about the little caged critter from Tobias.

I wonder what the bishop thinks of that fer-hoodled parrot Josh keeps in his kitchen, too.

Not long before Suzanne died, the large, talkative bird had arrived from parts unknown. Word had it that Josh purchased the pet from someplace outside Hickory Hollow.

Maryanna sometimes wondered how many other pets inhabited the house, though she had no desire to investigate. She did know, however, that her Benuel had found Josh to be a good and fun-loving friend. *With the emphasis on fun.*

Alone now with Benny, Leda, and Tobias, she managed to push away the memory of coming to after her faint and seeing Josh's concerned face so near her own. She had awakened with her head cradled in the crook of his elbow, of all things! She could not recall what he had been whispering. Surely nothing of consequence, not with his father right there witnessing her predicament. Was Josh Peachey praying, perhaps? Still, the recollection of what must have looked quite intimate set her mind reeling. Maryanna was disgusted with herself for having fainted in the first place.

Her mother peeked her head in the back door, asking with her eyes if Sarah had been found as she made a quiet assessment of the three children at the table, poking at their oatmeal. Who could blame them?

Maryanna herself had no appetite. How could she eat with little Sarah still missing? How could she function at all?

Dear Lord in heaven, help us!

She invited her mother to come in — *"Kumme esse!"* But Mamm waved and said she'd already eaten, and hurried on, a worried expression on her face. Both Mamm and *Daed* had thoroughly searched their own Dawdi Haus last evening, after Maryanna let them know about lost Sarah. In fact, Daed had gone with a flashlight all around the front, side, and backyards, looking to no avail.

Benny asked for more milk, his upper lip white from the first glassful. "I'll go an' feed the pigs right after breakfast," he said, obviously trying to sound all put together, poor thing.

Just as strong as Benuel would expect him to be, she thought, glad she hadn't shown the children Sarah's dress or hairpins. No, the dress was safely tucked away in her bureau drawer for now. *She'll wear it again,* Maryanna told herself, insisting this be true as she rose to get more milk from the gas-powered refrigerator.

"I'll help Benny feed the pigs, too," Leda offered, her voice shallow, like she had a sore throat.

"No need, *Schweschder,*" Benny said, his face sympathetic.

His twin sister shook her head. "Ain't fair otherwise."

Maryanna appreciated how caring they were to each other. She said not a word, knowing that, when all was said and done, Benny would give in and let Leda join him in the dirty chore of feeding their half-dozen pigs.

"Let's say the Lord's Prayer, children." She bowed her head and began in German. When they were finished praying, she led out in the song *"Gott Ist die Liebe"* — "God Is Love" — one of her and Benuel's favorites.

Once the boys and Leda had gone to the barn, Maryanna carried the dishes to the sink, thinking ahead to the long day. She felt rather lifeless knowing she must redd up the kitchen, mow the backyard, and finish up her orders in the greenhouse for a list of customers. *They'll understand if I'm not ready . . . if I'm unable.*

Sighing, she recognized again how a person's sudden absence could completely drain a day of its significance. It was all she could do to plod out to the little wooden shed and get the push mower. But soon, several Amish neighbors dropped by and mowed for her, as well as did other chores, not wanting her to be alone, for which she was so thankful. And as they worked, Maryanna fretted about her responsibility as a mother. She blamed herself — there was no getting around it. She should've insisted on Sarah coming up front and sitting with her last evening. *Am I really that lenient with my youngest?*

Maryanna glanced over at the Peachey farmhouse, a cornfield away, remembering sharing favorite dessert recipes, such as blueberry crunch cake, with Josh's petite wife. Oh, the glow of love in Suzanne's eyes when she'd confided in Maryanna that she was expecting their first baby. Maryanna also recalled the school board deciding to flunk Josh and make him take his eighth and final year over again, all because he'd slipped away to hunt or fish rather than attend the one-room school down the way. Being the oldest in the school and two years older than Maryanna, Josh was expected to be an example. But when he got caught playing hooky, he'd always tell the teacher he loved God's creation more than book learning *"any ol' day."*

Of course eventually he settled down and joined church, becoming downright responsible before he married lovely Suzanne.

Maryanna went indoors and washed her perspiring face, then headed out to the greenhouse, where she gathered up the necessary potting tools with help from her Amish friends, who'd congregated at the farmhouse, as was their way. Reaching for the trowel, she noticed for the first time the marks in her left palm, where she'd clutched Sarah's hairpins much too hard.

Trembling anew, Maryanna stopped to pray as sunshine splintered through the east-facing windows of the greenhouse. *Lord in heaven, hear the cry of my broken heart. Will you bring little Sarah back to me?*

CHAPTER 7

Well into the fifth mile of her morning run, just past the sign for Old Leacock Road, Jodi's cell phone vibrated on her waistband. She groaned but kept jogging as she reached to unclamp the phone. She checked to see who the caller might be.

I have to get this. She moved to the shoulder, running more slowly now. "Hey, Mom!"

"Hi, Jodi — you sound out of breath."

"I'm jogging." She laughed.

"I won't keep you, honey. Just thought you should know that Trent's father ran into us yesterday. Such a wonderful Christian man." Her mother proceeded to tell Jodi that her fiancé was going to Japan to teach English for a year, as if Jodi didn't know.

Jodi felt a stab of guilt. "I'd planned to tell you and Dad. Things just got away from me."

"We know you're busy."

"Mostly with training for the half marathon. But I am enjoying the scenic farmland here." Jodi described the great swath of earth to the south that rose up in the near distance to what the locals called Grasshopper Level. "You should come to Lancaster County sometime, Mom. I think you and Dad would like it."

A short pause. Then her mother said, "I'm sure we would, but we're just swamped right now. *Too* busy, I think."

Jodi knew that was true. Her parents had thrown themselves into outreach ministry after Karen's death, their days of pew warming over.

"Well, maybe just keep it in mind."

Mom sighed into the phone. "I'm not putting you off, it's just that —"

"Don't worry, Mom."

"There's so little time during the summer," her mother said. "We have a lot of catching up to do at the rehab center before school starts again. Our free time belongs to God now."

Mom's new motto: *Saving the world, one addict at a time.*

Jodi suddenly realized she'd stopped running. "It's all good, Mom . . . what you and Dad are doing."

"You'll be back in Vermont when?"

"Actually, I just arrived here the day

before yesterday. I have two days less than two weeks to hang out in the garden spot of the world. Not a bad place to house-sit. Oh, and did I tell you they have a cat?"

"It'd be so wonderful if you could come to New Jersey and help us at the center during your off days this fall."

Jodi cringed. *Teachers rarely have downtime,* she thought, and her parents knew this firsthand. "Weekends, you mean?"

"Sure, honey. Whatever you can do." There was a pause before her mom said, "Well, I know you want to get back to your morning run."

"Okay, nice to hear from you. Tell Dad I said hi."

"Keep in touch, dear."

"I'll text you, okay?"

Mom laughed. "If you insist."

"It's faster, you know."

"That's fine. We love hearing from you, whatever form it takes. We're praying for you, honey."

There had been a time when Jodi would've said, *"I'm praying for you, too."* "Be safe," she replied instead. "I love you."

They said good-bye and hung up.

"Okay, now I've totally lost my momentum." Jodi began to walk briskly. Truthfully, she'd lost her momentum in more ways than one. It wasn't hard to decipher the real reason for Mom's call. Since Karen's death, Mom called more frequently, which was fine. But today it was also obvious she'd wanted to let Jodi know they were on top of things, that she and Dad were in the know about Trent's plans. Of course, this news should have come directly from Jodi. And why not? Shouldn't it be a joy to share the details of life with the people you loved?

Sighing now, Jodi considered the uncomfortable new spiritual gulf between them. While her parents had raised her in a Christian home, their heightened focus these days on living as believers sometimes alarmed her, maybe more so because she'd gone in the opposite direction. In the end, Karen's untimely passing had affected their lives in very different ways.

Why wasn't just attending church enough? She considered the friendly community place of worship they'd attended as a family in New Jersey.

Jodi headed back toward the north, in the direction of her cousin's house. Feeling slightly exasperated, Jodi knew her mom meant well; she always had. It was the undercurrent in the conversation, what hadn't been said today, that troubled Jodi. Both of her parents had spoken to her on multiple occasions about her need *"to get things squared away with God,"* as her father had most recently put it.

Dad had taught high school English prior to becoming a department head, then a principal. And Mom was a middle school strings instructor. In fact, every adult in Jodi's family was involved in some aspect of education, for two solid generations on her father's side. *"Teachers aren't made, they're born,"* Dad often said with a winning smile. Jodi had always been proud to share in the family profession and delighted in the connection it gave her to her parents. But now . . . well, Dad's and Mom's fervent interest in their faith had put a serious wrench in things.

The sun felt warm on her right shoulder as Jodi steadily found her stride again. She enjoyed various new vistas in all directions — she could see why Paige had referred to the region as *"God's green earth"* when she'd been tempting Jodi to stay.

Jodi ran all the harder, eager to put an end to the numbness she still awakened with every single day. Running not only beat a counseling session, but it was the only time when things seemed almost manageable, as if Jodi had *some* control over her life. At one time, she might also have said that running was a good time to talk to God, but the last time she did that was the day Karen died, and she no longer remembered exactly what she'd said. She *did* remember, however, what she'd thought — that if the world were to stop spinning right then, it would be quite all right with her.

And if you don't mind, I'd like to get off.

Her plea now wasn't exactly a prayer, but very close.

Following a gentle turn in the length of road, Jodi zeroed in on a string of oak trees coming up on the left. From this far away, it looked to her like a small child was playing beneath them. Not thinking much of it, Jodi maintained her speed, enjoying her run now, relishing the breeze as she went. But as she approached the grove of trees, she noticed the youngster wasn't playing at all but rather curled up like a kitten, fast asleep.

To Jodi's surprise, the sleeping girl was wearing only a white undershirt and panties. The sight startled her, and while she hadn't wanted to stop or slow her pace again, she was helpless not to. Going directly to the side of the road, where tall grass grew and the sunlight sifted through wide green leaves overhead, Jodi stooped near the child, who looked about four years old, if that.

Certainly a shady spot for a nap, but why here, so near the road?

Glancing about her in all directions, Jodi scanned for a nearby neighborhood or a playground . . . anything. "So small to be alone," she whispered.

Moving closer, Jodi lifted a long strand of matted wheat-colored hair from the tiny tear-streaked face. *She's been crying!* There was also a large bruised bump on the girl's forehead. Jodi felt her heart pounding, and not from exertion.

A further inspection revealed brush burns on the child's right elbow and bare foot. Had she fallen? Was she a victim of abuse?

Jodi crouched low and fumbled for her cell phone. Quickly, she searched the web for a child alert in the Lancaster County area. Turning up nothing, she checked for the entire state, then for the surrounding states, but there had been no such report today or even in the past few days.

She touched the girl's wounded arm, her dimpled hand. *Her parents must be frantic with worry. . . .*

Jodi quickly dialed the local police station and the phone rang five long rings before she was transferred directly to the voice mail of her cousin, Lieutenant Scott Winfield. *Strange,* she thought and hung up.

She decided to call 9-1-1 to report her discovery, knowing she should act quickly. Just as she started to dial, though, the little girl's eyes fluttered open. *Blue as the waves of the sea.*

"Mamma," the adorable child whispered, big eyes searching hers.

"Oh, sweetie," Jodi said, her heart in her voice. "Are you lost?" Jodi inched back slightly, afraid she might startle the child, who was sitting up now. "Where do you live?"

The little girl started to cry. Sobbing, she whispered, "Mamma . . . Mamma." With each repeat, she sounded increasingly more forlorn.

"Please don't be frightened. I won't hurt you."

The tot began to shake all over, her eyes sorrowful beneath thick, long lashes. She lifted her arms to Jodi, as if pleading to be picked up and returned to her family.

"Come here, honey. Let me take care of you." Jodi reached for her and gathered her near, carrying her tenderly in both arms, like one might cradle an infant. All the while her heart raced — was she doing the right thing? She must get ahold of her cousin. Scott would know what to do.

The little one burst into heartbreaking

sobs, burying her face in Jodi's neck.

"You precious girl." She formulated a plan, deciding to take the lost child to Scott and Paige's house, then drive her to the police station. But the house and car were at least a mile away.

Gently, Jodi carried the terrified child, refusing to tell her not to cry when she obviously had every reason to do so.

"Mamma," the little girl whimpered between cries.

The tender way the name was spoken tore at Jodi's heart. "I'll find your Mamma, I promise."

CHAPTER 8

Jodi glanced at her cousin's garage but kept moving to the house and a cooler place for the little girl in her arms. She set her down on a patio chair to unlock the back door, then took her hand and led her inside, heading to the kitchen to put some ice on her forehead. "It will help the swelling," she said, but the child said nothing.

After showing the little girl how to hold the ice pack, Jodi carried her into the small bathroom near the kitchen to wash her face. Her bare feet and legs were also terribly grimy, as if she'd been walking for a very long time. *Why — and how far?* wondered Jodi, offering a tentative smile.

She crouched down to eye level. "What's your name, sweetie?"

Wide eyes stared back.

"Do you understand?"

The lower lip trembled again. "Mamma . . ."

"Aw, honey, I know . . . we're going to find her real soon." Jodi was heartbroken for her yet baffled as to why she spoke only one word.

Jodi knelt on the floor, patting her own chest. "My name is . . . Jodi." She gently pointed to the child. "What's *your* name?"

Again, the youngster's eyes brimmed with tears, and she looked anxiously around the small room, still holding the ice pack on her bump.

Jodi made another attempt. "Do you know your phone number?" Essential information all parents would want to drill into their child. "It'll help us find your family."

More quivers from the little girl, and soon, big tears spilled down her pink cheeks.

"It's okay, sweetheart." Jodi's maternal instinct intensified. "Let's wash your face and hands."

After not having much luck in getting the dirt off her face with a mere washcloth — and worried about hurting the bump on the girl's forehead — Jodi leaned to turn on the warm water in the tub. "Do you like bubble baths?" she asked, opening the pretty pink bottle and pouring in a capful. "See? A nice warm bath will make you feel better." She swished the bubbles around as the child's eyes grew bigger. "All we need now is a rubber ducky or two," she said, trying to keep the mood light — the girl seemed so painfully naïve.

In that moment, something cautioned Jodi not to bathe her. *What if there's evidence?* But the little girl dropped the ice pack and leaned over the tub, her tiny foot up on the edge, eyes wide with wonder. And just that quick, she splashed into the sudsy water, underwear and all.

Not wanting to leave her, Jodi reached for her cell phone and dialed Scott's cell number, which quickly went to voice mail. Hearing Scott's message, she changed her mind — she didn't want to bother him on his vacation with Paige. It was such a rare thing, their getting away together, as Scott worked long hours at the police department. Paige had mentioned as much when lobbying for Jodi to come and stay at the house. *House-sit, really?* Jodi had thought reluctantly at first, especially because it would eat up her last days with Trent before he left for Japan. But she'd empathized with their situation and finally agreed after promising to Skype with Trent every day.

"Ich will mei Mamma," the little girl said softly as she looked up from her soapy pool, where she'd removed her panties.

Jodi handed her a clean washcloth and the

bar of soap, but the girl gave it back.

"Wu is sie heit?" the child whispered. *"Wu?"*

"You want me to wash you, sweetie?" Jodi asked. But when she didn't respond, Jodi began to soap up her arms, then her back. The whimpering ceased for a time, and Jodi was relieved, though still anxious to find out where she belonged.

Her mother must be beside herself, Jodi thought as she shampooed the long, silky hair.

When that was done, Jodi wiped the preschooler's face carefully, then washed out her underwear in the tub, as well. Rolling them in a clean hand towel, she hung them up before swathing the child in a thick bath towel and lifting her out of the tub.

When she tried to set her down, the girl clung tenaciously. "It's all right. I'm just going to help dry you off," Jodi assured her.

But the girl wrapped her arms around Jodi's neck all the tighter, wet hair pressing against her face. Not wanting to frighten her further, Jodi carried her and the damp underwear to the laundry room. She stepped over the bag of clothes Paige's friend had dropped by earlier as she placed the clean items in the dryer and turned it on.

Still carrying the child, Jodi headed to the

kitchen, where she sat the waif on one of four kitchen chairs situated in a cozy breakfast nook. The girl's hair formed ringlets over the towel, and her blue, blue eyes scanned the sunny kitchen.

Jodi removed a banana from the bunch and peeled it, then offered it to her. The girl reached for it quickly and popped the end into her mouth.

She's famished!

"Ba-na-na," Jodi said slowly, pointing to it.

The girl smiled faintly. *"Friehschtick."*

"Friehschtick means banana in what language?" Jodie asked herself. "Is it German?"

"Meh." The child stared anxiously at the banana. *"Meh?"*

"What are you asking for?" Jodi whispered, terribly frustrated. If only she'd taken German instead of French in college. "You must be very hungry," Jodi said, getting up to go to the fridge to pour a glass of milk. She set the glass in front of the child and sat across the table, inching her chair closer.

"Mamma . . ."

Jodi grimaced. "Honey, do you speak any English?"

"Ich habb mei Mamma falossa . . . un Kaylee."

72

"Ich habb," Jodi repeated. "Has to be German."

From the intensity of the girl's tone, Jodi assumed she was asking where her mother was — and something about a person named Kaylee. The worrisome thoughts nagged Jodi again. Was the girl a victim of kidnapping? Abuse?

If so, might I be implicated?

She refused to wait a second longer. Jodi yanked her cell phone off her waist clip and dialed Scott's number again. This time, she left a voice mail. "It's Jodi, and I'm really sorry to bother you, but this is an emergency," she said. "Please call me ASAP."

Maryanna could stand it no longer — she simply had to do something. She tugged at the dainty white handkerchief beneath her sleeve and wiped her clammy forehead and cheeks. Sighing, she set aside a good half of the greenhouse orders and abandoned the potting bench, determined to put her faith into action.

She hurried to the stable and led Dandy out of her stall and down to the carriage, where she'd left it last night. She began the hitching-up process while Benny and Leda were busy with chores in the pigpen. Soon, Tobias wandered out from the chicken

73

coop, looking mighty dejected. "I wanna help," he said, scarcely able to get the words out, and Maryanna could see that he'd been crying.

When they finished hitching up, he asked if she'd take him along, wherever she was going, and she agreed. Right away, she called to let Benny and Leda know she was leaving to retrace last night's journey, taking Tobias with her. "We'll be back shortly," she promised before hurrying to the waiting horse and carriage. Lo and behold, Tobias had settled himself in the driver's seat, already holding the reins.

He moved over right quick when she climbed up. "Denki, son," Maryanna said, suddenly glad for his company.

On the way up Hickory Lane, she told him to keep a keen eye out for Sarah's little cloth doll. "Ya know, the one she takes almost everywhere. She had it with her last evening. I know she did."

"Jah . . . and she calls it Kaylee," he said, blinking fast. "That ain't even an Amish name, is it?"

"No, that's right." This wasn't the first fancy name little Sarah had chosen for one of her dolls.

"Why'd she pick it, Mamma?"

She looked down at her young boy. His

hair was all *schlappich* and a piece of straw stuck in the crisscross of his black suspenders. "I honestly don't know."

"How's she know 'em?"

"*Englischer* names?"

He nodded slowly, his face cheerless.

"Well, I s'pose from the tourists' children at market." It occurred to her then that Tobias had rarely accompanied her to the Bird-in-Hand Farmers Market. Typically, he spent market day next door, helping Josh feed chickens and running errands and whatnot. Of all her children, Tobias had most latched on to Josh after Benuel's passing.

"Are we lookin' for a doll, then?" Tobias asked innocently.

"Just let me know if ya happen to spot it anywhere, is all. . . ." Maryanna didn't say more. She couldn't reveal that she wished she'd gone searching with the menfolk last night — though how unconventional would that have been? No, Maryanna wouldn't let on that she was, in all truth, looking now for little Sarah herself.

CHAPTER 9

Joshua pressed onward with the other searchers, probing past the boundaries of Hickory Hollow with his German shepherd. All the while, he struggled with his recollection of Maryanna lying limp in his arms after she'd collapsed. Daed had awkwardly looked away for a time as Joshua quietly prayed she'd quickly come to. Thankfully, she had, and he hadn't made a fool of himself, though he certainly could have.

One long year had passed since he'd held a woman like that, his own sweet wife, gone to Gloryland. *Dear Suzanne, she suffered so,* he thought of his bride, who had died in childbirth. Maryanna's missing little girl had brought back thoughts of his own tiny daughter with soft hair the color of sunlight. *Our firstborn . . . who lived but a single hour.*

Joshua sighed. He was a widower, and from the looks of it, without any recourse to remedy that unless he found the courage to invite one of the area's younger widows out for a date.

Jah, I must ponder that. . . . Maryanna Esh would be his first choice, although it was unlikely she'd ever agree to go anywhere with him. She was clearly a determined woman with a mind of her own — qualities he admired. Not only that, he had been impressed with the way she'd held things together for her four young ones back when Benuel died without warning, and here again with this strange disappearance of little Sarah.

An admirable woman, he thought, bone-weary now. They'd tromped all over the county during the night without rest or sustenance.

Pulling on Buster's leash, Joshua bent to pick up something that might belong to Sarah Esh, just maybe. But alas, it was merely refuse stuck in the soil.

Several of the older men looked nearly stooped and sometimes paused briefly to press their strong fingers into their necks and shoulders, all done in. Joshua wished those who hadn't left for the early morning milking would simply drop out and head home to rest a spell. Made good sense, yet the remaining farmers kept pushing onward. As for himself, he refused any notion of stopping — more than anything, he wanted to find Maryanna's beloved child and bring her home.

Waiting for Scott to return her call, Jodi stood in the kitchen while the little girl slept on the living room sofa. If this were a summer ago, Jodi might be praying now. Her mother would not be reticent about it at all, leading out in a confident prayer and asking God for guidance to find the child's family. Jodi's father, too, would be praying aloud as he drove to the police station with the lost girl in the backseat.

So what am I waiting for?

Oh, but she knew. Too many times during her year of teaching, she'd encountered children who had been moved from one foster-care setting to another. There were plenty of wonderful foster families, but she felt fiercely protective of this innocent child.

Jodi grabbed a bag of carrot sticks and noticed Gigi standing near the food bowl again, staring her down. She dismissed the feline and her power struggles — there was plenty of food in there.

Jodi hurried back to the sleeping child, a wave of sympathy overwhelming her. The knot on the girl's forehead still concerned her. Glancing at her watch, Jodi realized it had been a couple hours since she'd found the child along the roadside.

The youngster opened her eyes and looked right at her, the rosebud mouth widening with a smile. The girl blinked sleepily, turning her head in time to watch Gigi leap onto a chair across the room, the cat's tail curling serenely around her body. Eyes brighter now, the little girl rose and scooted over next to Jodi, towel and all, leaning against her arm. Then, after staring at the cat for a few minutes, she promptly fell back to sleep.

She must be dreaming, Jodi assured herself, shaken by the child's easy affection toward a stranger.

Maryanna sighed heavily in the carriage seat, fanning herself with the embroidered hankie. Was it just her, or did the day seem remarkably hot and humid? She'd purposely slowed the mare from the outset and had scanned the roadside for miles, tears dimming her sight at times, though she hid them from Tobias.

"Does everyone have a guardian angel, Mamma?" he asked.

"What does the Bible say 'bout that? Do you remember?"

He shook his head and shrugged his slight shoulders. This was the young son who'd

79

chosen to sleep away his birthday the year after Benuel died, staying in bed, no doubt missing his father. Maryanna had known he wasn't sick because the very next day he was back to normal, out working with the twins once again.

Such a sensitive soul . . .

"The ninety-first psalm says angels will keep us in all our ways," she said, clinging hard to its truth.

Tobias nodded, his straw hat pushed back on his head. *Like Benuel always wore his . . .* "Just makin' sure," he muttered.

She reached to pat his shoulder. "There now, don't ya fret. We'll find her," she said. "In God's way and time."

Her words sounded forced. Did Maryanna truly believe that? Were the words from her heart in perfect unison with the Good Book?

"Thy will be done" echoed in her head.

Joshua became aware of the rumblings of a dispute when Smithy Riehl took up the notion of contacting the police. He'd said it loudly, like it was something folks might actually consider.

Joe Hostetler pulled a disgusted face and spared no one's feelings by stating emphatically that *he'd* never reported *his* daughter missing.

"Well, but your Lizzie was nearly grown and felt she knew her own mind," the smithy replied. "Back then."

"True, but we kept the Englischers out of it, like always." Joe's face was the color of ripe beets, including his earlobes, which stuck out from beneath his hair and frayed straw hat. "Ain't nothin' wrong with trusting the Good Lord, I say."

Mutters of agreement were heard all along the search line.

"The longer little Sarah's not found . . . well, I don't think it's wise." The smithy's voice faded.

"It's not that I don't want to find her," Joe replied. "Don't get me wrong."

" 'Course not — you're here, ain't ya?" Smithy put his head down just then, looking grimly at the meadow grass.

Hoping things might die down, Joshua glanced at the bishop, just four men to his right. Would the man of God speak up?

Joshua felt his chest tighten as he gripped Buster's leash. It wasn't the first time their blacksmith had pressed things with the Hickory Hollow bishop, who was known for standing hard on most positions. Even stricter than other bishops nearby.

Still, Joshua couldn't help but think the debate was sparked by the fact the whole

81

bunch of them were not just dog-tired but hungry. They'd seen the moon set and then the sun rise up over the trees, casting a hazy gold shroud over fields and barns and windmills. And they'd heard the sounds of family carriages clattering up and down Old Leacock Road on the way to market. And the kindly calls of "Gott be with ya" and "We're lookin' for her, too."

Now, though, the men were far from home, especially to be on foot like this.

"What say you, bishop?" asked Eli Lapp, Samuel and Rebecca's middle son, married and with a small brood of his own.

There 'tis, thought Joshua, wondering if they might not end up arguing in a circle under the morning sun, smack-dab near the intersection of Old Leacock and East Gordon roads. Just a short distance from the train tracks.

"If ya don't know by now, Eli, I daresay you haven't been payin' much attention for a *gut* long time," the bishop declared. "Ain't so?"

Has Eli forgotten what happened to his willful sister, Katie?

"How would ya feel if you were Maryanna Esh? Think of that." Eli posed the unspoken question on Joshua's mind.

The bishop nodded. "Well, son, we all

82

know the Lord God sees and understands the worry in Maryanna Esh's heart, and her youngsters, too." Bishop John stopped walking, and the whole line of men followed suit. "Some of you concern me greatly. You sound like the fancy English we rub shoulders with over in Bird-in-Hand and New Holland." He frowned. "If you can't trust almighty God to help us find one of our children, how can you trust Him for your crops . . . your daily lives?"

Joshua considered that. *Still, other Amish districts use 9-1-1,* he thought, knowing it was true.

More murmuring followed, and then the blacksmith dropped out of the line and turned to head northeast toward Hickory Hollow. His young partner, Eben Troyer, stayed put.

"Anyone else?" the bishop asked loudly, as if daring them.

Remarkably, a bunch more men, including Hank Kurtz, Nate's eldest, turned heel and left with a mighty swift gait.

They'll catch it later. Joshua wondered if Hank or the others would contact the police. Personally, he was torn between the two camps, wishing for a compromise. *Where's the middle ground?* There was a child at risk, after all.

The men abandoning the search would certainly feel like deserters once the rest of them finally found little Sarah. Joshua wished they might change their minds and stay the course, drained though they all were.

"C'mon — let's keep moving. Sarah Esh is still missing," Bishop John said and stepped ahead, toward Paradise to the south.

The remaining men followed, marching forward with renewed determination. Thankfully, about the time Joshua's tongue began to curl with thirst, they heard a spring wagon rumbling along. The bishop's young wife, Mary, and her neighbor Mattie Beiler were bringing sandwiches and thermoses of water.

The wagon pulled off the road, next to the grazing land, and the men flocked to it like parched birds.

CHAPTER 10

Maryanna had slowly become accustomed to making her own decisions over the past nearly three years. She no longer conferred with anyone about what to grow in the greenhouse. Nor did she hesitate to light a lantern on a sleepless night to read in bed, or think twice about cooking her favorite meals — and the children's — or just plain doing things the way she chose to. She wouldn't call herself set in her ways, exactly, but with God's help — and the help of her extended family — Maryanna and her children were doing quite well.

She and young Tobias had only been home a few minutes from their fruitless search for little Sarah when her sister Mollie Yoder turned into the lane with their family carriage.

"Hullo, Maryanna," sweet Mollie called while tying the horse to the hitching post. Maryanna's older sister by a few years, she wore her gray choring dress and black apron, some of her light auburn hair already falling free of her bun. "Came to keep ya company." Her brown eyes were sad, and the area around them was puffy and red. "Jeremiah and I heard the news and went right to prayer. I came just as soon as morning chores were finished." Mollie eyed the horse and walked toward Maryanna, bringing two of her girls with her. "Whatever needs done, we're here to help."

Twelve-year-old Bertie smiled timidly — she'd been born with Bardet-Biedl syndrome. Bertie wore thick glasses to help her failing eyesight and had a tiny sixth toe on her right foot. In part due to her poor vision, she struggled with learning difficulties. Bertie's genetic disorder was one of the reasons for Maryanna's and her husband's concern and faithful prayers for healthy children, each of whom had been tested in turn at the Clinic for Special Children. Bertie's younger sister, Fannie, was blond like Bertie and had recently turned ten. Both girls now followed their mother toward the house, across the newly mown lawn and up the walkway.

Right from the very first, when they were young girls, Maryanna had sensed something special about this sister. With Mollie near, everything was going to be all right, no matter the circumstance. Even today, when Mollie opened her arms in greeting, Maryanna felt much more secure. But she had a strong urge to cry as she clung to her, though she tried to compose herself in front of her nieces. Bertie was especially sensitive to outbursts of emotion by others. They made the dear girl awful panicky.

Once indoors, out of the heat, Maryanna composed herself under Mollie's sympathetic glances. She didn't feel much like being a hostess, but Maryanna washed several clusters of red grapes and quartered some apples, glad she'd changed out the old red-checkered oilcloth on the table for the new blue-and-white one. She returned to the gas-powered refrigerator and reached for a large pitcher of cold meadow tea, then carried it to the table.

"Jeremiah was out searchin' all night with the men," Mollie said, looking mighty tired herself.

"Truly glad for that."

"Some disbanded for rest a while ago, and to tend to livestock." Mollie added that she'd made something for Jeremiah to eat right before coming. "That's why it took us this long to get here."

Maryanna understood. "No need to

apologize."

Bertie nodded, her hazel eyes blinking fast. "Jah, we had to do all of *Dat's* mornin' chores first." She rubbed her plump belly. "But we didn't mind."

Fannie smiled, then looked quickly toward the window. "When did ya see Sarah last, *Aendi* Maryanna?" she asked.

It was all Maryanna could do to recount the story of last evening's trip home from Paradise for Fannie and the others. But she tried to put herself in her precious nieces' shoes — both Fannie's and Bertie's faces looked drawn as they listened to Maryanna's account.

"Mattie Beiler and the bishop's wife headed out to take food and water to the men looking for Sarah," Mollie mentioned. "And to bring back those who needed to catch up with farm duties and whatnot."

They settled down at the table, nibbling on the fruit, even though none of them probably cared much for a snack.

Where on earth is my Sarah? Maryanna shook her head, feeling dizzy again. *Where?*

Mollie touched her arm. "You didn't get a wink of sleep last night, did ya?"

Maryanna refused to admit she'd only dozed in a chair, not wanting to seem to complain.

"Why don't ya go upstairs and put your feet up for a while?" Mollie suggested kindly. "The girls and I will take care of everything — cook the noon meal and supper for ya, too."

Maryanna didn't need to say that her own children were out doing their many chores. Very soon they'd be running to the house to greet Aunt Mollie, one of their favorite relatives. She certainly could trust Mollie to look after them.

I should let myself rest, thought Maryanna, all in. *I need to be strong for Sarah's sake . . . for all of my children.* She held her breath so she wouldn't give in to tears. No matter how bleak things seemed, she refused to relinquish hope.

Joshua drank his fill of refreshing cold water, Buster panting nearby as the weary band of men, who were rotating in shifts, clambered onto the wagon.

In short order, they were on the way back to Hickory Hollow with Mary and Mattie. Many of the men promised to return later in the day, if need be. *If Sarah's still missing,* thought Joshua with a great sigh.

In the meantime, all of them were committed to praying for God's protection over the little girl and divine help in finding her.

Will someone defy the bishop and call the police now? he wondered.

A half mile or so from his house, Joshua and Preacher Yoder got out of the wagon and started walking home. Joshua released Buster from the leash and set him free, watching as the devoted dog headed straight toward home. Buster had not wavered during the search, and for that Joshua was grateful.

Once home, Joshua turned on the spigot in the barn to water his beef cattle, troubled at the talk amongst several more of the men. A growing number believed someone must contact the police if Sarah wasn't found by nightfall. The bishop had made yet another point of declaring God's sovereignty. *"It won't matter if we bring in Englischers or not, the outcome will be the same,"* he'd stated.

The men in question had bowed their heads, saying no more. The consensus was to heed their bishop.

Joshua was bone tired as he pondered all that had transpired, wondering how Maryanna was holding up. He imagined her look of happiness if he were to bring Sarah home to her. Ever since last night when the search began, he'd wanted to bring *gut* news — nothing like the heartrending news he'd delivered nearly three years ago.

He felt another twinge of guilt, the kind that occurred whenever he remembered the past, and he had to push it away. Maryanna didn't hold him responsible for Benuel's death. How many times had he told himself that? What had happened that day couldn't have been helped. Nonetheless, not a day passed that he didn't miss his dear friend, as close even as a twin brother.

Ach, so many losses. Benuel, Suzanne, and now . . . dear Lord God, please don't add young Sarah to the list.

A few minutes later, Joshua heard the barn door slide open. He was a bit surprised to see Tobias Esh standing in the blinding sunlight. "Hullo there," he called to the boy. "C'mon inside."

"I seen you were back." Tobias pulled hard on the barn door to close it.

"Saw," Joshua corrected him.

"Jah, sorry. I can't remember *gut* grammar."

Joshua patted his shoulder. "The minute I'm finished here, I'll be back out lookin' for your sister. Retracing every step I took last night and this mornin', too."

Tobias hooked his thumbs on his black suspenders and looked up at him. "Thought you might've found her by now." His voice sounded so forlorn, Joshua had to swallow to keep his own sentiments in check. In fact, he turned momentarily to conceal them. Then Tobias added, "I'd like to go along."

"Well, I'm not sure what your Mamma'd say to that."

"She won't know, 'cause she's resting."

This was a desperate boy. "I still think it's best you tell her where you're goin' . . . given the situation."

"You honestly think I'd get myself lost like little Sarah?" Tobias pushed out his lower lip.

"Nee." Joshua shook his head. "I know better."

"I ain't a little child . . . and I certainly ain't a *girl.*"

Joshua was mindful not to smile. "No, you're a determined young man, and I understand you want to help."

"I surely do." Tobias leaned over. "Mamma would never let me go."

"Then you best not."

"But we *have* to find Sarah. Mamma won't be able to keep goin' without my baby sister. I just know it." Tobias shook his head. "Please, won't ya just take me, too? We'll be back before Mamma even knows."

Torn between the pleas of his young friend and the fact that Maryanna Esh would never forgive him, Joshua put his hand on

Tobias's shoulder. "Listen to me, son. . . ."

Tobias frowned severely, his eyes glistening.

"I want ya to pay attention." Brushing aside his slip, Joshua proceeded to remind Tobias of the pain his poor mother had suffered during the past few years, including now, with Sarah's disappearance. "And what kind of people do ya think we'd be to add even a speck of worry to your Mamma's load?"

Tobias wiped his eyes with the back of his arm, and for the longest time he was quiet other than a few sniffles.

"I'm not belittling your desire to help," Joshua added. "*Begreife* — understand?"

Toby stared at him, the first time Joshua had witnessed the slightest hint of defiance in the lad. And then, ever so slowly, Toby's expression softened and he nodded his head. "All right, then. I'll stay put at home. Like ya said to."

"Thattaboy," Joshua said, his heart heavy as Maryanna's sympathetic son rose, stuck his hands in his pants pockets, and turned toward the barn door. Before he left, though, Tobias looked back at him and their eyes locked. It was then that Joshua realized he'd acted on behalf of his *gut* friend Benuel — Toby's father wouldn't have wanted to risk adding further worry to Maryanna. *Not for the world.*

And neither did Joshua.

Maryanna gazed out the tall window across the bedroom, attempting to rest. She'd left the green shade up, needing the consolation of the blue sky. As a child, she'd often thought of a clear sky as a promise of good things to come. She sighed as her chest rose and fell. Her head pounded from lack of sleep and the misery of yearning. "Oh, Lord, please . . . I must have my little daughter home again," she murmured. "How will I live, otherwise?"

She'd recalled the day of Sarah's birth a dozen times or more since her disappearance. The miniscule weight of her darling newborn in her arms — where she longed for her girl to be now. The cuddly way her Boppli looked up at her, hazy blue eyes still learning to focus. Benuel had been near, sitting just across the room from her until Mattie had placed the tiny pink body on her own. Benuel had stepped over quickly, sliding his hand beneath Maryanna's head as he kissed first her lips, then their baby's pretty round head.

She rolled over and closed her eyes. Now their last babe was gone, and she didn't know where.

How could I let this happen? She'd asked herself the question in various ways, gasping under the weight of guilt. One thing was certain — such a thing wouldn't have happened if Benuel were alive. Nor perhaps if her children had a good and loving stepfather.

Not until today had Maryanna considered the notion that she was depriving her children of a man to be their covering under almighty God — a father to love and protect her children. Truth be told, they needed someone to look up to and obey, and someone to call Dat. *Especially since it seems their mother hasn't done such a good job,* she thought, letting the tears roll down her face. *I've failed them miserably.*

"Thy will be done" came to mind again, and she felt as if she'd failed the Lord, as well. Had she made little Sarah an idol in her heart, binding herself up in what Sarah wanted or needed — Sarah's antics? Did she live her life to please her little one, like Abraham of old, who struggled to give up his hold on Isaac?

Do I adore my youngest child more than God?

In that moment, Maryanna knew what the Lord required of her. Too weary to get up and kneel, she folded her hands and lay prone before her Father in heaven, praying silently. *I am willing to release my daughter Sarah to you, O God, entrusting her completely to you. I do this with your help and yours alone, through your only Son, Jesus Christ, my Lord. . . .*

CHAPTER 11

Using the house phone, Jodi once more dialed the non-emergency number for the police department. Since Scott hadn't immediately returned her call, she'd leave her cell phone open. He and Paige were most likely enjoying the sun and surf on the Oregon coast.

While Jodi was put on hold to speak to an officer, her cell phone rang — it was George Stringer, her gregarious middle-aged principal. Deciding she might be on hold for an eternity, she answered her cell, hoping an officer wouldn't answer while she took George's call.

"Hello."

"Hey, Jodi. George Stringer here. How are you?"

"Doing well. How's your summer going?"

"Could be better," he said. "So I hear you're in Pennsylvania. Are you enjoying Amish country?"

She filled him in quickly on why she'd come, and they exchanged a few more casual remarks.

Then he paused, exhaling into the phone. "I'm afraid I have some bad news."

Now what? she thought, remembering the dreaded third-fourth teaching combo.

"The district is cutting back across the board," he explained. "It can't be helped. And I want you to know I tried my best to spare your job."

No . . . not my teaching position!

Jodi did her best to take the staggering news like a professional. Somehow she managed to calmly express her disappointment. "I'll really miss working with you, George, and all the teachers at the school," she said, realizing in that moment how proud her father would be of her . . . for taking the high road when she wanted to grovel and plead and ask if there wasn't something she could do to save her first-ever teaching job. But she kept her tone respectful.

She fought back tears, wishing she'd had one more year under her belt so tenure might have saved her. But instead she was discovering the meaning of "last in, first out."

"I know you'd be very welcome in the district as a regular substitute," George mentioned. "If you choose to take that route."

A sub when I was so close to tenure? Talk about starting over!

She thanked him, not really interested in considering that course, then said good-bye. No, she still hoped she could land another full-time position in a nearby district before school began.

While the little girl slept, Jodi cradled the house phone under her chin, still waiting for someone, *anyone* to pick up and take her call at the police station. She occupied herself by sending texts on her cell phone to several of her closest teacher friends . . . and to Trent. To think she had been so very proud of her first-year work ethic and teaching abilities.

If only it weren't so late in the summer. All the same, Jodi was anything but a quitter. Tonight she'd get busy tweaking her resume and send it out all over New England.

It struck her as ironic that Trent had taken leave of his tenured position to teach overseas. It was almost as if he had *two* jobs, and she had none.

Within minutes, she had responses from three of her teacher friends in Arlington, declaring their school day would never be as stimulating or fun without her. *Besides, who's going to bring healthy snacks to get us through the day?* wrote another. But none of them truly understood the sting of sadness and disillusionment Jodi felt.

Trent texted her next. *Hon, I know how upset you must be.*

She returned the message, saying she hoped to pick up some subbing for a while, if nothing else. *And who knows, if I hurry, maybe I can still line something up. But I really dislike the idea of moving.*

He didn't text back right away, and she sat quietly considering her principal's call. George Stringer had been such an encourager from the very first time she interviewed with him. And not only to her, but to the entire staff. She could only imagine how amazing things might be at this moment had she begun her teaching career earlier, straight out of college, and not opted to first get her master's degree in child psychology.

Jodi wondered how her parents might respond when she informed them of her lousy news. But that would have to wait until she'd had some time to process this for herself.

Suddenly, the house phone clicked off, giving way to a dial tone. She'd been disconnected! Determined to speak to someone, she dialed again, this time getting a busy signal.

Jodi forced air out of her mouth — she'd try again in five minutes. Carefully, she rose from her comfortable spot, not wanting to awaken the exhausted little girl. She wandered about the living room, then down the hallway, still in a daze, thinking of all the creative plans she'd made for her third graders — interactive bulletin boards ready to assemble; thematic centers for science, art, and writing; even a cozy rug for a reading nook — all stored in her apartment back in Arlington.

It's not the end of the world, she told herself. But if not, why did she feel such panic?

Jodi's gaze fell on the preschooler on the couch as she meandered back into the living room. Surely it was unreasonable to be so upset about losing a job when a mother somewhere out there had lost her child.

But she's safe, Jodi thought, staring at the girl. *And she'll be home soon.*

Jodi slipped away to the main-level guest room where she was sleeping and sat on the edge of the bed, trying to shake off her disappointment. *I can't let this get me down,* she thought, noticing for the first time a lovely carved plaque across from her, near the chest of drawers. How had she missed seeing this? *"Trust the Lord with all your heart, and do not rely on your own understanding. . . ."*

One of Karen's favorite verses. But spotting it now jolted her. " 'And do not rely on your own understanding,' " Jodi said softly, refusing more tears. It would not do for her to seem despondent when she returned to the living room and the lost little girl.

Back in the living room, Jodie used her cousin's phone to dial the police station, only to again be put on hold. She felt she might lose her wits, considering everything that had transpired this morning. She glanced at the youngster, who'd awakened and was presently sitting next to the cat on the living room floor, still wrapped in her towel. In spite of everything, Jodi had to smile as she listened to her talk soothingly to Gigi in her own language, leaning her head down to nearly touch the cat's nose with her own.

Lost in thought, Jodi started when her cell phone rang and Scott's number appeared.

She hung up the house phone and promptly answered her cell. "Am I ever glad you called!"

"Hey, what's going on?"

She filled him in on finding the child and calling the police station for advice. "But I haven't been able to connect with anyone yet."

"Do you think she might be abandoned?" Scott's voice was solemn.

"I wondered that, too. But it's hard to believe."

"Well, why?"

"She's just so beautiful . . . absolutely darling. And anyway, who would desert a child?" She watched the little sweetie pat Gigi's tummy. "And while she's worn out and hungry, she looks like she's used to being fed well. Yet on the other hand, when I found her, she was barefoot and without clothes."

"Really?"

Jodi described how meagerly she was clothed. "She also has a big bump on her forehead and bruises on her arm and leg."

"Did she tell you anything?"

"She speaks no English, far as I can tell."

"No kidding."

"Almost sounds German . . . but I'm not sure." Jodi told him the word for banana. "Ever hear it?"

"Might be Pennsylvania Dutch." Scott paused a second. "How's her hair cut?"

"Looks like it's never been trimmed."

"Parted down the middle . . . with a bun in back?"

"No bun, but definitely parted in the middle."

Scott paused, clicking his tongue like he did when he was deep in thought. Then he said, "Tell you what. Put her in the car and drive over to Hickory Hollow — use your GPS — it's not too far away. Turn right at the first road after Cattail Road and Hickory Lane, and go a mile or so. There'll be a one-room schoolhouse on the left. The next farmhouse on that side of the road belongs to Bishop John Beiler. He'll know what to do."

"So forget about contacting the authorities?"

"Well, you just *did*. An off-duty police-man."

She imagined his grin. "On vacation, no less."

"I'm glad to help."

"I did check for reports of a missing child," she further explained. "Nothing showed up."

"Right. It may seem strange, but if she *is* Amish . . . the People prefer to keep the English authorities out of their hair as much as possible."

"The People?"

"The Plain community there."

She considered this. "Why?"

"They're cloistered by choice, separated from the world — that's us, we who aren't Amish. They call us Englishers. And they definitely prefer to handle things themselves."

"Even in locating a lost child?"

"There are probably a bunch of farmers out searching for her as we speak."

Jodi shivered at the thought.

Scott paused, then added: "Try saying this to her: *Kannscht du Deitsch schwetze?* and see how she reacts."

"Um, something about Dutch?"

"Yep. Can you speak Deitsch? It's the mother tongue of the Amish."

"Terrific, I'll repeat it to her when I hang up."

"Just get to Hickory Hollow as quickly as possible."

"Okay, I'm on it."

"Update me later."

"Will do."

They said good-bye and hung up.

Jodi leaned down to reach for the child's dimpled hand.

Too much drama for one day, she thought, realizing how fond she'd become of the little darling. *The way she says Mamma just sounds so sweet.*

She attempted to say the phrase Scott had mentioned. "Kannscht du Deitsch schwetze?"

The little girl leaped up, clapping her hands and jabbering in her language.

"That's all I know," Jodi said, laughing as she received the child's hug. "Let's find you something to wear besides this towel."

Jodi led the child into the laundry room, where she opened the dryer and removed the warm underwear and handed them to the child so she could dress herself, smiling at her astonished look. It was at that moment she remembered the bag of donated clothing.

"Let's take a look," Jodi said, opening the sack.

Pulling out several dresses, she could see they were much too big. But there was a small skirt with blue and green polka dots, and a green short-sleeved top that matched. "Well, look at this," she said, holding it up. "What do you think?"

The girl frowned, clutching the towel closer and shaking her head. "Nee."

"Aw, but honey, you need something to wear." She paused. "And this is super cute," she said as she looked through the rest of the clothes. Nothing else was even remotely the right size.

Trent would call this providential. She closed the bag.

When she looked up, the little girl had left the room. Jodi found her in the bathroom, leaning over the empty bathtub and reaching for the bright pink sponge.

"Listen, honey, you can't just wear your undershirt and —"

"Sehne?" The child patted her tummy.

Jodi had her work cut out for her. "Let's just try on the skirt and top, okay?" Even though she knew the girl had no clue what she was saying, she attempted to persuade her with a gentle and hopefully encouraging tone. She held out her hand and led her into the guest bedroom, then stood her in front of the floor mirror. She put the skirt up next to her waist and dangled the green top above, making eye contact with the youngster in the mirror. "See how pretty you look? Very pretty."

Without waiting, Jodi slipped the green top over the girl's head. And, wonder of wonders, there was no further resistance. *So far, so good.* Jodi held the skirt open and the child stepped into it, although her eyes were wide, as if she'd never worn anything like it. She even let Jodi button the waistband.

"Okay, we're set." Jodi offered her hand again.

Then, thinking perhaps she should slip a skirt over her running shorts, Jodi hurried to the closet and did just that. She also grabbed two pillows, hoping to make her passenger comfortable in a seat belt. "Now, let's go find your mom."

"Jah . . . mei Mamma!"

Jodi smiled as she looked down at her. She hoped the Hickory Hollow bishop could help them find the girl's family. *Scott's so sure about this,* she thought, anxious that all go well. She was surprised by how very much she cared for the small child who now clung to her hand.

CHAPTER 12

Jodi squinted into the midmorning sun, surprised at seeing so many fruit and vegetable stands on a short stretch of road. She was also intrigued by the many hand-lettered self-serve signs. Other wooden signs posted at the end of lanes advertised food items: peanut brittle, jam, homemade root beer, cabbage, onions, squash. To her amazement, money boxes had been left out in plain view for potential customers at the unattended road stands.

"Amish folk must be very trusting," she murmured, looking back at the child in the rear seat, who was perched on the pillows and securely buckled in. Jodi had been vigilant to drive extra cautiously with such precious cargo.

The little girl's eyes lit up and she giggled as she pointed to the horse-drawn carriages coming toward them on the opposite side of the road. *Does she recognize them . . . or is it just a childish attraction to the horses?*

Jodi was captivated herself and gave the horses wide berth. It suddenly struck her that these back roads might be ideal for jogging — there was hardly any car traffic.

In the field to the right, a mule team pulled a strange-looking contraption that was bundling wheat. She slowed, astonished at the charming sight. Men and boys were setting up each bundle into sheaves by hand.

So these are the People. . . .

Two barefoot girls rode scooters just ahead, moving courteously onto the dusty shoulder when they noticed Jodi's car. Their strawberry-blond hair was pulled back into identical thick knots, and they wore matching long mint-green dresses and black aprons. She moved toward the left side of the road, giving them plenty of room. For a moment, she considered stopping to see if they might recognize the child she had with her. But remembering Scott's instruction, she continued on, watchful for the one-room schoolhouse and the lane to the Amish bishop's place.

Farther up the road, two boys walked side by side with fishing poles slung over their slight shoulders, talking and laughing and wearing straw hats, black pants rolled midway up their legs, and thin black cloth suspenders over blue short-sleeved shirts.

Jodi tried to remember if she'd ever seen anything like this — even on a postcard. The clothes and carriages were straight out of the nineteenth century. She observed the gray buggies with their spindly wheels and cringed to think of what damage a car might inflict on them even at low speeds.

Jodi braked again to accommodate a small cart pulled by what looked like a pony, with two youngsters tucked inside — a boy and a girl who certainly could pass for twins — hauling two chickens in a wooden box with wire mesh on both sides.

Jodi assumed things were done in pairs here in this place that time had seemingly passed by. She spotted the much-anticipated schoolhouse just as Scott had said. It was charming, with a bell atop its roof and what looked like individual outhouses for boys and girls. There was a baseball field on the south side, and she considered taking a picture with her cell phone. "We're almost there," she said over her shoulder, noting the little girl, who looked mesmerized by the surrounding farmland.

Is anything familiar to her?

Passing the school, Jodi saw the lane Scott had so aptly described, as well as a handful of gray boxlike carriages parked in the side yard. Six or seven Amishmen dressed in black pants and short-sleeved white shirts with tan suspenders stood around toward the side of the house, their straw hats nearly bumping as they huddled.

The small girl in the seat behind her pointed and babbled in Deitsch. Then, when Jodi slowed to turn into the lane, she began to shake her head, saying, "Nee, nee." She strained her body against the seat belt as she continued to point forward.

A wave of mixed emotions met Jodi, who was torn between what her cousin had told her to do and what the little girl was urging, speaking rapidly now in her mother tongue.

Jodi decided to follow the girl's lead, and the child nodded her approval, an eager smile on her face. So she *did* know where they were, and with that in mind, Jodi began to cautiously speed up, driving straight ahead.

Maryanna waved good-bye to Rhoda Kurtz, who'd come to pick up her order of late celery plants, seedlings Maryanna had started in Benuel's greenhouse. She stood near the house, watching the road horse pull out of the drive to make the turn onto Hickory Lane.

It had felt good to offer some comfort to Rhoda, who like Maryanna was beside herself with worry over Sarah's disappearance. In reaching out to her longtime neighbor, Maryanna had felt the hand of the Lord God consoling her, as well. They'd embraced and Rhoda had assured Maryanna of her prayers, also offering to bring food over, even though Mollie and her girls were there at Maryanna's cooking several dishes to store in the refrigerator.

Maryanna headed to the well pump to wash her hands before going inside again. She was conscious of the searing heat and was searching the sky for a rain cloud when a dark blue car slowed near the mailbox and gradually turned in, creeping now up the driveway.

Maryanna gawked and moved closer, curious. "Ach, who's this?" Other than the hired drivers she sometimes used, she knew not a single soul who drove a car.

A slender woman with brown hair, no more than her late twenties, quickly emerged from the driver's side. She wore a long white skirt and white top and kept her head down as she hurried around to the opposite side of the car.

Then, lo and behold, she opened the door, leaned into the backseat, and brought out a little girl in fancy getup: Sarah!

"O merciful Father!" Maryanna ran toward the car and her young daughter, who'd spotted her and was already dashing toward her, looking mighty peculiar in a polka-dot skirt and green shirt.

"Mamma, Mamma!" sweet Sarah called, tears of obvious joy rolling down her chubby pink cheeks.

Maryanna bent down to receive her daughter, and oh, the joy of this longed-for moment, holding her so near! Thanking the Lord and kissing her baby's face over and over, Maryanna's tears blended with her darling's.

In her childish voice, Sarah told her in Deitsch that the lady who drove her home had found her asleep along the road. "She took care of my bumped head, Mamma."

"Did ya fall out of the carriage, then?"

"Jah . . . and so did my dolly," Sarah said before going on again about the English woman, who she said was like the Good Samaritan in the Bible. She stopped talking long enough to show Maryanna her other minor injuries, then babbled on about looking for her *Dallbopp.* "Aren't ya glad the nice lady brought me back to you, Mamma?"

Maryanna inhaled quickly and turned to

thank the slight woman standing back near the car. But Sarah was itching to get down, and when Maryanna released her, she ran to the young woman and took her hand, affectionately tugging her along across the yard.

"Mei Gardien Engel," Sarah said, looking up at the woman clad in white.

Maryanna trembled at the thought. Wasn't that *exactly* what they'd prayed for? And here she was in the flesh — Sarah's guardian angel!

"I can't tell ya how very grateful I am," Maryanna told the woman as she extended her hand. She blinked back more tears.

They clasped hands. "It was your daughter who helped me find you," the woman said with a friendly smile, her eyes gleaming. Then, as if remembering to introduce herself, she added, "I'm Jodi Winfield."

"Maryanna Esh . . . Sarah's mother."

"I'm so happy to meet you." Jodi quickly explained how her cousin had suggested coming to the Hickory Hollow bishop's home. "But it was Sarah who led me right to your door."

Maryanna's heart was so moved, she wanted to do something for the sweet-spirited Englischer. "Please, won't ya come inside? My sister and her girls are here."

"Really, I don't want to intrude."

"Ach, you brought my daughter home to me!" Maryanna declared.

Still holding her angel's hand, little Sarah urged Jodi toward the house, and Maryanna fell in step with them on the walkway.

*O dear Lord, thank you for this wonderful-*gut *answer to prayer!*

CHAPTER 13

The warm reception from Maryanna Esh surprised Jodi, as did Sarah's show of affection. Jodi was led along a flowery path, where a curious menagerie of old children's shoes had been pushed into the soil and planted with flourishing red, white, and pink petunias. She'd never seen anything like it, though the same could be said for the unfashionable gray dress and black apron on Maryanna. Aside from her outfit, Sarah's mother was uncommonly pretty, and her blue eyes twinkled when she smiled. Her white net head covering had a distinctive seam down the middle that created the shape of a heart, and its long white ties draped loosely over Maryanna's shoulders. The woman's hesitance around a stranger was evident, but relief shone from Maryanna's clear countenance.

Delighted exclamations were coming from inside the house even before they set foot on the back porch. Sarah reached up to politely open the screen door for her mother. Another Amishwoman — evidently the sister Maryanna had said was visiting — wore a maroon-colored dress and apron similar to Maryanna's, and two girls wearing matching green dresses and black aprons rushed out to greet Sarah. The woman scooped up Sarah and kissed both her cheeks, her own face glowing. The older of the two girls clapped her hands repeatedly, grinning and blinking exquisite hazel eyes behind thick glasses.

A round of quick talk in Deitsch ensued, and Jodi noticed the other Amishwoman touch Sarah's skirt and shake her head. "Ach . . . nee," she said, eyeing Jodi as though she realized Jodi was somehow responsible.

"Mollie, I want you to meet the young woman who found Sarah," Maryanna Esh told her sister before turning to Jodi. "This is Jodi Winfield."

"Hello, Mollie." Jodi offered her hand.

"It's ever so *gut* to meet ya," Mollie replied, gripping Jodi's in a firm welcome. "You just don't know!"

"I can imagine how you must feel," Jodi replied. "Sarah is a precious little girl."

Mollie asked how long ago she'd found

Sarah, and Jodi was quick to fill in the details, as they were obviously eager to know everything.

Maryanna invited Jodi to sit at the wooden kitchen table near three windows, and offered her a tall glass of delicious homemade iced tea.

"We call it meadow tea," Mollie said, folding her arms and coming to stand right between Maryanna and little Sarah. Mollie looked first at her sister and then at her niece, tears springing up. "Such a reunion, this is!"

Maryanna bent down and put her arm around Sarah, leading her to the table, where they took seats across from Jodi. "We thank the Lord for bringing our lost lamb home," Maryanna said in a soft whisper, her voice cracking. She kissed Sarah's face, and Sarah reached up and wrapped her arms around her mother's neck, beginning to cry.

"Now, Boppli," Maryanna said, her cap strings getting jumbled in the embrace. Then, glancing at Jodi, she continued speaking in English. "She's home . . . *home,* I say! And I'll never let her out of my sight again."

"I knew Gott would lead her back to us," Mollie said, looking up as three more children came rushing into the kitchen.

"Well, for pity's sake! I nearly forgot to tell your sister and brothers the news," Maryanna said, setting Sarah on the bench and rising at the entrance of the older girl and two boys, who resembled Sarah a great deal. "Must be I'm ever so ferhoodled."

Ferhoodled? Jodi had never heard such a charming word.

The new girl leaned down and kissed the top of Sarah's head, but the slim towheaded boys hung back — the younger staring at Sarah's clothing and frowning in what looked like disbelief.

"Children, I'd like ya to meet Jodi Winfield. She found little Sarah," said Maryanna, motioning toward Jodi.

The boys removed their straw hats and held them over their chests. "Hullo," they said in unison.

"Denki for bein' my sister's angel," the older girl said, staring now at Jodi. "And ya surely must be, 'cause you're dressed all in white." She said something in Deitsch to Sarah, who had a ready response, and they all laughed pleasantly.

Maryanna quickly translated: "She says, 'Jodi doesn't have to wear white to be *my* angel.'"

Jodi smiled at this, still amazed by their

openness, allowing her to be a part of Sarah's happy homecoming.

Maryanna introduced her three older children more formally now. "This is Benny, Leda, and Tobias, who sometimes goes by Toby," she said, indicating each child in turn. "And these two girls here are Mollie's daughters, my nieces Bertie and Fannie."

Eventually, after chattering excitedly with Sarah, the girls scattered to different locations in the kitchen to finish making the noon meal. Meanwhile, the boys replaced their straw hats, though the older boy, Benny, seemed apologetic about needing to return to the barn.

Sarah scooted off the bench and wandered over to climb into Jodi's lap, surprising Jodi.

Maryanna's jaw dropped, and for a split second, she stared. "Well now, look at this," she said, finding her voice. "She's really grown attached to you. And so quickly, too!"

The poor girl looked content but droopy-eyed. "I wonder if she slept much last night, with all that wandering about after falling out of the buggy," Maryanna said. As if to punctuate her mother's comment, Sarah rubbed her eyes with tightly curled fists and yawned.

Jodi could not comprehend how she'd fallen out the back of the carriage. It was difficult to imagine. She and her sister, Karen, had once ridden in a hay wagon when they were younger, but they'd sat safely in the middle, as far from the edge as they could get. Other children were more daring, sitting with legs dangling over the side, and Jodi recalled being nervous for them at the time.

Sarah's mischievous personality was unfolding for her as Jodi pieced together the things Maryanna was saying. It seemed unlikely the average Amish child would connect with an outsider as readily as Sarah had.

"And she took off her dress, for goodness' sake. Such a fright she gave me!" Maryanna said to Jodi. "The neighbor and his father found it and brought it to me in the wee hours. She must've felt mighty hot for that." She said something to Sarah in their language and shook her head with obvious disapproval.

Little Sarah shrugged slightly. Then her eyes blinked shut and she gave a slow, deep sigh as she fell sound asleep, right there in Jodi's arms.

Maryanna gave a sympathetic smile, then gently took her from Jodi. "Ach . . . mei Boppli!" She carried her out of the kitchen, presumably to bed.

"Seems she's awful tired," Mollie said to Jodi over her shoulder, where she helped her girls tear lettuce for a salad.

"Might be she'll sleep through the noon meal." Fannie glanced at Jodi shyly from her place at the wooden cutting board.

"She's gotta sleep sometime," Bertie noted. She appeared to be having a hard time counting out utensils from the nearby drawer.

Beginning to feel out of place, Jodi rose, deciding that as soon as Maryanna returned, she would excuse herself and say a proper good-bye. Yet the thought of leaving this homey setting, somewhat reminiscent of *Little Women,* made her a bit wistful.

Jodi walked to the back door and scanned the wide, newly mown yard, noticing a latticed area surrounding a well pump, as well as a horse stable and a white gazebo. The size of the trees indicated their advanced age, and she assumed the house was also historic, though very attractive and well kept.

"Aren't ya stayin' for dinner?" Mollie asked, calling her back.

"Dinner?" Jodi was confused. Dinner was hours away.

"Round here it's supper at night and dinner at noon." Mollie smiled. "And I'm ever so sure Maryanna would want ya to stay and eat with us."

Bertie twitched and nodded her head.

Fannie, on the other hand, continued chopping cucumber, not making eye contact as she added it to the bed of salad.

Not knowing what to say, Jodi decided to wait until Maryanna returned. "It's nice of you to suggest it, Mollie. I should probably be heading out, but thank you."

Leda grabbed a towel from the counter, wiping her hands, looking Jodi's way. "You can't stay?"

"I don't want to impose."

"Impose?" Mollie replied. "We can never thank you enough!" Mollie continued, saying she couldn't imagine life with her niece gone missing. " 'Specially with all we've been through, losin' Maryanna's husband."

Jodi's eyes went wide. "Her husband is —"

"Gone to heaven," Mollie said quickly. "The accident happened so fast, he never had a chance."

The air nearly left her. "I am *so sorry,*" Jodi said, turning now to watch the three girls perform their individual tasks. A trio of cooks in long dresses and full aprons. When had she ever seen three children so well organized, yet without anyone outwardly in charge? This was not at all like recess, where nearly everyone had a vocal opinion about what they should do.

"We didn't know if Sarah would be found," Leda spoke again. "But Mamma did. She believed God would take care of my sister."

"Aendi Maryanna must have prayed a lot," Bertie added, glancing down at her handful of spoons and then recounting.

"We all did." Leda looked over again at Jodi. "And you're the answer the Lord gave us."

Such words stirred something deep in Jodi's heart, especially coming from a mere child.

Leda reached out for Jodi's hand. "Please, won't ya join us?"

And, of course, Jodi was unable to resist.

CHAPTER 14

The first thing Maryanna did before putting Sarah down was to remove her fancy attire. At least the Englischer had clothed her in *something* to bring her home. It was still beyond her why Sarah had removed her dress, though she'd sometimes been known to do so as a toddler. So many questions flitted about Maryanna's head.

As warm as it was upstairs, Maryanna just let Sarah lie there in her underwear, which looked as clean as Sarah herself — surprising, given all she'd been through. In fact, her daughter smelled of soap.

Gently, she covered Sarah with a light throw and knelt beside the bed, thanking God for bringing her baby safely home. *Help me be ever mindful of putting you first, before my children or anything else, O Father God.*

Rising to sit on the bed, Maryanna let her tears fall as the realization settled in — the dear Lord had answered their prayers. She began to hum one of the songs she'd taught her children since they were tiny. "I have a friend who loves me . . . and that friend is Jesus."

As she looked down at Sarah, she knew that her cloth doll would eventually have to be replaced. It would take no time at all to make her a new one. Even so, the likelihood of her naming the new doll Kaylee like the lost one was unlikely, persnickety as her young daughter was.

Kind though Jodi seemed, Maryanna was disturbed by this brush with the world and the connection her daughter seemed to have with the brunette woman. Never before had she known her youngest to be so familiar, even snuggly, with any of her grandparents or many aunts, let alone someone outside Hickory Hollow. Wherever had she gotten the idea she could be so with an Englischer?

But of course Jodi Winfield had *rescued* little Sarah, delivering her back to Maryanna's arms. Perhaps Sarah's relief at being found explained it.

Tiptoeing to the dresser, Maryanna opened the drawer and removed the dress Joshua Peachey and his father had delivered to her before dawn. Now that Sarah was safely home, she'd simply wash it up right nice.

Oh no! How had she forgotten? The men were still out searching for Sarah! "Someone must alert them," she said aloud, moving quickly through the bedroom to the hallway. "And Daed and Mamm must be told, too."

She dashed across the hall to Leda's room, where the windows faced east, toward the Peachey farmhouse. To her surprise, there was Josh, coming out his back door and walking briskly toward the long dirt drive leading to the road. Why, he might be heading back to search with the men even now.

Someone must get the word to him that Sarah was home, asleep in her own bed. Tobias, perhaps? *He knows Josh best. . . .*

Maryanna nearly flew downstairs into the kitchen. The girls were still preparing dinner, and Jodi stood looking rather out of place by the screen door. "I'm awful sorry," she told her. "I need to fetch one of my boys to run over yonder right quick."

"Oh, that's fine —"

"You *are* staying for dinner, jah?" Maryanna said.

Leda interjected. "Mamma, the boys took the ponies up to the high meadow. They'll be back for the noon meal, though. Do ya want me to go instead?"

Maryanna shook her head, waving her

hand. "Ach, I'll be right back," she said. "Must catch the neighbor an' tell him to call off the search."

She swept out the back door and lifted her skirt just enough so she wouldn't trip as she hurried over the yard, seeing Mollie over talking to Mamm on the small porch next door. She made her way through the vast field between the two farmhouses, then past Josh's old clackety windmill and the wood-shed piled high with logs. Next came the stacked-stone springhouse — Benuel had helped repair the exterior a year before his accident. He'd said then that Josh was a mighty dependable fellow. *A man to be counted on."*

Feeling slightly winded, Maryanna thought ahead to what she should say to Josh. Despite the good news of Sarah's homecoming, she felt tense and terribly uncomfortable. She couldn't shake off the remembrance of waking from her faint in Josh's arms, and mumbled now in disgust at herself as she neared him and slowed. Was it proper to call out to get his attention?

She supposed she had no choice, not unless she wanted to continue running after this man. *The last thing I want to do!*

"Hullo, Josh." She raised her voice a bit,

noticing he was without his large dog.

Joshua turned and looked at her, out there on the road. "Maryanna . . . what is it?" His eyes registered concern as he rushed back. "Is there some word on your daughter, maybe?" He put out his hand as if to touch her, then drew it back.

"Bless the Lord, she's been found."

"Such *wunnerbaar-gut* news!"

Tears of happiness threatened to spill down her cheeks. "Sarah's resting in her own room. Safe."

He raised his eyes to the skies. "I prayed this might happen. Did she wander home, then?"

"An English woman discovered her somewhere near the road," Maryanna said. Then, feeling a bit strange, she added, "The young woman's still at my house."

Josh fumbled to remove his straw hat. "This is the best news, ain't?" He grinned, his deep-set eyes searching hers.

"I need to get back. I came just to ask ya to let the men out searching know . . . 'specially the bishop."

"Oh, jah . . . jah," he sputtered. "I'll go an' tell them without delay."

But she couldn't let him leave just yet — not before she set the record straight. "I'm fit to be tied 'bout what happened earlier . . .

130

ya know, when I —" She felt her face grow warm.

"Passed out?" He merely shrugged and smiled pleasantly, if awkwardly. " 'Twas better than letting ya fall, ain't so, Maryanna?"

Was he teasing her? Maryanna wasn't sure what to think. "Jah . . . for that, I best be thankin' ya."

"No need to fret."

"All right, then. Denki, Josh."

He made a little sound. "It's *Joshua,* by the way." His eyes twinkled at her.

"Ach, forgot — no nickname." Oddly, she felt lighter, relieved she'd brought up the niggling topic.

Then, without another word, he ran off to spread the news.

Going back the way she came, Maryanna noticed what looked to be an old swing in need of repair. Nearby, a pair of wooden benches with peeling paint waited beneath the large shade tree across the driveway from the house. There was no evidence that either the swing or the benches had been used since Suzanne's passing.

Maryanna wondered if it had been a special spot for the young couple. Turning, she saw on the opposite side of the yard Joshua's meager attempts at a flower bed. A hodgepodge of flowers had sprung up all

131

along the west side of the house, like he'd scattered a variety of seeds without giving any thought to the arrangement. *For pity's sake,* she thought, but with a prick of sadness, sorry he'd lost his pretty young bride . . . and their baby, too.

He must be ever so lonely without even a child to welcome him home.

Hurrying now, Maryanna longed to see her own little ones again. She thanked the Almighty, promising to be ever grateful for her little family and home, as well as the cheery greenhouse where she loved to work and be mindful of her Creator.

Just then she heard squawking and carrying on coming through Joshua's open front room windows behind her. For a moment, it sounded like it might be the raucous parrot young Tobias was so fond of — one of Joshua's ridiculous pets. But how on earth could such a creature screech her name? "Mary-anna, Mary-anna!"

The clamor startled her, and she quickly made her way toward the grazing land. "Benuel would have a *gut* chuckle over this," she said aloud.

She glanced back at Joshua's house and saw Buster shake himself awake and leap down from the back porch, the sound of that parrot ringing in her ears. The squawking and the disarray in the flower garden caused her to shake her head.

Preaching service was to be held at Joshua's place come Sunday, in only two days. Had he even thought of sprucing things up for the sake of almighty God and the People?

What he needs is a gut *wife,* she thought to herself. *Anybody but me!*

CHAPTER 15

Jodi studied the hand pump not far from the back of the house, intrigued by the old-time contraption. She started to push down on the handle, trying her best to draw out some water. "Must be a very deep well," she muttered after a number of attempts. She wondered if Maryanna had gotten sidetracked on her mission to the neighbor's. And Mollie was still next door.

Looking about her, Jodi was amazed at how she'd stumbled into a little pocket of time where no one followed the rules of modern society. It was as if the dogged forward march of years had ceased.

Her mind wandered back to when she was in grade school. Dad had liked spending hours pruning his rosebushes and often waxed eloquent with trimmers in his smooth schoolteacher hands. *"Remember, each person you meet in life crosses your path for a reason. You can learn from everyone you encounter."*

Contemplating her father's remarks, she heard footsteps on the porch steps — Bertie was stepping outside. The girl came one step at a time and shuffled toward Jodi, a frown on her heart-shaped face.

"Takes awful long, ain't?" Bertie was looking at the hand pump.

Jodi nodded. "My arms are already sore." *I'm a wimp!*

"We don't get many outsiders here," Bertie said. She clumsily placed her chubby hands on the pump and helped Jodi push. "We prob'ly scare 'em off."

"Things *are* different here, yes."

"Where do you live?" Bertie asked, standing very near her now.

"I live in Vermont, but I'm house-sitting not far from here."

"House-sitting?"

Jodi explained the concept of taking care of someone else's home while they were away. "My cousin and his wife have a beautiful indoor cat that I'm caring for, too." She'd seen several barn cats running around and wondered if Bertie had ever seen an animal as spoiled as the prim and proper Gigi.

"So you're cat-sitting, too?"

"Strange as it may sound, I am."

Suddenly, the water started rushing forth, and Bertie squealed. She stepped back and clapped her hands, moving to grab the metal dipper. "Here, ya need this."

After all that work, only a dipperful? Jodi smiled, enjoying Bertie's enthusiasm. It was apparent she suffered from some sort of physical disorder, as well as developmental delays. The trunk of her body was very round and disproportionate to the rest of her. But her demeanor was sweet and her joy refreshing.

While Jodi sipped the cold water from the dipper, Leda stepped onto the back porch and held up a plastic pitcher, waving it at Bertie. "Wanna fill this up?"

"*Gut* idea," Bertie mumbled, as if she wished *she'd* thought of it.

"We'll be ready to eat in a jiffy," Mollie said, appearing around the side of the house. "Might as well wash up. Maryanna's headin' this way."

Jodi looked over her shoulder and saw Maryanna coming from the pasture, her face red in the heat.

"Sorry it took so long," Maryanna called, taking long strides.

"I've had good company," Jodi replied with a glance at Bertie.

This brought a bright smile to Bertie's

face, and she motioned for both Jodi and Maryanna to head inside with her. But Bertie stumbled on the porch steps and would have fallen if Jodi hadn't reached out and caught her.

"Ach, you're *gut* at takin' care of kids, ain't so?" Maryanna commented.

"I've had some practice," Jodi admitted.

"A family, then?"

"No, I'm a teacher." *Well, I was. . . .*

"Oh? What do ya teach?" Maryanna asked as they made their way inside and to the table.

"Third grade . . . I'm a classroom teacher." She couldn't bring herself to say that she'd been let go.

"A *gut* teacher's hard to come by." Maryanna frowned suddenly.

"That's for sure." Mollie looked up from the table, where she placed a large hot dish of creamy noodles with crumbled hamburger. "Just ask my husband, Jeremiah, and the rest of the school board."

"Ach, now, Mollie." Maryanna shushed her. "Best be eatin' our meal. Leda, go an' ring the dinner bell for Benny and Tobias."

Leda immediately turned and leaned out the other kitchen door, where she pulled a cord to make the bell ring.

"What about Sarah?" Fannie asked, going

137

to stand at the foot of the stairs, inclining her head as if to listen for her younger cousin.

"Let her sleep, poor thing. She must've been awake all last night," Maryanna said, a catch in her voice. With that she sat at the head of the table, where Jodi assumed her husband had once sat.

Then, pulling out the wooden chair where Maryanna directed her to sit, Jodi settled in at the quaint table. The picturesque wall calendar on the far end of the kitchen caught her eye. *"And be not conformed to this world."* ~ *Romans 12:2.*

Seeing it, Jodi felt she'd never been surrounded by a more visible example. She felt a sense of peace when Maryanna reached for Leda's and Benny's hands where they sat on either side of her, and Leda looked over and smiled shyly at Jodi, offering her other hand to her. Across the table, Mollie linked hands with her daughters.

Maryanna bowed her head reverently for a silent table grace as everyone else did the same, a gesture that Jodi mimicked out of respect.

When the lovely Amishwoman coughed a little, all heads bobbed up, and noticeable tears glistened beneath Maryanna's eyes. The sight nudged Jodi's heart, and she had to look away or she might have shed a tear herself.

CHAPTER 16

Maryanna's parents came over from next door just as Jodi and the others were beginning to eat the noon meal. Maryanna introduced Jodi to Zeke and Emmie Mast, who nodded and shook hands. Emmie placed a ceramic pot of what she called red beet eggs on the long table as they all took their seats again.

"So glad you brought the eggs," Maryanna said. "One of Sarah's favorites!"

"Guess we'll save some for when she wakes up," Mollie said. "Poor dear is all in . . . and it's no wonder."

Mollie started talking about food, saying, "Mamm knows a hundred or more recipes by heart — though she'd never brag."

When Jodi asked how she remembered, Grandma Emmie shrugged and said, "Just by doin'."

Leda nodded, seemingly anxious to say something. "Mammi and Mamma pass recipes down by showin' us girls how they do things," Leda said, her blue eyes bright.

Mollie wagged her head. "It's like havin' a backup for the computer."

This brought a round of laughter from the youngsters, and Jodi wondered how they knew anything about that.

Then Benny spoke up. "One of our hired drivers brings his laptop in the van when he takes us to the Bird-in-Hand Farmers Market or the general store. He likes to tell us kids all 'bout his English gadgets and whatnot."

"Much to your Mamma's dismay, ain't so?" Emmie Mast eyed Maryanna.

But Maryanna merely shrugged. "Well, we live in the world, but we're not *of* it. 'Least we're not s'posed to be."

Jodi glimpsed the words from Romans on the calendar again and assumed that any group, not only Amish, could support the idea of cloistered living with such a verse.

Later, after trying the pickled red beet eggs, Jodi asked if Leda might share the recipe.

"You just mix some canned beets and juice in with sugar, vinegar, and salt, and bring it to a rolling boil," Leda explained.

The boys teased her, rolling their eyes and leaning their heads together.

Leda ignored them. "After that, you pour the mixture over the hard-boiled eggs and let them set at room temperature for a bit . . . then put them in the refrigerator overnight."

"Sounds easy enough," Jodi said. "Thanks."

Tobias nodded his head repeatedly like a puppet while Benny attempted to squelch a laugh.

"Now, boys," Maryanna said quietly but firmly. "This isn't something most Englischers know."

"Or most *boys*!" Bertie declared loudly, and the whole table burst out laughing, except Benny and Tobias, whose faces reddened with embarrassment.

Jodi was intrigued by the clearly defined gender roles. Apparently, boys were not expected to know about the preparation of food.

She thought of Trent and realized he would most likely starve if *he* didn't know how to make a sandwich or open a can and use the microwave. After all, Trent's mother was a longtime career woman and not very interested in cooking or baking.

"Our neighbor Joshua Peachey, now, *he* knows how to cook," Tobias said, his eyes round little moons as he looked over at his mother. "For certain."

"Well, he'd *have* to," his grandmother said softly. As an aside, she explained to Jodi, "The poor man lost his wife a year ago."

Jodi listened, glancing back at young Tobias, who was still watching his mother, obviously waiting for her to respond.

But Maryanna was strangely quiet.

"He *does,* Mamma," Tobias repeated.

"Why, sure, I 'spect so," Maryanna said, giving her younger son a reprimanding stare.

"He's a right *gut* housekeeper, too," Tobias added, slipping it in as though he'd almost better not.

" 'Cept for all those filthy pets." Maryanna shook her head. "If God wanted animals to live inside, they wouldn't have fur coats, now, would they?"

Benny poked Tobias, who still wore a grin.

"Joshua's only got *one* cat and one small bunny . . . and one parrot. No other pets inside the house," Tobias replied while Benny fidgeted. "I wouldn't mind a pet or two myself."

"He has an indoor cat now, too?" Maryanna sighed loudly and waved her hand in exasperation.

Jodi's antenna shot up. It was evident Toby had tremendous affection for Joshua, and Maryanna did not.

"Doesn't he know cats are meant to be mouse catchers?" Maryanna continued.

"I don't know." Toby shook his head fast, his hair flying.

"Maybe he cooks for his *pets*," Bertie said, leaning forward on the table to peer down at Toby. "Animals need to eat, too, ya know."

"But what do indoor rabbits eat?" Benny asked rambunctiously. "Same as outdoor ones, ain't?"

Toby frowned. "Why are ya pickin' on our nice neighbor?" He appeared ready to say more when his mother nipped it in the bud and asked him to leave the table.

Toby hung his head. "Sorry, Mamm."

Maryanna apologized to everyone for her son's outburst. "Don't know what's got into him."

Mollie and Emmie looked at each other, then resumed eating.

What's going on? Jodi wondered as the table fell silent, except for the clink of utensils on plates and the occasional burp from Benny. *Why is Maryanna so rattled?*

Joshua was a bit surprised to see Preacher Ephraim Yoder cutting through his field, coming this way again, carrying what looked like a loaf of bread.

"Bishop John just told me the wonderful-*gut* news of Maryanna's daughter's safe return," Ephraim said, handing him the bread. "My wife sent me back over here . . . guessin' she's worried 'bout you."

"No need, but mighty kind of her. Denki." Joshua motioned for the minister to follow him to the house, where he deposited the loaf on the counter and offered Ephraim some ice water. "Heard your daughter Rosaleen's all done teaching."

Preacher nodded and bowed his head a bit. "Not sure I oughta say anything."

"Go right ahead." Joshua was a firm believer in giving folk plenty of leeway. Some folk might call it rope.

Preacher glanced at him and let out a guffaw. "That's what I like 'bout you, Josh."

"Joshua," he said quietly, wishing the reminder would stick. Counting Maryanna, Preacher Yoder was the second person today who'd slipped up and called him by his childhood nickname.

Preacher tugged on his beard, then continued. "Well, I rode over and gave my daughter's beau an earful last week."

"Oh?"

"Decided it was time he made up his mind to marry Rosaleen. The boy's been seein' her for two long years now. So I upped and told him right to his face: 'Are ya gonna dilly-dally through life or make something of yourself?' "

Joshua's ears pricked. "How'd he take it?"

"Must've needed the nudge, 'cause he proposed to her the very next day."

"Ah, so *you're* the reason the school board's frettin' over who to choose for a teacher this fall?"

"You heard this?" Preacher removed his straw hat and fanned himself.

"Sure. The grapevine's got your daughter hitched come November wedding season."

"At long last."

"Word's out that there aren't any scholarly girls suitable to take Rosaleen's place teachin'."

"Is that right?"

"The only graduate in last year's crop was a poor pupil, is what I heard. Not qualified to take on the task."

There was a long and awkward silence, and the longer he waited, the more Joshua wondered what the preacher was thinking.

"You're a rather young man yourself, Joshua," the preacher began slowly. "Why don't ya think of settling down with one of the younger widows in the district? Remarry?"

Joshua shook his head.

"Widow Ida's real nice — God-fearing, too. What are you waitin' for?"

He sighed, mulling that over. At last, he said, "If the woman you've got your eye on won't have you, what should ya do?"

"I'd say to set your sights on another."

Joshua pondered that. "But what if you don't care for anyone else?"

Preacher inhaled deeply, his chest rising. He stared at the cat all curled up in the sunshine near the window, and the parrot in its cage right above. "Is it all these pets of yours? Are they the problem?"

"Could be she doesn't know 'bout the cat."

"Well, if I know 'bout it, I 'spect she does, too." Preacher frowned, looking at him askance. He pointed to the parrot. "What about this big bird of yours? Any reason why a loud creature like that needs to live all cooped up inside a cage?"

"Malachi? The poor thing would die out in the wild."

"That's because you feed it," Preacher Yoder insisted.

Joshua didn't pay the minister any mind — what did the man know of exotic birds?

Preacher eyed him and leaned forward. "Who's the woman, if I might ask?"

Joshua shook his head. There was no

revealing that. "She thinks I'm peculiar, so we'll just leave it right there."

"Well, if this woman loves ya, she'll overlook it."

"Then it's *ummieglich* — impossible."

"So I guess that's that," Preacher said, looking at him sympathetically. "You've come to a sudden *schtoppe.*"

"Jah, and sadly so," Joshua admitted. *All too true.*

CHAPTER 17

Despite Jodi's largely warm welcome, there were several moments when she'd caught Maryanna looking at her charily. *She was startled when Sarah crawled on my lap,* Jodi realized. *She must be feeling protective.*

Maryanna declared the peach cobbler a special dessert to celebrate Sarah's return home. Presently, they took turns scooping vanilla ice cream to top off the dessert. Jodi took a bite and resisted the urge to inquire about the recipe for the scrumptious cobbler. With the heat in the house quite overpowering, she wondered how long it would be before the ice cream turned to soup on her plate.

Halfway through the meal, Benny had brought in a large battery-operated fan and set it in the middle of the kitchen. Jodi was grateful — she'd felt like she might melt, yet she refused to mention the heat the children seemed to take in stride. *Without air-conditioning, their blood is thinner,* she decided.

Maryanna called for Tobias, who returned looking humble and properly chastened as he sat next to Benny on the long wooden bench.

"You should see how much ice cream Great-Aunt Heddy eats," Benny said, picking up his fork and digging into the dessert.

"She had four big dips last night," Tobias added, eyes shining.

"Ach, boys . . ." Maryanna said, and immediately Benny and Tobias looked repentant. "Be respectful of your elders."

"Sorry, Mamm," Benny apologized first, followed by Tobias, who spoke more softly.

"Did ya know Great-Aunt Heddy's helping some of the Amish schoolgirls in the Nickel Mines area make a comfort quilt?" Mollie said between bites. "To show compassion for the families who were victims of the theater shootings in Colorado."

"Sounds like something dear Heddy would do," Emmie Mast said.

"Ever thoughtful, jah?" Maryanna spoke up.

Both Mollie and Jodi nodded in agreement.

"They want to send it to one of the Aurora public libraries," Mollie added. "As a gesture of caring." She smiled sweetly. "The children want the families to know they understand what they're going through."

Maryanna rested her elbows on the table, eyes moist. "Being Amish doesn't separate us from the pain and suffering others feel."

"I've never heard of a comfort quilt before," Jodi said.

Maryanna nodded. "For the longest time, there was another such quilt on display at Bart Township Fire Station 51. They were the first responders to the Amish schoolhouse shootings," she explained. "It was made by Catholic schoolchildren in Ohio for students at the St. James Catholic Grammar School in New Jersey." She sighed, visibly moved. "Many of the children in New Jersey lost family members in the 9/11 terrorist attacks at the World Trade Center."

Jodi was captivated by the idea of the quilt being passed on from one hurting group to another.

"Then, after the shootings at the college in Virginia, forty Amish folk took a bus to deliver the quilt with a letter to the campus that summer, hoping it would bring comfort to the families whose loved ones lost their lives."

"Did it go anywhere after that?" Bertie asked, eyes wide.

"Well, yes, unfortunately — to yet another university, sadly enough — this time in northern Illinois," Maryanna said.

Fannie looked away, face pale, and Bertie reached over and touched her shoulder. "I don't know why some folk can't just be kind," she said softly. "Live the Golden Rule . . ."

"Fighting's just terrible," Zeke said, looking round the table.

"Surely is," Emmie agreed.

"I wouldn't be surprised if the children in Nickel Mines got the idea to make this new comfort quilt from that first one," Mollie remarked.

"Maybe so." Maryanna offered more meadow tea to the children, who sat patiently while adult talk took precedence.

Jodi was curious about the interplay between Maryanna and Mollie, as well as the humble and respectful attitudes displayed by the children, Tobias's minor fit notwithstanding. *A far cry from the behavioral problems I've dealt with at school.*

Maryanna asked if anyone wanted more ice in their tumblers.

"Ach, why not just sit and rest awhile, sister?" Mollie urged her.

"Oh, I can rest tonight," Maryanna answered with a glance at Jodi. "I'll go now and check on Sarah." And with that, she rose and slipped from the kitchen.

Jodi found herself holding her breath, hoping Sarah might be awake. She hated the thought of leaving without saying good-bye to the little Amish girl and her very special family.

When Preacher Yoder left by way of the back steps, Joshua noticed the same car still parked over in Maryanna Esh's driveway. *Must be the woman who found Sarah.* This gave him pause. Although the community would be exceedingly grateful to her, the last thing young Sarah or anyone else needed was to fix their eyes on the fancy folk.

Hurrying out to check on his two young colts, Joshua made his way to the barnyard. The sun was blistering hot on his neck, and he wished for a breeze . . . and a ceiling fan in his house like he knew neighbor Samuel Lapp had installed in Rebecca's kitchen. Joshua could not recall a hotter summer, or one with less rain. Just yesterday he'd read in *The Budget* that a number of states were in severe drought, and as he checked on the water level in the trough, he prayed, *Lord God, grant mercy on those who need your blessed rain most.*

Pausing, he looked over yonder at Mary-anna Esh's expanse of land. *And thank you for bringing young Sarah back safely to her family,* he continued. *Look after her and lead her, all the days of her life.*

As Joshua returned to the house for a cold drink, Malachi began to caw, which turned into noisy squawking. "Josh-wa, Josh-wa," the bird parroted his name, then cackled, making fun.

"*Puh,* go on with ya, old bird." Joshua sat at the table, drinking, feeling the cold liquid slide down inside his chest.

"Hul-lo, Josh-wa," the bird said, staring right at him, daring him to reprimand.

There were times Joshua wished he hadn't spent hours teaching his pet to talk. He looked at the rabbit in its cage and joked back at Malachi. "See that quiet little rabbit? Take some lessons from Shadow, won't ya?" He laughed, wondering if Suzanne would think he'd lost his mind, talking to his pets.

But life without Suzanne was nearly unbearable most days. Especially the long nights. He'd heard of folks dying of loneliness, so it made perfect sense to populate the kitchen with a cat, parrot, and black rabbit. The ornery tabby cat, however, had tried its best to get past the barrier between the kitchen and the small sitting room. Joshua had seen the determined look in the tabby's eyes on more than one occasion. He could just hear the wheels turning. What Honey Lou wouldn't do to get upstairs and lie there in a puddle of sunlight all day, near Joshua's bedroom window.

Such is a cat's life!

Joshua had to squint to look across the field, but he could see the Englischer's car well enough. None of his business, really, but having been Benuel's closest friend, Joshua felt a strong sense of protectiveness toward the Esh family, and toward Maryanna herself. Although undeniably Maryanna would prefer that wasn't the case.

Am I envious? For the life of him, he wished he might've been the one to bring Sarah home. And come to think of it, he wished *he* was finishing up the noon meal with the Esh family just now.

Joshua sighed, pushing away the meddlesome thoughts. "Don't be a coward," he said to himself.

"Coward!" the parrot mimicked. *"Caw!"*

Joshua's ire rose. "Quiet now!" he commanded, and Malachi retreated in obedience.

Feeling remorseful, Joshua rose and fed

his bird a treat. "Sorry, little one. Just a bit tired, I guess."

Gently, the bird nuzzled Joshua's fingers, as though forgiving him.

Little Sarah was just waking up and stretching her arms when Maryanna came into the doorway. Going to the bed, she sat next to her daughter and smoothed Sarah's hair away from her face. "You've been sleeping ever so soundly," she said in Deitsch. " 'Tis *gut.* But I missed you, my dear."

Sarah sat up and moved next to Maryanna, cuddling with her. For the longest time, Sarah lay very still in her lap as Maryanna hummed a hymn.

Then, after a while, Maryanna dressed her and fixed her hair. Sarah looked up at one point, asking if the Englischer was still there.

"Just finishing up her dessert."

A slow smile spread across Sarah's sweet face. "I want some, too . . . with Jodi."

Maryanna smiled and was about to lean down to kiss her cheek, but Sarah slid out of bed and scampered out of the bedroom. And before Maryanna could say more, Sarah's bare feet pattered down the stairs.

When Maryanna returned to the kitchen, there sat Sarah on Jodi's lap again, leaning her head back against her, content as a kitten. If she wasn't mistaken, their guest looked a mite sheepish.

"Well, it seems Sarah has grown quite attached to you!" Maryanna said, trying to laugh it off.

Jodi's face flushed.

"Let's get Sarah some cobbler with ice cream," Maryanna told Leda, who rose quickly and took down another plate from the cupboard. "Anyone for seconds?"

Benny and then Bertie shot up their hands, and Tobias waved his mischievously in the air.

"Mamma's cobbler's a lot like her chocolate chip cookies. You can't eat just one helpin'," Benny said.

Soon enough, Leda carried over a plate with the cobbler and ice cream and put it in front of the English woman and Sarah. "Looks like she needs a spoon, too," Maryanna told Leda, motioning for her to go back and get one.

"She don't look helpless to me," Tobias muttered.

"Doesn't," Benny corrected.

Tobias grimaced. "I hate grammar."

"Shouldn't say hate," Benny spouted back.

Maryanna shook her head, mortified.

"Still, little Sarah's *home* . . . and we're all mighty happy 'bout it," Mollie intervened.

157

Maryanna smiled her thanks at Mollie, and Tobias dug into his cobbler, slurping at times, imitating his brother. Then, turning to Jodi, she said, "I'd like to talk with you alone, before you leave, if ya don't mind."

Still holding Sarah, Jodi looked surprised but agreed. But it was Mollie whose eyebrows arched.

"Can you come for breakfast sometime?" Tobias asked Jodi. "Mamma makes the best eggs and bacon. You'll see."

Jodi, looking ever more self-conscious, explained that she liked to run early each morning. "That's how I found your sister today . . . I was out jogging."

Tobias's eyes grew wide. "You're a runner?"

"It's just a hobby."

"I whittle sometimes," Tobias said. "That's *my* hobby."

Benny nodded. "Mine too."

Maryanna was taken aback — she'd never known her children to be so comfortable with an Englischer. First Sarah for understandable reasons, and now Benny and Tobias.

"I'd like to see some of your whittling," Jodi said, her pretty face beaming back at the boys.

As if lightning had struck, Tobias and

Benny left the table and hurried off to their room upstairs.

"Why do ya run, Jodi?" Bertie asked, putting down her fork and wiping her mouth with the back of her chubby hand.

"Well, it's a great way to handle stress, or to mull things over. And I get some good exercise, too."

Mollie leaned back in her chair. "Did ya know there's a half marathon coming up in a few weeks not far from here — in early September, I believe."

"Really?" Jodi's eyes lit up. "Where?"

"It's the Bird-in-Hand Half Marathon, between the villages of Bird-in-Hand and Intercourse. And a whole bunch of Amish young folk go running together every few evenings, once the sun goes down — 'cept Sundays," Mollie told her. "They call themselves the *Vella Shpringa* — Let's Run. Would ya like to join them?"

Maryanna didn't know what had gotten into her sister. Were they all falling under the Englischer's sway?

Jodi seemed pleased. "Will any of you be running?"

"My husband, Jeremiah, plans to," Mollie answered right quick.

"Funny you're telling me this."

"Why's that?" Mollie stole a glance at

159

Maryanna.

"Well, driving in from Cattail Road today, I noticed how Hickory Lane weaves and curves, and I thought it might be a relaxing place to jog."

"I think that's why the folk enjoy the back roads here, away from traffic."

"So it's a half marathon?" Jodi asked.

"That's right — an annual fall event." Mollie was looking now at Fannie and Bertie, and Maryanna almost wondered if she was going to ask them if *they* wanted to run with the stranger at the table.

Jodi's eyes twinkled. "I'll google it and find out more."

"Google?" Bertie laughed. "Such a silly word."

Jodi tried to explain about the Internet, but Maryanna inched into the conversation and changed the subject to the upcoming canning bee over at Rhoda Kurtz's place next week. And that was that.

Once the table was cleared, Maryanna was conscious of Benny and Tobias over with Jodi, showing off their whittling projects — a duck head and an egg. Jodi made over the pieces, complimenting the boys and asking questions.

Meanwhile, little Sarah pleaded in Deitsch

for her mother to invite Jodi for another visit as Maryanna stacked the last of the dishes in the sink. Maryanna was secretly glad Jodi didn't know what Sarah was begging for, although by the tone of her voice, most anyone could've guessed.

At last, Maryanna gave in and agreed to invite Jodi Winfield to come tomorrow. Sarah squealed with joy and scampered across the room to Jodi, whose cheeks sported a wholesome blush.

Where do I draw the line? Maryanna wondered, still grateful to the guest in their midst, but also wary of her youngest's strong attachment to her "guardian angel."

CHAPTER 18

"Kumme mit?" Sarah asked as she inquisitively looked up at Jodi. She held out her petite hand.

Leda translated the earnest request as the three of them walked to the main back door. "She wants to show you the hen house and Mamma's perty greenhouse, too."

Jodi smiled as Sarah bit her lower lip, obviously hoping the answer was yes.

Stooping to Sarah's level, Jodi shook her head. She'd already sensed more than a slight hesitation from her Amish hostesses. Regardless of Maryanna's gratitude, she certainly wasn't accustomed to Englishers hanging around. It was time to exit, once she and Maryanna had their "talk."

But Sarah's sulking face spoke a world of words.

"I'm sorry, sweetie."

"If you can spare the time, the tour of the farm will take only a few minutes," Maryanna spoke up from behind them.

Despite the few suspicious glances prior, Maryanna seemed genuine and so very kind in her invitation.

"Little Sarah can't seem to get enough of ya," Maryanna continued. "You're truly welcome to stay."

"It *does* sound like fun," Jodi said, glad when Leda fell into step with her, too. Jodi and Maryanna's two girls headed across the yard, past the now familiar hand pump, toward the chicken coop.

"Since my sister doesn't speak English yet, I'll come along so you'll know what she's sayin'."

"Thanks, Leda."

"I'll catch up on my chores later," Leda added.

Jodi was taken by her courtesy, so uncommon in a child. Was this typical of all Amish youngsters?

To think she was getting an astonishing firsthand glimpse into this unique culture Scott and Paige found so appealing. Jodi pinched herself to see if she was merely sleepwalking. But, no, she remained just as firmly planted in the dreamlike setting around her. It was as if she was somehow destined to stumble upon little Sarah Esh this morning, sleeping by the roadside.

■ ■ ■ ■

Maryanna inched away from the door after Sarah coaxed Jodi toward the hen house, with a bit of help from Leda. Honestly, she didn't know whether to smile or frown. The bond between her youngest and Jodi was ever stronger, and Maryanna felt helpless to interfere.

Mollie came over and stood next to her, tea towel in hand. "Relax — the young woman's harmless, far as I can tell."

"I *am* grateful to her." Maryanna sighed. "God does work in mystifying ways, using an Englischer to find Sarah, when our own men couldn't!"

"For certain."

"Still, she's an outsider."

Mollie nodded. "Yet the children are clearly fond of her. You saw how Benny and Tobias —"

"Jah, I did."

"I daresay Sarah's drawn to her 'cause she brought her back to you. That's all."

"If so, I can't blame her," Maryanna said, not entirely convinced. "I just pray that's the reason, and it's not because Jodi's right fancy."

Mollie agreed. "So what should we do?"

164

"Well, the Good Lord brought her into our lives, so I won't stand in His way." Maryanna returned to the sink and ran hot water on the dishcloth, then scrubbed the table clean while Mollie swept the floor.

Later, Preacher Yoder and his wife, Lovina, dropped in to check on Maryanna, asking specifically about little Sarah.

"Oh, she's just fine, out with her sister showing off the greenhouse to the young woman who found her," Maryanna said, appreciating the kindly gesture. She offered some cold meadow tea and sweets, and they stayed for a brief yet comforting visit.

"Der Molligrobbe," Sarah was saying as she tugged on Leda's apron.

"Do ya really think Jodi wants to see those ugly tadpoles?" Leda asked Sarah first in Deitsch, then grinned as she repeated it in English for Jodi's benefit. "You can show Joshua Peachey, maybe . . . next time he's around. Or our boy cousins."

But Sarah shook her head and babbled further.

"Jah, we'll go to the greenhouse next," Leda said softly, again translating everything. "Besides, Jodi might have other things to do today, ya know." She repeated it in Deitsch for Sarah, or so Jodi thought.

Little Sarah's face turned sad at that. "Nee."

Even without a translation, Jodi chuckled at this. "I can stay awhile longer," she said.

Leda recited that in Deitsch, and Sarah's frown quickly vanished. Then, turning to Jodi, Leda said, "My sister tends to get her way with most folk."

"I can see why."

"With Mamma, too."

Jodi nodded, unable to suppress a smile. "She's one determined little girl."

" 'Tis true." Leda pointed toward the small greenhouse, set back from the hen house. "Our father built this," she said. "And Mamma's ever so glad. She loves working out here."

Wondering if it was also their livelihood, Jodi followed Leda while Sarah continued to clutch her hand. "Do you also farm your land?"

"We rent it to another Amish family . . . for now."

Along the exterior of the greenhouse, Jodi noticed a row of pots where golden mums were beginning to sprout. "Do you sell lots of these?" she asked.

"Oh jah," Leda said. "And other plants, too, 'specially seedlings. But no tobacco plants. Mamma's a stickler 'bout that."

Considering Leda's remark, Jodi headed inside the smallish greenhouse, where the loamy smells of plant life reminded her of her father's own green thumb. *Wouldn't Dad be surprised to see me here?* She realized then that she hadn't told her parents her lousy news. But real life could wait. She would text or email them tonight about her job loss.

"Mamma's got some perennials on sale," Leda said. "This late in the summer, ya know."

Jodi gazed enviously at the beautiful flowers, as well as the lush houseplants — several large ferns in hanging baskets and numerous potted African violets, and a few leftover annuals. There were also cauliflower, celery, cabbage, and broccoli plants for the fall planting, in addition to birdseed and plant fertilizer for sale.

"Our vegetable garden needs watering every day 'cause of the heat."

"I noticed a number of road stands when I came in." Jodi was dying to ask if anyone ever helped themselves to the contents of the money box, but she thought better of it.

"Jah, most of us sell our extra produce pretty cheap," explained Leda. "Mamma says we don't have to make lots of money from our customers."

So the Amish didn't sound at all like modern businesspeople. Were they really not interested in getting the most for their produce? Though foreign to everything she knew, Jodi found this approach refreshing.

"Come outside a bit," Leda said after showing her around. "Sarah will pout if she doesn't show you the tadpoles."

"Molligrobbe, right?" Jodi teased.

A stream of giggles poured from Sarah, and she wrapped her arms around Jodi's knees.

Jodi patted the tight bun on the back of Sarah's head. "Can't miss out on seeing those slimy critters," Jodi said as she caught Leda's eye. "Need to keep everyone happy, right?"

Leda offered a knowing smile.

Jodi walked along the small walkway, a mosaic of stepping-stones, around to the side of the greenhouse and out toward the pastureland, where two horses and several ponies grazed. Sunshine spilled over the idyllic scene, creating shadows under the branches of willow trees and in the tall grass growing along the perimeter of the pond. And in that moment, she understood why little Sarah loved to seek out the tadpoles. As for herself, Jodi couldn't recall a more wonderful afternoon. Not at all what she'd expected following the bad news from her principal.

When Jodi and the girls returned to the house, Maryanna met them on the back porch with flour on her hands and cheeks. "Did ya have a nice look around?" She held out her arms to her daughters.

"I just had a crash course on hens and egg gathering," Jodi said, adding that she'd enjoyed the sights and smells of the greenhouse, too. "Oh, and I saw Sarah's tadpoles, as well."

Jodi thanked Leda and Sarah, and waited for Maryanna to say when she wanted to have their private talk. "I don't want to keep you," Jodi said. "You're obviously very busy."

"As *you* must be," Maryanna added. "You really didn't intend to spend all day with an Amish family, did ya, now?"

Jodi laughed. "It's been truly wonderful."

Maryanna brushed her hands on her black apron, leaving more floury handprints. "Come — let's go out toward the road. It'll take but a minute."

Leda quickly took Sarah inside, even though Maryanna hadn't prompted them. *Is everyone in perfect sync here?* Jodi wondered.

"I hope ya know how thankful I am to you," Maryanna began, her dress flapping against her shins.

"I did what anyone would've — Sarah's absolutely adorable."

"Even so, it's hard to think of anyone kinder."

"I guess I was in the right place at the right time."

Seeming less hesitant now that they were alone, Maryanna asked her a series of questions, including how Sarah could be so clean after a night of wandering about. Jodi was happy to reveal everything, as well as how she'd tried to discover whether Sarah had been reported missing. "I attempted to put myself in your shoes as her mother. I couldn't imagine anyone abandoning a child."

"Did ya think she was kidnapped?" asked Maryanna as they went.

"It crossed my mind."

"All of us were prayin', for sure and for certain."

"I would have, too." Jodi caught herself.

"And God covets our prayers every day, rain or shine. In *gut* and bad times."

Jodi could just hear Trent saying something comparable. *Karen too.*

"The Lord knows we forget to be thankful when things are goin' well," Maryanna said, lowering her voice. "Yet He still forgives."

Jodi didn't clench up as she did when her parents talked this way. There was something so gentle and down-to-earth about Maryanna and her view of God.

"Just think of a mother craving her child's love and only receiving it when the little one skins her knee or is hungry and wants something to eat. What sort of relationship would that be?"

Jodi heartily agreed.

They walked farther, not saying a word, but it felt natural, like they didn't need to fill the gaps of silence.

"It's almost blissful here," Jodi said at last.

"Folk tend to say that about Hickory Hollow. Maybe it's just quieter round here."

"Because of the lack of cars?"

Maryanna nodded. "The horse sets our pace — the tempo of our lives. When he stops for water and feed, we stop and pause for breakfast, and then the noon meal. When he needs to rest on a hot afternoon, we, too, have a natural break in the course of our daily routine. And like horses, we go to sleep early and rise with the dawn."

The idea of a life based on such simple rhythms did have its appeal.

"We ofttimes ask the dear Lord to help us be ever gentle with His creatures — to be *gut* shepherds of everything entrusted to us."

The dear Lord, thought Jodi.

"The best way to repay our animals — they toil so hard alongside us — is to give them our kindness."

"I've never thought of it quite like that, but it certainly makes sense." Jodi shared how she'd always been fond of animals, especially pets like cats and canaries.

"Well, I don't mean to take such affection to an absurd level," replied Maryanna. "Not like some folk do."

Jodi was surprised at the sudden edge to her voice. Was she referring to her neighbor Joshua?

After a time, Maryanna pointed out a large farmhouse, with a secondary house built onto the south side. "That's my friend Ella Mae Zook's place. The People call her the Wise Woman."

"Are you sure you're not the wise one?" Jodi replied. "You sound astute enough to me."

"Oh, nothin's like Ella Mae's homespun wisdom. I started goin' over there and talking out my heart after Benuel's death. For months, I must've cried all the tears I had."

Jodi held her breath, listening. *Such an openhearted woman,* she thought. *I've misjudged Maryanna.*

"Honestly, it was such a strange thing to watch my strong husband walk out the door after breakfast, and then struggle to take his last breaths in my arms but a few hours later."

Jodi felt terribly lacking. "I don't see how you got through."

"Apart from God, I doubt I would've." Maryanna slowed her pace. "Goodness' sake, why am I tellin' you this?" She began to apologize. "Those long hours last night wonderin' what had become of little Sarah must've set me back some."

"You've endured a difficult time."

Maryanna nodded slowly. "I feel so sorry for my children." She sighed. "But life isn't so much about circumstances as it is learning to look to almighty God. Just being aware of His presence, ya know. When all's said and done."

Jodi might have said the same at one time, but she'd pushed God away for so many months, it would feel awkward to let Him back into her life now.

Maryanna smiled. "I'm glad it was you who found Sarah." Her voice cracked and she pulled a hankie out from beneath her sleeve. "When I think what could've happened . . ."

Jodi shuddered.

Maryanna looked at her with somber eyes. "The Lord knew all about this day long before Sarah was even born — and all the many prayers God heard and answered." She smiled faintly, as if struggling to say more. "Jah, you're welcome to visit us again."

"Thank you, Maryanna."

"I'm not much for Englischers, I have to confess." Maryanna glanced at her. "But, you . . . well, I don't know. I s'pose not all English folk are alike. So the invitation's open. And I know for sure Sarah wants to see you again."

Jodi's heart was deeply moved by this remarkable woman. "I'd like that."

"Tomorrow, then?" Maryanna's eyes were smiling.

Jodi felt as if she were being swept up in a current, yet for once the thought that she wasn't in control didn't concern her. In fact, she was happy to agree.

CHAPTER 19

After Jodi Winfield backed out of the driveway and headed up Hickory Lane, Maryanna returned to the house. She went to the corner cupboard and took out a box of crayons and *An Amish Quilt,* a new coloring book she'd purchased just last week, and presented it to Sarah.

"Denki, Mamma!" Sarah clapped her hands with glee and crawled up on the long bench on this side of the table, ready to color.

"Be sure an' look for the cuddly bear."

Sarah opened the book and found it right away. "And, look, there's a little doll like Kaylee." Her mouth turned down just then. "But Kaylee's lost."

"I'll have your new doll all sewn up by tomorrow," Maryanna promised, happy to turn Sarah's sad face into a smile. "Won't take me long at all."

Sarah patted the bench next to her, and

Maryanna was overjoyed to sit awhile and watch Sarah's little fingers wrap around the red crayon. Her youngest always had preferred bold colors. She moved the crayon carefully on the page, staying in the lines.

Maryanna leaned close, enjoying the sweet nearness of her youngest, and let her memory waft back to the snowy November day she'd revealed to Benuel the news they were expecting their fourth child.

Her husband had been tired that cold day, rubbing his left temple as he came in from the barn, where he'd just lost a prized calf. Maryanna had made some creamed chipped beef with mashed potatoes to cheer him up.

But it was well after the children were tucked into bed that she'd pulled up a chair beside Benuel as he sat near the heat stove. "We're going to have another baby," she'd told him, sharing her joy.

Immediately, his demeanor had changed, and he reached for her hand with a broad smile. "*Gut* news, indeed."

She was pleased but pondered the worry she and Mollie and others in their family had experienced during each of their pregnancies due to the real possibility of genetic diseases.

"Let's pray," Benuel said, as if sensing her unease. And, still holding her hand, he asked God to bless their coming child, asking for a divine shield to cover him . . . or her. "Make this little child strong for you," he concluded. Maryanna had never forgotten.

When Sarah finished coloring her page and taped it to the refrigerator, Maryanna watched her run outside to find Leda. Meanwhile, she hurried next door to look in on her parents. Already beginning to second-guess the walk she'd taken with the Englischer, Maryanna realized she'd been much too plainspoken. Had she succumbed to whatever the children sensed in the fancy yet likeable brunette?

Was it her white clothing?

But, no, Jodi Winfield was not an angel sent from heaven. Maryanna laughed under her breath as she stooped to shoo away a pesky gray barn cat. Jodi was just an Englischer, for goodness' sake!

Maryanna ran up the steps to the back door, delighting in her mother's arrangement of red and white geraniums all across the back porch and the hanging basket of petunias, as well.

"Hullo, Mamm . . . Daed," she called through the screen door before she opened it.

Her parents were sitting in their small front room, on the side facing the road, away from the hot sun. The dark green shades were all the way up to let the faint breeze come in. It certainly looked like her mother was helping it along by fanning herself with Daed's blue paisley kerchief.

"You had yourself a pleasant visitor," her father said, looking up from his newspaper. "We liked her."

"Thank you for praying for little Sarah's return," she said.

" 'Tis a miracle she wasn't hurt more than she was," Daed said.

"Well, if anyone's gonna fall out the back of the carriage, it's Sarah." Mamm looked up from her cross-stitch sampler. Her hair was pulled tight into its bun, and her crisp white *Kapp* was freshly ironed.

"I never would've thought she'd lean so far as to tumble out, though," Maryanna replied as she took a seat next to her father on the upholstered settee. "It's beyond me what she was even doin'."

Her father folded the paper. "I 'spect she was curious 'bout the cars, just maybe?"

"You know Sarah well, I daresay."

"That we do," Mamm said, pushing her needle into the fabric and then folding her arms. "She's always been a curious sort."

Maryanna suppressed her smile. There was no doubt Sarah had enjoyed her momentary flirtation with fancy life.

But her mother wasn't finished. "And, not to worry ya unduly, but if somethin's not done, and real soon, I'm afraid you're going to have your hands full with that one."

"You're not the first to say so." Maryanna looked toward the window and sighed. Ella Mae had also said as much. Everyone, in fact, sounded worried about Sarah.

"Then what can be done?" asked Mamm, looking hard at Daed now, as if urging him to speak his mind. "You're bringing the children up in the fear and admonition of the Lord — we know that."

Such a long day, Maryanna thought. " 'Tween you and me, last night I began to wonder if God had taken her early," she admitted.

Her father's grim frown indicated his concern. "Some believe when such a little child goes like that, it's the Almighty's way of keeping them unto himself."

"Still, she's so young, Daed."

"Well, and she's safe now," Mamm piped up.

Daed ran his fingers through his thick, graying beard. "Have you considered the Lord God may have given a warning?" He stopped to punctuate his remark. "And will ya heed it?"

Maryanna felt her ire rise, but she bit her lip.

Her mother's brow puckered. "Don't take this wrong, dear, but we think it's time for the children to have a stepfather. Past time, maybe."

Maryanna gasped.

"Not to put our noses in . . ."

Dat spoke up. "I know just the man, too." He chuckled.

There were several local widowers, some older than others, but there was only one widower — Turkey Dan Zook, with five sons — that she was fairly certain they were thinking of. Dan was known as a man with some financial means, having received his grandfather's small turkey farm years ago. Even so, no one was a fit replacement for her Benuel.

"Seriously, ya might just ask the Lord to open your heart again to a man, is all," her father said, then pressed his chapped lips firmly together.

"Will ya give it to prayer, dear?" Mamm asked.

Maryanna shuddered. Her children were suffering without a father, especially little Sarah, as her parents had so aptly pointed out. But could Maryanna release her memories of Benuel, such a good man?

I'd hoped to grow old with my first love.

"Meanwhile, why not bring Sarah over to visit more often?" Daed said with a smile. "Spending time with her nearest grandfather might just be a *gut* thing, too."

Meanwhile? Do they think I can just snap my fingers and make this happen — this remarrying notion of theirs?

"Jah," Mamm was saying, rocking fast in her chair. "Your father and I want to help steer Sarah toward the church."

"I'll encourage her to visit here more," Maryanna said. "But that's all I can do."

"Nee, ya can't make a child go against his or her will," Daed spoke up. "But you can point them in the direction of the right path."

Maryanna wondered if he was referring to the old willow switch she'd tossed out a week after Benuel died. It wasn't in her to physically discipline little Sarah that way. Now the boys, that was another story, but she'd chosen the paddle for their backsides. As for Leda, all Maryanna had to do was give her a stern look and tearful repentance burst forth.

"Would ya like a fresh loaf of bread?" Maryanna asked, ready to change the sub-

181

ject. "I'll let the bread cool, then bring over a loaf."

"Got any blueberry jam?" Daed asked, eyeing Mamm. "I daresay we're all out."

Mamm laughed suddenly. "Can't keep it round here for long."

"Sure, I'll have Leda check the cold cellar. I know we've got a-plenty." Maryanna rose and waved. "I'll send little Sarah over with the bread in a while."

Daed's wrinkled face brightened, and he tugged on his black suspenders, letting them snap. "I'll spread blueberry jam on a piece of toast for her," he said. "That'll get her attention."

"Actually, she doesn't like it," Maryanna reminded him.

"What *does* she like on bread?"

"Mostly honey — and sometimes a sprinkling of cinnamon, too."

Daed shook his head. "No fruit jams?"

"Not a single one."

Mamm broke into the conversation. "She's a picky eater, I'll say."

"Leaves more jam for me, ain't?" Daed grinned.

Maryanna called good-bye and hurried back to the main house to find Sarah watching Leda carefully pull the loaves of bread out of the gas oven.

Standing in the doorway observing her daughters and recalling her parents' sobering words, Maryanna knew they were right. Without a doubt, Sarah's soul was more important than Maryanna's reluctance to remarry.

And yet, the mere idea of dating and remarriage made her shy away. Knowing what she ought to do, and doing it, were ever so different.

CHAPTER 20

Still under the spell of Hickory Hollow, Jodi put a small load of laundry in to wash, including the white skirt. Then, wearing her shorts outfit, she carried her laptop to the breakfast nook and sat in the very chair where spunky little Sarah had sat that morning.

Reliving her time with Sarah and her family — Sarah's insistence on sitting on Jodi's lap, the way she folded her hands in prayer at the table, and Jodi's long walk with Maryanna — Jodi touched Karen's gold bracelet. "I wish I could talk to you . . ." she whispered.

She had been struck by how cohesive Maryanna's family was, even without her husband, and the sweet way young Sarah's siblings had shown their delight at having her home, snatched from the worrisome unknown. In that moment, everything crashed down around Jodi — her sister's death, her job loss, Trent's going to Japan, and the prospect of starting at square one again with her teaching career.

Jodi refused to dwell on the earlier call from her principal, though, and gave herself a stern talking-to. Just like after a car accident, it was important to get back into the car and drive.

So she took time now to update her resume and began the process of submitting it online, deciding to focus on the few openings in Vermont, since she was already licensed there. But at the last minute, she also included school districts in New Hampshire and Connecticut. It didn't make sense to look for a teaching position too far from Trent's secure job in Bennington, after all. Yet if she landed a job this late in the summer, there'd be hoops to jump through to get recertified elsewhere. Still, she wasn't giving up on Vermont, not when she and Trent planned to make Bennington their home once they were married.

If we can see eye to eye!

Later, while making a turkey, tomato, and lettuce sandwich for supper, she received a text from Trent. *I talked to your dad — he wants you to take an unexpected opening at his school.*

She found it surprising that Trent had

already communicated with her father about her dilemma. Were they really that much in touch long-distance?

"Thought you were packing for Japan," she whispered, carrying a paper plate with her sandwich to the fridge for a can of juice and a bunch of grapes. Then, closing the door, she eyed the patio through the kitchen window, but it was still too hot to sit out there.

Her dad's eagerness to help and Mom's phone call that morning closed in around her like walls. Sitting at the breakfast nook, she sighed. *So much to consider . . .*

She opened the juice and had a clear vision of Maryanna Esh pouring iced tea. *Never heard of meadow tea before today.* After getting to know the woman better, Jodi actually felt drawn to her, despite Maryanna's admitted aversion to English folk.

Why, when we have nothing in common?

Then Jodi thought of Sarah.

Well, almost nothing . . .

When Jodi didn't answer Trent's text right away, he called. "Want to Skype, honey?" he asked. "We'll make it quick."

"Tomorrow, okay? I'm really tired," she begged off and guessed by his pleading that he wanted to offer more ideas for her job search. Knowing him, he had been online scouting out every school district in the tristate area. Always helpful Trent.

"You've ruined me," he replied. "I love seeing your pretty face, Jodi."

"Details, details." She laughed.

He told her how nice he thought it was of her dad to make an offer. "He has an opening for a third-grade teacher at his school — a perfect fit, really. What do you say?"

"I'd rather have my tonsils ripped out."

"That's what I love about you, Jodi . . . you're so subtle."

She cracked a smile. "I'm wiped out, is what I am."

"Are you okay . . . I mean —"

"Other than getting the boot from my job?"

"You sound pretty frustrated, hon."

"It's been a rough day."

"You were going to jog. Did you?"

"Yes." Then she told him about finding the little Amish girl and tracking down her family. "Though in all fairness, I had some help locating Hickory Hollow." She mentioned Scott's input. "But from there it was Sarah herself who guided me to her farmhouse."

"Remarkable." He seemed all too interested in the abandoned child, so Jodi toned down the part about being fond of Sarah and her mother and played up Amish farm life and the humble, sweet behavior and innocent playfulness of the other children she'd met. "For such secluded people, they were surprisingly friendly. Sarah's mother even invited me back."

He asked if she had any idea how the child wandered away.

"Fell out of the back of her family's buggy, evidently."

"Something you don't hear every day." He paused. "I've read that Amish families have an average of seven or eight children."

Please don't get any ideas!

"Sarah's mom has two boys and two girls. She's a young widow — possibly close to Karen's age. . . ."

"Sounds like you got well acquainted."

"It *was* fascinating." Jodi remembered her manners and asked about his day. "So are you settled on what you're taking overseas?"

"All decided, yes." Trent talked of his upcoming preparations for his trip to Japan in seven days. The JET program required participants to arrive by the twenty-ninth of July, but Trent was an overplanner and not one to leave any detail to chance. *A good thing,* Jodi thought as they talked about his hopes to sell his car before he left for the year.

"Really, your old beater?"

He laughed infectiously. "It's not worth much, and since I'm leaving my apartment there's no place to keep it."

She understood. Still, all of this was starting to sound so permanent. "You sure you're coming back home after Japan?"

"Let wild horses try to drag me away from you!"

She smiled, sufficiently reassured. "And you're still cool with me planning the wedding?"

"What guy wouldn't be?"

"Okay, I'm holding you to it."

"And I wish I were there right now, holding *you* in my arms."

She smiled. "You're such a dreamer."

"Well, get used to it, because I plan to be annoyingly romantic for the rest of your life."

She liked the sound of that.

"Yes, married life is going to be good . . . and we'll look to God for our help and direction," he added. "Don't forget that I'm praying for you."

She left the comment alone.

"Well, great talking to you, honey. We'll keep in touch."

"Have a good night," she said.

"I love you, Jodi soon-to-be Norton."

"Love you, too."

They said good-bye and hung up. But instead of feeling encouraged, Jodi felt inadequate. Trent's confident voice in her ears hadn't helped.

Leaning back in the chair, she closed her eyes, trying to remember the last time Trent's exuberance *hadn't* lifted her spirits.

She heard a *meow* and opened her eyes to see the cat headed this way. "I could use some company," she said, delighted when Gigi padded over and leaped onto her lap. "Aren't you sweet?"

The cat peered up at her and then began licking her front paws.

"Oh, now, that's lovely. You're taking a bath in my lap." She laughed softly, remembering how Sarah had sat on the living room floor with Gigi, seemingly content in the midst of missing her mother and longing for home. Such a trusting little girl.

Is that what Jesus meant when He said to come as a child? No qualms, no cares?

"Trent's praying about my next job," she informed the cat. "I suppose I should feel hopeful."

And with that, she turned off her phone,

needing to be alone with her thoughts for the rest of the evening.

Chapter 21

Midmorning the next day, Maryanna couldn't help noticing attractive Ida Fisher over talking to Joshua Peachey out by his mailbox on Hickory Lane. She was surprised at this obvious overture by the young widow and felt a strange prick of annoyance. *Surely not jealousy,* she thought, dismissing it.

Barefoot Ida was carrying a small wicker basket, possibly coming from visiting her parents up the road. Nonetheless, she had stopped at Joshua's mailbox around the time Maryanna wandered out to her own. And there was Joshua getting his mail, too.

How odd, thought Maryanna as she pulled out a few letters and some bills.

Glancing back at Ida and Joshua, she realized they were waving at her now. Joshua had removed his straw hat, just like yesterday when Maryanna had scurried over there.

Maryanna waved back, and it struck her that Ida was wearing her best blue dress and matching cape apron, and on a Saturday yet. Maryanna pondered the situation as she walked back to the house with the mail.

Has Ida come out of her shell?

Brushing aside her curiosity, Maryanna went through her letters and noticed one from her cousin Fay Mast, who'd gone to visit cousins in Westcliffe, Colorado, last week with her husband and several other Amish couples. Maryanna couldn't imagine traveling so far herself.

When she finished reading the letter, Maryanna wondered momentarily if Ida and Joshua were still talking together, but she didn't go to the front room window to look out. She could easily imagine lovely Ida marrying again and settling into Joshua's farmhouse.

She's ideal, mused Maryanna, *considering she has no children.*

After Jodi's short but invigorating run that morning, she turned on her phone and discovered, much to her dismay, three voice-mail messages from her parents. *I don't want to be rude. But I can't accept my father's offer, kind as it is,* she decided.

Uppermost in her mind was returning to Hickory Hollow today, once she showered and dressed. Unfortunately, she'd brought along only one skirt, and after being around Maryanna Esh and her family, she didn't feel it was appropriate to wear shorts or even capris to visit there. So she looked on Paige's side of the closet for a long skirt or flowing dress and found several options. Quickly, she texted her cousin's wife and asked if she'd mind loaning her a skirt for the day. *I'll take care of it,* she promised. And Paige wrote back immediately to agree.

Jodi skipped the makeup after her shower to feel better suited for her visit. And before heading out, she jotted down some grammar tips for Toby, including some easy jingles she'd made up for her students last year.

She jumped when her cell phone rang. It was her father.

I'll just listen for a change, she thought, feeling bad about ignoring him and Mom all last evening.

"Hi, Dad," she answered. "Nice to hear your voice . . ."

"Yours too, honey," he said. "I've been thinking."

She held her breath as he forged ahead, saying he'd heard from Trent about her job

194

being cut. Like any loving father might, he apologized profusely. But then, not realizing it was putting her in a tight spot, he offered her the job Trent had mentioned.

"Dad, that's really nice of you."

"Well then, say yes."

This was hard — Jodi didn't want to be in the position of saying no to her own father, yet she also couldn't accept only to please him. "I really need to think about it."

"Okay, I'll give you a week to come up with the right answer. How's that?"

There was such optimism in his voice.

"Sure, that's fair," she said, wishing there was a way out that wouldn't disappoint him.

For the life of her, Maryanna could not get Sarah to move away from the front room window. She'd sat there on the wide windowsill for a solid half hour already. "Why don't ya go over and see Mammi Emmie."

"I'm waiting for my angel," her daughter replied.

"You might have to sit there all morning, then."

Sarah said she didn't mind. And Maryanna shrugged, still stumped at her evident fascination.

"Have ya done your chores yet?" she asked.

"Jah," Sarah replied.

"So gschwind? — So quickly?"

Sarah nodded, her gaze still fixed on the road.

Maryanna kissed the top of her little head, her heart swelling with happiness yet again. "Sure ya don't want to help make some ice cream for the noon meal?"

Sarah turned and nodded her head, eyes sparkling. But she made it clear she wanted to help turn the crank while sitting at the table. "So I can watch for my Jodi angel," Sarah replied.

"You really think she's heaven-sent?" Maryanna managed to say.

"Don't you, Mamma?"

"The Lord watches over His children, for sure," Maryanna replied. "He uses many ways to do so."

Sarah's smile was priceless.

"Did ya have a nice visit with your grandparents yesterday?"

"Dawdi Zeke read me a Bible story and put honey on my toast." Sarah beamed. "Did you tell him to do that, Mamma?"

Maryanna nodded. *Such a bright little thing.*

"Does Jodi like honey toast with cinnamon, too?"

"Why don't ya ask her when she comes?"

Sarah's head bobbed up and down. "I

can't wait to see her again, Mamma."

"I know, dear one," replied Maryanna. "I know."

It crossed Joshua's mind that Ida Fisher might have been encouraged to walk past his house around the time of mail delivery. After all, Preacher Yoder's youngest sister was a close friend of Ida's, and the preacher had gone so far yesterday as to single Ida out. So Joshua was quite certain the encounter on the road a bit ago was not a coincidence.

He was heading out to the barn to feed, water, and groom his livestock when he saw the same blue car pulling into Maryanna Esh's driveway. This, too, could not be a mere coincidence.

He wasn't sure of the make of the vehicle, but the car looked identical to the one parked over there yesterday for hours. Was the Englischer smitten with Amish farm life? Or had Maryanna unwisely invited her back to visit?

He feared the latter considering Preacher Yoder's advice — it *was* about time to think of marrying again.

Mighty interesting of Ida to stop by. But it was the thought of Maryanna that tugged on his heart. Still, if Maryanna Esh rejected him, maybe he ought to think about Ida Fisher instead.

Can I give Ida my whole heart, if she'll even have me? Joshua shoved open the barn door. He drew a sigh as he stood there, able to see a dark-haired English woman being greeted by Tobias and little Sarah.

Well, what do ya know? Joshua shook his head, not sure what to think.

CHAPTER 22

Little Sarah and her brother Toby were walking back from the barn when Jodi arrived at the Esh farmhouse that Saturday morning. She reached across to the passenger seat for her list of lighthearted grammar tips and took it with her as she got out. She heard Sarah's happy calls first — "Jodi . . . Jodi!" — then was welcomed enthusiastically by both children, who ran across the yard to her. Jodi had a hard time concealing her surprise when Toby stuck his hand out for her to shake.

"We meet again," she said, smiling. "Hi, Toby and Sarah."

"*Guder Mariye,* Engel," Sarah said, grinning up at her and looking as lovable as she had yesterday.

"She's told everyone you're her angel," Toby said.

Jodi chuckled. "Well, I've been called lots of things, but never that."

"What's in your hand?" Toby asked.

"Ever hear the song 'The Farmer in the Dell'?" Jodi asked him.

He shook his head no.

"Well, it's real easy. Here, I'll teach you." She leaned against the car door and sang it on the syllable *lah.* After that, she hummed it a second time and was tickled when Toby and Sarah tried to chime in. By the third time, they had the melody down pat. "Now, even though Sarah won't understand the English words I made up for this tune, you will, Toby."

He rubbed his hands together fast, eyes alert. "Jah, teach it to me."

"Okay, remember what we just hummed?"

He nodded eagerly.

"All right. I'll add words to the tune we just learned." And she began. "Person, place, or thing. Person, place, or thing. These are nouns for us to sing: person, place, or thing."

The children's eyes twinkled, and Toby's head dipped and swayed to the song.

"There's more," she said. "Listen." And she continued on to the second stanza of her made-up ditty. "Sarah, house, and nose; Toby, garden, rose. These are nouns for us to sing. See how knowledge grows!"

Toby's smile spread across his face. "I like

it. Sing it again."

So she did, and he immediately joined in.

Sarah tried to sing along, especially at the part where her name came in.

"See?" Jodi said. "Learning grammar is fun."

Toby stepped closer. "I'm awful sorry I said I hate it yesterday." His face reddened. "Mamma said I should apologize . . . and I wanted to, anyways," he admitted. "Will ya sing the song again?" he asked as he motioned them toward the house. "I want Mamma to hear it."

If only Dad could see me now! Jodi thought. He'd always said, *"Once a teacher, always a teacher."*

Jodi folded her notes and stuffed them into the pocket of Paige's pale blue skirt. She wished Sarah spoke English. Despite that, Jodi seemed able to convey some of her meaning a good part of the time.

"Come inside," Toby said. "Mamma's waitin' for ya."

Sarah babbled something to Toby and pulled on his arm.

"My sister wants me to tell ya she's getting a new doll today," Toby said. "Mamma's makin' it to replace the one she lost."

Sarah added something, and Toby again translated for Jodi. "She's naming her doll

201

Engel, after you."

Jodi smiled, pleased. "Tell her that's sweet."

He frowned, clearly confused. "Like sugar?"

"No, like *very nice.*"

"Oh," he said and told little Sarah, who reached for Jodi's hand as they entered the kitchen filled with the yeasty, wonderful aroma of freshly baked cinnamon rolls.

"You're just in time for warm sticky buns," Maryanna Esh declared when she saw Jodi there with the children. She wore a green dress with a black full apron, and her golden hair was neatly tucked in a bun beneath the white net cap, just it had been yesterday.

"A mornin' snack, jah?" Toby said, rushing to the counter, where a whole sheet of rolls was cooling.

"Wash your hands first," Maryanna urged. "Those *Pattie* have been out in the barn and all."

Toby made a detour to the washing basin, and Sarah followed behind, pulling up a stepstool and climbing on.

Maryanna invited Jodi to sit at the table. "We're glad you could drop by," she said, sounding a bit more reserved than yesterday.

"Thank you." Jodi watched the two chil-

202

dren jabbering at the sink and wondered what was being said. Then they surprised her and burst out with the tune, Sarah humming as Toby sang, "Person, place, or thing . . ."

"For goodness' sake, where'd they learn that?" Maryanna asked, looking back at Jodi.

"Sarah's angel made it up," Toby told his mother, drying his hands on his pants as he came over to the table.

"Facts set to music are a quick way for children to learn," Jodi explained.

"Why, sure . . . you're a teacher." Maryanna didn't seem to know what to make of her children singing and showing off. "I nearly forgot."

"Well, I *was*," Jodi said, then wished she hadn't.

"You ain't now?" Toby asked.

"She isn't," Maryanna corrected.

"Aren't," said Toby, grinning.

"It's a long story," Jodi replied as she finally took a seat at the table.

"Well, all of us enjoy a story, that's for sure," Maryanna urged.

Jodi nodded, watching Sarah and Toby take turns getting their cinnamon rolls. "I lost my teaching position recently."

"Oh?" Maryanna took a bite of her cinnamon roll.

"Budget cuts in the school district — not enough children enrolled to justify having as many teachers."

"You look sad 'bout it."

"Do I?" Jodi nodded. "Well, my principal notified me just yesterday, so the news is still sinking in. But I'm going to try for another school."

"*Des gut.* Teachers are important, jah?"

Jodi agreed. "My whole family's involved in education."

Maryanna reached for her cup of coffee. Then, after taking a sip, she nearly gasped. "Ach, I'm ever so sorry! Would ya like coffee or something hot with your roll?"

"Water's fine, thanks."

Instantly, Maryanna rose from the bench. "I hope you find a *gut* school come fall," she said at the sink.

Jodi nodded. "So do I."

"If you were Amish, you might step in and take Rosaleen's place, just maybe. Since she's newly engaged."

Toby's eyes lit up, and he leaped up from his chair. "Oh, can she, Mamma?"

"Mind your manners and take your seat," Maryanna said, snapping her fingers.

"Sorry, Mamma." He sat quickly.

Maryanna set a tumbler of tap water on the table before Jodi, and Sarah came around to her. She whispered something to her mother.

"She'd like ya to see her new dolly, but I'm not quite done with it," Maryanna explained.

"That's all right."

"It was goin' to be faceless like most of her dolls," Maryanna told Jodi, "but Sarah wants her to look like you."

Jodi smiled.

"She even wants her dolly to wear a tiny gold bracelet." Maryanna pointed to Jodi's right arm. "Sarah said you wore it even when you helped her in the bath."

Jodi tensed. She wasn't ready to talk about her deceased sister. "It's a special piece of jewelry" was all she cared to say. But knowing that Sarah had been so observant endeared the little Amish girl to her all the more.

"Mamma," said Toby, looking at his mother, "is it okay for me to say something 'bout the last teacher we had?" His tone was meek.

"*Gut* manners are very important." Maryanna put more sugar in her coffee after she again took her place at the table. "It might be best if ya wait, since we have a guest now, son."

"Jah, but all the other pupils would say it, too."

Maryanna's brow rose — she looked frazzled. "What is it, Tobias?"

"Rosaleen's beau sometimes visited her during lunch recess — just the two of 'em in the schoolhouse."

Maryanna shook her head. "Ach! Such a breach of principle."

"Benny told her beau he'd get her fired if he didn't quit stoppin' by."

"And did the young man return?" asked Maryanna, her neck reddening.

"The very next day, jah."

"Well, then, it's a *gut* thing Rosaleen won't be teachin' this school year."

Toby bit into his cinnamon roll and nodded. Then he reached for his glass of milk and washed down his mouthful.

"These courting couples," Maryanna muttered almost under her breath.

Jodi assumed she should stay out of this conversation. It certainly seemed as though Maryanna had forgotten she had an outsider sitting at the table.

Toby began to sing Jodi's song quietly. "Person, place, or thing. Person, place, or thing. These are nouns for us to sing: person, place, or thing."

Little Sarah burst into giggles next to him.

As tense as the atmosphere had been, Jodi eased into a smile, too. *Toby knows what a noun is now . . . and both children can sing on pitch!*

CHAPTER 23

Maryanna didn't have the heart to tell Tobias and Sarah in front of the Englischer that she wasn't too keen on their singing worldly songs, even for the purpose of learning grammar. She was still mum on the subject when she set about clearing the table later with the help of Leda, as well as Jodi, of all people.

Then, when the dishes were in the soapy water, she finally went upstairs and brought down Sarah's unfinished doll to show Jodi. "I marked where her features will go." She pointed to the doll's right wrist. "And the bracelet."

Jodi glanced at her own wrist. "What will you use?"

"Tiny gold rickrack ought to work," said Maryanna. "If I can find some at the Hickory Hollow General Store, that is."

"Well, if you don't, I'll be glad to drive you to look elsewhere," Jodi suggested.

"It's very nice of you to offer," Maryanna said to Jodi. "We'll see what Preacher Yoder has on hand at his store."

"Your minister works there?" Jodi seemed puzzled.

"We don't have paid ministers," Maryanna explained. "If a man is chosen by lot — by divine appointment — to become a deacon or a preacher, then he continues what he's been doing for his livelihood."

Jodi nodded as if she understood, but her greenish eyes studied Maryanna as if still taking in what she'd said.

"I'm sure it's real different with your minister."

Jodi looked slightly embarrassed. "Actually, I don't attend church anymore."

Maryanna was stunned. "Sorry to hear it." She couldn't imagine not going to Preaching, so central to the life of her family and community. She shooed the children out of the kitchen — outdoors — and held up the doll, looking it over. Then she handed it to Jodi. "What do ya think? Does she look like you?"

The Englischer scrutinized the doll closely, her eyebrows rising. "Sure . . . other than her Amish clothes."

"Well, Sarah wants her to resemble you, but she also wants her to look Amish."

"And what Sarah wants, she gets?" Jodi surprised her by saying.

"Ain't that the truth!" Maryanna glanced out the window to see her sister Mollie and more of her family with her today. "Looks like Mollie's here for her African violets. Come, you can meet the rest of her children."

Jodi handed the doll back to her.

"Mollie's gonna wonder 'bout this doll, let me tell ya," Maryanna said, placing it on the hutch across from the table.

Smiling, Jodi followed her outside. And as they hurried to greet Mollie — all four of her girls had squeezed into the carriage this time — Maryanna could feel in her bones that the brunette woman had been sent their way for a reason.

Joshua Peachey had never seen anything like it, and he told his neighbors so when Paul Hostetler and Nate Kurtz dropped by to help him get things ready for church tomorrow. Hot as it had been, it was a better idea to set up the church benches in the barn than the house.

"Just look over there," Joshua said as he pointed to Maryanna Esh's place, where the Englischer was sitting in the gazebo with a whole bunch of children, mostly girls.

"Who is the brunette woman, and what's she doin'?" asked Paul, moseying over nosy-like toward the horse fence separating Joshua's driveway from the paddock.

" 'Tis the young woman who found Sarah and brought her home to us," Joshua said. "Er . . . to her mother." He felt his face flush red, but neither of the men caught it while gawking at the sight across the pasture.

"Looks like she's teaching them something," Paul said.

Nate mumbled something indistinct.

"Wonder where Maryanna and her parents are," Paul added.

Joshua wasn't about to say he'd seen Maryanna at her folks' place not long ago, while he was out pulling weeds along the side of his house. Things there were getting out of hand, and his wilting flowers looked pitiful.

"Doubt Zeke and Emmie know," Nate said.

Joshua smiled. "Oh, but they must," he insisted. "Mollie drove in with her girls just a few minutes ago."

Now Paul turned to cast a searching look at him before leaning on the fence again, seeming lost in thought. Nate, however, still faced the Esh farm.

"Are either of you planning to run in the

211

Bird-in-Hand Half Marathon?" asked Joshua, suddenly feeling a need to direct the subject away from his neighbor.

"My son Michael might," Paul said. "But not me. Not since I broke my foot."

"Might limber it up," Nate said, offering a rare grin. And finally both men moved away from the fence.

"Guess we should get started before the bench wagon arrives." Joshua motioned and they made their way toward the barn, ready for the big job. Before heading inside, Joshua stole one more glance over yonder, wondering what Maryanna was up to, and why she was this friendly with the Englischer. *Isn't like her.*

The fancy woman might have carried Sarah home to the People, and for that they were obliged, but if Maryanna wasn't careful, this same Englischer might just carry Sarah right out of the church . . . one day.

Jodi was pleased at the children's attention and wholehearted interest in learning. She was surprised, too, that Maryanna didn't seem to mind this impromptu gathering in the white gazebo near the large oak tree. It had been Toby and Sarah's idea, and their excitement had been contagious. The older girls had carried worn blankets and spread them on the wooden floor, and Benny had mentioned his mother would bring snacks out later.

"Let's practice arithmetic," Benny said, nudging Fannie on one side and Fannie's younger sister, Ellie, on the other.

The other sister, the youngest of the four girls, was a few years older than Sarah, from what Jodi could tell. Darla and Sarah could easily pass for siblings, they looked so much alike. Even as first cousins, they were clearly tuned in to each other's way of thinking — and as sparkling and eager as any students Jodi had taught.

"Do you have any flash cards?" Jodi asked.

"Just at the schoolhouse," Benny said, raising his hand before he spoke.

"We're not in class," Leda said, laughing.

"I almost forgot," Benny replied.

Jodi had an idea and began to go around, starting with the youngest children and giving easy addition questions to review. "Darla, what's two plus three?"

"Five," the little girl said, looking at Sarah, who was trying to fit in despite the language barrier.

"Two plus seven?" Jodi asked Ellie.

"Nine," the slightly older girl said.

Working around the circle, she gave the easy problems more quickly now, turning it into a game as she decided to time them, too. She moved on to ask who could say first how many inches were in a yard and other units of measurement.

"Let's sing our song — the one you taught us before," Toby said later, hopping up and speaking to Sarah in Deitsch, no doubt asking her to join him.

But Sarah frowned and shook her head at him, cousin Darla's hand still clasped in hers.

Toby launched into Deitsch again, apparently attempting to persuade Sarah to change her mind. But by her flashing eyes, she wouldn't hear of it.

Suddenly, little Sarah pointed directly at Jodi. *"Du . . .* Jodi *singe!"*

"She wants *you* to sing," Leda said, though this time Jodi needed no translation.

"All right," Jodi agreed. "Do you know 'America the Beautiful'?"

The children shook their heads but leaned forward like young birds reaching for sustenance, their interest firing Jodi's own enthusiasm. So she took a deep breath and began to sing, and noticed Maryanna at the screen door, watching cautiously.

Am I stepping out of bounds?

"She must be singing an English song,"

214

Maryanna said to Mollie as she observed Jodi Winfield. "Never heard it before."

Mollie set down her mending and joined her at the back door. "Me neither."

Maryanna couldn't help noticing the children's attentiveness. "Have you ever seen the likes of this?"

" 'Tis mighty curious, I'll say."

"A true teacher has a gift from God, Ella Mae always says."

Mollie touched her arm. "Even an Englischer teacher?"

Maryanna paused as she saw how enthralled little Sarah was by Jodi. "I pray I wasn't wrong to invite her back."

"You wanted to thank her, is all."

"Even so."

"Time will tell, sister," Mollie said.

As she continued to watch, Maryanna mulled over the conversation she'd had with Daed and Mamm. Was this association with Jodi feeding into Sarah's apparent curiosity for the English world, fueling what could become a problem?

Have I erred in judgment, Lord?

It occurred to Maryanna that if she could rein in her youngest, her parents might leave her be about remarrying. She smiled at that. For one thing, her best efforts weren't working, and even if they were, she doubted her parents would *ever* let up.

Truth be told, Maryanna knew it wasn't just Sarah who needed the firm yet loving hand of a stepfather, but also Benny, Leda, and Tobias. She sighed so heavily that Mollie asked if she was all right.

CHAPTER 24

Jodi noticed Maryanna step onto the back porch, her face shiny with perspiration.

"Would ya like to stay and eat with us, Jodi?" Maryanna asked.

The sun was creeping closer to the housetop, shining through the slats on the gazebo's roof and into the children's eyes. None of them had complained of the heat, but Jodi was quite aware of it dressed in Paige's long skirt.

"Thanks, Maryanna, but you really don't have to invite me again."

"Well, most of the children have come in to whisper to me, askin'."

Jodi looked into their adorable smiling faces and noticed Toby appeared particularly mischievous. "So *that's* what you've been up to, sneaking off one by one!"

The older children grinned sheepishly. "We like havin' ya here," Toby said softly, and the others nodded their heads.

"I'm enjoying myself, too." Jodi was surprised when shy Fannie leaned against her and looked up with her big eyes. "Thank you — it looks like I'll be staying for dinner," she added to Maryanna, who nodded before walking back into the house.

"We'll hurry with our afternoon chores — and polishing all the shoes for Preachin' tomorrow," Benny said, explaining before Jodi asked.

"I don't want to keep you from your work." Jodi slipped her arm around Sarah, who'd managed to burrow under Jodi's elbow.

"Joshua Peachey's hostin' church tomorrow, and his flower beds are all schlappich," Tobias announced.

"Us girls should slip over there," Leda said. "While Joshua and the men set up the church benches."

"We," Benny said, looking to Jodi for approval. "Take 'girls' out of the sentence and what do ya have? *Us* should slip over there. . . ." He laughed and gave Toby a high five.

"When did you get so schmaert?" Bertie asked, giggling.

Benny replied, "I went and found some of my old school papers, that's what."

"Why? Just 'cause Jodi was comin' today?"

218

Toby teased.

Jodi stifled a laugh.

Benny wisely changed the subject. "Mamma still has some blue fan flowers and red and white geraniums in the greenhouse you girls could plant over there."

"*Gut* idea!" Leda said, clapping her hands.

"Better ask first," Benny chided.

It certainly sounded as though the neighbor's flower beds needed some attention. Apparently nothing was too insignificant to be overlooked when preparing to host church at one's house. *What a major undertaking that must be!*

"Will ya come, too, Jodi?" Leda asked, her eyes pleading.

"If your mother doesn't mind." Jodi wanted to be sensitive to Maryanna's wishes.

"Oh, she won't." Toby stood right up. "Mamma'd prob'ly go and redd up Joshua's garden herself, but his pets annoy her somethin' awful."

"And that ain't all," Benny whispered, eyes flashing.

Leda gave him a stern look. "Best be still!"

"Ach, you too," Toby replied.

Jodi found the cryptic talk interesting and wondered what else besides his pets annoyed Maryanna about the mysterious

Joshua.

Jodi offered to help with the dishes so Leda, Sarah, and their cousins could run over to plant flowers at Joshua's, once they'd asked permission. Maryanna hesitated so long about it that Jodi could practically see the wheels turning. Eventually, Maryanna agreed. "Since it's for the Preaching service," she said, not blinking an eye.

But when the girls begged for Jodi to go over and help, Maryanna stepped in. "It's the hottest time of the day, for pity's sake."

Jodi went along with Maryanna's wishes, since she was a guest. Maryanna said no more about the widower Joshua Peachey, which only served to pique Jodi's attention.

Drying dishes the old-fashioned way, with an embroidered tea towel, took Jodi back to occasional visits with Karen to see their great-aunt Leora, who'd never married. Leora had also never bothered to purchase a dishwasher, not even after she moved into a smaller house on the outskirts of Rutland when she eventually retired from teaching. The long dirt driveway up to Leora's white-frame two-story house was a magical recollection — a green passageway through overhanging trees and brushwood. An abandoned woodshed stood on the left, and on the right there was a small brick structure where, long ago, a slow fire had dried up to five bushels of apples at a time on wooden racks.

The memory of hot, sticky days came back to her, and Jodi recalled picking blackberries in the rain, getting thoroughly drenched. Karen had laughed and danced in the downpour, flinging her auburn hair about, just as pleased with the wet weather as their great-aunt, who also harvested her garlic in the rain, taking it indoors to her laundry room to hang and dry.

Finishing up with the pots and pans now, Jodi wished Benny had left the big fan he'd brought in for the meal but promptly took to the cellar afterward. Still, she assumed it must be even hotter with the horses and other livestock.

"You've stirred up some excitement for book learnin' round here . . . and before school starts, yet," Maryanna said unexpectedly. "Benny was in his room looking over last year's schoolwork last evening. I happened upon him long after he should've been in bed."

Jodi was happy to hear it.

"Toby, too, talked 'bout paying more attention to his grammar and workin' on speaking correctly."

"They're really wonderful boys, Mary-anna. You must be very proud of them — and your girls, too."

"Ach, not as proud as I am glad they're mentally fit and healthy in body." Maryanna admitted she'd nearly held her breath during her pregnancies, praying daily that each of her children would be born hale and hearty.

Jodi listened as she stacked the plates where Maryanna instructed. "That's something every parent wants," she said.

"As you can tell, Mollie's girl Bertie is a special child. And there are a few other children on my side of the family who are also affected by genetic diseases." Maryanna sighed. " 'Tis awful sad . . . and hard to take, at times."

"No wonder you're glad yours are healthy in every way."

"It's not something my husband and I ever took lightly. We understood that our children were at risk for the same disorder as Bertie — other things, too. Each time we had another baby, we believed it was a miracle that he or she was fine. Sooner or later, we thought the odds would be against us." Maryanna paused and put her hand on her chest.

"So, with little Sarah, we again prayed for

the divine provision of health, that we'd be blessed with another healthy child. And when she was born, Benuel and I felt a tremendous sense of relief that once more God had answered prayer."

Jodi's neck muscles tightened. *Answered prayer — there it is again.*

Yet God had allowed *her* only sibling to die. Why? *How could a loving heavenly Father deny what an earthly father would gladly give?* In light of Maryanna's remarks, these lingering questions tormented Jodi.

"Of course, there are other couples amongst us who've also prayed for healthy babies, but their little ones have serious, even fatal diseases," Maryanna added while rinsing one of the pots. " 'Tis not for us to understand."

"My sister suffered terribly with leukemia," Jodi said, testing the waters. "Died of it."

Maryanna looked stunned. "Oh . . . I'm so sorry. Was it recent?"

"Six months ago, but it seems like last week." Then, taking a deep breath, Jodi told Maryanna the whole story, struggling to maintain her composure. She described the initial tests, the days at the hospital, the rounds of treatment, and the endless prayers. All for nothing.

Maryanna was quiet for a moment. "I can't imagine losing a sister."

"Well . . . I can't imagine losing a daughter," Jodi said, thinking of Sarah. "And so I can't bear the thought of taking that risk . . . by having a baby someday."

"Grieving takes plenty of time." Maryanna's eyes shone with tears. "But we Amish believe children are a blessing."

Jodi nodded. Despite the gulf in their backgrounds, she felt a connection to Maryanna, as if it was safe to share her heart with her. "Unfortunately, my fiancé and I have recently come to disagree on having children," she said quietly, looking toward the window. "It's becoming a problem."

"Aw, dear girl, no wonder you're upset. . . ." Rinsing her hands, Maryanna dried them and motioned Jodi over to the table. "Come sit."

Jodi followed, feeling so hot she could hardly breathe.

"You're betrothed to this man?" Maryanna folded her hands on the table.

"Yes."

Maryanna's eyes searched hers. "Might this alter your commitment to marry?"

"All I know is we'll have to work things out," Jodi said.

"And your young man — where does he live?"

She told her about Trent's plan to work overseas for the next school year. "Might actually be a good thing, considering this."

"You do love him, don't you?"

"Absolutely — he's my other half. Now that my sister's gone, Trent's the dearest person on earth to me." Jodi breathed deeply. "I can't imagine my life without him."

"Well, he must be just wonderful" — Maryanna smiled — "if he's anything like you."

Jodi felt her face redden at the unsought affirmation, so like something her sister might have said.

"Getting back to the question of having children, I daresay that's one issue where things boil down to sheer trust in our heavenly Father. I honestly don't know any other way to peace."

"Or maybe just not having kids, right?" Jodi forced a laugh.

Maryanna smiled across the table. "Some might think so, I s'pose. But having our babies only deepened Benuel's and my marriage. We blended our love for each other and spread it to our children."

Jodi absorbed this. While her doubts

remained, she'd never heard anyone describe it quite that way before. Maryanna had certainly given her a lot to think about. And for this she was glad, even thankful.

CHAPTER 25

When Joshua and his helpers finished carrying the backless wooden benches to the upper level of the barn, they began to place them in orderly rows. There was the occasional remark from one or two, but for the most part, the talk was subdued as they went about the Lord's work.

The men were hauling up the old *Ausbund* hymnals and stacking them in neat piles when Joshua spotted the Esh girls working in his flower garden down yonder. He chuckled at the sight of Leda pressing soil down around some newly planted geraniums while her little sister and two cousins helped.

"This looks much better," he said as he ambled outside, wondering why they'd come with the colorful plants.

"Just wanted to help out," Leda said, her eyes sparkling.

"Your mother didn't send yous over here,

did she?"

Leda and her cousins exchanged furtive glances. But they didn't fess up as they shifted their weight from bare foot to bare foot.

So it was *Maryanna's idea!*

Well, he felt as light as duck feathers.

It was just then that Lovina Yoder, the preacher's wife, and his four sisters-in-law arrived to clean the kitchen. They and a number of Lovina's relatives and friends would be in charge of assisting with the shared meal following the Preaching service tomorrow, as well, since Joshua was not expected to be adept in the kitchen. The rest of the house was in fine shape, since his female relatives had been at work for several weekends now, shining up all the windows and cleaning the house from the attic down.

What'll I do with my indoor pets? Joshua wondered after he said good-bye to the Esh children and greeted the new arrivals. Two of his brothers' frank wives had not so gently suggested putting Honey Lou out in the barn *"from now on."* They'd simply rolled their eyes at his rabbit in the cage, scoffing when he'd said its name was Shadow. But, now, the way they'd taken to Malachi was quite remarkable. They'd declared his parrot *"downright perty."*

Taking all that into consideration, Joshua figured it would be best to move Honey Lou and Shadow upstairs to one of the several empty rooms while the womenfolk were redding up. So he carried up the necessary food and water, and then made another trip for the cat's litter box before taking some time to make a small sleeping pallet for Honey Lou from a shabby blanket. Looking around the room, Joshua was pleased with this choice, the ideal place for the two pets to stow away during tomorrow's reverent gathering.

Joshua reached for the rabbit's cage when he returned to the kitchen and hauled it and Honey Lou to the second floor. When he'd shut the door behind him and returned to the kitchen, Joshua saw the parrot cock its head and stare fiercely at him, as if wondering what trouble he might be up to. Joshua glared back. "Best not be sassin' me, bird!"

Lovina Yoder eyed him curiously, and Joshua shrugged, shaking his head.

Then he contemplated what to do with the noisy parrot. It was out of the question to move Malachi to a different location — the finicky bird would start carrying on if the environment were radically changed. And, too, a rise or fall in temperature — the least little draft — also posed a problem. *I daresn't put him down in the cellar or upstairs.* Joshua didn't want his wife's former pet to catch a cold. That would never do.

Since Preaching was being held in the barn, why not simply keep the parrot and its large cage in the kitchen? *Especially with the other animals out of the way.* Joshua opened the cage and let the bird fly free. Then he held out his hand, waiting for the bird to land. After a time, the fickle parrot landed on him, and Joshua took ample time to pet and talk to Malachi, being careful what he said, because this bird was mighty smart. Almost too smart, having picked up words and phrases Joshua had never intentionally taught it.

Joshua returned Malachi to the cage while the women got rid of cobwebs before sweeping and washing walls and polishing everything in sight.

He envisioned the crowd of people coming to worship at his farm — he hadn't hosted church on his own since Suzanne's passing a little over a year ago. The People typically rotated homes for Preaching service every nine to ten months, but the ministerial brethren had taken pity on him and given him a reprieve. Best of all, more than a handful of the womenfolk had quickly volunteered to assist with the shared meal, including Ida Fisher.

Soon the kitchen was tidy and gleaming, and Joshua was thankful — and pleased. How long had it been since this room had gotten the once-over?

It would never do for Maryanna Esh to have seen it dirty!

After the women left, and Joshua had polished his black shoes for Preaching service, he washed his hands and made a ham and cheese sandwich for supper, then took it outdoors to eat without even a paper plate.

Tired but pleased, he sat on the willow chair on the back porch with Buster nearby, marveling at all he'd accomplished that day. "With help from *gut* friends and family," he muttered. They'd moved things around outdoors, whacked weeds, and even repaired some horse fence. But not everything had been taken care of, because his lawn hadn't been edged of late and his old swing still needed painting . . . something he'd planned to do himself but hadn't gotten around to.

Joshua was in over his head, trying to host a worship service. He even started to wonder if he'd made the right choice in moving the cat and rabbit upstairs, because just now he heard Honey Lou scratching at the window screen above him. But, no, if he could manage through till the People left for home after the common meal, things could return to normal here. "S'pose I should see what I can do 'bout getting the widows to agree to take a spin in my carriage." He chuckled. "One widow at a time, of course!"

Finished with his sandwich, he rose from his chair and hurried down the porch steps and around the side of the house to marvel at the Esh children's quick work. The flower bed had been thoroughly weeded, the way it had always looked when Suzanne was alive. He felt giddy at the thought of Maryanna's prompting the girls to surprise him.

"Can it be that Maryanna does care for me?"

His gaze wandered over to the east, to the familiar exterior of the Esh farmhouse. Seeing the glow of the gaslight in the Dawdi Haus, he assumed Maryanna's parents were already having their family worship, reading the Good Book together.

Oh, but he yearned for a wife and family to have worship with each morning and night, just as he and his brothers had enjoyed as children. As lonesome as Joshua felt at times, he'd even thought of moving his father in with him, but the truth was Daed was comfortable staying with Joshua's oldest brother, Ned, and his wife, Sadie.

Joshua looked forward to welcoming his own extended family tomorrow. They would arrive very early. Other church members would come around eight-thirty, since the worship service began at nine. He needed to pray for divine help in what to say especially to reluctant Maryanna Esh, because he was fairly sure Ida Fisher would be agreeable to the invitation he'd planned.

But the notion of putting his hand and heart out there, especially to Maryanna, made Joshua so nervous he went right upstairs, sat down on the only chair in the spare room, and let Honey Lou purr in his lap for a good half hour. "I'm sorely out of practice," he muttered to the cat.

I'll ask Ida first, he thought, because if he asked Maryanna and she said no, he'd be so ferhoodled he wouldn't have the courage to ask even Ida. And if Ida said yes, he'd be emboldened to ask Maryanna next.

Joshua sighed and thought that it wasn't so much a matter of getting *one* of them to go out riding. "But rather, will I make a fool of myself?"

Jodi made a raw vegetable and tofu salad

for supper, watching the small TV in the kitchen as she worked. Gigi paraded past, meowing loudly. "Aw . . . did you miss me?" Jodi bent down and rubbed the cat behind the ears, smiling as Gigi leaned into her hand, purring for more.

Later, while eating, Jodi checked her email and text messages, reliving the day in Hickory Hollow. Before she left the Esh farm, Maryanna had reminded her that at dusk a group of Amish and Mennonite young people planned to meet and practice for the Bird-in-Hand Half Marathon. *"Feel free to join in,"* Maryanna had encouraged her. *"Anyone's welcome."*

Jodi couldn't imagine running in a long skirt, if that's what it took. So she went online to research the actual September event, wanting to see if there was a website. Sure enough, there was an informative web page, complete with a video telling about the upcoming event. On the video clip, she noticed some English women wearing running shorts and modern-style tops and decided she might actually fit in. Not for the marathon — she would be long gone by then — but it would be fun to run on the back roads with a group. There was some intangible good in running with others.

Jodi waited for the sun to slip down

toward the horizon before driving to Bird-in-Hand, where she parked her car along the road near the designated farmhouse on South Harvest Road. There she found twenty or more young people already gathering, mostly Amish. There were also a handful of non-Amish runners, two of them women her age wearing shorts and trendy running shoes. The few Amish girls wore their long dresses with matching aprons, but with socks and running shoes. The young Amishmen sported similar footwear, and wore long black pants and short-sleeved shirts.

One of the girls mentioned a hot air balloon launch and other festivities surrounding the run at seven-thirty on the morning of September eighth. Jodi wondered if it might make sense to scrap her plans to run the Boston half marathon in October and run in Bird-in-Hand instead. But all of that would depend on where she landed her next teaching job. *If I do,* she thought. Her time earlier today with Maryanna's and Mollie's children had been such an encouragement. Their excitement had infiltrated her teacher heart, and she could hardly wait to see them again. Unfortunately, there had been no further specific request for her to return again, although Maryanna followed her out to the car and offered an open-ended invitation to visit *"any time while you're in the area."*

When Jodi considered it, two days in a row might be all Maryanna and Mollie cared to be involved with an English woman, as they referred to her. Besides, tomorrow was their church service, and Jodi had things to do. *Top priority is finding a job!*

Warming up now with the other girls — Amish and English alike — Jodi thought of texting Trent to let him know what she was up to. Would he be amused at this diverse group of runners?

But, no, maybe it was best to have some silence and space between them. Jodi wanted to embrace every aspect of this twilight run, and the thought of Trent's hope for a family made her depressed if she dwelled on it. She longed to preserve their beautiful love, their life as a couple. It took a whole lot of faith in the future, and in God, to bring a child into the world . . . and it was faith she just didn't have.

CHAPTER 26

Joshua rewarded his work with a lukewarm shower, then sat on the back porch again, enjoying the slight drop in temperature with Buster's nose resting on his knee. He had been tempted to watch the courting carriages rumble by from the front porch. Those young folk from other church districts had a no-Preaching Sunday tomorrow and could sleep in some, unless of course they had cows to milk.

Near the white barn, a red-tailed hawk seized what must've been a mouse or other small rodent and flew off with it, squealing. Soon, lightning bugs dotted the yard and meadowland beyond, and he recalled sitting there with Suzanne as they discussed names for their coming child, Suzanne talking also of all the many things she'd sewn.

She was living for that baby — our firstborn.

Joshua still shuddered at such thoughts. He recalled discovering little Sarah Esh's discarded dress in the ditch with his father. Truth be told, Joshua's own heart had dropped to his feet at the sight, and he'd feared the People would be grieving another one of their own. But thank the dear Lord, Maryanna's little one was safely home.

He sighed, embracing the pending nightfall and longing for his wife.

Safely home. If there ever was a young woman who loved her heavenly Father, it was his young bride. On the worst days of his sorrow, Joshua drew comfort in knowing that to be absent from the body is to be present with the Lord.

Getting up, he headed into the house. He wandered through the kitchen and gave it an additional inspection. *Another Sunday without her.* He walked toward the steps, despising the long nights and eager for tomorrow's dawn.

Yet was he truly ready for the Lord's Day?

Maryanna prodded Sarah to finish up her bath and get dressed for bed. Benny, Leda, and Tobias had sailed through their Saturday-night preparations without a speck of prompting, including lining up the for-*gut* shoes on the back porch, polished for church tomorrow. But as was typical, her youngest poked along.

"Mamma, will Jodi come see us again?" Sarah asked.

"Maybe." Maryanna had guessed this might come up.

"I wish she lived round here."

Maryanna finished drying her off and held up her soft, pink nightgown. "We must wrap up your hair in a towel and then get the snarls brushed through before you put your head on the pillow."

"Can we sit outside?"

Always pressing for more time . . .

"We need to get to bed early so we're up and ready for Preaching in the mornin'," she reminded.

"We don't have to hitch up Dandy to the buggy, jah?"

"No, that's right."

"Can we just cut through the meadow?"

Maryanna could see where this was going. "You don't want to go to bed too early, I s'pose?"

Sarah grinned and wrapped the towel around herself. "This is how Jodi let me sit and eat a banana at her cousin's house."

Maryanna was tired and anxious for bed, but she was patient, waiting to hear what was on her youngest's mind.

Sarah began to giggle. "There was the cutest cat there, too, Mamma."

All the talk of Jodi. Sarah rarely ceased talking about her angel. She'd also made it clear she wanted to keep the fancy little outfit she'd worn home. Sarah had hung it on a peg, and when Maryanna tried to remove it to wash and return it to Jodi, Sarah cried like her heart was crushed. Sarah had even named the cloth doll Maryanna had finished just today Engel.

"We'll sit on the back porch for a while to read the Bible while your hair dries," Maryanna said, hoping the quiet time might be an opportunity to redirect her youngest toward the ways of the Lord.

"Does Jodi read the Good Book?"

Maryanna wasn't about to divulge any confidences. She did not think it wise to reveal that Sarah's "angel" was out of sorts with the Almighty.

Helping her daughter dress, Maryanna scooted her out to the porch, where the air was still warm. One of their horses neighed suddenly. It crossed her mind that Joshua might've noticed the difference in his one and only flower bed by now, and she hoped he hadn't put together who'd gone over there . . . unless he'd seen Leda and the girls, maybe. The latter made her fret — the last thing she wanted was Joshua Peachey coming over here to thank her for what had been solely the children's idea.

"Let's read now, Mamma." Sarah patted her arm as they sat together on the wooden settee.

"All right." She turned to Psalm Ninety-four, verse fifteen, and paraphrased for her little daughter, " 'Right must remain right, and to this all the upright in heaven will submit.' "

Sarah sat still for a change and listened.

"I want you to remember this," Maryanna told her little girl. "Dressing Plain as we do and leading a simple, quiet life is important. Do you understand?"

Sarah's eyes were fixed on the pastureland, and she nodded absently.

"It's important never to take the first step away from the People."

Sarah turned to look at her now, eyes wide.

None of her other children had ever needed this kind of talk as little ones. "If you don't take the first step toward the English world, you'll never take the second or the next, taking you far away and out of sight."

Maryanna hoped this would suffice. She suggested they pray before going to bed, and Sarah willingly folded her hands. They sat there in silence, heads bowed. Maryanna thought of leading out in prayer as some of her Mennonite neighbors often did, because she had no idea what her darling girl was thinking or praying just now. As for herself, she pleaded with the Lord God heavenly Father to keep all her children safely in the fold of faith. She recommitted her heart to passing on the Old Ways and God's will to her children, like a relay runner holding out a baton to the one coming behind — something she'd recently read in her daily devotional book.

The thought of her four-year-old already having such strong leanings put not only the fear of the Lord in her, but caused Maryanna to again ponder her own parents' pleas that she remarry. *How do they expect me to go about getting a date, though?*

Could it be that they'd already set things in motion, perhaps? She recoiled at the thought of her father talking to any of the area's few widowers. Especially Turkey Dan — at age forty-five, more than ten years her senior. Mamm had gone so far as to make a point a couple months ago about how happy Mary Stoltzfus Beiler always looked, married to the bishop and all. *"There's twenty years difference 'tween them, ya know."*

Her father hadn't minced words, either, declaring nothing wrong with that. And now yesterday, they'd made it clear they were done hinting around. They were certainly moving her marital status to the front burner! Even so, Maryanna was somewhat relieved to think they didn't have Joshua Peachey in mind. She could not imagine her own house overrun with critters, including an obnoxious parrot!

Besides, wasn't it a good idea to actually care for a man — not just marry for convenience?

CHAPTER 27

Jodi noticed the cars parked along the narrow road and in the lane leading to the farmhouse that evening. It surprised her so many others besides Amish had come here to run. She'd read online that whoever hosted the run was also responsible for planning the routes, either a ten-mile course or a four-and-a-half-mile route, as well as refreshments.

The friendly group of mostly Amish and Mennonite men and women runners, the Vella Shpringa, met frequently at different farms. An even larger group ran the night of each full moon. Jodi found it fascinating, thrilled for the company.

While doing a few stretches, she discovered she was next to Barbara Yoder, Mollie's sister-in-law. "I met Mollie at Maryanna Esh's," she said, shaking the younger woman's hand.

Barbara tilted her head, eyes fixed on her

all of a sudden. "Then you must be the one who rescued little Sarah?"

Jodi smiled. "I'm just glad she was okay when I found her."

Barbara looked at her with rapt attention. "Nothing but the hand of God, you findin' Sarah like that."

"More like an *angel* of God," the woman next to Barbara spoke up. "By the way, I'm Rosaleen Yoder, Barbara's cousin."

Turning the conversation away from herself, Jodi mentioned how calm the evening was, perfect for a nice long jog. Both Barbara and Rosaleen had been running with this group for more than a year, they said. "It's loads of fun," Rosaleen said. "So glad you joined us."

The group set out into the darkening night, the women running behind the men. Jodi's companions were quiet for a while; then Barbara said, "I'm ever so anxious for autumn."

"For the wedding season?" asked Rosaleen.

"Well, that and for a break from the hectic pace of gardening, canning, and weeding," Barbara said. She ran between Jodi on her right and Rosaleen on her left.

"I feel the same way, believe me," Rosaleen replied, laughing a little, somewhat out of breath.

Jodi loved how they broke into Deitsch or mixed it sometimes with English, sounding so carefree.

"Is it nosy to ask why you have to quit teaching when you're engaged?" she asked.

"Well, it's simply our tradition," Rosaleen explained. "I'm expected to start preparing to make a home for my husband-to-be and our future family. There's much to accomplish in a short time."

"Makes sense." There was a huge difference between the soon-to-be Amish bride and one in the modern world, where career women juggled work and wedding planning and shared the task of setting up a household. "But I'm sure the children will miss you as their teacher."

"I'll miss them, too."

They ran a bit farther, then Rosaleen asked, "I heard ya quizzed the children on their arithmetic at Maryanna's."

"I did." Jodi chuckled, surprised at the speed of the Amish grapevine.

"That sort of thing rarely happens during the summer," Rosaleen said. "Maybe ya didn't know."

"Really? Why not?"

"Book learning's reserved for the school year. The summer break is to be a carefree time for the scholars."

Scholars? Jodi mentally tried on the word for size. She'd occasionally heard older teachers refer to students as pupils before, but never scholars.

"It's nice of Maryanna Esh to permit you to review with 'em a bit. She's not known for leniency." Rosaleen smiled at her. " 'Cept with Sarah, that is."

Jodi realized then how very unusual that morning had been, and she felt almost flattered.

"Bertie sure likes you," added Barbara. "I was over at Mollie's to drop off a box of canning jars, and Bertie couldn't stop talking 'bout Sarah's English friend."

"I'm fond of Bertie, too," Jodie replied.

"Seems everyone in Hickory Hollow knows 'bout you," Rosaleen said. "Even Ella Mae."

Barbara was quick to interject. "Jah, the Wise Woman wants to meet you."

"Meet *me?*" Jodi remembered Maryanna pointing out the small house yesterday, when they'd gone walking.

"No worries," Barbara said. "She's not at all intimidating."

"I haven't met anyone in Hickory Hollow who isn't super nice," Jodi said, matching her pace with theirs.

"Oh, jah, plenty of fancy folk say that," Barbara said, her arms close to her body.

"*Most* Englischers do," Rosaleen corrected her, laughing softly.

Jodi smiled, glad for the twilight and the katydids and crickets. The day was cooling down, and the dew point didn't feel as high, either. Moonbeams drifted down through several trees as the runners whisked past.

"You might've missed out on finding our little hollow if it wasn't for Sarah Esh," Barbara said with a glance at her.

Jodi didn't care to show her ignorance. "I'm house-sitting for my cousin and his wife, and they're pretty fond of Amish lore and food. So it's possible I'd have stumbled onto your charming community eventually."

"Well, we're glad the Good Lord brought you along that stretch of road where Sarah was sleepin'," Rosaleen said.

"Ach, come to think of it, maybe that's why Maryanna was so easygoing 'bout letting you spend time with the children," Barbara added thoughtfully.

Nevertheless, Jodi held no high hopes for future involvement with Maryanna's family, or Mollie's, for that matter. She was content with what had taken place and assumed the story had climaxed to a happy finish. And it was just as well, considering her massive job search ahead. Trent had even put in an appeal with his own principal in Bennington. *"For anything, including a position other than classroom."* She was grateful for even a snippet of a possible lead, of course, but wasn't counting on it.

"What's your favorite thing to do in the fall?" Barbara asked, breaking the stillness after they'd run silently to catch their breath.

"I'm looking forward to running even more when the weather's brisk."

"So how often do you run now?"

Jodi laughed a little. "Let's just say that sometimes I overtrain."

"Sounds like you've got some time on your hands," Barbara said. "House-sitting and running."

Jodi considered that. "I usually have a little time to myself during the summer, yes . . . but right now I'm job hunting. I'm a teacher without a school."

"Ach, sorry to hear that," said Rosaleen, and both Amishwomen grew quiet.

Jodi fell easily into her own thoughts. She'd missed something of the slackening and quickening of the seasons this past year. Teaching, though she loved it, was all consuming. If she wasn't actually working with students, she was preparing exciting new lesson plans. Her career was her life, especially with dear Karen gone . . . and Trent leaving the country. *Except now I don't even have my teaching,* she thought ruefully.

The runners arrived in excellent time at the designated five-mile point and made a U-turn in the road to head back to complete ten miles. There was no air of competition, yet the Vella Shpringa really cut loose and ran.

When Rosaleen or Barbara slowed along the way to drink the bottled water in their fanny packs, Jodi kept her pace, drinking from her hydration pack.

Eventually, they came to the end of the run, back at the Glick farmhouse, where refreshments were served — delectable-looking whoopie pies, ice cream, water, and chocolate milk. *Not exactly my usual post-run nosh . . .*

"We'll run again on Monday evening," Rosaleen told Jodi, leaning down to catch her breath. "Nothin' happens on the Lord's Day, though."

"Other than Preaching, that is," Barbara said, twisting her upper body as she cooled down.

"I might see you Monday," Jodi said, thanking the girls for being her running companions. "I'll see how things go."

"Hope you do," Barbara said with a wave. "The half marathon's not too far off now."

She didn't have the heart to tell them she'd already paid the registration fee for the half marathon in Boston. "Good night," she called, deciding against staying to have refreshments.

"Nice meetin' ya," Barbara said.

"You too!"

"Gut Nacht, Jodi!" Rosaleen called.

Smiling, Jodi headed to her car. A feeling of well-being washed over her as she got in and pushed the key into the ignition.

Just as she was about to back up and drive to her cousin's house, a text came in from Trent. *I miss you, hon — would love to spend the weekend together!*

I miss you, too, she wrote back. "More than you know."

Want to chat? he asked.

I'm ready to drive back to Scott and Paige's. I'll talk to you when I get there, OK?

Sure. See you!

As much as she wanted to talk to him, she also dreaded it. She disliked the idea of depriving him of children. Was that fair to him? She worried they might end up coming apart at the seams even before Trent left for Japan. The thought choked her up, and Jodi struggled to see through her tears as she turned onto Route 340.

What would Karen say to do? She'd always talked everything out with her sister, but those happy years were gone. *Forever.*

CHAPTER 28

Jodi inched her car into her cousin's garage, then parked and turned off the ignition. Ready to call it a day, she headed into the house, where she was met by Gigi, who appeared around the corner, meowing in a suspicious tone. "You don't like being left alone, do you?" Jodi said.

She slipped to the kitchen floor and allowed the cat to wander into her lap. She felt sorry for Gigi, remembering what Maryanna Esh had said about caring for God's creatures. *The only way to repay the horse is with kindness.*

"Tomorrow we'll hang out, okay?" she told Gigi.

The cat paid no attention, and she felt silly. *Do cats even understand English?* Jodi laughed, enjoying the quiet house and her downtime with this beautiful feline. It was amazing how the world just fell away when a cat was purring in her lap.

Then, hearing what sounded like a knock at the front door, Jodi rose and turned on the overhead light in the living room, wondering who this could be. Looking through the peephole, she could not believe her eyes!

She unlocked the door and opened it to her smiling fiancé, who held a bunch of red roses and wore a grin to wipe away all doubts. "Trent! What are you doing here?"

He reached for her and wrapped her in his arms, pressing her close. "Hey, can't a guy visit his girl?"

She loved the strong feel of his arms and kissed him sweetly on the lips. "What a nice surprise, honey!"

He kissed her back several times, lingering on the last kiss. Then, seeming reluctant to stop, he followed her into the house.

She took the flowers from him, lacing her fingers into his as they walked to the kitchen. "You really shouldn't have been so surprised," he said. "My text said I'd see you."

"Oh, you!" They nestled close again and his lips found hers. Then reluctantly, she pulled away. "I still can't believe you're here!" She studied him — his light brown hair and gorgeous green eyes — and the way he seemed to adore her.

"Are you hungry?" she asked.

"Only if you are."

"Well, I just ran ten miles, so I could eat, sure. You want take-out or home cooked?"

"Steak sounds good."

She laughed and snapped her fingers. "I'll serve it right up."

"Seriously, I'll eat whatever you want, honey — a sandwich would be fantastic."

She grabbed the loaf of bread Maryanna had given her yesterday and waved it around, chuckling at his humorous moans of delight. "When was the last time you had homemade bread?"

"Whenever it was, it was too long ago!"

She went to the fridge and began pulling out mayo, lettuce, sliced turkey, and bacon. "How does a club sandwich sound?"

He grinned and folded his arms, standing back against the counter to watch her.

"I ran with a group of mostly Amish and Mennonites tonight," she said, spreading the mayo. "It was kind of fun . . . and really different."

"You don't look all that tired, hon. How'd you do time-wise?"

"I didn't bother to keep track." She mentioned how interesting it was that no one was really into timing the run. "Maybe they get more serious closer to the actual race, I

255

don't know." She filled him in on the Bird-in-Hand Half Marathon.

"Thought you were running in Boston this year — your big dream."

"I am. And I probably can't afford to do both. Besides, I'm hoping something comes through for me on the job front."

He nodded thoughtfully. "Have you called your dad back?"

"He called *me.*" She sighed. "And he gave me a week to decide if I want to accept his job offer."

Trent studied her intently, as if he hadn't seen her in years, and she soaked it up as she topped each sandwich with a thick slice.

"You know how Dad is."

"I do, yes. And he'd love to have you there in New Jersey. So would your mom."

"Because you're going to Japan?"

He explained, with obviously measured words, that while her father wanted to look after her, he was also concerned it was too late to locate a position anywhere else, especially the classroom job she wanted. "Teaching is your passion, after all."

"Right, but for one year I can get by with most anything. And I don't see myself working for my dad." She sighed. "I just don't."

She found the paper plates and placed the sandwiches, one on each. Then she wiped her hands on the towel.

He was actually staring at her. "Jodi, there's something else. . . ."

Her heart clenched. *Please, not this again.*

"I've been thinking. Maybe it was God's answer to our dilemma, you know . . . the loss of your job."

The look on her face must have said it all.

"Just listen, honey," he urged, reaching for her hands. "Please, Jodi, hear me out."

She pulled away. "Trent, I —"

"I know our marriage is a ways down the road, but what if it's best that you aren't teaching then? Just, please, think about it, hon."

"I love teaching, Trent. You know that."

"And I love *you.* But if you're not tied up teaching, we could —"

"What? Start a family?" She beat him to the punch line.

"I'd really like you to pray about it. Will you?"

"Is this why you came to see me?" She blinked back tears.

"Jodi . . . *honey.*"

She sniffled, feeling more exhausted now than during her run. "We agreed on a you-and-me kind of life. And with Karen gone . . . well, I honestly can't bear to think of bringing a baby into the world, and . . ."

He touched her arm, but she backed away again.

She carried the plates past him to the bar and sat down. "What's changed, Trent? Why do you want children now and not before?"

"It just seems so final to me . . . closing the door like that." He came over and turned her around on the stool to face him. "I'll never see your smile on our children's faces, never —"

"Right." She looked into his beautiful eyes. "But I haven't changed my mind."

"And I have." His eyes were serious.

Her emotions were brimming over. "Do we have to talk about this now?"

"No." Trent shook his head slowly. "But will you pray about it?"

"I haven't done much praying lately."

"Sweetheart . . ."

"Karen's illness came out of nowhere. And there was no stopping it." She bowed her head, tears threatening again. "You just never know. . . ."

"Jodi, darling." He coaxed her off the barstool and took her in his arms. He tucked her head beneath his chin. "Honey."

"Please, let's just drop this talk of having children." She didn't want him to hold her anymore. "I'm sorry, Trent. I really am. But I'm not ready to pray about this . . . or anything else."

She faced the bar, staring at her sandwich as she stepped away from him to slide onto the barstool.

Trent sat next to her, momentarily bowed his head, then took an enormous bite of his sandwich.

Jodi picked at her food, no longer hungry.

CHAPTER 29

The Lord's Day dawned with even warmer temperatures. Thin clouds veiled the fair sunrise as Joshua single-handedly watered his beef cattle and got breakfast, too — cold cereal, juice, toast with the homemade raspberry jam left by Ida Fisher yesterday, and black coffee. A second cup of the latter made him break out in a sweat once he'd cleaned up right good for the Sunday gathering, wearing his best black broadfall trousers and white shirt and tan suspenders beneath his black summer vest.

It occurred to him to walk over and thank Maryanna Esh outright for redding up his flower bed, but he didn't want to embarrass her. Instead, he pictured what it might be like to speak with her later today. Somehow he'd manage to greet her and the children before or after the shared meal on the back lawn. Knowing Tobias, the lad would seek out his grandfather Ezekiel before filing into the barn for church with his mother and siblings. Old Zeke was about as friendly a man as Joshua had ever known. Benuel, too, had enjoyed spending time with good-natured Zeke, who was always looking to tell a story from his boyhood. But since Benuel's passing, Zeke's health had gone downhill some. *Maybe Zeke is someone I could befriend.* Then, thinking on that, Joshua didn't want anyone, least of all Zeke or Maryanna, to imagine he was worming his way into their lives for ulterior motives.

Joshua went around his house and porch, looking to see if things were up to snuff for today's meeting. Satisfied, he headed upstairs to the second level of the barn to double-check the tidy stacks of Ausbund hymnals and saw to it that each row of benches was straight. He used this peaceful time to ask God to pour a divine blessing on the day, still concerned things weren't entirely as spick-and-span as when his wife was alive.

He heard the rattle of the first horse and carriage as it came into the long driveway. Behind it were a good many teenage boys walking single file, duplicates in black trousers and vests and white long-sleeved shirts. They'd come early to tend to the road horses and lead them one by one to the stable to shelter them from the sun as the many families arrived. The same young men would fill a watering trough in the barnyard for the hot, thirsty horses and park the carriages, as well as a few spring wagons for larger families, in an orderly fashion. These young men were the hostlers, and Joshua was mighty grateful for them. He waved now to the oldest of the teens, Caleb Stoltzfus, the bishop's strapping step-nephew. "Hullo, and Guder Mariye!"

"*Gut* mornin' to *you,* Joshua!" Caleb called back, looking mighty *schee* today, his light brown hair clean and combed and his face freshly shaved.

"All set to do the Lord's work?"

Caleb gave a quick nod. "Mighty honored to help. Denki."

"The gratitude's all mine." Joshua nodded and headed out to the road to greet the various families, including the extended Beiler family — Ella Mae Zook, the Wise Woman, smiled as the enclosed carriage made the turn into his lane. The Nate Kurtzes and Paul Hostetlers came in next, followed by the Mast and Stoltzfus families and then Benuel Esh's siblings' families.

But it was impossible for Joshua not to notice Maryanna Esh and her four walking this way, along the road. Maryanna's blue dress and white apron looked crisply ironed, as did her girls'. Tobias hung back a bit with Benny, and it was obvious the two of them had been scrubbed till it hurt. Joshua tried his best not to stare, but the sight touched him to the core, and he yearned to go and say hello but held back.

Shortly, when his brothers and their families arrived, Joshua quietly engaged himself with the men in his family, walking to the barnyard to wait till the ministerial brethren showed up. It was the oddest thing, but no matter where he stood, Maryanna was in his line of vision, looking prettier than ever. And if he wasn't mistaken, she'd caught his gaze, as well.

Ida Fisher arrived a few minutes later with her older brother and wife, the carriage creeping into the driveway as they waited for Caleb and the other fellows to unhitch their mare.

Seeing him, Ida nodded discreetly, her smile warm.

Joshua returned a quick nod. *O Lord in heaven, I entreat you for divine guidance.*

A reverential frame of mind was expected upon entering into worship with the other members. When the service began later, Joshua focused on the familiar hymns, tuning his ear as the preacher took his place before them to give the first sermon. During the first prayer, Joshua asked for wisdom in finding the right wife. *A man like me needs a helpmate, O Lord God. . . . If you have put this in my heart, may your will be done.*

Well into the second sermon, Joshua's cat began to meow, mildly at first, then more loudly. The ruckus swelled till it was just plain shrill, and folks shifted uncomfortably and turned to look back at the house. As if being attacked by a wild dog, Honey Lou's caterwauls escalated to the point where they became a disruption to Preacher Yoder's fervent preaching.

Joshua wished he'd closed the windows to the upstairs room where he'd put the cat. But when the preacher himself paused in the midst of his rhythmic delivery, his serious eyes fixed suddenly on Joshua, it crossed Joshua's mind that he should go immediately and see what the world was happening. Then, to compound the problem, the parrot began to call and screech like it, too, was being assaulted.

Honey Lou's upsetting Malachi!

And it didn't stop there. In short order, there was a duet — if not a duel — going on between the kitchen downstairs and the guest room upstairs. It sounded like the bird was trying to out-holler the cat.

O dear Lord, I beseech Thee for help!

Standing quickly, Joshua was conscious of heat rising from his neck to his face as he kept his gaze on the barn floor while making his way out of the somber meeting. Nevertheless, if he was not mistaken, Maryanna Esh actually sputtered as he walked past the benches of womenfolk. He groaned inwardly. What had started out as a glorious Sunday had rapidly deteriorated. Heaven knew Maryanna would be the first to say it was Joshua's fault for keeping *"those wretched indoor pets."* And his hopes of getting Benuel's widow to accept an invitation to go riding had just flown quickly out the window.

Maryanna had not erased the memory of Joshua Peachey's ill-mannered parrot calling out her name the other day. Oh, goodness, now her neighbor's pets had literally stopped the sermon. When the unreasonable man finally took leave of his seat and exited, it was all she could do to curl her toes in her best black shoes and hold her breath as he walked past her row. What if that horrid bird started shouting out names next? *What then?*

She felt light-headed at the dreadful thought. Everyone would know the truth about Joshua — that he'd either taught the bird to say her name, or that it had heard him speaking of her so much the parrot had begun to mimic him. Her neck turned stiff and sore, and she had visions of the People turning and staring at *her* next, as if such a thing were her fault.

As a result, Maryanna did not hear another word Preacher Yoder spoke, and she silently pleaded for the bird's beak to remain shut during the solemn moments when they all turned to kneel at their benches. *If this is the last prayer you ever see fit to answer, O God, I ask for mercy in this matter!*

With Leda on her right and little Sarah on her left, Maryanna folded her hands so tightly, it reminded her of when she'd squeezed Sarah's hairpins into her palms, frantic with concern. And right then, she again thanked the Almighty for returning her baby safe and sound.

Suddenly, the hushed serenity was broken by Joshua's all too audible voice, as in the house he reprimanded first the parrot, and then, a few moments later, the cat. " 'Tis the Lord's Day," he was heard to say. "You must be still. You must!"

To make matters worse, in another minute she could hear one window after another being closed upstairs, followed by a loud clattering, like a cage or something else metal falling. Maryanna could not imagine what was going on. She did know one thing, however: Suzanne would be just horrified. And it was beyond her what Joshua's dear, patient wife must have had to put up with.

As for herself, Maryanna did not care to know what had set off Joshua's raucous animals. It was anyone's guess.

Doesn't the man have any sense?

CHAPTER 30

Jodi dragged out of bed much later than usual Sunday morning, heavyhearted with the memory of the dismal turn in her conversation with Trent last night. She couldn't remember the last time they'd disagreed so vociferously. Raising the blind, she peered out and was glad to see a slight cloud cover. In the yard below, three robins flicked water about in the stone birdbath. The sight was restful, and she briefly considered Maryanna Esh and her little family, wondering if they were already sitting in church.

Inadvertently, Jodi bumped the window, and the pretty birds flew away.

With a sigh, she assumed that Trent, too, had managed to locate a house of worship to attend while here in town.

Groaning, she made her way to the closet to decide what to wear for her morning run. Prior to Karen's passing, Jodi had rarely missed church and even looked forward to going. When she and Karen had visited their parents in Jersey, all of them enjoyed the early morning service and then went out to one of Dad's favorite Italian restaurants for lunch.

"Everything's changed," she murmured sadly as she reached for her long white skirt. She wanted to see what it was like to run dressed like Rosaleen and Barbara Yoder. She pulled on the skirt and top she'd worn the day of Sarah's return to Hickory Hollow and combed her hair into a ponytail. Carrying her athletic socks and running shoes, she meandered down the short hall to the sun-drenched kitchen, where she noticed Trent's roses on the counter. She'd taken her time arranging them after he headed off to a hotel nearby to unwind before bed.

Red roses for love . . .

She added water to the vase, then went to the fridge and grabbed a cup of natural yogurt and cut up a few strawberries to mix in. She sat at the bar to enjoy the light, simple breakfast, along with some organic apple juice she'd purchased at a nearby Whole Foods. As was her habit, she'd wait until after her run to eat more heartily.

How can I possibly move forward with our

269

engagement? she wondered, realizing how strange it was that the man she loved was in Lancaster but she didn't feel like contacting him. The whole thing boiled down to one simple fact: She did not want to be a mother.

What point is there in communicating every day as planned?

Everything about Trent's change of heart made her wonder what had truly transpired. She didn't understand where he was coming from.

Noticing the cat's empty dish, Jodi went to pour some fresh food before doing her stretches and warm-ups. She itched to check for email and possible phone calls regarding her resume. *But it's the weekend,* Jodi reminded herself. What chance was there of a nibble on a job?

As she rinsed out the yogurt dish, she recalled the things Trent had said. Sharing her heart with him had never been so exasperating. And if he *did* call today and want to see her before driving back to Vermont, wouldn't the elephant in the room inevitably spoil that visit, too?

Is it best not to see him? Not if he was going to pressure her for a commitment to pray, especially for the purpose of getting her to change her mind.

She gritted her teeth as she pulled on her socks and shoes. "Why is this happening now?"

She removed her phone from its charger and checked the weather. "Lovely," she whispered when she saw that the dew point was already miserably high at seventy-two. But she was eager to run despite that. Pushing herself physically always helped to manage stress, and a run down Hickory Lane might prove to be interesting, considering the Amish folk were attending house church.

"It's Sunday," she declared to the cat as she reached for her purse and car keys to drive there. "I won't be long," she promised.

After the shared meal, Joshua kept an eye out to calculate when might be the best time to discreetly approach Ida Fisher. She and several other women were in his kitchen now, finishing up the dishes. Thanks to the ruckus during Preaching, his heart was in his throat.

A few minutes later, Ida was walking alone toward the carriage, her brother and his wife having been called by the deacon. Increasing his pace, Joshua fell into step with her, offering a smile. Her eyes instantly brightened, and he took that as an encouragement.

271

He helped her up into the carriage, then stood below, reminding himself to breathe. "I wonder if you might like to go riding with me in the next week," he said so quietly he scarcely heard himself.

"Sorry?"

He repeated his request, ignoring the rapid beat of his heart. "I'd like to take ya riding sometime, if that's all right."

"Oh," Ida said and broke into a smile. "Well, would ya like to come for dinner instead?"

He was stunned. "Why, sure. Denki."

"When's a *gut* evening?"

"Anytime, really."

"Well, ya have to eat anyways, so just pick the day."

This was much too easy!

"How's next Saturday, then?" he asked.

"Just fine." She nodded warmly. "Come around five o'clock."

Joshua agreed.

"I'll see you next weekend, Ida."

"All right." She waved good-bye.

Pleased, he hurried toward the stable to see how the young men were managing the many horses, matching them up to the right carriages and all. But as he watched, his earlier elation began to dissipate, and he began to feel foolish. Truth be told, his heart did not sing at the thought of sharing a meal with Ida, and now he'd be doing just that. He looked toward his house, and there was Maryanna Esh calling softly to Sarah, who was still mingling with other children. Benny, Leda, and Tobias waited patiently with Maryanna, evidently ready to walk home.

I should have asked her first, he thought, kicking himself.

Tobias spotted him just then and made a beeline to Joshua. "I didn't see ya earlier," the boy said, face flushed and grinning.

"I've been here all day."

"Just had to ask ya — what happened to make Honey Lou and Malachi carry on during Preachin'?"

Joshua should have guessed Tobias would start with that, but he didn't mind — the boy shared his love for pets. "Honestly, it was the rabbit that got things goin'."

"Oh?"

"When I left church to check, I found Shadow running around out of his cage. Got loose somehow or other."

Tobias's eyes grew wider. "I hope Honey Lou didn't try 'n' catch Shadow."

"Well, Shadow's still cowering under the bureau, I'm afraid. Poor thing's had a fright."

Tobias frowned hard. "Shadow's not hurt, is he?"

"Not to worry, son," he reassured him.

Benny ran over to get his brother, and Tobias said he'd see Joshua tomorrow. "I'll come help water the steers."

"Denki." Joshua glanced at the boy's mother, but Maryanna looked away. "Wait just a minute," he said. "I'll walk down there with ya."

Benny looked surprised, but Tobias stayed right beside him, matching Joshua's purposeful stride toward their mother.

CHAPTER 31

As soon as Jodi turned onto Hickory Lane, she tried to remember which driveway led to the Amish bishop's house. She figured it would come to her in spite of the fact she had been so concerned for the lost little girl sitting in the backseat that morning.

Pulling onto the right shoulder, she parked and got out, breathing deeply of the fragrant air. Up and down Hickory Hollow Lane might equal three or more miles, she guessed. If she wanted to, she could run it twice, which would be about six miles and therefore even better. She was enamored with the area and hoped to see some of the carriages going to or from house church, perhaps.

She heard the inviting trickle of a nearby stream as she began to run, slowly at first. In the near distance, horses rambled through tall grass, and along the roadside, robins tugged at earthworms.

275

It was impossible not to think of Karen in such a setting. Their great-aunt's home in rural Vermont had been a place for both girls to unwind and run through the meadows with the breezes in their faces. Before Great-Aunt Leora moved there, stinging nettles and other weeds had sprung up where once a vegetable garden flourished. But within a few months' time, the place was alive with colorful flowers and fresh produce. Jodi and Karen were some of the first benefactors, enjoying moist zucchini bread, carrot cake, and raw cucumbers drenched in Leora's creamy homemade dips.

Jodi recalled nightly walks with Karen and their aunt, who knew the constellations so well she simply pointed out the names of one star after another.

The world, my world, was upright back then. . . .

At the farmhouse on the right, just before Maryanna's house in the distance, row after row of gray carriages were parked on one side of the yard. Jodi slowed her pace as she took in the sight. She was sure she'd spotted Maryanna with Leda and Sarah standing close by. A bearded man dressed in black, except for his white shirt, was walking toward Maryanna and her girls, accompanied by Benny and Toby, his smile wide as he removed his straw hat.

Jodi continued to run as she watched, her long skirt bunching up between her knees. She wondered how many tourists viewed this world from afar each day after stumbling upon the remote road. To think she had personally sat in Maryanna's kitchen twice, enjoying two home-cooked meals.

Definitely something Scott and Paige would give their eyeteeth for!

The Amishman held his straw hat, turning it steadily as he talked. Jodi presumed he was the neighbor for whom Leda and her cousins had gone to plant flowers. Craning her neck, Jodi looked to see the side garden the children had discussed but was unable to tell from so far away.

It was odd to see Benny and Toby standing so erect, listening with almost exaggerated respect to the man as he spoke directly to Maryanna.

He's nervous, she realized, watching him twist his hat in his hands.

Joshua drew a deep breath as he stepped near Maryanna Esh. "If ya don't mind, I'd like to thank you for beautifying my flower garden for today's service."

"Oh — well, Leda's the one to thank,"

Maryanna replied quickly, glancing at her older daughter.

Joshua's spirits fell. "Then I'll have to say I'm mighty grateful to you, Leda."

The girl nodded shyly, her cheeks turning rosy.

"Leda's bashful today," Tobias said next to him. And Leda pulled a face at him.

"I was, too, when I was her age." Joshua was surprised when Maryanna cracked an appreciative smile. He felt slightly encouraged. *Maybe she even remembers what I was like as a boy.*

"Hope it was real nice for Preachin' service to be held here — so close and convenient for you and your family." He tried not to focus only on Maryanna but wondered how on earth he was going to get her alone, as he had Ida Fisher. Or maybe this was not the time the Good Lord had in mind.

"The bunny's frightened, Mamma," Tobias said suddenly, looking up at his mother and explaining, evidently for her benefit. "The cat chased it and tried to catch it and —"

"Tobias, don't speak out of turn," Maryanna said.

"Sorry, Mamma." Tobias glanced at Joshua now, which Joshua deemed a mistake. He felt sorry for the lad.

"Shadow's all right," Joshua reassured him. "I saw to it."

But now little Sarah looked like she might cry. Her lower lip pushed out, and a big frown emerged on her face. "I wanna see Shadow, Mamma."

"We best be goin', children" was all Maryanna said as she reached around both Leda and Sarah to guide them toward the driveway leading to the road. "Come now, Benny and Tobias."

"Da Herr sei mit du," called Joshua as the boys left his side.

"God be with you, too," Benny spoke up.

Tobias smiled back at him, waving with his fingers as he always did.

Joshua knew he must do something. The time was now! "Excuse me, Maryanna — might I speak with ya, right quick?"

He was shocked when she walked back toward him, leaving the children within earshot. "What is it, Joshua?" She forced a smile, though with some difficulty, he was all too sure.

Putting his hat back on his head, he changed his mind and removed it again, holding it over his heart. "Walk with me over yonder," he said, pointing to the rickety bench.

"Is everything all right?" she asked, still following.

Then, lest he lose all courage, he looked at her in earnest. "Maryanna, I'd like to take ya ridin' sometime next weekend. If that's all right."

She blinked, then looked away. "Oh my."

You're pressing your luck.

"I'm just not sure . . ." She stared at the field between their houses.

He felt like a *Lump* putting her in such an awkward position and was about to politely retract his invitation out of mercy for both of them when she finally answered.

"Exactly how many pets *do* you have, Joshua?"

He cleared his throat. "Well, now, there's Honey Lou and Shadow, Malachi and —"

Maryanna's face was not nearly as pretty this way, all serious-looking, her mouth in a straight line. "They caused quite a disturbance today," she added.

"Entirely my fault."

"Yours?" She tilted her head innocently, and for some reason it endeared her even more to him. "How can that be?"

"Well, I left the cat in the same room with the rabbit. Poor judgment on my part."

"And the parrot?"

Joshua explained that the hypersensitive

bird had been distressed by the noisy cat in the room overhead. "I thought it was a *gut* idea to make an apology to Preacher Yoder for disrupting his sermon."

Maryanna's expression evolved to sympathy, or at least something more like it.

Then, taking him off guard, she said, "All right, Joshua, I'll go with ya."

His heart pounded nearly out of his ears. "Jah?" he replied, standing straighter and pushing his shoulders back, chin up.

"How's Saturday evening?" she asked.

He was flabbergasted at his success. "Just fine," he said cheerfully. "I'll pick you up after supper, round seven o'clock."

"Might be a bit late."

"Six-thirty, then?"

She nodded and glanced back at the house. "And the pets?"

"They'll stay put, of course."

She nodded and joined her waiting children without commenting further.

Joshua didn't dare watch them walk toward the road. And he was altogether persuaded that Maryanna's bark was fairly convincing, but surely worse than her bite.

He was heading back to the house when it hit him. A broad smile erupted on his face. *Maryanna said yes!*

But just as quickly, he realized his terrible

blunder. He had two dates with two women on the selfsame evening!

CHAPTER 32

Jodi was greeted by Sarah in a pale blue dress with a sheer white apron on top. The little girl came running to see Jodi on the side of the road, Benny and Toby close behind in look-alike black pants and white shirts with black vests. Leda hung back slightly, a white apron over her deep purple dress, too.

Maryanna smiled from where she stood farther back with her sister Mollie. Both seemed surprised to see Jodi as Sarah threw her arms around her knees, jabbering in Deitsch.

"We didn't know you were comin' by today," Leda said, grinning.

"Nice ya did, though," Toby said, inching closer.

"I wanted to see you again." Jodi also mentioned she'd gone running last night on one of the roads near the route for the Bird-in-Hand Half Marathon. "I met your former schoolteacher, Rosaleen Yoder, and another girl you probably know — her cousin Barbara Yoder."

Benny nodded. "Rosaleen's right over there." He pointed toward the group of women near his mother who were standing and staring at Jodi and the children.

Am I interrupting their Sunday?

It did look like church had already disbanded, although many people were still lingering about the side and front yards. Jodi was most interested in knowing if the man talking earlier to Maryanna and the children was their neighbor Joshua. And if so, how remarkable that he was so youthful and good-looking — not at all like she'd pictured him.

"I hope you'll come home with us," Leda said softly, her eyes shining.

"We still have ice cream from yesterday," Toby said with a glance back at his mother. "Will ya come?"

Jodi didn't quite know how to respond. "I really should run some more," she said, thinking that might suffice.

But now Fannie and Bertie, along with Ellie and Darla, had spotted her, too, and were calling her name as they hurried down the driveway, all dressed alike in maroon dresses and white aprons.

"You're back," Bertie said, blinking. "We didn't think we'd see you again."

Thrilled, Jodi smiled and greeted each of Mollie's four girls by name.

"You remembered us!" Darla said, wiggling in between Sarah and Toby toward Jodi.

"We've been practicing our arithmetic," Ellie said, her light brown hair slicked back on both sides.

"You'll be all set when school starts," Jodi replied.

" 'Cept there's no teacher yet," Bertie told her, and the children's faces drooped as they nodded their heads.

It was Leda who spoke next. "If the school board can't find someone soon, we might have to start late."

"Ain't never happened before." Toby frowned.

"How do you know this?" asked Jodi.

"Well, 'cause Uncle Jeremiah's on the school board," Benny volunteered.

Toby looked over his shoulder at Rosaleen. "Least we won't have to worry 'bout the teacher this year."

"Ach, Toby," his cousin Fannie said, stepping even closer.

With eight children pressing in around her, Jodi wondered if they shouldn't move closer to the front yard.

When Jodi suggested it, Leda said there was rarely any traffic on the road. "Just horses and buggies, mostly."

This made Bertie giggle for some reason. And then all the children began laughing, Sarah still with her arms around Jodi's knees. "Mei Engel," she said again.

Despite the fact that the Amish folk were milling about, talking with each other, Jodi felt their collective eyes on her.

Maryanna watched Jodi with the children — the young woman seemed so comfortable with them. Why didn't such a delightful woman want children of her own when it was apparent to everyone watching that the Englischer was a magnet for them?

"Just look at her," Mollie said softly next to Maryanna.

"Jah," Rosaleen agreed. "Barbara and I ran with her last evening, and she's not like some of the English folk we know. Both of us remarked 'bout it."

"Oh?"

Rosaleen continued. "She fit right in, and we had a *gut* time together. Odd, though . . . she never once had to stop to drink water, and goodness, we ran a long ways."

"Don't be silly," Barbara interjected. "She

has one of those water carriers on her back to drink from. Look, she's wearing it now."

Maryanna smiled. *So Jodi's human, after all!*

"Jeremiah's over talkin' to Bishop John — wants to call a school board meeting at first light," Mollie said, seemingly anxious to impart the news she'd heard just a bit ago from her husband. "Even the bishop noticed Jodi out there with the children."

"Does he know she's the one who found Sarah?" asked Maryanna.

"Oh, he seems to know *all* about it."

"So what do you think'll happen tomorrow morning?" Maryanna asked.

"I heard something but best not say." Mollie glanced at her husband and the bishop, deep in discussion with the two other fathers who were decision makers in appointing the next schoolteacher.

"Bishop must think Jodi's a godsend, then." Maryanna could see why, despite Jodi's spiritual wavering since losing her only sister.

The children were still pressing in around Jodi on the lawn, some of them sitting on the grass as they pleaded for her to sit with them, too.

"You don't think they'd ask an outsider to teach, do ya?" Rosaleen asked.

"It's never been done," Barbara Yoder spoke up.

" 'Tis true," said Mollie. "Not ever."

"I do know she's lookin' for a teaching job," Maryanna revealed. "She said so herself."

"Ach, that's right . . . she mentioned it last night." Rosaleen seemed excited suddenly.

"Of course, that doesn't mean she'd ever consider what you're thinkin'," Maryanna added.

"Well, the pay's not what she'd get as a public schoolteacher, I'd guess," Rosaleen said. "It's all right for a single Amishwoman, still living at home, of course."

"You're forgetting she has a place somewhere up in New England," Mollie said.

"Vermont," Maryanna was quick to say.

"Does she own a house there?" Barbara asked.

Mollie stroked her Kapp strings. "Ain't for us to be talkin' this way."

"Isn't," Rosaleen corrected.

They all tittered, trying to keep their voices at the appropriate level for the Lord's Day.

Maryanna saw little Sarah reach for Jodi's hand and begin to head up Hickory Lane, all seven children following close behind.

"Where are they goin'?" she whispered.

"To your place, must be," Mollie replied with a gentle poke on her arm. "Better follow an' see."

"A Pied Piper's come to Hickory Hollow," Maryanna heard Jeremiah say from back amidst the menfolk.

"And just in time, too," the bishop stated.

"Well, mercy's sake," Maryanna's own mother said.

What have we prayed into our community? Maryanna wondered as she followed behind the children with Mollie, scurrying to keep up.

"What if Jodi refuses?" Mollie whispered.

"Don't get your heart set on this, sister. She's not Amish, remember."

"Well, but look at *us* . . . we, too, are steppin' to the Pied Piper's music."

This brought another chortle, but Maryanna was more concerned about Sarah, who looked to be leading the entire procession.

CHAPTER 33

Jodi had asked the children if it was all right to head over to the Esh farmhouse without getting permission from their mother. Both Benny and Leda had insisted it was fine, so off they'd gone. And now Joshua Peachey's German shepherd was following them, panting in the heat of the day.

"Will the dog find its way back home?" she asked Benny.

But it was Toby who interjected that the big dog knew his way all around the neighborhood. "Buster's our watchdog at school, too," he said.

"Really? You take him along to school?"

"Joshua brings him every day when we all walk together," Benny explained. "And he comes back for Buster when the bell rings at the end of the day."

Jodi wondered why but didn't have to ask.

"Joshua says it's a *gut* idea," Benny added. "Buster keeps an eye out for tourists. And to be extra careful on the road, we all wear our new yellow safety vests — even Joshua."

"There are so many picture-takin' folk in their cars," Toby offered, his face serious. "It bothers the brethren no end."

The brethren . . .

Smiling at the idea of Joshua walking with the schoolchildren, Jodi followed Sarah into Maryanna's driveway. *So much for getting a jog in today. And poor Trent must think I've disappeared.*

She'd left her phone in the glove box of her car, still parked at the eastern end of Hickory Lane. For now at least, there was no way to check if he'd sent her a text or tried to call. Regrettably, she was out of reach.

By the time they'd all sat down at the table in the very warm kitchen, Maryanna and Mollie were coming indoors, smiling and talking cheerfully. They went to the cupboard and lifted down a stack of bowls for the ice cream that Leda and Sarah had already gotten from the freezer.

"Hullo there," Maryanna said as she placed the bowls around the table. "It's nice to see you again, Jodi."

"You too," she replied. "I hadn't planned to drop by unannounced."

"Well, you're always welcome."

Jodi was quite aware of it. "I can't seem to stay away from this lovely little hollow."

"We invited her for ice cream," Benny said with a glance at Jodi, seeming to speak in her defense. "And I think Mammi Emmie and Dawdi Zeke might come, too."

"That's fine," Maryanna said, hoping her parents would indeed do so.

Little Sarah held up her new cloth doll, making it bend and bob its head on the table until Leda gently pushed her arm down, and Sarah made the doll disappear.

Mollie came over and distributed spoons and paper napkins. "We heard you were out runnin' by moonlight last evening."

Removing her hydration pack, Jodi nodded. "It was really quite pleasant and much cooler."

"Well, Rosaleen and Barbara surely enjoyed meeting you," Maryanna said as she came to sit next to Jodi.

Mollie added, "Word has it you kept up real *gut* with all the rest."

Jodi smiled. "There were about twenty-five of us. Actually, it was perfect. Incredibly peaceful, too."

Leda brought over the big tub of vanilla ice cream, Sarah behind her carrying the chocolate syrup. "Will ya go runnin' with them again?" asked Leda.

"I might. But my fiancé's here in town."

Maryanna's eyebrows rose. "Was that a surprise?"

She nodded.

"Hope things are goin' well," Maryanna said more softly as she leaned in closer.

Shrugging, Jodi indicated not so much.

"So sorry," Maryanna whispered.

Jodi thanked her and looked around the table at the many sets of beautiful eyes on her.

"Time to say the blessing. *Pattie nunner* — hands down," Maryanna said and bowed her head.

All of them did the same, including Jodi, who managed to be grateful for the blessing of these friends. She hoped above all that Trent might understand her heart.

Joshua closed the door on the parrot's cage and hurried upstairs to rescue Honey Lou and Shadow from the warm room. Below him, just outside the window, the bishop and the three school board members were putting their heads together about a replacement for Rosaleen Yoder. *On the Lord's Day, yet!*

"Even if the Englischer did agree to fill in as teacher for a number of weeks, we still have *Druwwel* — trouble — on our hands," Jeremiah was telling Bishop John, Ned Peachey, and Noah Mast. "Who will we get for a permanent replacement?"

Pausing at the window, Joshua felt peculiar eavesdropping.

"And this outsider knows nothin' about our curriculum or expectations," Jeremiah continued. "Rosaleen would have to instruct her as to how things are done."

"Which is a mighty big undertaking in just a few weeks' time," Ned said.

"It'd be a *gut* idea to have her attend a seasoned Amish teacher's schoolhouse once the school year begins. Could that be done, maybe?" This was Noah's idea, and a mighty fine one, Joshua thought.

"Well, if you're in favor of that, school might need to open late," the bishop suggested.

"Honestly, I'm not sure we're in agreement on any of this," Ned declared.

"Keep in mind this would only be for a short while — if the young woman's even willing," Noah said. "We haven't proposed the idea."

"Let's meet again in the morning," Jeremiah said. "Bishop, are you free to join us?"

Joshua leaned closer to the window, wondering what on earth Bishop John might say to that, known as he was for being a stickler. Of course, there was nothing in the church ordinance about teaching appointments, although this was such rare territory Joshua doubted it had a precedent. Not here in Lancaster County, at least.

Yet, come to think of it, he had read somewhere about an Englischer woman who was a substitute at a one-room Amish schoolhouse somewhere in Kentucky, if he remembered correctly. The school board of four Amish fathers had asked her to wear Mennonite-looking dresses and comb her hair back in a bun, though they hadn't required a prayer veiling, as far as the story went.

Just then Honey Lou began to chase her tail, as if bored. And Shadow was clearly frightened, still as he was in his cage. Joshua had rescued the poor thing earlier from under the dresser, glad to see there wasn't a scratch on him.

Gathering up the cage and the cat, Joshua headed back down to the kitchen to the sound of Malachi cawing, having another tizzy. *Such a day it's been,* Joshua thought as he poured cat food into Honey Lou's dish and gave the parrot something to nibble on.

He considered his terrible error in judgment, making plans with both widows for dates on the same evening. When Maryanna had agreed and suggested the day, he'd been so ferhoodled it hadn't occurred to him he'd just agreed to meet Ida on the exact same Saturday.

I have to make it work, he thought, nervous all the same.

Walking out toward the barn, Joshua noticed the school board members still in a huddle, though there was no further sign of the bishop.

But it was the subject of the men's former conversation that intrigued him most — Jodi, the lovely young woman in their midst earlier. He could see why the children were impressed with her. The vivid memory of the Englischer dressed in white came back quickly, standing with all the People's children gathered near, fancy woman that she was. She seemed to have an uncanny sense of what to say and do around Amish. He considered again how Jodi had, for some reason, not involved the police when she found Sarah — was it out of respect for their Plain culture? If so, no wonder the bishop was talking of setting an extraordinary precedent for a teacher!

Maryanna's parents joined them in her

kitchen while they were having their ice cream, all busy eating and talking around the table. It was only a short time later that Ella Mae Zook came into the driveway in her son-in-law's family carriage. She halted the horse, still holding the reins.

Leda whispered, "Mamma, the Wise Woman's here."

Secretly pleased, Maryanna had hoped Jodi might have occasion to talk with the kindly sage. "Excuse me," she said as she left the table to help the elderly lady out of her carriage.

As soon as Maryanna slipped out of the kitchen, the table erupted into a rush of even louder prattle, and she found it both curious and comical, wondering what was being said in her absence. Her father loved to get the children laughing at his own long-ago childhood antics, especially the tale about the time he'd used his suspenders to shoot kernels of Indian corn at his father's scarecrow. *At least* Jodi *hasn't heard this story yet. . . .*

"How are ya, Ella Mae?" Maryanna asked, extending her hand as they walked across the driveway.

"Doin' fine," Ella Mae said. She was without her cane. "Even though I feel like a hundred years old today."

"We all do, some days." She smiled at the dear woman.

"Isn't that the truth!" Ella Mae chuckled. "I appreciate your help, I daresay."

Maryanna kept an eye out in case her friend should stumble as she sometimes did, despite having surprisingly good balance for her age.

"We have an English visitor," Maryanna told her as she reached for the back screen door.

"Hoped so. Spotted her over at Joshua's a bit ago."

"Did ya see her with the children?"

" 'Twas somethin' to behold." Ella Mae sounded breathless as she stepped into the utility room and reached to steady herself against the wall where wooden hooks held the family's sweaters and jackets.

"You all right?"

"I will be in just a second — a mite dizzy." Ella Mae lowered her head, taking her time to regain her balance. "Denki kindly."

Maryanna waited right beside her until at last, Ella Mae slowly proceeded into the kitchen, waving hello to Maryanna's parents, who were sitting across from each other.

Maryanna took the liberty of introducing her to Jodi and made a place at the table.

Ella Mae seemed not only pleased to have the opportunity to eat some ice cream, but she showed an immediate interest in Jodi, asking her how long she'd been in the area.

Jodi said she was house-sitting nearby for her cousin and his wife, which brought a smile to Ella Mae's face.

It was odd seeing the older woman on a Sunday afternoon, since she typically slept for a couple hours on the Lord's Day, all tuckered out from Preaching service or going visiting.

The children, especially Benny and Tobias, seemed far too excited about recounting the *Unzucht* — rumpus — caused by Joshua's pets during the sermon. "Malachi was the loudest of all," Benny was saying, his eyebrows touching his bangs.

"Malachi?" Jodi said.

"The parrot's name," Tobias said.

"I see." Jodi shook her head, grinning now. "Sure sounds like a mouthy bird."

"Is he ever!" Tobias seemed to know.

Maryanna's father laughed right out loud. "Ain't that what parrots do — yackety-yak?"

"I daresay whoever's hosting church in two weeks surely won't have all those animals to contend with, ain't?" Ella Mae said as she looked right at Maryanna.

"One can only hope not," Maryanna

replied. "The day should be a reverent one."

Fannie and Bertie nodded silently, eyes darting toward their younger sisters, who were too busy adding more chocolate sauce to their ice cream to pay any mind.

"Reverent, jah . . . and a day for a bit of mingling with, well, certain folk, I noticed." Ella Mae eyed Maryanna again.

She couldn't believe her ears — Ella Mae talking like this in front of the children and Maryanna's parents. And their English guest, too! Maryanna gave the older woman a look and hoped that might keep her mum. She got up to bring over some cookies, hoping to distract Ella Mae, known for her wisdom. *Most of the time,* thought Maryanna, unwilling for her children to be made privy to the plans Joshua had made with her earlier. There was no doubt Ella Mae had been referring to Maryanna's conversation with just that neighbor.

"Not sure what I was thinkin'," she whispered to Ella Mae as the woman selected a couple of cookies.

"Well now," Ella Mae said softly. "You just never know. . . ."

I accepted Joshua's invitation to please my parents, Maryanna told herself.

She heard the clatter of wheels and looked out the window. Dan Zook's horse-drawn spring wagon was moving quickly into the lane, all five of his sons still dressed in their Preaching clothes. Two boys were sitting clear at the back, their legs hanging over the edge.

"Who's this?" Benny said much too loudly.

"Like I said," Ella Mae sputtered with a few dips of her head as she spooned up some ice cream.

Jodi had obviously heard and looked up from her dessert with probing eyes, as did Mollie. Maryanna's mother pulled a handkerchief from beneath her dress sleeve and began mopping her brow.

"I'll be right back," Maryanna said as she hurried to the back door.

What's Turkey Dan want?

CHAPTER 34

Things had ramped up a notch as Jodi finished her ice cream, enjoying the children's banter and their grandfather Zeke's down-home humor. From where she sat, she could easily observe the man outside in the wagon as he handed the reins over to one of the older boys. Presently, he was getting down to talk with Maryanna, looking very happy to see her. Since there was no woman with him, Jodi assumed he must be a widower, though he was years older than Joshua and not nearly as good-looking. The man's full beard almost touched his chest when he spoke.

Not wanting to be nosy, Jodi forced herself to look away, and Sarah leaned against her arm, making the little cloth doll with its stitched facial features lay facedown on Jodi's hand. "Somebody's getting sleepy," Jodi said.

"Sure looks like it to me," Grandmother

Emmie said.

Leda shook her head. "Sarah rarely sleeps on a Lord's Day afternoon anymore. Mamma sometimes does, but not Sarah."

Toby turned to look at them from down the long table. "Sarah ain't tired," he seconded. "She just thinks you're gonna leave soon."

How sweet, Jodi thought with a glance at Mollie. "Well, I *should* finish my jog." She leaned down to kiss the top of Sarah's head. "But I'll visit again."

"You will?" Bertie asked, her eyes hopeful.

"Do ya promise?" asked Ellie as she twisted the thin white strings of her little cap.

"Of course I do," Jodie told them.

"When?" Leda's pretty eyes were very serious.

"Very soon."

Both Sarah and Bertie perked up, but Ellie and Toby still looked concerned, as if they weren't convinced.

But Jodi knew she needed to get in touch with Trent. She felt terrible for abandoning him after he'd driven all that way to see her.

Maryanna's friend Ella Mae sat across from Jodi, smiling silently and batting her blue eyes.

"It was very nice to meet you, Ella Mae,"

Jodi said.

The older woman smiled and pointed her finger at them and waved it in a circle. "I daresay you've got yourself a lot of young friends here."

Jodi agreed with a nod at Maryanna's parents, as well. "I certainly do."

"And you're the one who brought Sarah home, jah?"

Jodi smiled down at the little sweetie next to her. "That's right."

"Well, I want to thank you for being a handmaid of the Lord," Ella Mae surprised her by saying. She went on to tell how many of the men in the community had walked through miles of fields and roadways all night long and into the morning. "Believe me, you were the answer to all of our prayers."

The woman's words and the depth of her sincerity touched Jodi in a way she hadn't expected. "Sarah deserved to come home," Jodi said, looking down at the little girl still leaning near.

"The Lord had it all planned, that's for sure," Ella Mae replied. "There's nothin' He doesn't see and know."

Benny and Toby nodded their heads. "We asked God for Sarah's angels to guard her," Benny added.

"But we never thought we'd meet one of them," Leda said quietly.

"Ain't that the truth?" their grandfather Zeke said.

Although it could've been an awkward moment, Jodi found their words endearing. She glanced at Sarah, whose twinkling eyes shone despite not understanding what was being said.

Rising, Jodi tried her best to tell the children good-bye, but they didn't make it easy. They popped out of their seats, talking and following her to the main back door, prolonging their farewells.

Mollie and Grandma Emmie rose and came to Jodi's rescue just as Maryanna's man friend and his brood of boys left. As Jodi headed out the screen door, Maryanna came hurrying up the walkway. "You leavin' already?"

"Trent will be disappointed if I don't see him today."

"Will we see you again?" Maryanna wore an anxious frown.

Jodi said they would.

"It'd be right nice if you could get to know Ella Mae better one of these visits."

"I'd like that." Jodi smiled and waved as she headed down the driveway toward Hickory Lane. When she turned east onto the road, she glanced back at the house and saw Sarah and her cloth dolly waving from the front porch.

She experienced a momentary pang of sadness and waved back. How would she ever be able to say good-bye to the dear little girl when she returned to Vermont?

Time to get back on the road. Jodi looked down at her long white skirt and realized she could actually become accustomed to wearing such feminine attire, though maybe not for running. Actually, there was a lot about this little place called Hickory Hollow that appealed to her.

Slowly, she began to run, and with each stride, she realized she could hardly wait to see Trent again, no matter their differences.

After a time, she heard a dog panting behind her, and she turned to see Buster keeping pace. "Good dog," she said, encouraging him to move up beside her. "I could get used to running with you."

Through some quirk, Joshua's brother Ned looked especially distinguished when he was frowning. Two identical deep lines furrowed his brow as he hurried into the barn, looking for Joshua. "May we use your Bible for a bit?"

"The bishop must've gone home, then?"

Joshua wiped his hands on his work pants.

"Jah, some time ago." Ned stood there, still scowling. "Jeremiah and Noah are here yet, though, and we wanted to look up a Scripture verse right quick."

"My English Bible's in the cupboard, second shelf, if that's what ya want," Joshua said, returning to scoop feed for his road horses and mules. The chickens were next, and he thought of Tobias just then and wondered how long it would be before the lad would come running over and offer to help.

He still could not quite believe that Maryanna had agreed to go for a ride with him. Or that he'd gotten up the nerve to ask. He bit his lip as he recalled how especially pretty she'd looked today. How was it he'd never really noticed before the way the sunlight shone on her hair, or the lively sparkle in her eyes?

Joshua was dumbfounded to think that here he'd been without the least inclination toward asking a woman out during the year since Suzanne's passing, and now he had two dates on one day!

Boy, oh boy, such a pickle I'm in!

He wished he'd conferred with someone regarding this — his brother Ned, perhaps? Certainly not Preacher Yoder, who was seemingly much too eager for him to get hitched again.

Joshua kept busy in the barn, thinking ahead to the next big slaughter for his grass-fed steers. The demand for his organic beef seemed ever growing, even in a down economy, and he was thankful for the Lord's provision. Now for the Lord to provide a wife, as well!

Happy to have logged a few more miles today, Jodi noticed several text messages from Trent when she retrieved her phone from her car. She called him while she drove. "What's a girl gotta do to get a little attention?" she teased when he answered.

Trent chuckled. "I was just thinking the same about you."

"Want to meet for coffee somewhere?"

"I'd meet you anywhere, Jodi."

She smiled into the phone. "Somewhere with AC, please."

He chuckled, saying she would have liked the church he visited. "They had the air-conditioning cranked way up."

"Did you eat dinner?"

"Lunch?"

"Right." Now she laughed.

"What's funny?"

She told him the Amish referred to the

noon meal as dinner. "Actually, all I had for lunch was some ice cream."

"That doesn't sound like you," Trent said.

"Doesn't it?" She laughed again and told him she'd gone running in Hickory Hollow.

"The little Amish girl's community?"

I miss her, she thought. "I ran into Sarah and her family as they were coming out of church."

"Let's see, the Amish have house church every other week, right?"

She was surprised. "Since when do you know so much about them?"

"Um, since I googled them last night, after you sent me packing."

Again she smiled. At least he wasn't upset.

"Seriously, theirs is a unique culture. Little known and quite misunderstood, too," he said.

"And rather enchanting, I have to say."

"I want to hear all about it," Trent said. "Where do you want to meet?"

"How about the coffee shop across from your hotel?"

"Which is right where I am — so, perfect."

"I'll grab a shower quick and meet you there." She said goodbye and clicked off. "I guess he still loves me," she whispered, relieved.

She drove west on Route 340, to Ronks

Road and then south toward Route 30, pondering all that seemed to stand in their way. They were so good together . . . and yet so far apart on things that mattered.

Despite Maryanna's protestations, Ella Mae headed out to her carriage, saying she needed to get home for a nap. "It was awful nice to see Sarah's guardian angel up close."

"Glad you dropped by." Maryanna walked out with her, at the ready in case Ella Mae faltered.

"We're havin' church next door at Mattie's in two weeks," Ella Mae said, sounding matter-of-fact. "She and my granddaughters have been scrubbin' and scouring for weeks already." She paused and looked away. "Something your friend Joshua might've put himself into a bit more, jah?"

"My neighbor," Maryanna insisted.

"Doesn't look like that's *all* he's aiming to be."

Maryanna hadn't known Ella Mae to be such a tease. "Daed thinks my children need a heavier hand."

" 'Specially Sarah, no doubt."

Maryanna nodded. "And the boys would love a father."

"Well, that's not the best reason to marry again."

Marry? The word lodged in her brain, and Maryanna must have looked startled. Ella Mae gave her a knowing smile. "When was the last time courting didn't lead to that?"

Maryanna chuckled. Ella Mae had her there.

Sighing, she hovered near as the Wise Woman untied the horse at the hitching post, then teetered around to the side and climbed into the carriage. "You can't go wrong with a man whose best friend was your own husband, my dear."

"We'll just see" was all she would say.

"You know where I am if you need to talk . . . or pray." Ella Mae picked up the reins and smiled sweetly. "This can't be easy, going out again with single men and all." She paused and scratched the back of her head through her Kapp.

For a moment Maryanna thought Ella Mae might ask why Turkey Dan had ventured this far south. But for once on this day, Ella Mae remained mum.

"It's always good to see ya, Ella Mae." Maryanna hesitated, then added, "You won't say anything 'bout seeing Turkey Dan here, jah?"

This brought a chortle, and Ella Mae nodded. "Who's that, ya say?"

Maryanna smiled. "Denki." She meant it.

No one needed to know why Dan Zook had stopped by today. No one at all.

CHAPTER 35

Maryanna cleared off the ice cream bowls with her daughters as she considered Turkey Dan's request to watch his three youngest sons next Saturday afternoon. Dan and his two older boys planned to pick up a new driving horse down near Kinzers.

"A mighty fine gray mare," Dan had said, standing a bit too close for her comfort.

She wondered why Dan had asked her and not one of his relatives. It wasn't that she minded, but it just seemed so out of the blue. Or was she being naïve? After today's earlier encounter with Joshua Peachey, Maryanna guessed she shouldn't be too hard on herself for being a bit jittery about *two* men showing her such interest.

Still, it was altogether unsettling. Especially Joshua, since he had always been simply Benuel's friend and a good neighbor — he and Suzanne were so kind and helpful. Maryanna had never thought of him in any other light. Till now.

The coffee shop was nearly vacant by the time Jodi hurried in after showering and changing clothes. She spotted Trent over in a comfy corner, near the window. The afternoon sun filtered through the wood blinds, and his handsome face lit up when he saw her. "Sit beside me," he said, moving over.

"Good, you want to snuggle," she said, happily scooting in and letting him kiss her twice on the lips. "Mm, I'm going to miss this."

"The year will go fast . . . I hope." He winked at her.

They leaned forward together to study the menu board above the counter. Jodi decided on an iced chai tea and Trent chose a mocha. She insisted on going up to place their order and then returned with their drinks to her grinning fiancé.

"By the way, you're cute when you're mad." His eyes were full of mischief.

She sighed. "I hope you're not referring to last night."

"Not specifically, no."

"Well, I think you are."

So much for the sweet tone of their date.

He stretched back in the booth. "Look,

Jodi, I know you're in a bad place right now, and I would be, too, if I lost my brother or sister. But you've got to know the feelings you have toward prayer and God won't last."

"How can you be sure?" She wished he'd validate her grief. "You can't possibly know. You've never experienced what I'm going through."

"Mourning comes in waves, hon." He kissed her again, but this time she didn't return it.

"You sound like a walking textbook. Losing Karen keeps me awake at night — gives me nightmares. I watched my sister die. I held her in my arms while she struggled to take her last breaths. I felt so . . . well, helpless."

"Jodi, I'm sorry. I don't mean to trivialize your sadness."

"As for having children, you don't get it, do you? I really just want us. *You and me.*"

He agreed with a hearty nod. "I want that, too. More than you know."

"Right, but *us* plus kids." She sighed, then covered her face and leaned her elbows on the table. "I'm supposed to start planning our wedding, Trent. But how, if we're at this kind of standstill?"

"It doesn't have to be this way." His voice sounded strained.

She moved her hands away from her face, cringing at what he'd said. "Do you think I'm sticking with our original plan to spite you, Trent?"

He shook his head, eyes searching hers. "No. I just don't get why you're not willing to pray about it. That's all."

"I can't explain that because I don't understand it myself." She breathed in slowly and made herself stay there next to him when she really wanted to move to the other side of the table.

"I'll wait for you, Jodi." His voice was softer now. "You know that."

"Wait for me to accept the family you want?" Her anger was rising. "And what if you wait in vain? What then?"

Trent shrugged. "We'll figure it out." He reached for her. "Come here."

Reluctantly, she let him hold her, glad for the privacy of the corner.

"I don't love you any less — do you believe me?"

She nodded.

"Let's keep talking, though," he said. "It matters most that we love well."

"I agree." She sat up straighter again, half tempted to add *minus kids.* But she held her tongue.

"God brought us together for a reason,

Jodi. You're the only girl for me."

She nodded, holding back tears. She felt the same way about him. But Trent couldn't just toss out spiritual stuff and compel her to see the light. The fact was, she wasn't so sure anymore they should go through with a wedding next summer. Not with their hearts in such different places.

CHAPTER 36

With help from her mother and Leda, Maryanna hung out the laundry early washday morning in a precise and orderly fashion from smallest item to largest. She considered Joshua Peachey and Turkey Dan, still somewhat perplexed at yesterday's unexpected attention.

"Mamma, oops! You put Sarah's dresses next to Tobias's britches," Leda said, giggling.

"I believe your Mamma has other things on her mind," Maryanna's mother said, smiling as she tried to put two wooden clothespins between her lips.

But Maryanna refused to own up.

"I wonder if the school board meeting's done," Leda said.

Maryanna turned toward her daughter. "You know 'bout this?"

Leda nodded. "But it's prob'ly over by now," she said. "I just hope we get to start school on time, like always."

"You're a right *gut* scholar — no wonder you feel that way." Mamm bent down to reach for more wet clothes from the basket. "You'd be a right *gut* teacher one day."

"I love school." Leda smiled prettily. Then she said, "Did ya know Sarah slept with her new doll last night? It wonders me."

"No doubt she'll remember Jodi Winfield for a long time," Maryanna said. "I 'spect it's that way when someone practically saves your life."

Mamm sneezed and pulled a hankie out from her sleeve. "We must give the dear Lord the glory, remember?"

Maryanna agreed and noticed tall, blond Ned Peachey walking briskly up the road, coming this way.

Evidently Mamm spotted him, too, because she looked quickly at Maryanna and motioned her head toward the road, a question in her eyes.

When Ned turned to come into the driveway, Maryanna said she'd be right back and headed round the house to meet him.

"Hullo, Ned," she said when he looked her way. *"Wie geht's?"*

"Guder Mariye. I'm fine. You?" He removed his hat politely and held it to one side.

"Keepin' busy — it's Monday, ya know."

He glanced about, then asked, "Do you happen to know how to contact the young woman who found Sarah?"

"Not offhand, no."

"No idea, then?"

"Jodi's never said where she was house-sitting."

He stared at his hat for a moment before putting it back on. "Well then, can ya let me know if you happen to see her again? I'd appreciate it, Maryanna."

"I surely will."

Not waiting a second longer, Ned turned and headed back from whence he'd come, which was most likely several farms over, at Noah Mast's place.

What do ya know! Maryanna dashed back across the driveway to finish the morning chore, deciding it best to keep mum that Ned Peachey had come so unexpectedly, asking for Jodi. Maryanna had more than an inkling why the school board member was asking.

Why else?

Ready for some fresh air, Jodi wandered outside to the secluded patio, where splashes of color reigned in the clay pots of pink and white geraniums and multicolored petunias.

She picked up the large watering can and turned on the outside spigot, still in her shorty pajamas. She'd stayed up late last night, searching online for recently posted teacher openings.

Feeling discouraged at only a few possibilities, most of which were out west, Jodi thoroughly watered each of the eight pots, then set down the watering can and strolled along the path near the willow trees. She welcomed a breeze, though the morning was still very warm and humid for the hour. Would the heat never let up?

Jodi tried to wrap her thoughts around what it might be like to teach at her father's school in urban New Jersey. Even if she agreed to Dad's job offer for a single year, she'd prefer to have her own place, although it was reasonable for them to want her near.

Her sights were set on her beloved Vermont, however. *Where Trent wants us to live after we marry.*

She sighed. *If we actually go through with it.*

Going back indoors, she wandered to the living room, still hazy from lack of sleep. She stared at the spot on the sofa where Sarah had slept so soundly. Jodi pressed her fingers to her temples.

Why can't I get her out of my head?

Restless and hungry, she went to the

kitchen to check her cell phone. No texts from Trent or any of her girlfriends. She scrolled down through his recent messages and felt sad at the way things had gone over the weekend. At least each knew where the other stood.

She went to sit on the barstool and forlornly eyed Trent's roses. She lightly touched one of the petals, noting the buds were opening beautifully.

She reached for her iPhone on the counter, put in the earbuds, and selected her favorite playlist — a little jazz to start the day. As for food, she liked the idea of something light. Fruit and yogurt sounded good . . . and maybe some eggs. Not so light, but how long had it been since she'd made an omelet?

A full breakfast made her think of Maryanna and her delightful foursome. How did she manage farm life and care for her children so well? Were Amishwomen simply more adept at domestic life?

Jodi went to the fridge and pulled out a variety of ingredients, including black olives, onions, and green pepper. Once the eggs were stirred and blended, she sprinkled in some goat cheese, along with a small amount of milk, still engulfed in her music.

Then, while the omelet cooked on the

stove, she sifted through her saved texts from the last week of Karen's life, savoring each one.

Don't hibernate when I'm gone, Karen had pleaded. *Live your life, sis. I'm counting on you.*

Jodi remembered the several good-byes she and Karen had said to each other. The hospice nurses kept calling to say the end was near. And all of them, including Karen's husband, Devin, had rushed to her side to sing Karen's favorite hymns and take turns praying, only for Karen to rally on three separate occasions. At the time, Jodi had believed it was Karen's way of saying she wasn't ready to relinquish this life. She wanted to stay with them, embracing the love from her wonderful husband and her family.

"I won't forget her." Jodi checked the eggs. This was the sister who'd shared nearly all of her passions — cooking, running, jazz . . . and their heavenly Father.

And Jodi cherished something of Karen's besides her memories — the special bracelet. *"A bracelet to last a lifetime and beyond,"* Karen had said, her expression so solemn Jodi had thought she was being a little over the top. *"I wanted to give it to my daughter someday, when she was all grown up. But instead I'm giving it to you."*

The memory of Karen's dying day plagued her now. Sadly, Jodi turned up her music and checked her email on her phone.

But there was nothing.

She glanced at the cat wall calendar and recalled Rosaleen and Barbara's invitation to return to run at dusk again this evening. Jodi hadn't promised to show up, and she was somewhat glad now, considering her morose, down-on-her-luck feeling. There was no way she had it in her.

She wanted to be alone . . . unless she was with Maryanna Esh and her family.

Jodi surprised herself with the thought. "Why?"

Maryanna chopped carrots for a salad two days later, instructing Sarah as she often did when cooking. "Stand back a bit, dear." She looked at her little daughter on the wooden chair next to her at the counter. "I don't want you to get cut."

"I'll be careful, Mamma."

"Leda, go an' ring the dinner bell, won't ya?" Maryanna said, and her big girl hurried right out to tug on the rope.

"*Wu is* Jodi?" asked Sarah, the cloth doll clutched in the crook of her arm.

"I don't know, Boppli." Seeing how glum

Sarah looked just now, Maryanna felt sorry for her. After all, her youngest had been on the verge of tears all morning. "But don't worry, I have a feeling we'll see Jodi again."

"Wann?"

She shook her head. Jodi hadn't appeared for three days now, not since Sunday afternoon, so it was anyone's guess. Still, it broke her heart to see Sarah so forlorn.

A few minutes later, the boys came bounding in, and once they'd washed up and were settled at the table, Maryanna brought the food over, and they bowed heads to give silent thanks.

When they were nearly finished eating, Tobias cocked his head and said in their first language, "Mamma, what would it be like if we had a stepfather . . . like Joshua, maybe? I really like him."

"Oh, mercy!" she gasped, not sure where this came from.

"He was Dat's best friend, after all."

Leda and Benny stared at their plates, but Sarah looked up all of a sudden with an alert expression.

Maryanna guessed she shouldn't be too surprised at Tobias, since he enjoyed working alongside Joshua. Surely, though, he hadn't overheard Joshua's invitation to Maryanna. Or had he?

"Mamma needs to finish eating," Benny said, raising his head and looking square into Tobias's face.

"Jah, 'cause there's some delicious berry pie for dessert," Maryanna put in right quick to defuse the tense moment.

Tobias, however, looked crestfallen, and Maryanna's heart went out to him.

She studied little Sarah, whose doll lay next to her plate. And thinking of her baby's keen interest in Jodi Winfield, Maryanna wondered, *Would it be so awful to marry a man for my children?*

CHAPTER 37

Dan Zook and his boys showed up later than planned Saturday, well after three o'clock. Maryanna fidgeted at the tight timeframe, even though she was fine about helping out as she'd promised. Telling Sarah to stay inside, she hurried outdoors and made it clear to Dan how imperative it was for him to return *before* suppertime. The last thing she wanted was for him to drive up when Joshua arrived for their date.

"That won't be a problem," Dan assured her, smiling with his light brown eyes and thanking her as he headed back to the horse and wagon. She couldn't help noticing his teenagers, lean Daniel and shy Willie, sitting in the spring wagon with their straw hats pushed forward on their heads, grinning at her.

Well, for goodness' sake!

Dan's younger sons, Yonnie, Jonathan, and Sam, hurried to the barn to find Benny and

Tobias. Maryanna watched them go, glad to provide a bit of care for these poor, motherless boys.

Shrieks of laughter commenced once Yonnie pushed open the barn door and his younger brothers followed him in. *Benny'll assign them chores right quick,* she thought as she headed back to the house, eager to get out of the heat.

On the way she saw Leda still weeding one side of the vegetable garden, thankful for such a willing worker. She recalled her own father joking that he'd planted weeds just for his children to pull, so they'd learn to work hard. Working and obeying were the hallmark of her upbringing, and she hoped and prayed she, too, was as successful with her children.

Maryanna stepped indoors. There, in the middle of the kitchen floor, sat little Sarah in a puddle of tears, cradling her doll and whispering to it. Maryanna held back, observing. It was still baffling to think how in the space of such a short time, she'd bonded so thoroughly with the Englischer. Was that attachment inspired by the Lord God, perhaps? Sighing, Maryanna honestly did not know.

She scuffed her bare feet against the spot on the floor where the linoleum had worn thin as she entered the kitchen, going to the pantry for a box of baby pearls to make tapioca. "It's awful hot for baking cookies," she said, glancing down at Sarah, "but I thought we might make some pudding while Leda's in the garden."

This brought a look of glee, and Sarah dried her eyes on the hem of her little black apron. Then, getting up, she pushed a chair over to the counter and climbed up, still holding the doll.

"Mamma's little helper," Maryanna said, and Sarah slowly nodded her head. "But I daresay you're much too sad today."

"Jodi's not comin' back, is she?"

"Well now, darling, we don't know that." But Maryanna wondered the same herself, what with the week passing and no sign of her.

"I remember the house, Mamma. The one where she's staying." The words were forlorn. "I do."

"I s'pose so."

Little Sarah nodded emphatically. And Maryanna worried she might press the issue and want to go out in the carriage and ride all over Lancaster County looking for an Englischer's house in hopes of locating Jodi.

She handed the measuring spoons to Sarah. If only her sweetheart might forget about the fancy woman, at least while they worked to make the dessert. "Let's sing now." Maryanna started the favorite song. " 'Wo ist Jesus, mein Verlangen, mein geliebter Herr und Freund?' "

Sarah joined in and sang a little off pitch, but that didn't matter.

"All right, now the same part in English. Listen to Mamma."

Little Sarah nodded, her face still gloomy as Maryanna sang, " 'Where is Jesus, whom I long for, my beloved Lord and friend?' "

They sang the hymn in German, and soon little Sarah's face began to brighten. Maryanna knew firsthand that singing while working had a way of cheering the soul and wanted to pass that joy on to each of her children.

"After we make the pudding, we'll have some nice cold watermelon," Maryanna said when they'd sung the song twice through.

Sarah blinked her eyes. "Can we eat our watermelon outside?"

"That's a very *gut* idea." She leaned down and kissed Sarah's cheek. "And we'll see who can spit their seeds the farthest." Maryanna laughed, knowing this would please the other children, as well.

A new online posting for a part-time art

teacher in Trent's very school district popped up on Saturday morning. Jodi would have laughed it off if she weren't so desperate to get another teaching job, but for a moment, she actually considered it.

I'm not qualified.

Jodi rose and checked Gigi's food dish, then decided to dust and vacuum to clear her head. Should she call her dad and talk things over?

Plugging in the hose for the central vac, she saw Gigi run for cover, squeezing her fluffy body under the low antique sofa table at the end of the living room. She could hardly blame the cat. Loud noises — and lately life itself — had a tendency to make *her* want to run and hide, too.

When her cell phone vibrated, Jodi fished in her jeans pocket and saw a new message from Karen's husband, Devin. With no siblings and only Jodi as a sister-in-law, he usually copied Jodi and her parents when he sent out email updates to his parents and a few close friends. So what was this?

Thought you'd like to know, sis, he'd typed. *Karen's headstone is engraved and set in place now. Next time you're in town, we can go to the cemetery together . . . if you'd like to.*

Jodi trembled — she hadn't even managed

to attend Karen's burial service after the funeral. Why would Devin think she'd want to actually see the gravestone?

Later, when the vacuuming was done, she put away the hose and its attachments in the hallway utility room, thinking the place looked better, despite the fact there was no real need to clean this much in the first place. Maybe a little cat hair, but the effort was more about her need to focus on something other than her life.

Letting Devin's text simply float, Jodi decided to call her dad, needing a new distraction and feeling bad about not checking in more often. She also needed to give him an answer, as it wasn't fair to keep him guessing.

While she was talking with him, she noticed a book on the shelf in the living room titled *The Amish Way,* and pulling it out without knowing why, set it aside. She felt tugged back to Hickory Hollow.

"I can't hold the position much longer," her dad said, sounding uptight and unlike himself. "You interested or not?"

"I understand, Dad." Sighing, she was at a loss for words. Besides, it might come across as a slap in the face for her to turn down a sure thing. "I just can't decide," she fibbed.

"You'd be foolish to turn it down, honey."

"I know." She held her breath. "But I need to."

There was a horrid, awful pause; then he said, "Well, how's everything going there?" Was he ignoring her decision?

She pressed onward. "I met some Amish people recently . . . even jogged with a few of them."

"Trent mentioned that, yes."

He talks to my parents more than I do, she thought. Any other time she would've found this to be rather sweet, but on the heels of Trent's difficult visit, she kept her thoughts to herself.

"You guys doing okay? Trent said he'd been by to see you."

She didn't like what she was hearing. "It was a short visit," Jodi said, grimacing. Surely, he hadn't unloaded on Dad!

"We're praying for you, Jodi."

She really didn't know what to say. "Tell Mom hi for me." That was the best she could do.

"We love you, Jodi . . . and Trent, too."

And if you don't pull yourself together, you're going to mess up a good thing — is this what he's saying?

She scratched her head literally and figuratively, scanning the flyleaf of the Amish book and wondering if she'd made a mistake by calling. "I love you, too, Dad. We'll talk soon."

"Sorry the job isn't going to work out." His voice was stronger now. "Nice to hear your voice, honey."

"You, too, Dad. Good-bye." She hung up, not sure what to think.

Opening the book to the table of contents, she scanned the four parts, her interest piqued by the third section: "The Amish Way in Everyday Life" and the chapters on children and family.

Dare I read this?

Joshua Peachey had only savored such a fine, tasty meal a handful of times in his life. Ida Fisher had seen to it that he was exceptionally well-fed at her table, which was laid with china and good silverware.

When he'd first arrived, Ida made complimentary statements about how nice things looked at his place for last Sunday's Preaching service, including his *"pretty flower bed."* She'd even noted how well-groomed Buster always was, and did not bring up the sermon-stopping chaos his parrot and cat had caused. By all signs he was certain she was as lonely for companionship as he. And a bit too eager to let him know, he was beginning to discover as she removed the dishes and offered a slice of fruit pie, her face aglow. She stood behind her chair waiting for him to decide, her eyes twinkling.

He was restless now and uncomfortable, too, as in that moment he not only chose the strawberry-rhubarb pie, but his mind sped back to his first impression of her immaculate house. Goodness, it appeared to be scrubbed down like she was hosting Preaching service. So Ida was a fine housekeeper, as well as an incredible cook.

"Whatever you'd like, Joshua," she said, all smiles.

The way she said it embarrassed him.

Then he remembered his manners and thanked her for the jam she'd left at his house last weekend. "It was yours, jah?"

Ida nodded, her cheeks pink at his remark. "Ever so glad ya liked it. And there's lots more where that came from." She kept looking at him, eyes blinking several times, her hands resting lightly on the back of the chair.

If I didn't know better, I'd say she's smitten.

At last, she turned to go tend to the slicing of the pie, and his neck muscles began to relax a bit.

For pity's sake, is that how I act around Maryanna?

If so, Joshua decided then and there to change his ways, starting right after he left here and headed for his second date of the evening. But with the wonderful-good thought of sitting next to Benuel's lovely widow — in the relative privacy of his carriage — came pins and needles that prickled his feet. How was he ever going to suppress his affection for *her*?

CHAPTER 38

Maryanna paced in her kitchen, waiting for Dan Zook to return for his sons. She was making herself perspire needlessly when she'd taken care to enjoy a longer bath than usual first thing. Tonight would mark her first date since her courtship days with Benuel.

She paused to check on the children — Turkey Dan's and her own. All seven youngsters were sitting in the gazebo telling stories, having worn out the game of hide-and-seek. To her amusement, Tobias was doing most of the talking.

Turkey Dan had guaranteed he'd return before suppertime. But supper dishes were already cleared, washed, and put away, thanks to Leda and even little Sarah, who'd looked surprised when Maryanna said she must run upstairs for a while, leaving them with the stack of work.

So just in case Joshua Peachey showed up

before Dan, Maryanna hurried next door to speak to her mother, all the while peering down Hickory Lane, hoping it wasn't her neighbor's carriage she'd see first. Thankfully, thus far there was no sign of either him or Dan.

She poked her head inside her mother's kitchen and asked, "Would ya mind going out to sit with the children awhile?" She felt breathless.

"Where are *you* headed, all dressed up for church?" Mamm's eyes were slits.

Maryanna paused. Should she say?

Mamm pressed. "You're not . . ."

Maryanna nodded right quick. "I took your suggestion. Yours and Daed's."

Her mother's face broke into a surprised smile. "Ach, well, isn't this —"

"Jah, and that's all I best be sayin'." Maryanna glanced toward the gazebo. "I'd also rather the children not be told." She didn't reveal that a collision of male suitors was about to take place, either. "I need to leave right now, just so ya know."

The collective laughter of youngsters came through the open back window, and Mamm gave Maryanna an inquisitive glance before looking out. "Well, I *thought* I heard more than just yours out there. I see a few of Turkey Dan's boys. It appears you've got yourself in a jam, ain't?"

Maryanna shrugged, feeling silly. "Their father promised to be prompt." She shook her head. "Should've known, since he was late arriving here, too."

Her mother's eyes were serious. "*Gut* thing your Daed's not here. He'd be out there greetin' both men, welcoming them. You know how he is."

"Well, I'm just putting my toe in, I guess, seein' what courting might be like," Maryanna said. "This doesn't mean I'm ready to wed, so please don't misunderstand."

Mamm's sober expression was difficult to read. Maryanna could not determine what her mother, typically an open book, was thinking.

"Best be headin' out if you're going," Mamm urged. "Gott be with ya, dear."

Maryanna hugged Mamm and thanked her.

"Anything I should say to Turkey Dan?"

"Tell him Sam spit the watermelon seeds clear to the woodshed."

"Sorry?" Mamm's eyebrows lifted.

"His sons had a very *gut* time here, is all."

Mamm nodded, still eyeing her. "You never know, Maryanna, you just might enjoy yourself tonight." Her expression softened. "Please try, jah?"

She didn't promise. "I won't be late."

Mamm chuckled. "All right, then."

Rushing back to the main house to get her shoulder bag, Maryanna smiled at the peculiar exchange just now. Her smile actually evolved to laughter as she slipped out the front door and down the driveway.

Last night, I did not dream of Benuel. . . .

It had been the first day in three years that Maryanna hadn't awakened with the memory of her husband's light cologne on her mind . . . or the memory of his strong arm curled around her as they slept.

"Does that mean I'm ready for this date, just maybe?" she whispered, suddenly feeling terrified.

As she hurried along a cluster of trees near the road, Maryanna was careful to conceal herself from the familiar carriage presently coming from the west. She made her way toward the *other* carriage she saw moving up Hickory Lane from the east.

"Ach, no!"

Joshua slowed the mare, aware of a distant carriage coming this way. Reminiscing about the exceptionally nice supper and overly animated Ida Fisher, he felt uneasy as he held the reins. Going from one woman's house to another on the same evening was never a smart idea. Yet there he was all the same.

Slowing even more, he was astonished to see Maryanna step out from the trees to walk briskly on this side of the road. She looked mighty nice dressed in her plum-colored dress and matching apron. The sight made his pulse pound, and he pulled to the side and stopped the horse.

Quickly, he got down and greeted her with a smile and a "Hullo, Maryanna" — but not too warmly, as he'd promised himself. "Out for a short walk?"

She nodded, an anxious look on her face, and he assumed her feelings were similar to his own.

To his pleasant surprise, Maryanna let him help her into the carriage on the left side.

When he hurried around to jump back inside, she looked much more relaxed, and it wondered him. "Busy day?"

"And hectic, too." She kept her hands folded securely in her lap.

Joshua clicked his cheek to urge the horse forward. "Did ya have plenty of time for supper, then?"

Maryanna nodded and offered a brief smile. "Did you?"

The last thing he wanted to discuss was

his meal with Ida. So he merely dipped his head to concur. Then he raised his eyes to the sky. "No rain in sight."

"Seems so."

He filled his lungs slowly. "Benuel used to say the Lord would send us rain when He's *gut* and ready. That most of the time, the answers to prayer come at the eleventh hour."

She smiled. "To teach us patience, jah?"

He nodded.

"Benuel had plenty to say 'bout many things," she added.

"I'm sorry . . . didn't mean —"

"Nee. Not to worry," she kindly replied.

"Benuel was the best friend I ever had," Joshua confessed. "In every way, he was an encouragement to me."

"And he always spoke kindly of you."

"Suzanne said the same of you, too," he said. "She'd hoped to be as sweet a mother as she observed you to be."

"Well, I know she would've been a loving Mamma." Then Maryanna seemed to catch herself. "Suzanne liked to spend time with my children, I remember. Did ya know she gave little Sarah a big needle once with some thread and showed her how to sew a little stitch — her very first?"

"Did she, now?" He couldn't help but

chuckle. Things were going along more than a mite better than he'd hoped. "Suzanne enjoyed sewing, too. I kept the baby blankets she pieced together . . . but never got them quilted."

"You saved them?"

"It seemed the right thing to do. I missed her so. . . ."

"Did ya sort through her clothes with her sisters, or —"

"Tellin' the truth, I couldn't part with them right away," he revealed, feeling surprisingly at ease. "Did you, with Benuel's things?"

Maryanna shook her head. "Guess I needed to hold on to what belonged to him for a while, ya know."

Joshua knew all too well. And when she sighed, he hoped he hadn't caused her unnecessary pain.

"It was a full year before I could part with them," she went on. "Never told a soul, other than Ella Mae."

"It's certainly no one's business how another person grieves, or for how long."

"Jah, Ella Mae said as much."

"You surely struggled. I know I did when Suzanne passed so suddenly." He was opening his heart much too wide, and too quickly.

343

"The way of sorrow can be ever so thorny."

" 'Specially with children, I would guess," he said, thinking of her four.

Maryanna explained there were days when she would have preferred to sleep away the day, yearning for sundown. "But then when it did come, I'd stay up late, so the nights weren't so long."

"I feel the same way." He directed the horse to turn at the next intersection, not paying any mind to where they were headed. Just being with Maryanna was enough . . . for now. "Suzanne wouldn't have wanted me to pine so, I can tell ya. And Benuel would have felt the same 'bout you."

Maryanna looked surprised and she unfolded her hands and touched her neck. "I 'spect you're right."

"One fall, when we were out small game hunting, he said he worried you might mourn too hard . . . if somethin' ever happened to him."

Slowly, she nodded. "We talked about it at times, too . . . how it would be for each of us if the other passed. Honestly, though, I'm glad it was me left with the children."

"For their sake . . ."

"Jah, 'specially for Leda and little Sarah," she said.

A catch was in his throat, and Joshua didn't know how to move ahead with this tender exchange. It had gone down a track all its own, delving deep into his heart. And hers, it was obvious.

"You don't feel sorry for them, do ya?" she asked out of the blue. "That Benuel's gone."

"Well, sure I do. We all do."

She looked at him with a frown. "But that's not why ya asked me out riding."

"No," he was quick to say. "Truth is, I want to get to know ya, Maryanna." He turned slightly.

She smiled so broadly, he didn't know what to expect. "All those years, livin' neighbors to you and Suzanne and spending time together as couples — making homemade ice cream and eating it out on the porch, the four of us — doesn't that count? Seems to me we've known each other for quite a while."

" 'Tis true," he replied, completely surprised by her response. Did she want him to pursue her now, when before she'd given him such bleak hope? "But our spouses' deaths have changed us in every way."

"That's for sure." She sounded sad.

"What I meant is, I'd like to get to know you as Benuel's widow, not as his wife. Do you understand?" He felt like he was holding his breath as he spoke the words. "I find you . . . well, beautiful, Maryanna."

He'd never seen a flush of color look so becoming. "Oh, goodness," she whispered.

"I certainly do." This moment had plagued him, the thing he'd kept in his mind and heart for the past few months, letting it grow and flower. All the times he'd seen her with her youngsters, going somewhere past his house in their family carriage, or out hanging clothes with Leda and Emmie. All of it had warmed his heart toward her. But, no, he'd promised himself he mustn't scare her off.

"Guess I should say Denki to ya, Josh." She laughed quietly. "I mean, *Joshua.*"

"Denki back." Now he was the one chuckling.

"You've always been Josh to me," she admitted. "Ever since our school days, ya know?"

"I recall."

"Doesn't it fit anymore?"

She was looking at him now, and if he wasn't mistaken, she'd somehow managed to slide closer to him. *Must've happened when we turned the corner,* he guessed, secretly enjoying it. "I was most definitely Josh then. I'd like to think I've grown up since that time, though."

"Well, in some ways, maybe." She actually giggled a little.

"Oh, I know what you must be thinkin'."

She was nodding her head insistently. "I'll give ya one hint."

"Let's see. Is it about something furry that lives in a cage?"

"Could just be," she said coyly.

"Well, on that subject, I've thought of givin' Shadow to Tobias, maybe. What would ya say to that?"

"I'd say no."

"Ach, that's mighty quick."

"If you were payin' attention all the years you and Suzanne came for supper, you'd know *I* don't have indoor pets. The Lord God meant animals for the barn and the meadow."

Joshua chuckled. "According to what Scripture verse?"

"Well, you have me there," she said, smiling.

He felt inspired by a newfound joy. Maryanna spoke so freely and seemed downright spunky. And to think he'd vexed himself into a near stew.

She continued, "I won't tell Tobias 'bout your idea, though . . . it would break his heart."

"Well, then, why not reconsider?"

"Change my mind about an overgrown critter in my house?" She'd stopped smiling.

"I think your son would enjoy having Shadow. Such a clean and quiet pet."

Maryanna looked away.

"Won't ya think about it?" he asked, hoping he wasn't pressing too much. "For Tobias's sake, at least?"

Now she was frowning. "I said no pets."

"So then, I guess I'd better not ask you to marry me, is that it?"

"Not if you've got yourself a houseful of animals, no."

The exhilarating atmosphere fizzled right then and there. Instantly, a dreaded silence took its place between them. Maryanna sat tense and unmoving. So she'd turned him down flat. And didn't he deserve it, having made himself worse than a fool? How ironic that after Joshua's earlier resolve to guard his heart, Maryanna Esh already knew he wanted her for his second wife — all within the space of this jubilant, then miserable hour.

CHAPTER 39

Maryanna had been having such an unexpectedly good time till Joshua brought up his pet. And his startling talk of marriage came clear out of nowhere. What about just getting to know each other?! Although, now that she considered it, she wasn't positive he'd meant a word of his ill-conceived proposal.

It was nearly embarrassing as she relived their frivolous banter earlier. Had they just felt freer somehow, riding together alone like this under the heavens?

To think that only a few minutes prior she was beginning to wish the evening might last. Not so now. But she was certainly not going to be the one to recommend they head home. Was there any hope of returning to the carefree sharing they'd so surprisingly enjoyed?

She waited, hoping he might say something. Then, thinking back to how they'd

left things — well, how *she* had — Maryanna supposed it was her place to speak
first. But what to say? A woman didn't
refuse a man's proposal because of his fondness for animals, whether indoor pets or not.

"Would ya care for some ice cream, Maryanna?"

Was he really asking to treat her after what
she'd said?

"Would *you*?" she managed to say.

"It's still early yet, so why not?"

They were giving questions for answers.
Regrettably there was no looking back, no
way to repair the damage she'd done. Maryanna sighed and clenched her folded hands.
Given another chance, she still would not
know how to respond any differently. Truth
be told, she loathed the thought of a rabbit
or a cat living in her house, let alone a loud
parrot.

But now, Buster, *he* was a right nice pet.
*An outside dog — living where animals be-
long.*

"All right," she said at last, though the
exciting energy had all but disappeared from
the confines of the carriage. They were
merely going through the motions till he'd
take her home and they would say goodnight.

Maryanna felt certain she'd never be

invited out again. Not by Joshua Peachey, anyway.

Long after returning Maryanna to her home, Joshua mentally kicked himself for glibly proposing marriage to the woman he loved. And surely it was love that made him feel the way he did. He wanted to care for her — and for her children — for all the days of his life.

Joshua pulled back the covers on his bed but did not retire for the night. Instead, he strode back and forth in the dim light of his lonely room, watching for the Esh farm-house windows to darken, as well. "What was I thinking?" he muttered, pushing his hands through his hair.

Sweet Maryanna had made it all too clear what stood in his way, but the thought of giving up his beloved pets just because of her sharp retort irritated him. The animals had become his family, sharing his lonely days — a comfort to him. And, too, Suzanne had always had room in *her* heart for pets.

He wore himself out going up and down the steep staircase, having first forgotten to cover Malachi's cage for the night, then go-ing back to check on Honey Lou's water dish. Back and forth, as if a nervous exer-cise.

Joshua slipped to the kitchen window and stood there, just staring at the moon, his hands at his side. He'd promised himself he would be prudent and move slowly where Maryanna was concerned, taking into consideration her regard for Benuel. Yet the careless words had slipped out, and it was too late to retrieve them. He'd offended her and probably came across as much too eager.

I should've kept my mouth shut. . . .

Honey Lou meandered near, shunning the bed in the corner as she purred loudly. The cat rubbed against his ankle, rumpling his pajamas. *I've ruined my chances,* he thought, disheartened as he reached down and lifted Honey Lou to his chest.

"Did ya have a nice time?" her mother asked as Maryanna sat down at the table. Mamm slid a tumbler of homemade root beer over to her.

"It was all right."

"Well, not by the looks of ya."

Maryanna shook her head slowly. "I must not have been thinkin' too clearly, accepting a date with such a man."

"Ach, wasn't he kind to you?"

Maryanna didn't feel comfortable going into detail. "Joshua was just fine, Mamm."

She sighed as she relived the evening. "I'll just leave it at that."

"So it *was* Joshua, then. All right." Mamm sipped her own glass of root beer. "Sorry I asked."

Now she felt bad, pushing her own mother away like this. "No . . . ain't your fault. I just . . ." She stopped. Dare she tell her Mamm how she'd turned down a marriage proposal over a trio of pets?

"Turkey Dan gave me a private message for ya," Mamm said. "Took me aside, away from the children."

Maryanna tensed. "Oh?"

"He said he'd be callin' on ya next Sunday evening, after supper."

She lowered her head. *Oh, goodness.* Was she ready to spend time with yet another man?

"He's awfully nice," Mamm said, her face softening. "And you'd never have to work another day in that greenhouse, ya know."

The remark smote her heart. "Mamm, I *love* what Benuel built for us. I surely do."

"Didn't mean to meddle, dear."

"I have my opinion, is all," stated Maryanna. Opening the door to dating widowers was laden with problems.

She thought again of Joshua's impulsive comment. And for the life of her, Maryanna didn't know why she'd shared her thoughts without restraint during their carriage ride. She ought to have known they could only ever be neighborly friends.

Nothing more.

Just as the sun was coming up Sunday morning, Jodi watered the potted patio plants prior to her early run. The dawn was less humid — a good thing — but already she felt things warming up. And minutes later, as she jogged the now familiar route, she considered the fifth-grade position that had just popped up in Bangor, Maine, not thrilled about moving that far away.

On the flip side, it wasn't sensible to be too particular this late in the game, even though she'd put away enough money to coast for several months, or longer if she ended up subbing in her own district . . . or Trent's. Her passion for teaching had driven her since being hired in Arlington, but oddly, she was reluctant now.

So she ran faster than usual to work things out in her head. Nearby, a handful of purple martins soared from their tall four-sided birdhouses, and in the distance, the golden sun floated over the horizon line. This early morning hour had become her second favorite time of day. The twilight run with

Rosaleen and Barbara Yoder had taken first place. They'd urged her last week to think of coming back to Lancaster County for the Bird-in-Hand Half Marathon in September, and while she rather liked being welcomed and included, she still hadn't decided.

Jodi once again passed the spot where she'd found little Sarah Esh nine days ago, lost and crying. The memory of that discovery, and the child's family — Maryanna especially — had embedded itself in Jodi's mind. Each day this past week, she'd had to purposefully keep herself from driving to Hickory Hollow as she kept busy following up on teaching leads, only to learn she was a few minutes or days too late. She had also talked to Trent by Skype quite frequently, including Friday, when he'd flown to Japan. And then again last night, when it was already this morning in eastern Asia. He was jet-lagged and glad he'd arrived a day before needing to report to the Japan Exchange and Teaching Programme coaches. He admitted how terribly he already missed her.

It was hard to think about Trent so far away . . . and Karen even farther. Jodi needed to pull herself out of the doldrums and do something these last few days before Scott and Paige arrived home. The thought of not seeing little Sarah and Maryanna again once she returned home to Vermont was disheartening. And when Jodi spied a tall white silo in the distance to the east, she knew exactly where she wanted to spend the rest of today — this Sunday was a no-Preaching day for the Esh family.

What could I give as a surprise? she wondered, wanting to do something to thank them for their kindness and, most of all, acceptance of her as an outsider. Maryanna grew the most gorgeous flowers in her gardens all around the house, and in the greenhouse, too. So flowers were out. There was also plenty of produce thriving in the fertile soil surrounding their stable and woodshed.

But the town practically rolls up on Sundays, so there's nowhere to shop. So what could Jodi bring as the perfect farewell gift for Maryanna and the children?

CHAPTER 40

During dessert, there was a gentle knock at the back door. Maryanna rose quickly, having just noticed the dark blue car parked down toward the end of the lane. "Ach, children — Jodi's back!"

Sarah let out a little yelp and scampered to the door. Maryanna didn't have the heart to shoo her daughter away, not when Sarah had knelt at her bed again this morning, her tiny hands folded in prayer.

Maryanna greeted the young woman, who looked clean and neat as always, especially minus any eye makeup. She wore the long pale blue skirt and beige blouse. "*Willkumm,* Jodi . . . so nice to see ya."

"I hoped you might be home."

Sarah raised her arms to Jodi, who leaned down quickly to give her a hug. She babbled to Jodi in Deitsch, looking sweet in her for-*gut* clothes. "I prayed you'd come see us again, Jodi."

Maryanna told Jodi what Sarah had just said, and Jodi beamed. "Come have a piece of strawberry pie and ice cream with us," Maryanna said. She laughed lightly, adding, "When I think about it, the kitchen table is the most important furniture in the house — it's where we talk, pray, and eat. And entertain our special guests." She smiled at Jodi. "It's so *gut* to see you."

Following Maryanna with Sarah's hand in hers, Jodi accepted the chair little Sarah pulled out for her. She spoke to each of the children warmly, careful to include all four.

"I was anxious to see you before I leave for home in a few days," Jodi said when she was seated.

Maryanna noticed she wore no earrings this time. "You say you're leavin' so soon?"

"Yes, Scott and Paige will be home this Wednesday."

The children's faces wilted, especially Sarah's, when Maryanna translated in Deitsch.

And then, just that quick, Maryanna recalled what Ned Peachey had come over to ask her last Monday morning. "Oh dear, I nearly forgot. One of the fathers on the school board was here lookin' to contact you recently."

Jodi frowned. "Me?"

" 'Twas Ned Peachey, wanting to know the next time you dropped by."

Jodi glanced at Benny and Tobias, who were sitting together on the bench. "Am I in trouble for the lesson time I had with the children?" She paused, looking now at Maryanna. "Is that why Ned wants to meet with me?"

Maryanna shook her head. "That's not the reason, I can assure you."

"I guess we should take Jodi over to Ned's after dessert," Benny said. "Ain't so, Mamma?"

"Would ya feel comfortable ridin' in the carriage with us, Jodi?" asked Maryanne.

"Or I can drive us, if you'd rather," Jodi offered.

"Well, we don't ride in cars on the Lord's Day," Maryanna let her know. "It's against the church ordinance."

The children leaned forward, curious eyes on Jodi. Suddenly, Maryanna wondered if they, too, suspected what Ned had in mind to ask the Englischer.

During the ride in the delicate, boxlike carriage, Jodi and Maryanna sat on the only bench seat as little Sarah nestled in Jodi's lap, her cloth doll, Engel, in her arms. Behind them, in the small area near the

359

back of the buggy, sat Benny, Leda, and Toby.

The leisurely pace and the sound of the horse's steady breathing and its hooves plodding against the road gave Jodi an otherworldly sensation. It was as if she'd been propelled back to another era.

She saw things she'd never noticed before when driving — the shape of tree branches sculpted by the wind and the dappled sunlight showering down through copious leaves. And she saw Buster wagging his tail at the end of Joshua's lane, a near smile on his striking canine face.

Maryanna made good use of the time, asking the children to practice singing "Jesus Loves the Little Children" in German. The sweet unison blending of their voices touched Jodi.

Benny asked his mother if he could tell Jodi about practicing the *"Loblied"* with his Dawdi Zeke.

Maryanna agreed. "It's something I've asked Benny to memorize before I'll let him sit with his grandfather over on the men's side of the church," she explained. "A very special ritual for a boy, when he's old enough to sing it."

"Jah, and that hymn's real long, too. It has four verses with seven lines," Benny

added, sounding excited. "And it's in German, so I still have a lot of practicing to
do."

Toby piped up. "Practice makes perfect."

"That's a terrific goal." Jodi laughed.
"And there's another way to say that, by the
way: *Perfect* practice makes perfect."

Benny laughed behind her, and Jodi
hugged Sarah.

"You're ever so *gut* with them," Maryanna
said, looking fondly at her. "All the children.
Even the bishop noticed."

Jodi's mother, too, had observed this from
the time Jodi was eight years old, the year
she began asking to help in the church
nursery. Jodi had even subsidized her appetite for books as a young teen with baby-
sitting jobs.

Later, Toby described how he thought
little Sarah had tumbled out the back of the
carriage. "She leaned over so far that *ker-
plop,* she fell out onto her head."

Jodi winced at the vision of the precious
dumpling tumbling onto the road like that.

"No wonder there was a knot on her
forehead," Toby said, sounding empathetic.

"Jah, no wonder," Leda said more quietly.

Jodi wished Karen could see her now.
Never in her sister's dreams would she have
expected Jodi to be received like this — even

doted upon — by an Amish family.

"I'd like to give your family a gift," Jodi mentioned. "Something you might need or want, just to remember me by."

"Awful nice of you, dear, but we do have our happy memories, ya know." Maryanna smiled brightly. "And Sarah right here to remind us, too, of how special you are to all of us."

"Well, if you think of something, let me know."

Then, looking at Jodi holding her youngest, Maryanna said softly, "Seems to me *you're* the gift, Jodi Winfield. *You.* And the splendid answer you were to our prayers in finding our Sarah."

Jodi shifted in the seat, feeling humbled and deeply moved.

CHAPTER 41

When they arrived at Ned Peachey's big stone farmhouse, Jodi, Maryanna, and the children were ushered inside, where Ned's six youngsters sat around the table playing quiet games or coloring.

Jodi was struck by the solemn demeanor of Joshua's bearded brother Ned. It was quickly apparent that he would not speak to her privately without his wife, Sadie, present. They led Jodi into another room, expecting Maryanna and the children to remain in the kitchen, something Ned communicated with the mere raise of an eyebrow and a jerk of his head.

She sat on a stiff brown settee near a window as Ned took a seat on the sofa next to his wife. "We've been lookin' high and low for a teacher to take Rosaleen Yoder's place," Ned began. He went on to explain that they had a good lead on a young woman in another Amish church district, but she was helping an elderly relative in Apple Creek, Ohio, and wouldn't be able to return for six weeks or more. "Peculiar as this may be to you, Jodi, it seems you're the only possibility we've got at present."

He paused, sighing, and Jodi wasn't sure what to make of his words — all of this was slightly surreal.

"What I'm getting to is . . . would you consider filling in as teacher for our Amish scholars for the time being?" Ned was dressed all in black, except for the long-sleeved white shirt, as if he'd been to church. "This would be for no more than two months, until the school board can locate a permanent teacher."

"This is quite a surprise," Jodi replied, stunned. "I don't know what to say."

Sober Sadie did not even blink, as far as Jodi could tell. She sat silently draped in a green dress and long black apron, scarcely more than a breathing fixture.

"Jah, no doubt." Ned tugged on his thick brown beard. "But if you agree, we'll see to it you receive thorough instruction and some help from Rosaleen between now and when school opens the last week in August. You'll have plenty of assistance."

Jodi was still trying to process his request. "Unfortunately there is less than a month to familiarize yourself with our curriculum and the many expectations of the board."

Many expectations . . .

Before she could respond again, he added, "No one amongst the Amish community here has ever hired an Englischer substitute that we know of, so admittedly we're in uncharted waters."

So why would they even consider me?

"When do you need to know?" she asked.

Ned rubbed his forehead. "Well, as soon as you feel you can submit to the board's requirements and start to prepare." He turned and gave his wife a gentle smile. "Of course, we don't expect you to teach without pay. We'll offer you the sum of nine hundred dollars per month. And provide a place to stay, as well, since our typical Amish teachers still live at home."

Jodi didn't permit herself to react, not wanting to insult him. *Oh, my goodness.* Was she hearing this correctly? This offer by no means matched the master's degree salary level to which she was accustomed in the public school system. But the free lodging was quite generous and unexpected. Where did he envision her staying? *If I agree to do this.*

"How many students attend the school?" she asked, still numb from the direction of the conversation.

"There are twenty-two children this year in all eight grades."

Such an ambitious undertaking for any teacher, let alone a very young woman like Rosaleen. And even more so for someone unfamiliar with Amish tradition.

"Would it be possible to review the curriculum — the various subjects — before I decide?"

Ned wore a solemn, scrutinizing expression. "Either Sadie here or our friend Maryanna can answer your basic questions about that."

Jodi agreed to talk with Maryanna.

"Perhaps you'd like to go and walk on the field roads out yonder. Give this some further thought?" He raised his callused hand and pointed behind the house. "It's peaceful out there, and one feels closest to the Good Lord near farmland, I daresay. It's the ideal place to quiet one's heart."

It was then Jodi realized: *He wants an answer today.*

The rippling alfalfa field quivered with flying insects, bluebirds, and silvery green willows in the near distance as Jodi walked with Maryanna on the dirt path.

"Ned's eight-mule team goes back and

366

forth to the barn on these perimeter lanes," Maryanna explained. Then she said nervously, "By the way, Sadie whispered that Ned encouraged you to come out to talk with me."

She's curious to know what's going on.

Jodi shared Ned's proposal on behalf of the school board.

"I kinda wondered if that might not be it." Maryanna nodded, her white cap strings flying.

Jodi confided that she wanted Maryanna's company — and advice. "I feel like a lone, floundering fish far from sea. And even more than that, why would the school board choose an outsider to instruct the children . . . even for a few weeks?"

"Well, there was some talk that our bishop took note of how all the youngsters were attracted to you after the Preaching service. From what I heard, he was very impressed with how ya conducted yourself."

Jodi remembered being encircled that Sunday afternoon. She guessed she could see how the children's fondness for her might astound the Amish bishop.

"Bishop Beiler believes it was nothin' short of a miracle that Sarah was brought home safely by you — and that you knew just where to bring her, too."

Jodi inquired about the curriculum, and Maryanna told her everything she knew about the subjects taught: arithmetic, spelling, penmanship, and reading. "There are also history and geography lessons, and some time in the afternoons for drawing, singing, and storytelling," said Maryanna. "Of course, the first graders are taught English, too, since up till then they've spoken only Deitsch."

Taking it all in, Jodi thought the three R's sounded most prominent. Then, without saying more, she made an attempt to submit to Ned's suggestion to quiet her heart. *Praying is what he really wants.*

As she walked, she enjoyed the solitude of the dirt path and the thousands of maturing plants. She was tempted to reach out and float her hand across the tip-tops of the alfalfa, much as she and Karen had sometimes done. All the walks — and runs — they'd taken together through the years had been so precious, though she hadn't realized it then. *"The soul yearns for tranquility,"* Karen had said once. *"But the only real peace comes from communing with God."*

"In prayer," Jodi whispered, startling herself.

Maryanna looked at her. "Sorry?"

"Just talking to myself."

"I tend to do that, too."

They walked along in silence for a while. Jodi contemplated Trent's arrival in Japan. He seemed so eager to work with children of a different culture, offering them something more than mere education.

Would he be surprised if I accept the Amish school board's request? She could only wonder, as Trent was out of reach right now. She walked on and let the magnificence of the countryside soothe her heart.

Jodi considered the possibility that finding Sarah along the road had been an answer to her own personal plea that morning — that the world would stop so she could step off and catch her breath.

"Jodi . . ." Maryanna broke the calm and slowed her pace. "Have ya ever thought that it's not what we think we ought to do that's essential for happiness, but what the Lord's leading us to do . . . and to be?" She smiled. "Ofttimes that can be two very different things."

Jodi drank in the clean air and the truth of Maryanna's words.

"God has a plan for each of us — I believe that." Maryanna tilted her head, eyes sparkling. "Maybe you were led here for an important reason."

Jodi had definitely considered that, as well.

369

"To fill in for Rosaleen, perhaps?"

Maryanna shook her head. "Not necessarily." She stopped moving altogether. "Walkin' the soil of God's green earth is what I'm talking about, for one. All of *this* . . ." And here Maryanna stretched out her hand at the expanse of land, smiling up at the sunlight. "Honestly, there's an atmosphere of healing here in Hickory Hollow — many a soul passing through has said as much."

"Fueled by the prayerful attitude of the People, maybe?"

Maryanna smiled. "I think so, jah."

"Prayer's a real struggle for me," Jodi admitted.

"But it hasn't always been, right?"

Jodi shook her head.

"Well, God's not limited by our wants and wishes," Maryanna stated. "Isn't our faith in Him more important than what we demand in our prayers?"

Jodi was taken by her fervor.

Maryanna went on. "I've learned that sometimes I have to give up my right to know and simply believe that God's knowing is enough. Not that I don't want to question. Ach, I surely do. But in the three years since Benuel's death, I've learned that peace comes with that kind of givin' up . . .

and, not to boast, but my faith has grown because of it, too."

Jodi knew she'd hit on something. "I never would have admitted it before coming here, but I've missed talking to God all these months. But . . ." She fought back tears.

"I'm sure you did." Maryanna reached out and touched her arm.

They continued to stroll along, farther away from Ned and Sadie's big barn. Anything Jodi might try to say or explain to Maryanna about her anger dried up in her throat. Anyway, it would make absolutely no sense to this prayerful, God-honoring woman.

Ned Peachey appeared relieved when Jodi agreed to take on the temporary teaching position. "I'll appreciate all the help your community is offering to get me up to speed," she said. "Thank you for putting your trust in me."

Ned nodded and said Rosaleen would be in touch.

Later, prior to Jodi's leaving with Maryanna and the children, Sadie Peachey offered sewing patterns for a basic long skirt and modest blouse, as well as several pieces of plain blue fabric.

"You may hire a seamstress to sew your

clothes, if you'd like," Sadie told her.

Jodi had almost wondered if she was expected to sew her own outfits, but on the ride home Maryanna said she thought her mother, Emmie, could get them sewn up in no time.

That's a relief, thought Jodi, ready to dive instead into her crash course on Amish curriculum.

Joshua could not believe his ears or eyes as he rose from the table where he'd laid out his German and English Bibles — his customary Sunday afternoon activity. He'd detected the motion of a carriage in his lane, and when he looked out, there was Ida Fisher, tying her horse to the back hitching post. Lo and behold, if she wasn't reaching into the buggy for a hot dish.

It was awkward to think of inviting her inside, given their single state, which Ida undoubtedly was hankering to change.

If Joshua hadn't felt so drained from last night's disappointing end with Maryanna Esh, he might've taken care to put on a pleasant face for this woman who'd cooked up a meal for him, as she described the baked beef stew while standing there on his back stoop.

"Denki, Ida," he said as he received the

372

large casserole.

"No need to bother reheating it," she said, eyes bright. " 'Least not if ya plan for an early supper."

Like last evening, she thinks.

"It should be fine if ya keep it covered." She tapped the quilted top and smiled up at him. "I hope you enjoy your supper, Joshua." She said it so kindly, it tore at his heart.

"I will, indeed" was all he could say. Nothing else came to mind as she returned to her horse and carriage. Nothing at all to encourage her thoughtful benevolence.

Still holding the hot dish, Joshua looked over the meadow at Maryanna's farmhouse, the sting of her rejection still vivid in his mind. Then, realizing how rude he'd been just now to poor Ida, he felt truly sorry.

I refuse to hurt her. I simply will not.

Joshua hurried into the kitchen and set down the casserole dish on the stove top, then rushed back out the door, down the steps, and all the way down the lane. "I appreciate your thoughtfulness," he called after Ida, waving his hand high as her carriage slowed. "I'll drop by to visit soon," he promised.

Her responsive smile gave Joshua a sense of resignation, and he was uncomfortably aware of his Adam's apple, wedged in his throat.

CHAPTER 42

On the carriage ride back from Ned Peachey's, Jodi thoroughly enjoyed the pent-up energy of Maryanna's children, who were laughing and jabbering in the back of the carriage. Benny, Leda, and Toby had not been told of her decision to accept the school board's request, since the three fathers, along with Mary Beiler, the bishop's wife, and Preacher Yoder's wife, Lovina, first wanted to meet with Jodi tomorrow afternoon at the bishop's house.

Things had happened swiftly once Jodi made up her mind during the leisurely wander along the field road with Maryanna. Yet Jodi had no second thoughts. *Teaching Amish children will be an interesting experience.* She smiled, remembering how she'd viewed with some apprehension the idea of teaching a two-grade combination class at her former school. To think she'd now be teaching eight grades in a single day! At least Rosaleen was staying around for the first week, and Jodi would have good support from the People, as well.

As she let the horse and carriage carry her along, Jodi realized she did not miss her playlist. Usually when she drove anywhere, she required her music, anything from light pop or jazz to Aaron Copland. And it struck her that perhaps some of her habits might begin to change because of her short stay in Hickory Hollow.

She recalled the fabric Sadie Peachey had handed off to her for clothing, and she wondered what else might change.

Will everything?

Maryanna pointed out Samuel Lapp's dairy farm, where she bought fresh raw milk for the family. "Rebecca and I've made a *gut* many quilted wall hangings to sell at market in that house," she told Jodi.

They rode past the large spread of land and the local harness shop. A chubby man still dressed in his Sunday clothes waved when he spotted them. "We get our harnesses oiled frequently," Maryanna told her. "If they dry up, they'll crack . . . and we sure don't want that."

A while later, Maryanna pointed to what Jodi recognized as the bishop's farmhouse. "In the late fall and winter, I go to quilting bees over there once a week. Bishop John Beiler and his wife, Mary, live there with their blended family."

"Oh?" Jodi's ears perked up.

"John was a widower when he married young Mary Stoltzfus."

"It's the bishop's second marriage?"

"Jah." Maryanna gave her a curious look. "There are presently several younger widowers in the community — you already know 'bout one of them."

"You mean Joshua?"

Maryanna nodded without looking her way. "I doubt there'll be many widowers for long, though. Men tend to remarry right quick, within a few months to a year, especially when there are children to raise." Maryanna gave a faint smile. "Not so the widows."

Jodi didn't probe.

They were coming up on a large white barn, which Maryanna mentioned had been raised a few years back after a lightning strike burned the original in a massive fire at Stephen Peachey's old homestead. "That's Joshua's father's former place. Just look at all the Dawdi Hauses."

Jodi counted three. "Looks like at least three relatives live there."

Maryanna affirmed that. "You can usually

tell how many generations are living in a place by the number of additions built onto the main house."

Jodi paused to think how different her own life might have been if her grandparents had lived in close proximity to her parents when she and Karen were growing up. "Where do Benuel's parents live?" she asked, hoping the question wasn't too intrusive.

"Several years ago they moved northwest of here to Smoketown to be near their next oldest son and family."

"Do you ever see them?"

"When we do, we make the trip to visit them," Maryanna explained. "They're both up in years, and it's too hard on them to travel even a short distance. Which makes our time together all the sweeter." She sighed and gave Jodi a quick smile. "The children love goin' — their grandmother reminds them of Benuel — her smile, the way she rolls her eyes and tilts her head back to laugh at funny stories. Let me tell ya, Benuel's parents truly love my children . . . maybe more so because Benuel's gone."

Jodi took it all in. "A reminder of their loss?"

Maryanna dipped her head slightly. "The first year, it was very hard. But not so much anymore. Families are, after all, the heart-beat of our existence."

Jodi was thankful the children were back there talking and playing clapping games now. "I hope I'm not being too nosy," she said softly.

"Not at all." Maryanna looked over her shoulder. Then, leaning her head so as not to be heard by them, Maryanna quietly offered Jodi a room. "A place to stay, once you're ready to settle in."

"Oh, I'd love that!" She glanced down at Sarah, tucked between them. "Thank you."

Jodi had told Ned and Sadie that she would need to briefly return to Vermont once she finished house-sitting. She hoped to temporarily sublet her apartment, and she wanted a day or two to gather up some clothing and personal effects before returning to Hickory Hollow. "I have lots of curriculum to study between now and the end of August, Ned says."

"Well, Rosaleen knows a seasoned Amish teacher over in New Holland who has a few workbooks she's actually written," Maryanna said as they passed the road sign for Hickory Lane. "Maybe you could glean from her, too."

Benny must've overheard them, because he said from the back of the carriage, "We

379

use the blackboard a lot at school."

"Jah, we like it when the teacher calls our grade up to do our spelling words," Toby said.

"And long division," Benny added.

"I like ringing the last bell at eight-thirty," Leda said, evidently not to be left out. "And singing the three morning songs . . . and the German song, too."

"Same ones every day?" asked Jodi.

"We get to choose," Leda replied.

"See?" Maryanna nodded her head. "The children will teach ya, and right quick."

"Jodi's gonna be our teacher, then?" Benny and Toby asked together, their words laced with exuberance.

Maryanna urged them to keep this information mum. "Till I tell ya it's all right to say . . . you hear?"

Jodi couldn't keep from smiling. Here were three of her twenty-two scholars.

She thought ahead to what time it was in Japan and realized Trent was most likely sleeping now — thirteen hours' difference. How fun that he would be teaching English to Japanese students while she taught Amish curriculum in Hickory Hollow.

What might have seemed unthinkable weeks earlier, she actually welcomed, thanks to the emotional roller coaster of panic and now . . . was this the peace Maryanna had spoken of as they walked on the field road earlier? The peace of submission — a yielding of the soul?

They must believe I'm called to do this. . . .

Maryanna's invitation to stay with her family surprised Jodi, as well. Did Maryanna view her as a friend now, or did she simply feel she could trust her? What had changed?

She spotted the Esh farm coming up, and Joshua Peachey's farmhouse just east of it. A horse and carriage with a woman driver was ready to pull out onto the road where Jodi and the children had stood talking a week ago today, after their church gathering.

Jodi observed the lovely woman with the radiant smile. Then, turning, she saw Joshua himself run after the carriage, waving and calling something to the woman.

Jodi glanced at Maryanna, who was watching this, as well. She couldn't put her finger on exactly what she was seeing on Maryanna's face. Was it surprise? Or dismay? Surely not jealousy!

CHAPTER 43

Before Scott and Paige pulled into the driveway midmorning Wednesday, Jodi had cleaned their house thoroughly, with the exception of the master bedroom, which she had not used. Inspired by Maryanna's polished kitchen, Jodi wanted everything to be picture perfect for her cousin's arrival.

I'd love to return to a clean house! She thought of her own apartment — she'd have some dusting to do there for sure. As for subletting her place, Jodi's old church friend Carra Mason was tickled by the short-term opportunity.

The details of her autumn stint in Hickory Hollow were falling neatly into place, but it was the future beyond that still looked unclear, with no job openings in the school districts she'd contacted.

In a matter of three days, Jodi had covered the daily school schedule for grades one through five with Rosaleen Yoder, as well as much of the course study for those grades. She had also learned at the meeting with the school board last Monday afternoon that the twenty-two pupils came from six families, all within walking distance of the one-room school. None of the three first graders spoke English, so Lovina Yoder had been appointed to help them communicate with Jodi. Lovina would also attend each school day to keep an eye on things, as was planned.

Rosaleen had loaned her a handbook, *Tips for Teachers,* as well as the *Blackboard Bulletin,* which included solid advice, fun riddles, and interesting stories to appeal to Amish children. Jodi was still getting used to hearing Rosaleen refer to "keeping her school." While Rosaleen enjoyed her freedom as an engaged young woman planning her November wedding, she seemed happy to help Jodi, even pinpointing various students on the school roll who could assist some of the younger scholars.

Jodi didn't feel overwhelmed, though she was concerned with the school board's assessment of her work ethic. It was impossible to erase the memory of Ned Peachey's near scowl when she'd first arrived at his home Sunday afternoon. Ned and Sadie hadn't even cracked smiles when she'd agreed to be the teacher substitute. But educating Amish children was exceptionally serious business, she realized, far more sobering than any school setting she'd ever encountered. Or ever would again! Jodi had felt almost reprimanded when Ned's wife took her aside and asked, on behalf of the Hickory Hollow community, that she pull back her hair at school and not wear pants or immodest clothing while teaching. *"Nothing form-fitting,"* Sadie had said. *"You know what I mean. . . ."*

As soon as Jodi packed her books and a few casual clothes back home — no need for makeup or many toiletries — she planned to move into Maryanna's vacant guest room. She wondered how she'd manage without electricity anywhere in the hollow. Then, smiling, she realized she'd have to see if Scott and Paige would mind her coming there to Skype privately with Trent.

Something I've taken for granted, she thought.

Before departing for Vermont, Jodi stopped in briefly to see the Esh family. By now, the children had been told Jodi was coming to stay with them for the interim. "In fact, news of the fancy teacher has spread to all the scholars," Maryanna said as Jodi and the children joined her at the kitchen table to drink ice-cold meadow tea.

"Your room's right across from mine!" little Sarah declared in Deitsch, which made Maryanna and the children laugh heartily, until they realized Jodi didn't understand what she'd said. Once Maryanna had translated, Jodi laughed, too.

"Ach, there'll be an angel sleepin' upstairs," Benny teased from the other end of the table.

"No, a teacher," Toby insisted, his bangs sticking up.

"An angel of a teacher," Leda said, eyes soft and smiling.

Maryanna reached out and hugged Leda. And when it was time to leave, Jodi felt a lump in her throat as she headed out to her car and set her GPS for home.

Before putting the car in reverse, she looked up and saw the children running out of the house, all of them waving. Sarah held her angel doll high over her head and blinked back tears.

Jodi opened her window. "I'll be back in a few days," she called to them as she inched back toward the road. When she looked again, she saw that Maryanna had joined her little ones outside, her arms around all four children, hugging them near.

■ ■ ■ ■

Jodi was halfway between Albany, New York, and Arlington, Vermont, when her mother's ringtone sounded.

"Hi, Mom," she answered the phone. "How are you this beautiful day?"

"Well, don't *you* sound perky?"

"I'm driving home to pack for my return trip to Hickory Hollow."

"So you must be planning to go through with the short-term teaching position?"

Jodi said she was. "In a way, it's on par with what Trent's doing in Japan," she said. "Minus the terrific pay, of course. But money's not everything, right?"

"Will you also be teaching English?"

"Well, to three first graders, yes. The rest of the children speak it fairly well."

"You sound *so good,* honey."

Hearing that, Jodi realized she hadn't felt quite like this since before Karen's diagnosis. "I'm actually feeling pretty confident — and content — strange as it sounds."

"I'm happy for you." Mom paused. "Keep in mind, though, that you're potentially tying up the first two months of the new school year. Your father is concerned about what that might do to any job prospects."

"Right. But I'm viewing all of this as the chance of a lifetime, Mom. I'm really looking forward to it."

"What will you do for the rest of the school year?" her mother pressed.

"If nothing else comes up, I'm leaning toward subbing in my old school district."

Mom sighed into the phone. "So far from us, Jodi?"

"It's not any farther than it has been the past year."

"I guess I was just hoping." Mom paused a second. "*We* were . . ."

Jodi tried to put herself in her mother's shoes. "I know you understand, Mom."

Her mother sighed and said she certainly did. "Well, your father sends his love along with mine."

"I love you both," Jodi replied. "And I'm glad Dad's not upset."

"Well . . ." Mom laughed softly. "I'll just say that he's getting over it."

"*Is* he offended?"

"He really wanted to take care of his little girl."

Jodi smiled. *I'm not little anymore.*

"Someday, if you have children, I think you'll understand."

"Mom . . ."

"I know, I know. You're not interested, but

I hate to think what our lives would have been like without you and Karen."

"Mom, we *lost* Karen."

Her mother fell silent for a moment. "Just think, though. What if we'd never known her . . . or you? Our lives are so much richer for having loved both of you, dear."

Deep down, Jodi knew she was right. "I miss her so much, Mom."

"Oh, honey, your father and I do, too. We think of her every day and count our blessings. But we can't stop living just because we're afraid of losing."

"That sounds like something my friend Maryanna would say."

An awkward silence ensued.

"I don't mean to sound pushy, Jodi."

"I know."

"Please drive carefully, and we'll talk again soon."

"Okay."

"And text me when you're home."

Jodi sputtered. "Text you, really?"

Now they were both laughing.

"Guess I'm a little desperate, eh?" her mother said.

No kidding!

"Bye, Mom."

"Good-bye, dear."

When they hung up, Jodi sighed and

plugged her phone into the charging port. "*Still* lobbying for grandkids," she whispered.

CHAPTER 44

Needing a few basics for tomorrow's breakfast and lunch, Jodi stopped at a convenience store before driving to her apartment. Once there, she unloaded the car and carried her laptop, food items, and luggage inside, placing them on her bed. She glanced at her watch and quickly changed into comfortable sweats to prepare for her chat with Trent.

Glad to be home, she went to the small living area, settled onto the sofa, and signed on, waiting for Trent. Her heart did a little skip when she saw him appear on her laptop screen. His light brown hair was mussed from having just rolled out of bed. It was, after all, morning in Japan. "Well, hello there . . . how are you?" she asked, grinning at him.

"Ready to hit the ground running — don't I look it?" He ran a hand through his bed

hair. "And you must be home from Pennsylvania."

"I am. And it looks like you slept *really*
well."

"Must've needed it." He shrugged. "So
we've had the big kickoff teachers' meeting,
and I met my students. A whirlwind here,
but I'm having loads of fun."

"Sounds terrific."

"There are so many kids here who want
to learn English. And their parents do, too."

"Have you picked up any Japanese yet?"

"Maybe by osmosis." He laughed, adoring
eyes squinting nearly shut. "I've got the bare
bones. You know: Hi, bye, and what's for
dinner?"

"Knowing you, um, the latter's very helpful."

He was smiling . . . always smiling. "I've
been here, what, four days?"

"Is the culture everything you imagined?"

He said it was. "And much more. But let's
talk about you. How's it feel to be home
again, hon?"

"Actually, I won't be here very long." She
reminded him about her temporary move
to Amish country — Trent had been astonished to hear the news from her Monday,
after her meeting with the school board.
"And get this: I'll be teaching English to

391

first graders, among other things."

He nodded. "Interesting, our parallel lives."

"I'm starting to think that, too." She told him her plan to return home to be on the sub list until the end of the school year, if something more permanent didn't open up. "I'll only teach in Hickory Hollow for two months at most. They're working on securing an Amish teacher."

"Well, don't get hung up on the end game, okay?"

"I'm not." She shook her head. "I mean, I'm starting to believe I'm meant to do this."

"That's my girl."

"You sound like my dad." She mentioned that her father was licking his wounds over her not going to Jersey to teach. "You know how protective he is."

"Hey, my parents are the same way. According to my sister, it's the classic symptom of caring."

"As long as it's not coupled with inflicting guilt."

They talked longer, primarily about his getting acclimated to eastern Asian culture — the food, the tight living quarters, and his students' keen interest in education.

She noticed how tired he looked. "Are you still jet-lagged?"

"Well, if I am, I'm bouncing back." He paused and looked right into the screen. "I really miss you, Jodi . . . not sure how we're going to manage living this far apart."

"I miss you, too. Keep in mind how busy we'll both be. Work's a huge help."

He nodded, smiling. "The cross-cultural aspects of this program are eye-opening, hon. I'm gaining new perspectives and finding an incredibly warm welcome from everyone. And my students are so excited for English. They pull the passion for teaching right out of me."

She could relate and told him about the times spent with Maryanna Esh's children and how eager they seemed to learn.

"Excellent." Trent continued, "My students are so outgoing and friendly, it's amazing. They treat me like a rock star."

"Sounds like you're falling in love with them."

"It's fascinating to discover how many other countries are represented in the exchange teaching program, too. The rewards, thus far, outweigh any negatives."

"I'm thrilled for you." She meant it.

"I wonder, sometimes, if I'll ever love teaching this much in any other setting."

She smiled, delighted they were connecting on this level once again. "Just so you come home to me," she whispered.

Eventually, they said a reluctant good-bye and signed off so he could get ready for his day.

Jodi was glad to see Trent so elated about this present calling. As for herself, she decided to put off packing until tomorrow and call it a day.

By nine-thirty she was in bed, yearning for tomorrow.

She thought of fluffy Gigi, remembering how Scott and Paige's cat liked to sleep near her feet, on the bed. What if she could adopt a forsaken feline from the Humane Society? The right cat would be ideal company for the long year ahead.

She slipped her hand beneath her pillow, glad she'd put fresh bed sheets on before leaving for Lancaster County. Drowsy now, Jodi caught herself breathing a prayer for her darling fiancé. Was it just an old habit reasserting itself, or was she beginning to open her heart . . . to trust God again?

The waning side of a full moon shone impatiently through the undrawn blinds. But Jodi was too tired to care as her subconscious skipped toward dreamland . . . and Hickory Hollow.

After a breakfast of fruity yogurt and healthy

granola, Jodi began sorting through some of her books, including several Karen had given her. One was a leather-bound edition of *Jesus Calling,* a devotional she'd read faithfully up until Karen's heavenly Home-going.

She turned the pages to the selection for the day. Just as in the past, she was astonished at the pertinence of the Scripture references, the way they seemed meant for her alone. She went about her packing, setting that book aside as a definite yes.

Maryanna checked to make sure the wash-bowl and water pitcher on the bureau were clean as she prepared the guest room for Jodi Winfield. She solicited the girls' help, and the three of them stripped the bed, even though no one had slept in it. Maryanna wanted the sheets to be absolutely fresh, along with the pillow slips, which she'd embroidered herself with yellow and orange pansies.

She fussed over the summer-weight quilt, asking Leda if she thought it, too, should be washed. But, no, Leda didn't think so and reminded her that they'd washed it after the last time they'd had visitors — second cousins of Benuel's from Sugarcreek, Ohio.

There were no curtains in this room,

although with an Englischer here, perhaps she needed something to dress the three windows. Then, thinking twice about it, she knew it wasn't the best idea to push things such as that. The typical green shades were the norm, although she'd seen cotton and lace curtains over the same green shades when she and Benuel had visited his Amish relatives in other states, especially Kentucky and Indiana.

"We need clean hand towels and two washcloths," she told little Sarah, asking her to fetch them. "And let's air out the room, too." She suggested Leda have Benny bring in the fan again. "And see if there's some room freshener somewhere in the pantry."

"All right, Mamma." Leda turned and paused in the doorway. "Do we need more furniture in here?"

Maryanna looked about the room, noting the bed, single cane chair, and small bureau. "I don't know — what do you think?"

"Depends on how much Jodi's bringing."

"True . . . true. Thank goodness your father added those shelves." She pointed to the alcove on the far wall.

"But there's no closet," Leda remarked. She looked flushed up here in the heat of the day.

"She'll just have to hang her things on the

wooden pegs like we do," Maryanna said, thinking there were plenty of things Jodi would be quite unaccustomed to. More than that, she hoped having Jodi under their roof would be a blessing to all and not a mistake. She hadn't actually second-guessed her decision to invite Jodi Winfield until just now. Especially not after little Sarah confided in her that Jodi's coming was an answer to her secret prayers.

Joshua never expected his rushing after Ida Fisher last Sunday would prompt her to show up at his back door again that Thursday morning. But she was there all the same.

This time, she'd brought him warm rhubarb pie and had it all wrapped in a cardboard box, saying she hoped he might enjoy it over a period of days. Hesitantly, he invited her inside to share some of the pie. Right quick, he discovered Ida was happy to accept. She even offered to cut two pieces for them, prior to the noon meal. He was not in any position to present her with anything more substantial, given his penchant these days for quick sandwiches.

The parrot seemed to be well behaved enough, which put Joshua more at ease. Anymore, he was never sure what Malachi was going to say. Sometimes it just wasn't pretty.

"I'll take ya riding this coming Saturday evening, Ida," he said. "All right with you?"

"That'd be nice as can be, Joshua."

She seems so willing to please. He'd noticed her resolve at her supper table last weekend, as well.

There was no way to explain away his feeling of obligation to the woman. He had tasted her delicious food and suspected there was much more behind the bait she'd flung out to him — a fish in the sea of singleness. Yet was he merely comparing Ida to the high standard of good-hearted Suzanne?

Or is it Maryanna?

Still, he could do a lot worse than making Ida his wife, he decided. And Joshua *did* like her cooking. Besides that, she didn't despise his pets.

CHAPTER 45

After the noon meal Friday, Maryanna and her children worked in the greenhouse preparing orders for mums and other potted autumn flowers, as well as broccoli and cauliflower plants. Leda busied herself in the area set aside for starting Christmas poinsettias while the boys carefully watered the ferns. Maryanna and little Sarah worked together to mix soil for potting future plants, as well as a few dozen flowering cacti.

The sight of them as the girls sang "Jesus Loves Me" made Maryanna smile. Benuel had intended their life to be this way — *a family that works together and prays together will always be close.*

She could hear Benny telling Tobias that there were one hundred and forty words in the *"Loblied,"* and he was close to having all of them memorized. "Won't be much longer now," Benny said.

Young Tobias's eyes shone with admiration for his brother.

"Just think, you'll be over there, too, one day, walking into church with the other men and boys," Benny told him.

Instead of with Mamma, Maryanna thought sentimentally. How quickly her young ones were growing up. *Benuel has missed all this. . . .*

Jodi surveyed the Amish guest room that afternoon. The walls were a subdued forest green, a paler hue of the shades rolled high on each of the tall windows. The wood plank floor was covered in two places — this side of the bed and in front of the old bureau — with large braided rugs in variegated colors. There was a pretty yellow, green, and ivory quilt adorning the double bed, bookended by its head and footboards. The bed's style was one she'd seen only in the flea markets and musty antique stores her mother adored.

Maryanna pointed out the row of pegs on the wall, apologizing for the lack of a closet, though that suited Jodi fine. But it was the bureau with its small white candle in a brass holder that intrigued her. She noticed a book of matches tucked partway underneath the candle holder, and an Amish prayer book set off to the side.

"The drawers are all empty." Maryanna pulled the middle one out to show her. "And a washcloth and towel are on the washstand."

Jodi was shown where the upstairs bathroom was located, a simple room with commode, sink, and a tub shower. "It certainly can be just for you, if need be," Maryanna offered.

Knowing there were already five of them, Jodi refused politely, saying she could easily share with the girls. The downstairs washroom was primarily used as a mudroom, and the boys showered down there, just as Jodi had suspected. "You really don't have to treat me like a guest," she said.

"You're almost family," Maryanna said with a smile, motioning Jodi over to Sarah's room to show her the little English outfit she'd worn home the day Jodi found her. "She's determined to keep it for always."

Jodi told her the skirt and top had been pulled out of a clothes donation bag. "Now that I think back on it, the clothing was providential — the timing of it."

Maryanna smiled at that. "Well, you've got some skirts and blouses to make, right?" Maryanna said, offering Leda to help lay out the patterns in the sewing room down the hall. Mammi Emmie next door had agreed to sew them once the fabric was cut and ready to go. "Meanwhile, I have some eggs to gather with Sarah."

Leda came upstairs soon, and Jodi spent a half hour with her, pinning patterns and cutting out fabric in the cheerful sewing room. When Emmie Mast arrived and sat down at the treadle sewing machine, Jodi was grateful. It reminded her of Aunt Leora's old pump organ, bequeathed to her from her own grandmother in Barre, Vermont.

"Yous did a nice job," Leda's grandmother said, smiling as she worked.

"Thanks to Leda." Jodi thanked both of them yet again and admitted she'd never sewn a stitch in her life. "Maybe I should learn." The thought of Trent's desire for a family suddenly skipped across her thoughts.

He might be surprised at what I'm picking up here!

By the next afternoon, Jodi had become well versed in pressing skirt seams flat — the blouses were yet to come — with a gas iron. She also took time to visit with Rosaleen, who dropped by with curriculum for the upper grades. They discussed the first-day quiz, including such questions as: What is the capital of our country? Do your parents subscribe to a newspaper? Can you manage without any whispering in school? Jodi smiled at that one — she remembered getting caught doing the latter herself in grade school.

Rosaleen reviewed the daily school schedule and promised again to be there starting Monday, August twenty-seventh, for the first week, which would consist of only half days.

Before Rosaleen left, she began to teach Jodi the Lord's Prayer in German, as well as the children's morning song, also in German, which they opened with each school day.

Later, Jodi helped Leda and little Sarah groom the ponies with their grandfather Zeke. She also helped carry water for the pigs and the road horses with Benny and Toby, though they insisted that it was "men's work." For the time being, Jodi wanted to immerse herself in all things Amish and enjoyed every second of this extraordinary lifestyle she'd stumbled upon.

Mamm had not exaggerated about the breeze on this side of the house that evening, Maryanna thought as she settled onto the front porch rocking chairs. She'd enticed

Jodi to join her, which was nice — the younger woman was fitting in with all of them quite well. She seemed surprisingly willing to wear long skirts and modest blouses and even switched to a tidy hair bun in place of her usual ponytail.

Leda and Sarah sat on an old blanket under a tree on the front lawn, playing their clapping games while the boys played tag, bustling about with intermittent laughter.

Despite the heat, the evening was pleasant enough, and Maryanna could see her parents strolling arm in arm, talking near their flower beds on the opposite side of the yard. No doubt they would amble over here in a while. *They'll want to be on hand when Turkey Dan and his boys arrive,* Maryanna guessed.

Several enclosed carriages passed by, and each time, Maryanna waved as she recognized a neighbor. But when Joshua Peachey headed up this way with Ida Fisher, Maryanna caught herself leaning forward.

"Isn't that your neighbor?" Jodi asked.

"Why, it sure is," she said. "And that's the young widow Ida Fisher."

"Oh." Jodi sounded disappointed.

"I wonder if she's fond of loud birds and rambunctious cats," Maryanna said quietly.

"So this is considered a date, riding around in a carriage?"

"Saturday evenings are a *gut* time for that, jah. Once the couple is, well, goin' steady, they visit relatives on a date, or sometimes go to a restaurant."

Jodi wore a sudden frown. "Joshua must be interested in remarrying."

Maryanna shrugged. "Guess we all need someone, ain't so?"

"True enough."

"We're drawn to the folks we're meant to be with, my Benuel always said . . . if we hearken to almighty God, that is."

Jodi smiled thinly. "I've never heard it expressed quite like that."

"I knew, for instance, that I was s'posed to be with Benuel." Maryanna watched her girls giggling together, Engel lying in Sarah's lap. The breeze came up a little, cooling her neck and face. "I daresay my children are in need of a father." She surprised even herself, stating the truth right out into the air, where it carried who knew how far. Certainly, it didn't need to wend its way to Daed and Mamm just now as they smiled and walked toward them.

"Your children appear content," Jodi replied, turning to smile and wave at Maryanna's parents.

Things aren't always as they seem, thought Maryanna.

Daed clicked his tongue against his cheek and pretended to be a horse, making his feet prance when he caught little Sarah's eye. The two girls rose immediately and ran across the yard, throwing their arms around their grandparents, and Maryanna's father rewarded them with hard candy from his pocket.

Is Dawdi Zeke enough of a father figure for my little ones? Maryanna wondered, dismissing Joshua's rather gallant riding with Ida.

When the children's grandparents reached the front porch, Jodi was tempted to inquire further about Ida Fisher, convinced this was the same woman they'd seen last Sunday afternoon following the visit to Ned Peachey. But judging from Maryanna's cautious responses, she decided against it.

Jodi wandered to the edge of the porch and glanced over at Joshua's house. Maryanna strolled behind her, following her gaze. Ida's buggy was parked there in full view.

"I didn't know Amishwomen were so . . . *forward,*" Jodi said, hoping she wasn't stepping on any toes.

Maryanna nodded. "Ida hasn't been one to assert herself around any of the widowers, not till just lately."

"Assert? Meaning what?" Jodi wasn't sure what the term indicated here in Hickory Hollow.

"Oh, taking food to impress a single man, for one." Maryanna sighed. "Not to speak out of turn, but she's come a long way since she told her young husband that if he wanted a nice hot breakfast every day, she'd be happy to set his cornflakes on fire."

Jodi burst out laughing. "She said *that*?"

Maryanna had crossed her arms to punctuate the comment. "Like I said, Ida's mellowed quite a lot since then."

"Well, for Joshua's sake, I certainly hope so!" Jodi replied.

Maryanna never once blinked, nor did she move a muscle. Her expression was completely deadpan.

So does she care for him or not?

Chapter 46

Not even a half hour later, Turkey Dan Zook arrived in the spring wagon filled with his lively boys. Two large watermelons teetered in the back between Daniel and Will, the oldest of the five.

Benny, Tobias, and then Leda ran first to greet them, followed soon by little Sarah. Maryanna's children were clearly surprised — she'd kept mum, not wanting to point up the visit as anything but two families getting together for some good fellowship. But Daed and Mamm were plainly aware of Dan Zook's interest in Maryanna, and Daed mentioned to Mamm in Maryanna's hearing that he should let Dan sit next to "you know who."

Turkey Dan and his sons unloaded the watermelons, along with a bundle of fishing poles and bait, too, enough for Benny and Tobias.

How nice, thought Maryanna, knowing her

own boys' enthusiasm for fishing in the big pond out back. Maryanna smiled and wondered what Jodi thought of this display of activity for Dan's sons' sake. *Surely, she's put it together.* . . .

Outgoing as usual, Turkey Dan smiled broadly and initiated introductions all around when Jodi walked over to meet them, accompanied by Maryanna. "This is your new schoolteacher for a few weeks — Jodi Winfield," he told his boys, offering a firm handshake. And each of the boys shook her hand in turn, as well.

Dan and his eldest, Daniel, proceeded to carry the watermelons around to the back of the house as Maryanna directed. Mamm, Daed, and all the children moved quickly up the driveway to the back porch, where Dan helped Maryanna cut the watermelons into manageable slices on the steps.

In no time, everyone was leaning over and slurping as they enjoyed the cold, sweet treat. In between bites, Maryanna's father brought up Dan's small turkey-growing operation. He and Dan filled up the silences with a discussion about the high cost of organic feed and the public demand for free-range poultry.

Jeremiah and Mollie pulled into the driveway then with their youngest girls, Ellie and

Darla. Maryanna caught Sarah's look of pure glee when she spotted her cousins, and she excused herself to Turkey Dan and the rest, wiping her sticky hands on her apron and hurrying out to say hello.

Soon, more watermelon slices were distributed, and a few of the boys wanted seconds. When they were finished eating, Benny and Tobias and the five Zook boys took their fishing poles and headed to the fish-stocked pond behind the barn.

The girls washed up at the well pump and scampered to the sidewalk to play jacks, which left Maryanna and Jodi alone with the other adults, including Turkey Dan.

Maryanna was glad to be ensconced in the midst of her family and friend, thinking it far less awkward than sitting and talking alone with a potential suitor. Maryanna was fairly sure Dan Zook had dropped his sons off here last weekend to see how they got along with her four. Understandable, especially if he had courting in mind.

Such an undertaking to mother all of those boys, thought Maryanna as she cleared away the watermelon rinds.

She was amazed when Dan began helping with the cleanup and even more surprised when he followed her into the kitchen and made short work of the mess.

He glanced over his shoulder, then said, "I'd like to take ya out for a nice supper at a restaurant sometime soon, Maryanna. Would you enjoy that?"

She didn't know what to say. He was very nice and polite, but being around him made her miss Benuel all the more.

"Denki, but I'd like to think about it, if you don't mind," she said at last, not wanting to sound as though she was brushing him off.

"Of course, take your time," Dan said, his brown eyes hopeful. "I understand . . . I truly do."

Maryanna gave him an appreciative smile, dried her hands on the kitchen towel, and went back out to the porch, lest her relatives wonder.

Jodi came in from feeding the ponies with Maryanna and her children, ready to have a quick breakfast of cold cereal, toast, and bananas. Maryanna's eyes flickered in the direction of Mattie Beiler's farmhouse, where church was to be held this rainy Sunday morning.

The weather had changed in the night, and Jodi had even gotten up to close her window around two o'clock, marveling at the sounds pouring into her room. "You're welcome to join us for Preachin' service," Maryanna invited as she carried a pitcher of raw cow's milk to the table. "We could've walked through the pasture to get there, but not in this downpour."

Jodi thanked her but didn't commit. In fact, she was hesitant to attend, since she didn't understand the language, for one thing. And she wasn't sure how she felt about diving back into church, even if it only meant for the weeks she'd agreed to teach at the Amish schoolhouse. "I guess I might pass," she told Maryanna as she washed her hands and offered to set the table. "If that's all right."

"Entirely up to you," Maryanna said, her voice crimped.

Jodi noticed the children glance at her when it was time to say the Lord's Prayer, after Maryanna's signal for the initial silent grace. Little Sarah smiled across from her, then folded her dimpled hands and bowed her head, leaning her forehead against her knuckles. The sight put Jodi to shame, and she stumbled along in German.

As she ate, she thought of driving to her cousin's place but knew they'd be at church, as well. Maybe she could simply go to the coffee shop where she'd met with Trent before he left for Japan. There, she could get plugged in and catch up with her fiancé, since it was already evening there.

She heard the children talking happily about going to "the house of worship" over at the Wise Woman's former home, and Jodi had second thoughts about not going. Besides, she didn't wish to discourage the school board fathers by not showing up, even though church attendance hadn't been discussed as one of the several requirements she must adhere to.

When she thought about it, Jodi realized the twice-a-day family worship had begun to grip her heart. Each time the family bowed their heads and said the Lord's Prayer, Jodi felt more miserable. The excess of emotion she'd suppressed since Karen's passing threatened to burst, and she realized her rejection of prayer had taken a terrible toll. She longed to express her sadness, even anger, to someone who would not condemn her. *Someone besides God.*

Pondering this, she wondered if there was a flesh-and-blood person who could understand what she'd been through. Someone in Hickory Hollow, perhaps?

"You know what?" Jodi said suddenly. "I think I *would* like to go to church with you, Maryanna."

Toby clapped his hands and whispered in

little Sarah's ear as Maryanna's face broke into a wide smile.

"It's a long time to sit on the hard benches," Benny volunteered.

"Well, she'll sit along the back wall, with the non-baptized members," Maryanna said, nodding her head repeatedly, as if delighted. "Just take a white hankie along to cover your head, jah?"

"I have one she can wear, Mamma," Leda offered, all smiles.

Jodi thanked her and dropped a tea bag into her cup of hot water. And observing the excitement her sudden decision had garnered, she was glad she'd changed her mind.

The scent of rain was on the People as they crowded into the open space of several rooms, their wall partitions removed for the occasion, something Maryanna had explained to Jodi on the damp ride over.

Benny hadn't been wrong about the church bench — it was indeed hard, as was the wall behind her back. And after the first German hymn, which sounded similar to a Gregorian chant and lasted a solid twenty minutes, Jodi understood why Benny's goal to learn the words to the *"Loblied"* was such a challenge. *It would be to anyone,* she decided, very aware of the reverent spirit in the large room. Even the many teenage boys sitting in front of her were solemn and respectful.

She felt she had been watched earlier in the long line of women and younger children. She and Maryanna and her children had waited in the downpour beneath umbrellas, prior to entering the farmhouse. Jodi could see she was definitely the odd woman out — the only one present without the typical Amish head covering and dress with long apron.

When everyone rose and knelt at their bench, she did so quickly, as well, glad for a change in position, and wondered what everyone was praying. Had they been instructed in German as to what to meditate upon, perhaps?

It felt strange at first, as unaccustomed as she'd become to prayer, and more than a little uncomfortable. *Hello, God. It's been a while. I guess I don't know what to say. . . .*

But no sooner had Jodi begun when a sense of appreciation washed over her. She missed Karen desperately, but she really couldn't feel sorry for her sister. *She's with the Lord.*

It's myself I pity, Jodi realized.

She tried it out. *Dear Lord, I know Karen's*

happy with you — and completely healed, too.
Thank you for taking care of her. . . .

As for herself, she had much to be thankful for, didn't she? So she spent the time on her knees offering her gratitude for the numerous blessings in her life — caring parents, a fiancé who loved her dearly, and this strange fall down the rabbit hole of Hickory Hollow.

Why me, God? she asked. *What have you prepared for me to do here?*

Although fractured, injured, and imperfect, Jodi realized she was willing. And it felt "*ever so* gut," as Maryanna might say.

Maryanna rose from kneeling and saw Jodi several rows back, brushing away tears. Her heart ached for one so marred by grief. *Oh, that the spirit of this meeting might soothe her soul and bring her peace,* Maryanna prayed as she turned around and took her seat between her daughters.

It was then, when Preacher Yoder moved to the front of the room and began the first sermon, that Maryanna wondered if she was supposed to think of Jodi Winfield as a type of sister, just maybe.

Might that be?

Nothing should have surprised Jodi, the way

things had been happening lately — finding little Sarah and being asked to sub at the Amish schoolhouse. But when Ella Mae Zook wandered over and sat down next to her during the shared meal, she was indeed surprised and quite pleased. "I've heard such nice things about you," she told the elderly woman, whose dress was the same color as Maryanna's.

Ella Mae glanced at the white hankie on Jodi's head and twinkled a smile. "And you, as well."

"Is it time to take this off?" Jodi reached up and removed the handkerchief.

"Well, sure, if you'd like to." Ella Mae leaned closer. "Did ya understand anything at church today?"

"A few things."

"Such as what?" There was mischief on her face.

"Everyone seems so humble," Jodi said.

Ella Mae nodded. "If a body ain't humble, he or she ain't truly Plain."

Jodi folded the hankie.

"Isn't that Leda's?"

Jodi said it was.

"If ya look closely, you'll see the *L* embroidered on it."

Jodi unfolded it and looked. She traced her finger over the ornate letter. "This must

417

be a special handkerchief. Is it?"

"I gave it as a birthday present when Leda was just a wee five-year-old."

Jodi liked the woman's personal approach. "That's lovely."

"Tellin' the truth, we're not s'posed to teach our young girls to embroider and whatnot. Basic sewing skills are thought to be more important, ya know." There was a twinkle in Ella Mae's eyes. "I'm not much-a one for rules that make no difference. If you know me for long, you'll learn this soon enough."

The woman was refreshing. "Really? What else aren't children supposed to do in Hickory Hollow?"

"Well, if ya come over to my little Dawdi Haus next door when you're through eating, I'll tell ya. It might be a *gut* idea to know, 'specially with the more ornery pupils, since I hear you're going to be the new schoolteacher."

Jodi suppressed a smile. To think she'd stumbled upon an eighty-something dissenter of sorts — and a rather sassy one — also known as the Wise Woman!

CHAPTER 47

Jodi followed Ella Mae through the alcove at the far end of what she called the front room of her daughter Mattie's home, where the church service had been held. Soon, she found herself in a smaller version of the main farmhouse — Ella Mae's own Dawdi Haus. Before Jodi left with Ella Mae, Maryanna had said to take all the time she needed. She seemed to derive a measure of happiness in seeing the two of them together.

Ella Mae moved directly to her gas stove, snatched up the teakettle, and filled it with water. "I like to offer my guests some tea, as you may have already heard." She offered a smile. "My peppermint tea hits the spot, hot or cold."

"Sure, I'd love some . . . iced."

"You'll enjoy my special tea, Jodi. For sure and for certain. And, I hope," she paused a beat, "our conversation, too."

Jodi could already see why folk liked her. "I'm anxious to hear what the children are expected to do and not do."

"Well, they're taught to accept simplicity in all things. There aren't many toys, for one, and those they do have are handmade or right simple, for the most part. Girls won't name their dolls anything but what their sisters and aunts are called." Ella Mae's eyes beamed. "Although I did hear there was once a dolly named Kaylee — little Sarah's, ain't so?"

Jodi had heard Sarah say the name before. "Are English names off limits, even for dolls?"

"Oh my, are they ever." Ella Mae sighed loudly and fanned herself with a tea towel. "Children are also not to talk back or be restless in school or church. They mustn't be idle, for it is the devil's workshop. And, of course, they must not yearn for the world."

"I expect some children are more curious about the so-called world than others."

"I daresay some are." Ella Mae held Jodi's gaze. "Maryanna knows this all too well. Ain't really my place to say more."

Jodi remembered what Maryanna had told her. "Grief tends to make people weary. Exhausted."

"Ach, 'tis true." Ella Mae motioned for her to sit at the cozy table. "When I lost my husband ever so suddenly, I was *bedierlich* — pitiable — let me tell ya. Really beside myself. 'Twas a *gut* thing I wasn't raising children then."

Jodi found it interesting that she wanted to talk about grief. "I understand something of that. My only sister died recently."

"Did she, now?" Ella Mae frowned slowly and shook her head. "I'm awful sorry."

"Thanks."

"I've told just a few souls this, but I want to tell you," Ella Mae said, stopping to wipe her eyes. "After my husband died, I plumbed the depths of anger. No one knows how upset I was. Oh, I tried to hide it, but it was there, oozing from me all the same."

Jodi nodded, no longer hesitant to bare her soul. "I've felt that, too, over Karen's death."

"It may be quite natural — some are depressed or bitter, but I was just plain mad, sad to say." Ella Mae's voice softened, and her eyes filled with tears again. "Until one night, the Lord met me in my room while I was prayin'. I poured out my anger like a big mixing bowl full of pain and ire, and you know what happened? He took my pain as His own . . . reached right into that bowl of emotions and removed all of it. And I knew from that time on, I was not alone and never would be."

Jodi felt like crying herself, she was so touched by Ella Mae's account. "I'm glad you told me," she said in a near whisper. "I really needed to hear this. You just don't know how much."

"Well, dearie, the Good Lord knows, jah?"

Smiling through her tears, Jodi nodded. "I guess He does."

Ella Mae reached across and patted her hand just as the teakettle began to whistle. "My dear girl, deep down in your heart you know He's been there all along . . . ain't so?"

While the peppermint tea steeped with sweetener, Jodi pondered that. Then Ella Mae poured ice cubes into large tumblers to serve the tea with a flourish. She brought over embroidered yellow rose placemats to adorn the table and matching dessert napkins, then a few homemade sweets on a pretty plate: peanut blossoms and hermits.

"I realize we just ate, but the common meal's not intended to be substantial. Rather something to tide the farmers and their families over. They need to return home in time for afternoon milking and chores, then they feed their faces more heartily in the evening."

Making a mental note, Jodi thanked Ella Mae for inviting her to the delicious tea party of sorts. She commented on the table setting, as well. "If mothers aren't to teach their young daughters embroidery, how did you learn to make such lovely things?" She fingered the placemat.

"Well, these are compliments of Maryanna, whose mother taught her to embroider and crochet when she was a teenager. She and I have the same birthday month, and they were a special gift on my eightieth birthday, a few years back."

"And a very nice one, I might add." Jodi looked at the yellow roses. "Is June your birthday month?"

"It is. Why do you ask?"

Jodi could hardly get the words out. "June is my sister's month, too. Well, *was . . .*"

"Aw, dear girl, your sister's with the Lord, jah? And waiting to be reunited with you, one sweet day. It's our blessed hope when our loved ones go home to Glory."

"Yes," Jodi managed to say. But hearing that Ella Mae and Maryanna shared Karen's birthday month stirred up more sorrow than anything. "I think about her every day."

"And you have a tender heart, which makes you miss her even more." Ella Mae went on to say she'd heard Bishop John Beiler was so impressed with Jodi in part because of this. "He saw into your spirit, so to speak, the way you attracted the little ones over at Joshua Peachey's place two weeks ago."

"I've always loved children."

"That's evident, dear, and it's a gift from God."

Jodi sipped some more tea. "I think I needed to come here and talk to you. My sister's passing has been eating me alive."

"Loving someone never has to end, ya know? Your love for Karen will carry you through till you see her again. Never forget that." Ella Mae rose then and stuck her hand into a cookie jar and brought over three large carrot cookies. "I almost forgot to offer ya some of these. I made 'em yesterday afternoon."

"I'll just have to run off the calories," Jodi said, accepting one and peering down at her dessert plate.

"Who was it who told me you were out running with a group of Plain folk here recently?"

"Maybe you heard it from Rosaleen or Barbara Yoder."

"That might be." Ella Mae picked up a cookie and placed it on her napkin. "Awful nice havin' you visit me."

"Thanks for sharing your response to your husband's passing," Jodi said. "You have no idea how helpful it was."

"Ah, well, I believe I do, dearie . . . I can see it on your face."

Jodi hoped she'd have the opportunity to visit with the Wise Woman again, because she could hardly pull herself away.

"You come drop by anytime, ya hear?"

"I appreciate that. Thank you."

"And if there's anything you've missed while preparing for school to start, don't worry your perty head. Those children can nearly teach themselves, is what I've heard." Ella Mae tugged on her earlobe. "That's not sayin' they can't benefit from a teacher . . . 'specially a bright one like you."

Jodi hardly knew how to take the woman at times. "I'll keep that in mind," she said with a laugh.

But as she walked back through the opening into the main house, she cherished the image of the Lord comforting Ella Mae in her great need. *Her heartache became His!*

CHAPTER 48

"Even the air feels different here," Jodi whispered to Maryanna as they headed for the stairs Sunday night three weeks later.

Maryanna was heartened to see Jodi putting in so many hours of study in preparation for school's opening tomorrow. Thank goodness Rosaleen had been faithful to come every weekday, answering Jodi's many questions. The two had even gone to visit two other Amish teachers in the area, which helped immensely, or so Jodi had confided in Maryanna earlier this evening, before family worship. It was also apparent that Jodi had learned to say the Lord's Prayer fluently in German, as well as sing several hymns in Deitsch.

Weary now, Maryanna climbed the stairs after praying with Benny and Tobias in their shared room downstairs. She stood in the hallway near Leda's room and remembered the first time she'd shown her how to dry dishes. Just three years old and so anxious to imitate her Mamma, Leda had stood on a chair.

My precious helper, she thought, going in to pray quietly with her, grateful down to her toes for this darling girl. Maryanna held her hand as Leda nestled in her cozy bed, looking peaceful as she closed her eyes, ready for sleep. When she'd said amen and "I love you," Maryanna kissed her on the cheek and reluctantly closed the door.

Then, going next to little Sarah's room, Maryanna watched her sitting on the bed in her white sleeping gown, talking to her new doll.

"Mamma and me will be alone tomorrow, when school starts for my sister and brothers," Sarah said quietly.

"But you can walk with Joshua and Buster to and from school," the doll replied. "And with Jodi and the others, ain't?"

"Still, it's not the same as when everybody's home," Sarah answered the doll quietly.

Engel began to tremble and made whimpering sounds.

"Are you all right?" asked Sarah, tilting the doll toward her.

Sarah helped Engel wipe her eyes. "I'll miss Jodi when she's done teaching here," the doll said.

Sarah held her right close to her face, then slowly pressed the doll against her heart. "I know you will, but don't cry, little one. I'll miss her, too."

Maryanna caught herself and stepped back into the hallway to take a deep breath. Then, coughing a little, she moved into the doorway. "Time for a Bible story, dear one."

Quickly, Sarah put her doll on the pillow next to her own, pulled back the quilt and sheet, and scooted into bed.

"Did Tobias tell you his secret?" Maryanna reached for the Good Book.

Sarah shook her head, her long hair swirling about her face.

"I gave your brother permission to bring Joshua's rabbit home tomorrow."

"Fer schur?"

She sighed — it hadn't been the easiest decision. "Jah, for sure."

Sarah's smile lit up the room, and she reached up to wrap her arms around Maryanna's neck, pulling her face near. "Denki, Mamma. Maybe you'll like Shadow after ya meet him."

It was impossible not to smile.

Later, after she'd read the story of Jonah and the great fish and they'd said their prayers, Maryanna tenderly tucked in her little one. She slipped past Jodi's closed door to her own room at the end of the hallway. *Such a lonely place.*

Sitting on the bed, fully dressed, Maryanna wondered what had come over her to agree to Joshua Peachey's suggestion about the black rabbit, all these weeks ago now.

She rose and went to the window and peered out at the white-cast landscape. She recalled that Jodi planned to go running again tomorrow evening with the Vella Shpringa. *"By the light of the moon,"* their English guest loved to tell the children.

But it was not talk of the moonlight on the practice route for the Bird-in-Hand Half Marathon that tugged at Maryanna just now. No, it was the way the shimmering light played down on the tip-top of Joshua's barn and silo, and the house, too. The grazing land was washed in the silvery light. She looked in awe at the light shining on her neighbor's property. A blue moon was coming soon — the second full moon in a single month. Was it a sign?

"No," she murmured, refusing such nonsense. "Joshua's taken with Ida Fisher, plain and simple." Maryanna knew it was true, for she'd seen Ida over there two, maybe three times in the last weeks. Always delivering a hamper of food — *the most direct path to a man's heart, lonely or otherwise.*

Closing the shades, Maryanna dressed for bed. Eventually, she outened the light and sat in her bed, the plumped pillows behind her, and relived the lovely evening with Turkey Dan two weeks ago. She'd let his sister, dear Nan, tell Dan she wished to accept his supper invitation, asking Nan not to share the matter around.

So far, so good. Thus far, no one but Maryanna and Dan themselves knew of their exceptional evening together. Yet despite the delicious food and animated conversation, primarily concerning his sons and her children, she had again yearned for Benuel. And more than ever, if that was even possible. There was something about the great void in her life that was accentuated by being with Dan Zook, and she felt terrible about it.

Did I feel that way when I was out riding with Joshua? Maryanna disliked comparing the two, not sure what she'd felt the evening she'd ridden off with her longtime neighbor. Was her knowledge of Benuel's close friendship with Joshua some kind of roadblock for her? Could that be?

She bowed her head and prayed for some direction. Dan Zook was eager to move forward and start their courtship, but she'd put him off, needing time. Two weeks had passed as he'd waited word from her, all the while sending her a pretty card and a couple of letters.

Because of his strong connection to Benuel, Joshua, on the other hand, was nearly like a brother in her thinking, or had been for so long, she thought. Joshua, master bow hunter and fisherman that he was, had shared his life and love of the outdoors with her own Benuel for so many years.

How would it feel to hold hands with Joshua, anyway? Maryanna wondered. Or to be kissed by him? But she mustn't let herself think that way. Not when word had it that Ida was hoping for a marriage proposal here before too long. So they were serious, nearly engaged.

For sure and for certain, Joshua had ceased pursuing Maryanna, like a turtle vanishing into its shell. Who could fault him? She'd put the nix on things, and now that she considered it, she could easily recall *that* aspect of their time together. Her words of rejection had sent him away.

So, to soften matters between them, she'd decided to let Tobias have Joshua's rabbit after all. "Of all things."

Maryanna slid down into her bed. *Might not be the best way to make amends,* she thought, glad Joshua would have a wonderful-*gut* cook in the house, if he and Ida married. *Like Suzanne.*

One of the things Jodi had learned in her twenty-seven years was that heavenly scenes like the one she was now a part of didn't just happen by sheer accident. She considered this while walking up Hickory Lane with Maryanna's children, including little Sarah, and Joshua Peachey, who held his black rabbit while keeping faithful Buster on a leash.

They were all wearing their new yellow safety vests, looking like a page out of Jodi's grandparents' *Saturday Evening Post.* This stroll to school along a curving, peaceful road, with a stream trickling nearby and the sweet sound of birds and horses in the distance, was a memory to cherish. Time was such a precious commodity. No one had enough of it. But *here* . . . here in Hickory Hollow, time stood still.

The happy chatter of children the first day of the new school year made Jodi ponder Trent's change of mind about desiring a family all his own. The feel of little Sarah's hand in hers had to be the reason for such thoughts.

"Have you ever seen a prettier day?" she

remarked to Joshua next to her, his straw hat square on his head.

"Why, sure," he replied, his grin infectious. "It's beautiful *every* day."

"I guess it is." She smiled.

"Have ya lived in the city all your life, then?"

"I grew up in New Jersey and attended college in Madison, Wisconsin. So, yes, I'm a city slicker." She told him she presently lived in a small town in Vermont. "There, everyone knows your name, what you do, and who you belong to." She smiled. "A little like here."

"Oh, that's the truth."

The older children waved their hands high to alert the younger ones each time a car passed, which thankfully wasn't often. Jodi was touched by the gesture. "It's sweet how the older children look after their younger siblings." She thought again of Karen.

"Amish families have something of a pecking order. From the top down, there are unique expectations for each child," he said. "You'll soon learn the specific responsibilities," Joshua explained, "if ya haven't already."

Sarah looked up at her just then, waving her angel doll and smiling but never letting go of Jodi's hand. "I guess Sarah will walk back home with you," she said to Joshua.

"Oh, jah, and that one's *gut* company, ever since Tobias started school a year ago," Joshua said. "She missed him a lot, Maryanna said, so Sarah started walkin' to and from school with me and the other children. She pretty much told her mother she was goin' to, and that was that." He chuckled. " 'Tween you and me, I think she'd be attending school, too, if they'd let her start early."

"She's a little corker." Jodi glanced down at her. "Good thing she doesn't know what we're saying."

Joshua nodded, his dwarf rabbit held close to his chest. Then he stopped to hand the rabbit to little Sarah, who squealed gleefully. All the children turned around and came back, oohing and aahing, wanting to take turns holding the little creature.

This man needs a family, Jodi thought as she watched him patiently stand near Sarah, making sure Shadow didn't get dropped.

After Joshua took back the rabbit, they began walking again, and along the way, more and more children ran down their lanes to join them. By the time the old schoolhouse was in view, Jodi noticed more than half the children in the entire school were walking barefoot two by two on the roadside.

Before arriving at the schoolhouse, Jodi mentioned hearing that Tobias was ecstatic about getting the rabbit. "According to Maryanna, anyway."

Joshua looked shocked. "First I heard it," he said, his expression brightening considerably.

"Oh." Jodi wondered if she'd spoiled something.

Joshua walked silently for a while. Then he turned toward Jodi. "Tobias is welcome to Shadow, of course — the cage, too."

Jodi listened, all ears.

"Naturally, it would be best if I heard from Maryanna directly, though, just to . . . uh . . . confirm her permission. Actually, why don't ya tell her to come get the rabbit herself."

"I'll let her know." Jodi suppressed the urge to smile. *What's he have up his sleeve?*

"I daresay I was wrong to worry 'bout you, Jodi," Joshua said softly. "I can see why the bishop was willin' to take this chance."

She smiled. "I'm determined not to disappoint you . . . or him. And the children most of all."

He held her gaze for a moment. "I believe that, jah."

Lovina and Rosaleen were waiting outside

435

the schoolhouse gate and greeted Jodi warmly when they spotted her. She planned to run the Bird-in-Hand Half Marathon with Rosaleen and Barbara — and still hoped to run in Boston in October, as well. Her father had recently urged her to do so, even suggesting they make it a small reunion, of sorts, bringing Mom so they could spend the weekend together. Jodi welcomed this idea, glad her parents understood her need for independence.

Presently, Joshua unlocked the gate and swung it wide, and all the children rushed inside. They removed their safety vests and piled them on the front porch of the quaint schoolhouse. Jodi had relished several afternoons with Rosaleen last week inside the one-room building, quickly navigating her way, noting where each of the so-called scholars would sit, with the smallest desks set closest to the row of windows, medium-sized desks in the middle rows, and the largest on the right.

Little Sarah squeezed Jodi's hand before letting go, then smiled past her frown while she waited for Joshua to link Buster to a long chain near the schoolhouse door.

"Have a *gut* first day of school," Joshua called with a wave.

"Thank you." Jodi watched him take

Sarah's hand and head out the gate, toward the road. *Why is Maryanna so resistant toward him? He's wonderful!*

Jodi turned to step inside, eager to begin. But it was the feel of Sarah's hand tucked securely in hers that implanted itself in Jodi's brain — from Leda's ringing the eight-thirty bell at starting time, all through singing the three morning songs.

Next came a Bible story about Joseph and his multicolored coat, which she followed with questions. The dear memory of Sarah lingered as Jodi took attendance and handed out the first-day quiz from *Tips for Teachers*. She gave them ten minutes to answer as many questions as possible, having Rosaleen assist her with the three first graders, whispering the question and helping to write their responses.

Later, when most of the students were finished, Jodi gave the first graders their easy English spelling words, which she'd written on the board before the last bell. She then called the second graders to the long bench at the front to recite their long and short vowel sounds.

While Jodi gave the third graders an assignment in their arithmetic notebooks, the rest of the students waited quietly for their grade level to be addressed as Rosaleen roamed among the rows of desks.

The boys looked glossy clean and combed. Most wore colored short-sleeved shirts, and their black or brown suspenders formed large X's over their backs. The girls, too, looked exceptionally neat, attired in clean dresses and matching aprons, their hair pulled back in tight knots or, in the case of the youngest girls, worn in braids wrapped around their heads.

Fourth and fifth grades were comprised of only three students, including Benny and Leda, who worked on penmanship. Jodi was very aware of the preacher's wife seated in the back of the spacious room, crocheting a small afghan, possibly for a baby cradle.

The three remaining grades, sixth through eighth, were assigned to the opposite corner of the room, where they marked a large map with the state capitals.

There was so much to juggle; Jodi admired Rosaleen's easy-going style. And later, when two of the first graders looked like they might cry for Mamma, Lovina went over and offered to quietly read a story to the three of them, which was a big help.

It was time for the middle graders to read for Jodi, so they came to the wooden bench next, while the second graders retreated to their desks and began working on writing their names in cursive, following the lesson in their notebooks.

By ten o'clock, recess was quite welcome. Jodi was actually thankful that week would only be half days. *Maybe I'll find my rhythm by next week,* she thought, going outside to watch the children play and pet Joshua's beautiful dog.

"If only you could talk," she said softly to Buster, thinking again how Joshua wanted to receive consent directly from Maryanna concerning the rabbit.

Why did *Maryanna change her mind?*

Was she warming to the idea of Joshua's house pets, and perhaps to the man himself? *Could I be right?*

CHAPTER 49

Joshua left Shadow at home when he returned to the schoolhouse for Buster and to walk back with Jodi and the children. He was still astonished at the school board's uncharacteristic decision. But from what he'd heard from Ned, the young woman was cooperating in every way, even going the second and third mile with Plain attire and hair. He smiled to himself, recalling his double take, seeing her hair pulled securely into a bun.

All she needs is a bonnet! He suppressed a laugh.

Little Sarah looked mighty disappointed when she saw Shadow was absent. She stood there at the end of his lane, sporting a mild yet steady scowl. And, well, if she didn't continue to frown all the way to school, even refusing to hold his hand. It crossed his mind to say something, but it wasn't his place.

When they arrived at the schoolhouse, Joshua spied the *Willkumm* sign strewn across the chain-link fence, there along the road. The schoolchildren had evidently pressed leaves into the fence, creating a unique welcome for all who passed by.

On the porch of the schoolhouse, Lovina Yoder was already helping Rosaleen and Jodi put the safety vests on the smaller children. He liked the idea of investing in safety — too many English drivers were inconsiderate on the road. He shuddered to think of a car hitting one of these precious ones.

Tobias ran to greet him, asking about the rabbit's whereabouts. The difference between him and his younger sister was that the lad took the news with grace, going along with Joshua's decision to leave the pet behind this time. And he didn't press about receiving the bunny, as young Sarah certainly would have.

Jodi walked with Benny and Leda, and he could hear their happy chatter. It was evident that the Englischer had made a good connection with each of the children, especially Maryanna's.

Zeke Mast sat whittling and whistling on the front porch when Joshua turned into his driveway, which was a bit of a surprise.

"Hullo, Zeke!" Joshua called.

"Hullo," Zeke replied. "Hope ya don't mind if I sit here and nick my fingers with a dull knife," he added with a wink.

Joshua set Buster free to run without the leash as he sat down on the porch steps. "Got yourself a day off?" he asked.

"Taking a short break from fillin' silo over at Preacher Yoder's."

Joshua turned and looked at him. "What's on your mind, Ezekiel?"

"Truth be told, I've taken a fancy to your parrot, Joshua."

"What's that?"

"Was thinkin' of taking your parrot off your hands, for a price."

"Well, Malachi's not for sale."

"Anything can be bought for the right price, least according to Preacher Yoder."

"What do ya mean by that?"

"Just that I want to buy your bird."

"Why on earth?"

Zeke rose with a groan and moseyed toward the steps, then turned around. "Just think 'bout it, all right?"

Watching Zeke walk down the driveway toward the road, Joshua was befuddled at best.

Remembering what Joshua had said earlier, Jodi passed along the message to Maryanna. "He'd like you to give permission directly."

"I have to go over there?" Maryanna asked, placing homemade corn bread in the middle of the table. "To get the rabbit?"

This tickled Jodi, but she kept a straight face. "That's what the man said."

Maryanna made an unintelligible remark under her breath and turned back to the stove to bring over a large pottery bowl of potato soup with German sausage sliced into it. "I'm awful busy today."

"Well, I doubt there's any rush," Jodi suggested as she boosted little Sarah up to the sink to wash her hands.

Maryanna turned to look at her, then shook her head in apparent disgust. "Don't know why I ever said Tobias could have that bunny rabbit."

Jodi smiled. And it was definitely a good thing Sarah had no idea what was being said.

A while later, Maryanna was happy to see Mollie drop by with all her girls, bringing two strawberry pies for dessert. Evidently,

Jeremiah was up the road assisting Nate Kurtz to mend his cow fences after more than half the herd had gotten out last night. Mollie and the girls, including Maryanna's pair, went out and dug new potatoes in the family vegetable garden. Later, the older girls and Mollie hulled lima beans, which Maryanna insisted on dividing up between them.

When Jeremiah returned for them, Maryanna figured now was as good a time as any to go to Joshua's and get the dwarf rabbit for Tobias. *Shadow . . . such a name for a rabbit!*

She washed her hands and then pushed a few loose hair strands back into her bun before she headed over there and found Joshua in the barn. She felt odd, seeing Ned working with him, not wanting word to get out that she was chasing after a man who was nearly engaged. Stumbling over her words, she offered to return later for the rabbit.

"No need." Joshua told Ned he wouldn't be but a minute.

"Thought I'd come over right quick," Maryanna said as Joshua fell in step with her.

"Tobias could've easily come for Shadow. Hope it didn't put you out. I just wanted to be sure you were serious."

She shook her head. "I understand. This is fine."

Joshua looked extra nice in his light brown work shirt, which accentuated the deep hazel in his eyes. Smiling, he said, "Tobias knows how to water and feed Shadow, so ya won't have to prompt him."

That surely wasn't something she cared to discuss. Just having the squirmy pet in the house was an enormous step. *I'm doing this for my children. . . .*

Joshua led the way into his kitchen, which was as remarkably clean as it had been on the Sunday they'd met in his barn for worship. Maryanna hadn't offered to help with food or tidying up after the shared meal, but she *had* sneaked inside just to see how a widower like Joshua kept things. Today, however, she noticed the addition of a litter box in the corner and scrunched her nose at it. Seeing the cat curled up on the wooden bench next to the table was downright alarming, and she looked away. *All that cat hair in the kitchen!*

"I'm sure Tobias and the other children will look after Shadow," Joshua was saying, yet he sounded nearly reluctant as he leaned down to peer into the small cage. "Suzanne enjoyed this little critter, believe me." He moved even closer. "Hullo, little one. . . ."

"And you do, too," Maryanna said.

He straightened, smiling. "Ever so much."

"Then why give it away, may I ask?"

He scratched his neck. "Tellin' the truth, I like your children, Maryanna. They're bright and energetic, and Tobias, especially, is such a *gut* help. Reminds me of myself when I was young, full of curiosity about nature and how things work." He smiled. "Industrious too."

"And has no aversion for school, jah?" She couldn't help herself, remembering Joshua's own reluctance to attend back when.

"I regret now my distaste for book learnin'."

It dawned on her then. Was this partially why Joshua walked to and from the schoolhouse with the children each weekday, taking such an interest in their safety? Was he trying to make up for the lost years of his own boyhood?

"Guess from time to time we all have distractions from the things we oughta be doin'." Maryanna gave him the benefit of the doubt.

"The cage ain't heavy at all." He reached to lift it and handed it to her. "Or I could carry it over to the house, if ya like."

"No, no . . . I can manage."

446

She wanted to simply pick up the cage and exit, but instead she found herself asking him what he thought of their substitute teacher.

He nodded. "Strangest thing, ain't? And yet I daresay Jodi Winfield's one of the best teachers we've ever had, least from what I can tell when she interacts with the children." He paused, his gaze lingering on her a mite too long. "She really cares 'bout them. And Ned says she's abiding by the curriculum set out by the school board."

"I believe so, too."

He went on to describe Jodi's gentle way not only with the youngsters but with Buster. "His tail just wags and wags when he sees her, I'll say."

Maryanna found herself sharing a sweet scene — of Jodi and her own four, when they were out watering the potted autumn plants and checking on the Christmas poinsettias. "She's nearly like a second mother to them." She laughed as she also recounted the Saturday morning last weekend when Jodi had learned how to whitewash the picket fence, with Benny and Tobias instructing her.

Maryanna and Joshua must have stood there talking for a good fifteen minutes or more, before she realized. Glory be, didn't she still have work to do?

Joshua looked at her more seriously, and it crossed her mind that he was a good-looking man, well above average. And it appeared he was itching to tell her something. "Maryanna, I . . ." he began, then hesitated.

"What is it?" she asked.

He stopped talking just that quick.

They both heard it, someone pulling into the driveway.

Turning, Maryanna saw Ida Fisher get down and tie her horse to the hitching post. "Ach, I shouldn't be keepin' ya," she said, absently placing the rabbit's cage on the kitchen counter.

Joshua's flabbergasted expression surprised her.

Flummoxed, she hurried out of the kitchen, not wanting to run into Ida or cause a lick of trouble here.

But alas, she saw the shock rising on Ida's face, though Ida said nothing as Maryanna fairly fled away.

She felt foolish and miserable as she rushed across the pasture. To think she'd allowed herself to get caught up in conversation with a man who was practically betrothed. *Honestly!*

But what was Joshua about to tell her, just before Ida arrived?

Well, Maryanna could just about guess. More than likely, he wanted to say they really shouldn't be having long conversations like that. "Jah, must be it," she muttered.

She huffed out an angry breath and smiled wryly to herself, remembering Ida's expression, fairly sure Joshua had some serious explaining to do.

Have I missed the boat?

To think she'd had her chance with Joshua, and what had she done? Maryanna fumed all the way to the edge of the backyard, then realized, *For pity's sake!* She'd left the rabbit back at Joshua's!

As she frequently did when frustrated, Maryanna took herself off to her room to sort. She began to pull out everything in each of her dresser drawers, as well as the blanket chest at the foot of her bed. This was a cleaning tirade, and she was glad of it.

What'll I tell Tobias?

Oh, for goodness' sake, she'd just send him back over there for the animal, since she'd already given consent in person. "Like Joshua wanted," she said right out. "But why was that even necessary?"

Turning her attention to the bottom

drawer, she attempted to open it, but it stuck. She jiggled it and could see several pieces of paper pushed clear in the back. She reached in and found what looked to be some old receipts — and a picture.

Turning it over, she saw Benuel's mother's handwriting on the back. *Benuel Esh, one year old.*

So long ago . . . She stared at the photo — those chubby cheeks and bright eyes so like Sarah's at that age.

She remembered when Benuel first showed her the precious picture. A rarity, to be sure, and something only a very few church members did when their children were small. As long as pictures weren't taken later in life, the ministerial brethren paid no mind.

Maryanna studied it as tears welled up. "Such a sweet-spirited little boy," she whispered, recalling her husband from their earliest childhood days, first at Preachings and later at the schoolhouse. Benuel had always sought out companions similar to himself . . . friends like Joshua Peachey. And Benuel always remarked about Joshua's *gut* heart, too. A heart for the Lord God . . .

And hadn't Maryanna observed that, too, in all Joshua had done for her family these last years, walking the children to and from school, checking in with the boys, searching for little Sarah? Truth be told, even his willingness to give Tobias that ridiculous rabbit showed the depth of the man's caring heart.

She thought again of Ida prancing up Joshua's back steps, obviously quite comfortable doing so.

So it's too late for me. She still held the picture of her dear husband. Then, sighing, she whispered, "Or is it?"

Brushing back the last remnant of tears, Maryanna carefully tucked the picture into the small drawer on the table next to her bed. *I've already lost one man, but I don't want to lose another!*

Chapter 50

The next day, Maryanna went out to get her mail and discovered yet another letter from Turkey Dan. He was inviting her out again to talk about *moving forward.*

She carried the letter up to her room and tucked it into a dresser drawer, starting to feel pressured. Oh, she liked him well enough — it wasn't that. Things with Dan Zook could take off like a wildfire, she was afraid. He was in a hurry to find a mother for his boys, a noble cause, of course. But when she pondered this, it reminded her of the main reason she'd accepted Joshua's invitation to go riding in the first place — prompted by her parents, no less.

And Sarah's need for a firmer hand.

The rabbit in its cage — in the utility room as of last evening, when Joshua briefly dropped by — was a tangible reminder of that man's interest in Maryanna's dear children. And in the midst of her chores and the busy afternoon ahead, she closed the door to her room and dropped to her knees beside the bed. "O dear Lord in heaven, if you want me to marry again, will you, by your great grace and wisdom, make it clear who that man should be? I give you all praise and gratitude for the many blessings over our lives. In the name of Jesus, I pray. Amen."

That afternoon, Jodi insisted they take her car to purchase canned goods at the "bent and dent" store — BB's in Quarryville — leaving Mammi Emmie in charge of the children, who were doing their outside chores.

Maryanna was not at all accustomed to riding in the front passenger seat of a car. She'd always sat farther back in the vans when their Mennonite drivers took her and the children to more distant destinations, and she felt a bit tense and wished Jodi might slow down a bit. Twice before, she'd gone with Jodi, who wanted to help out with groceries, refusing to *"sponge off"* them, as she put it.

"Are you nervous?" Jodi looked over at her.

"Jah, a little." Maryanna didn't mind admitting it and was glad when Jodi slowed significantly as they drove west on Hickory Lane, toward Old Leacock Road.

"I think the rabbit will be content with all the extra attention," Jodi said out of the blue.

Maryanna tried not to roll her eyes.

Jodi laughed a little. "Shadow was special to Joshua. Wasn't the rabbit his wife's?"

"As I understand it."

"His pets must be a comfort to him."

Maryanna hardly knew what to say.

"But he *did* give up the rabbit," said Jodi.

" 'Tis true."

"And," Jodi continued, "Joshua probably wouldn't ever have wanted all those pets if he wasn't so lonely."

"Hard to say."

"I've actually thought of getting a cat myself, when I return home. It's going to be a long year without my fiancé nearby."

"Japan's awful far away."

"So I can see why Joshua likes to have several pets, especially indoors." Jodi paused. "You've got your children, and he has none."

Maryanna guessed that was a logical way to look at it, although she still didn't equate her children's wonderful-*gut* company to that of furry pets or a loud-mouthed bird.

The sky was exceptionally pale, nearly

white, like a vast bed sheet on washday. Maryanna kept her eyes focused on it instead of the road.

"How long has Joshua been a widower?" Jodi asked.

Maryanna told her.

"I'm surprised."

"Why do you say that?"

Jodi looked over at her. "I didn't mean —"

"No, I'd like to know."

Jodi cleared her throat. "Well, on the walk to and from school yesterday, I noticed how patient and gentle he is with the children. From what I've come to know of him . . . Joshua's rather remarkable."

"You think so?"

"And very attractive."

"Oh," Maryanna said, blushing at that. She'd certainly noticed as much herself, at least here lately, but she hadn't expected the Englischer to think so, too.

CHAPTER 51

In the days that followed, little Sarah encouraged Jodi to kneel beside her during morning and evening prayers as Maryanna and the children went around the room and said a short prayer of gratitude.

Ever since her prayer in the back row at church, Jodi's heart was softening — something was loosening up in her. *Trent was right,* she thought. *I can't stay mad at God forever.*

Jodi had missed praying while jogging all those months during her standoff. Now she looked forward to family worship before going to bed and at other times during the day. She prayed for guidance and help, too, especially regarding the care and teaching of the Amish children to whom she was growing more attached as each week passed.

At the end of every day, there was time for reflection and sometimes just sitting and watching the lightning bugs sparkle across the meadow while the children played with the ponies. And, oh, the sound of the katydids!

One such night, Maryanna probed a bit, just as Jodi had with her on the drive to Quarryville some time ago. Only Maryanna was far more tactful, asking quietly how things stood between Jodi and her fiancé these days.

"We're careful not to talk about certain topics — like having kids." Jodi assumed that fact showed Trent's consideration for her, that he'd bundled his frustration and given it to God in prayer.

"Well, maybe you can think of it another way," Maryanna said sympathetically. "I almost lost Sarah when she fell out of the carriage."

Jodi nodded.

"But do you think I wished I'd never had her because of that mishap? Even if she hadn't been returned to me, I would have cherished every minute we'd had, for always." She paused. "Do you see?"

Jodi listened, reminded of her mother's similar words about Karen last month.

Maryanna sighed. "And, too, I loved Benuel so much . . . our little ones are a constant reminder of him."

Jodi hadn't considered this before, but she

was beginning to understand. "You know, if a little girl like your Sarah could steal my heart, maybe I haven't really resolved this issue. And who knows, maybe I would be a good mother."

"Oh, goodness' sake, I know that for sure!"

It really wasn't about that, anyway. Nor was it about losing anymore, either. Jodi wanted to give of herself, for whatever time God allowed her. It all came down to trusting, embracing His sovereign will.

At such a time, it was impossible for Jodi not to consider her own argument for why Joshua had his pets — he seemed to regard them as part of his family. But wasn't she doing that very thing with Trent, asking him to give up his unborn children, so to speak? Maybe it was a stretch, but she saw the parallel and it struck her heart.

In the tranquility of the moment, with a choir of crickets crowding out the world and slowing down the night, Jodi recognized that somewhere along the way, she'd begun to change her thinking.

"I think I need to talk to Trent," she said, wanting to share her new resolve, although she hated to do so via Skype. She wished they could be together at Thanksgiving or Christmas, but that was impossible. Besides, why wait to tell him then?

So that evening, she took her laptop and drove to the coffee shop where she and Trent had argued. There, she composed a heartfelt email, taking her time to explain — and apologizing for — what she felt was her very selfish, even stubborn, position. *It was absolutely unnecessary,* she wrote, struggling to see the screen through her tears. *I've learned a lot about myself here, Trent, and I've rediscovered my desire to pray again. I'm sure you'll be happy to hear this, unquestionably an answer to your own prayers. And I believe it is one reason why I have become more open to being a mother to your children someday . . . if you're still interested.*

When she'd finished writing her heart on the page, she happily pressed Send. Jodi was surprised to see an email from Trent had arrived in her inbox. In her haste to write, she'd missed seeing his note!

Clicking on it, she began to read.

Hi, Jodi,
The days are so full of activity associated with my students, all of whom have captured my attention. For more than a week, I've wanted to see you face-to-face, but we both know that can't hap-

pen till next summer. I've been compos-
ing this email to you in my head awhile,
and I'm ready to tell you what I'm thinking. After much prayer, I've come to see
your position.

Life is fragile, which is why I didn't
want to lock the door on having a family
with you, honey. The reason I initially
changed my mind is because of my love
for you — I wanted to see your eyes,
your sweet spirit, your Jodi-ness in
another soul . . . in our future children.
But causing you stress or pain — heaven
forbid! — by insisting on my way is not
what I wish to do.

So I'm going to honor our original
decision, Jodi. I love you that much . . .
enough to give up the hope of children.
You will be my family, and I am content
with that.

With all my love,
Trent

She gasped, crying, "What have I done?"

During the next two weeks, Joshua's neighbors kept dropping by unsolicited to inquire
about his two remaining indoor pets. It was
the most peculiar thing, really. Why would
not only his own sisters-in-law and neighbor

Rhoda Kurtz stop by, but also Lovina Yoder and even Rebecca Lapp? The women brought fresh-baked sticky buns or pumpkin whoopie pies from the Bird-in-Hand Bake Shop or their own kitchens, seemingly for the purpose of asking to purchase Malachi or to take Honey Lou off his hands.

Not a one had said boo about faithful Buster. That, too, was very odd.

What's going on? Joshua wondered as he tended to his young steers.

The last week Jodi Winfield was scheduled to substitute teach, Joshua decided to pay a visit to Maryanna while the children were at school. He'd seen little Sarah going next door to visit her grandparents, so the coast was clear.

If Maryanna's busy, I'll just make it snappy, he decided.

Maryanna greeted him at the back door, and he immediately felt awkward. "Just thought I'd ask 'bout Shadow." He removed his straw hat.

"Well, so far he hasn't eaten more than his fair share," she said with a straight face.

"Have to say I miss the little critter." Joshua looked down at his feet, standing there on the back porch. "My house pets have all been farmed out."

461

Maryanna wrinkled her nose. "I imagine Ida must be happy 'bout that."

"Ida?"

Maryanna seemed to hedge. "I didn't mean to —"

"No worries. Besides, I'm not seein' her anymore."

Maryanna turned pale. "Well, why not?"

"It just wasn't meant to be, and I'll leave it right there."

Maryanna looked at him intently, as if unable to grasp what he'd said. In fact, her expression was so curious, he felt compelled to explain further, even though warning bells were sounding: *Don't put your foot in your mouth!*

"Ida's nice enough," he said. "Ain't that." He hesitated, then thought better of what he had in mind and plunged right ahead. "But I figure a man shouldn't marry someone, no matter how nice she is, when he can't stop thinkin' about another." His heart was on the ground, but Joshua had said what he'd wanted to since before his first date with Maryanna.

And now, what was this? She was blushing to beat the band. He'd embarrassed her. Again.

They stared at each other, Joshua shuffling his feet, hardly knowing what to say or

462

do. "Heard the school board's finally found a replacement for the Englischer. Did ya know?"

Maryanna, still red in the face, nodded. "Jodi did mention something."

"An unmarried older teenager from the Harvest Road church district, evidently. She'll teach for the rest of the school year."

"The children will miss Jodi, I'm sure."

He agreed, returning his hat to his head. "Well, I'd better be on my way."

She looked nearly dejected. "Must ya, Joshua?"

"Sorry?"

Maryanna softly cleared her throat. "Would you like to come for supper, I mean?" She glanced in the direction of his house. "Since your pets aren't around, it must be awful lonely over there."

He gazed at her pretty face, and she smiled sweetly. And if he wasn't mistaken, it looked a little like the way she used to smile at Benuel when they were first courting.

Joshua said simply, "I'd love to join your family, Maryanna . . . for supper."

CHAPTER 52

It was Jodi who uncovered the mystery behind the neighbors who'd given new homes to Joshua's pets. On her final day of teaching in early October, she listened as Lovina Yoder let the information slip while she helped gather up lunch coolers and a few stray backpacks.

"My husband always thought Maryanna and Joshua would make a happy couple — this was after their spouses passed away, of course. But he was also aware of Maryanna's dislike for the man's indoor animals." Lovina began to look sheepish.

"So your husband prompted the neighbors to take Joshua's pets?"

Lovina said it was so.

Jodi smiled, touched yet again by the interconnectedness of the People. She found it especially interesting that the parrot had gone to Maryanna's parents and the cat to Ella Mae Zook.

Standing in the schoolroom for the last time, Jodi's eyes swept over the familiar space, saying a silent good-bye before she moved to the door and locked it behind her. Then, following the children out to the gate, she spied Joshua with little Sarah, who came running to her, eyes shining.

All the way back to the Esh farm, Sarah helped carry some of Jodi's teaching handbooks, less clingy than all the weeks before. Jodi guessed it had something to do with her explanation to the Esh children while Maryanna and Joshua had a date after supper last evening. Leda and Toby took turns telling Sarah in Deitsch that a permanent teacher had been acquired, and that Jodi was returning home to Vermont. *"But she'll keep in touch with us,"* they assured their sister.

Jodi enjoyed the walk but already missed these darling youngsters. She would also miss running with Rosaleen and Barbara, and interacting with all the other Plain folk, too. During the Bird-in-Hand Half Marathon weeks ago, she'd joined with twelve hundred fifty other runners from thirty-eight states and four countries, helping raise money for the Bird-in-Hand Fire Company, so essential to the Amish farmers. *The least I could do . . .*

Suddenly, Joshua stopped walking and leaned over to retrieve something from the roadside ditch. "Well, lookee here." He held up a muddied cloth doll. "Isn't this just like the one —"

"That's Kaylee!" Tobias exclaimed, running to look. "Sarah's lost doll." When little Sarah saw it, her whole face shone.

Leda hurried to see, too. "She needs washin' but *gut.*"

"Now my little sister's got two dolls with fancy English names," Benny said, looking glum and shaking his head.

"Maybe she oughta rename them?" Joshua said, offering the soiled doll to Sarah, who quickly handed off the teaching books to Jodi, then accepted the doll. She held it at arm's length, making a face at its condition.

Jodi smothered a laugh as she recalled her recent chat session with Trent, truly thankful when she considered his very trusting way. He still wanted her to plan their wedding, giving her free rein to do whatever she wished, as long as it was simple. And he didn't want to be given a single hint until he arrived back from Japan early June of next year.

So she'd decided that if he really agreed to a mystery wedding, he'd have one. And Jodi loved him all the more for it. Best of all, Trent was overjoyed at her email describing her change of heart about having children. His initial shock had quickly given way to elation.

Maryanna stopped weeding at the far end of the vegetable garden as she heard Jodi and the children returning from school. She moaned inwardly at the thought of losing her not-so-fancy friend. Well, it wasn't really a loss, but it would feel like one, for sure.

She did not seek out little Sarah first upon seeing her children striding up the lane with their teacher and friend. No, today she embraced each of her four darlings with her loving gaze. They were all special, each and every one, and she had the dear Lord to thank for that realization. *And Jodi Winfield.*

She was also learning the benefits that could be reaped by disciplining a child who had been too favored. *"It's a gift for the child's heart,"* Joshua had said last night. *"Discipline leads to happiness."* Maryanna knew he was being gentle with her, and both of them believed their recent efforts with little Sarah had begun to yield fruit.

Dear, wise man. Her children would be delighted to soon discover Joshua's and her secret.

Leda and little Sarah hurried over to show

her a grimy-looking doll. "The lost is found," Leda told her, her arm around her younger sister.

Jodi caught up with the girls, smiling.

"In more ways than one, I'll say." Maryanna looked lovingly at the three of them. "We'll get the doll cleaned up in no time," she promised.

"Joshua said it needs an Amish name," Leda spoke up.

"*Gut* idea," Maryanna agreed. She would explain this to Sarah later when they were alone.

In the house, the doll was relinquished to warm water and suds in the sink while Benny helped Jodi carry her bags and books out to the car.

Maryanna was happy for Jodi, who'd just learned she was to be a long-term substitute for a teacher who was about to go on maternity leave — in her former school district, yet. *The Lord had plans for her all along.*

Back inside, the children encircled Jodi, and Maryanna joined hands with them, bowing her head for a final prayer for traveling mercies and guidance as Jodi resumed her teaching in the English world. "And please give Jodi's young man a special blessing, too, as he teaches children in a faraway land."

They said the Lord's Prayer in German, and tears welled up in Tobias's eyes as he shook Jodi's hand. Benny hung back a little. Then he went to the corner cupboard and brought out a hoot owl he'd whittled with Dawdi Zeke, just for Jodi. He gave it without saying a word, eyes wide.

Leda opened her arms and hugged Jodi, as did Sarah.

Smiling graciously, Jodi offered her thanks to Maryanna — "for absolutely everything." She pressed her lips together for a moment, then shook her head quickly. "Actually, that's far too general." She glanced at the sky. "I'm grateful for each of the beautiful gifts I've received here, Maryanna. Miracles to me, in many ways. The gift of balancing life's pain with divine healing — for body, mind, and soul." Now looking at Benny, Leda, Tobias, and little Sarah, she whispered, struggling to speak. "And the gift of love in the innocent eyes of your darling children." She turned to Maryanna, tears rolling down her face. "And you, my dear sister-friend . . . just *you.*"

Such farewells were ever so hard. Maryanna reached for a tissue for her and then, when Jodi had composed herself, she wrapped a piece of shoofly pie and thought of pleading with her to stay the night. Why not have just one more evening together? "You're more than welcome to stay over, if you wish," she offered.

The children joined in, cajoling, their pleas like sweet music.

But Jodi, while seemingly grateful for the invitation, was ready and appeared reluctant to prolong the sting of separation — something Maryanna felt, too.

After more good-byes, they all walked with her to the car and watched her get in, back out of the lane carefully, and wave to them one last time.

"She promised to write," Tobias said, his small voice breathy.

"Oh, and she will," Benny assured him.

Leda sniffled, speechless, struggling not to cry.

"Bye-bye, Angel. Come back soon!" little Sarah said as clear as anything in English. The first words spoken in her new language!

"Well, bless your heart," Maryanna said. *Too bad Jodi missed this!*

The children returned to the house and to their chores, but Maryanna strained to see the dark blue car make its way down Hickory Lane, east toward Cattail Road. And she stood there counting her blessings, which sincerely included Jodi Winfield, watching till she could see the car no longer.

The next afternoon, the Bird-in-Hand Bake Shop was abuzz with tourists and an abundance of local Plain folk. Maryanna headed up the front porch steps into the familiar, welcoming bakery. Yeasty smells of baked goods, every delicious treat a body might crave, greeted her senses.

She made a beeline for the pastry counter and chose a dozen chocolate whoopie pies, eager to surprise Joshua and the children. More and more, he was thrilled to be invited for supper, and it warmed Maryanna's heart to see not just Tobias delighted with his good company, but all the children, as well.

The Amish clerk counted out the goodies, adding a thirteenth for the baker's dozen, and wrapped tissue paper around each one. Turning, Maryanna happened to see Ida Fisher standing over in the next room, looking at small wooden rocking horses. *Must be for one of her young nephews,* thought Maryanna.

Then, lo and behold, Turkey Dan and his youngest boy, five-year-old Sam, appeared and turned to talk to Ida, Dan's eyes bright with attention. Seeing the lovely sight was heartening, as Maryanna had regretted the way things fizzled with Dan Zook, although she'd written him a letter in answer to his even before she knew Joshua and she would be courting. There was no reason not to be friendly when they all lived and worshiped in the same church district.

She went right over and greeted them, talking also with young Sam. Ida simply sparkled as she glanced up at Turkey Dan, who grinned down at her.

Later, when Maryanna paid for her treats, she felt good, knowing Dan had someone who cared for him and for his boys — and the same for Ida. The Zooks were getting a wunnerbaar-*gut* cook if a wedding was in their future. Of course, she didn't know for sure, but they certainly looked happy together.

Maybe she'll get a shiny new gas stove from her new husband. Maryanna thought of her own plans for a rather small wedding in a few months in her farmhouse. Only immediate family and spouses would be invited — one hundred fifty relatives in all. Not the more typical wedding she and Benuel had shared as young folk, of course, when four hundred fifty souls had come to witness their vows to God and to each other.

Maryanna made her way outside, feeling

the nip in the autumn air. She pulled her woolen shawl closer and walked toward gentle Dandy and the waiting carriage. Looking at the sky, she thought again of Benuel, but without the usual twinge of sadness. She was past her mourning years and looked ahead with expectation to the joyous future . . . just around the corner.

EPILOGUE

The mid-June sunshine showered the smiling bride and groom with plentiful blessings, and I was ever so sure I'd never seen a prettier day. Jodi and Trent exchanged wedding vows in the newly painted white gazebo behind my house as my own husband, Joshua, and I and the children were privileged to witness the special love between our English friend and her adoring betrothed.

The couple's well-dressed parents stood on either side of them, and Jodi's brother-in-law, Devin, along with Trent's siblings and their spouses, filled up half the gazebo.

Ella Mae Zook had been invited, too, and she sat attentively on a wooden lawn chair in the yard, petting Honey Lou in her lap. My parents sat and observed curiously, as well, none of us ever having attended an English wedding.

Wearing navy blue trousers and a white

shirt and tie, Trent leaned down and sweetly kissed Jodi, who looked lovely in her simple wedding gown, just like the angel clothed in white who brought my Sarah home to us. The sun filtered through the gazebo slats above them, falling gently on their shoulders.

Twenty-two barefoot young scholars made a human circle with their hands as they sang "Jesus Loves the Little Children" in German, the only song Jodi had planned, which delighted Trent — I could see it in his eyes.

Then, unexpectedly, little Sarah stepped forward and began to sing in English, her childlike voice ringing out ever so clearly, " 'Where is Jesus whom I long for, my beloved Lord and friend?' "

Never having heard Sarah sing in English, Jodi turned and, with an affectionate smile, reached for her hand.

There wasn't a dry eye amongst the adults present, including the English minister from Vermont — Trent and Jodi's pastor — who fumbled for his white handkerchief before offering a benediction.

For refreshments, Jodi served iced peppermint tea — Ella Mae's secret recipe. And for Trent's benefit and to the delight of all the children present, there were dozens of whoopie pies in several flavors.

Trent declared it "the best-ever simple wedding and reception," clearly taken with Jodi's surprise.

As for myself, I can say that marriage to Joshua is truly a joy. Honestly, I wish this kind of loving relationship for any woman yearning for a godly and loving lifemate. The Lord God had answered before I ever knew to ask.

Suzanne's unfinished baby quilts will soon be ready for a new little one — my first baby with Joshua, who was surprised when I showed him the pretty cradle quilts Suzanne had started were now finished. When he realized what I was doing and why, he reached for me — much too gently I must say — and took me into his arms to kiss me. Of course, I told him I wouldn't break just because I'm in the family way.

My children have received the daily blessing of a loving stepfather, and when Joshua and I tuck them in each night, we see the contentment in their eyes and thank the dear Lord for erasing the loneliness and replacing it with such happiness.

Jodi and I exchange letters faithfully once a month, and I recently shared with her that Joshua sold his farm, thankfully to another Amish couple. It's always wonderful-*gut* to keep the land with the People.

When Joshua and I have family worship with Benny, Leda, Tobias, and Sarah, we always end by giving thanks for the Lord's protection over their little sister that frightening night nearly a year ago. Truly, God's love is the greatest miracle of all.

AUTHOR'S NOTE

While on a springtime book tour, I stumbled upon an intriguing article in a homespun Southern newspaper. I leaned in, gasped, and reread the lead line: *Amish child falls out of carriage and goes missing.*

"What an incredible story idea!" I told myself. After reading onward and discovering — much to my relief — that the real-life child was found twenty-four hours later, I began to write my own version, pouring all the angst of my own mother-heart into poor Maryanna Esh's. I truly felt little Sarah's terror, as well as Jodi Winfield's astonishment. And my heart was ever so tender to dear Ella Mae Zook's sincere wisdom.

As always, there are many wonderful people to thank, beginning with my own darling husband and partner in fiction, David Lewis. I *could not* manage all the ideas whirling in my brain, let alone get them down on paper, without Dave's encouragement and loving support. And his helpful cooking!

I'm beyond grateful to David Horton, the head of Bethany's terrific fiction team. And I offer my ongoing appreciation to my amazing editor, Rochelle Glöege, and to Ann Parrish and Helen Motter.

My heartfelt gratitude to Dr. D. Holmes Morton for his remarkable work at the Clinic for Special Children in Strasburg, Pennsylvania — located in the middle of a former cornfield. Also, deep appreciation to my astute consultant, Donald Kraybill, whose book *The Amish* is enlightening to anyone eager to understand Amish life and tradition.

I am thankful to Jim Smucker, Erik Wesner, Brad Igou, and Hank and Ruth Hershberger. Other Amish and Mennonite research assistants requested to remain anonymous but are equally important to my work and to its accuracy.

I am devotedly indebted to my partners in prayer, including Dave and Janet Buchwalter, Dale, Barbara, and Lizzie Birch, Donna DeFor, Debra Larsen, and my loyal Facebook friends, who take prayerful intercession seriously. What a difference it makes!

My cheery friend Martha Nelson offered her very own "fiery cornflakes" anecdote for this book, for which I am still smiling . . . and thankful. And where would Tobias Esh and his siblings be without my sister, Barbara Birch's, original and catchy lyrics ("Person, Place, or Thing") set to the tune of "The Farmer in the Dell"? Thanks for sharing with my reader-friends!

Denki to Eli ("Small") Hochstetler of Berlin, Ohio, who prayed the Lord's Prayer in German at my request as we shared a special dinner, his eyes filling with tears as he said the reverent amen. I'll never forget!

If you're interested in information regarding the annual autumn Bird-in-Hand Half Marathon or the *Vella Shpringa,* please check online.

While the fictitious bishop in this story staunchly rejects contacting the police in the case of little Sarah Esh, many other present-day Amish communities in Lancaster County *do* utilize 9-1-1 for emergencies.

Saying thank-you is simply never enough, my faithful reader-friend. An inspiring and compelling story is always my cherished goal . . . from my heart to yours.

Soli Deo Gloria!

ABOUT THE AUTHOR

Beverly Lewis, born in the heart of Pennsylvania Dutch country, is the *New York Times* bestselling author of more than ninety books. Her stories have been published in eleven languages worldwide. A keen interest in her mother's Plain heritage has inspired Beverly to write many Amish-related novels, beginning with *The Shunning,* which has sold more than a million copies. *The Brethren* was honored with a 2007 Christy Award.

Beverly lives with her husband, David, in Colorado.

The employees of Thorndike Press hope you have enjoyed this Large Print book. All our Thorndike, Wheeler, and Kennebec Large Print titles are designed for easy reading, and all our books are made to last. Other Thorndike Press Large Print books are available at your library, through selected bookstores, or directly from us.

For information about titles, please call:
    (800) 223-1244

or visit our Web site at:
    http://gale.cengage.com/thorndike

To share your comments, please write:
    Publisher
    Thorndike Press
    10 Water St., Suite 310
    Waterville, ME 04901